THE KISS THAT MADE HER REALIZE . . .

"Why have you agreed to marry him?" Ford demanded abruptly. "You don't love him."

He lowered his lips to hers, firm and warm and seeking, letting the sweet taste fill him. He released his hold of her arms and wrapped his own round her, holding her close to him, feeling the heady throb of her heart that echoed his own. He knew at that moment that the same fire that burned within him was in her as well.

He was right. Amity knew it as surely as he did. Somehow his lips managed to touch her in a way that bewildered her, that caused a liquid heat inside her that melted her. Justin's kiss had not done this to her, had not left her feeling breathless and weak. She could not understand what it was Ford did to her, but she knew she did not want it to stop. Whatever magic his lips held, she wished she could drink in enough of it to sate herself of it, enough for a lifetime. But she knew it would have to end . . .

FIERY ROMANCE

CALIFORNIA CARESS (2771, $3.75)
by Rebecca Sinclair

Hope Bennett was determined to save her brother's life. And if that meant paying notorious gunslinger Drake Frazier to take his place in a fight, she'd barter her last gold nugget. But Hope soon discovered she'd have to give the handsome rattlesnake more than riches if she wanted his help. His improper demands infuriated her; even as she luxuriated in the tantalizing heat of his embrace, she refused to yield to her desires.

ARIZONA CAPTIVE (2718, $3.75)
by Laree Bryant

Logan Powers had always taken his role as a lady-killer very seriously and no woman was going to change that. Not even the breathtakingly beautiful Callie Nolan with her luxuriant black hair and startling blue eyes. Logan might have considered a lusty romp with her but it was apparent she was a lady, through and through. Hard as he tried, Logan couldn't resist wanting to take her warm slender body in his arms and hold her close to his heart forever.

DECEPTION'S EMBRACE (2720, $3.75)
by Jeanne Hansen

Terrified heiress Katrina Montgomery fled Memphis with what little she could carry and headed west, hiding in a freight car. By the time she reached Kansas City, she was feeling almost safe . . . until the handsomest man she'd ever seen entered the car and swept her into his embrace. She didn't know who he was or why he refused to let her go, but when she gazed into his eyes, she somehow knew she could trust him with her life . . . and her heart.

MOONLIGHT CARESS
SUSAN SACKETT

ZEBRA BOOKS
KENSINGTON PUBLISHING CORP.

ZEBRA BOOKS

are published by

Kensington Publishing Corp.
475 Park Avenue South
New York, NY 10016

First printing: December, 1990

Printed in the United States of America

Chapter One

"I must admit, Beatrice, your sister has turned out to be quite a surprise to me. I'd rather expected her to resemble that gawky, round-eyed waif I remembered from our wedding. It seems she's turned into a rather handsome young woman."

Beatrice Ravenswood St. James dropped her brush into the lap of her gown, turned away from her dressing table, and watched her husband adjust his collar studs with critical, knowing eyes.

"Nine or ten years does have the habit of forcing little girls to grow up, Charles. And if I see what I think I see in your rheumy little eyes, let me assure you that although I may ignore your occasional peccadilloes, I will not countenance any such thing in my own home. And certainly not with my sister." Her husband considered his reflection in the mirror one last time, then turned, strode up behind her chair, and leaned over her shoulder to press his lips against her bared skin.

"I'm shocked, my dear, at the casual way you wrong me. You know you are the only woman in my life." He let his fingers play slowly along her shoulder. "You are my life."

Beatrice seemed unimpressed with his words and the kisses he pressed first to her shoulder, then to her neck. She lifted her brush once again. "I may be many things, Charles, but please do me the honor of not thinking me a fool," she muttered angrily as she stared at her reflection before she brought the brush to attack a perfectly arranged curl.

His hand reached out and held hers before she managed to disturb the arrangement of her hair too seriously. He took the brush from her hand and put it firmly down on her dressing table.

"You are my life, my love, and you wouldn't have me any other way than as I am," he told her confidently. "I don't suppose this would be a diplomatic moment to remind you that technically this isn't your house, that we live here only so long as I continue to be consul?" he asked her lightly. He considered the small storm that filled her dark eyes. "No," he answered his own question, "that certainly wouldn't be wise. And I am, after all, the most diplomatic of men." He smiled at her knowingly. Then he put his hands to her shoulders, turned her to face him, and brought his lips to hers.

As he knew it would, his wife's anger melted and she wound her hands around his neck.

"Oh!"

The small exclamation was enough to redirect Beatrice's attention. She turned and saw her sister turning to leave the room.

"You needn't go, Amity. You aren't interrupting anything," she called to her sister, then let her glance move meaningfully to her husband, only to find he, like she, had turned to face Amity and, unlike her, had not tired quite so quickly of the view.

"I ought to have knocked," Amity apologized. She hesitated a moment, not quite sure of herself, before she started forward. "The door was ajar, you see—"

"No matter," Charles interrupted her, his manner hearty in a way that seemed not entirely genuine to Amity. He smiled at her, and Amity realized there was something besides cheerful friendliness in the smile, but she was not sure just what that was, either. "We were actually just saying how delighted we both are to have you here with us."

Amity found herself feeling a bit on edge. Just why that

6

was, she couldn't say, nor did she wish to consider the fact at that moment. Instead she hurriedly addressed the matter that had brought her to her sister's bedroom in the first place. "Caroline and Paul asked me to intercede on their behalf," she said, addressing her words to Beatrice.

"Intercede?" Beatrice never felt quite at ease with herself when she was around children, her own included. That fact was reason enough to make her puzzled as to how Amity had forged such an obvious bond with her offspring in the short time she'd been with them.

"They thought they might be allowed a discreet visit to the kitchen for a small sample of the party cakes before bed," Amity explained. "I promised them I'd remind you what absolute little jewels they've been all day," she added with a grin.

"Jewels?" Charles asked. "I suppose that means they haven't terrified their nanny out of her wits or thrown the dog down the well?"

"Well, if that was their usual modus operandi before I arrived, then they really have behaved like angels today," Amity laughed.

Beatrice lifted a heavy string of pearls from her jewel box. "I suppose, under the circumstance, the little beasts do deserve a small treat," she said as she held up the necklace and let Charles fasten it for her around her neck. "Would you be a darling, Amity, and ask Nanny to take them down? For one cake each, no more. Then straight to bed."

"I'll take them myself," Amity offered, and once again turned to the door.

"Just a minute, Amity," Beatrice called. She assured herself with a quick glance in the mirror that the necklace properly set off her pale skin and the décolletage of her gown, then stood and crossed the room to her sister, her hands automatically settling the silken folds of her skirt as she moved. "Let me have a look at you. I should hate to have to introduce my sister to the whole of Cairo society—what there is of it—looking anything less than magnificent."

Amity felt a small stab of panic at Beatrice's words. For a moment she was a child again, one who feared her older sister's disapproval far more than even that of her parents. She'd felt the same way when her boat had docked at Alexandria five days before, and she'd stood, terrified that she wouldn't pass muster under Beatrice's critical gaze, wondering childishly if she might be sent back to Boston without even being allowed to disembark and meet her young niece and nephew. The moment of fear had passed then, just as it did once again. Amity performed a neat pirouette, then a curtsy.

If Beatrice was aware of the fear she had inspired, she made no move to dispel it. Her practiced inspection was unhurried and objectively judgmental, taking in her younger sister's tall, slender form, her waist, encircled by the sea-green ribboned trim of her white silk gown, seeming impossibly narrow, the thick mane of chestnut hair, of which Beatrice had always been secretly jealous, caught up in a becoming arrangement of curls that framed her delicate features most attractively.

Strange, Beatrice thought, *how different the two of us are,* and she cast a quick glance at her own far more womanly figure in the pier glass before turning back to consider Amity's slender willowiness. Even though Beatrice realized most men preferred women with ample curves like her own, she decided Amity's charms were more than sufficient to find her an acceptable husband.

In fact, there was the strong possibility she'd already made a firm step in that direction. Unless Beatrice was entirely mistaken, and she very much doubted she was, Amity had completely charmed that young banker, Justin Gardiner, when he'd stopped by to see Charles about some small matter regarding a visa three days before. Beatrice had wandered into her husband's office, and, finding an eminently eligible bachelor in her parlor, had taken the opportunity to introduce Amity to him. And quite to her expectation, Gardiner had suddenly found himself at his

8

leisure for the afternoon, and more than willing to accept her invitation to stay for tea. Upon due consideration, Beatrice found she had no complaints with her sister's appearance, no complaints at all.

"Well?" Amity demanded with a smile. It was odd, she thought, how the feeling of panic seemed just beneath the surface. She hoped it was just because she was still relatively a stranger in Beatrice's house, that the feeling would soon disappear entirely.

"You'll pass in a crowd with a push," Beatrice replied, but then she smiled. "And only a very small push at that."

"I strongly disagree," Charles put in as he made his way between the two sisters. He, too, considered Amity's appearance judiciously. "You are stunning this evening, my dear," he said as he took Amity's hands in his own. "I daresay there will not be a man here this evening who will not soon be groveling at your feet." He brought her hands to his lips. "Myself included."

Amity drew back, the feeling of disquiet once again nudging at her. She barely managed a smile at Charles. "I think flattery comes entirely too easily to a diplomat, Charles," she said and she threw a slightly embarrassed look at her sister. "I think I shan't be able to believe a word you say." Then, to forestall the objection it seemed he was about to make, she turned to the door. "I'd better get back to the nursery or your progeny will never forgive me," she murmured hastily.

"Don't let the little beasts muss you, Amity," Beatrice warned.

"And remind them they have a nanny to wash their messy little faces and get them into bed after," Charles added. "I will need both the lovely Ravenswood sisters at my side to greet the khedive."

When Amity had gone, Beatrice stood facing her husband, her eyes blazing with a fire he knew only too well.

"I warn you, Charles," she hissed at him through tight, pale lips. "Not in my house, not with my sister."

He stared at her for a moment, then smiled and

9

shrugged as he turned away. "I think, my love, you misconstrue my gestures of hospitality." He peered at his reflection in the mirror, and slicked back his sandy blond hair with the heel of his palm, then adjusted the perfect white linen of his cuffs. "And may I suggest you hurry yourself? You wouldn't want to be late to your own party, would you?"

"Would you think ill of me were I to confess I only accepted the invitation to this reception because I knew you would be here, Miss Ravenswood?"

Amity looked up at Justin Gardiner's sharp blue eyes. They seemed momentarily oddly bright in the flickering light cast by the garden lanterns, but the effect passed as they walked along the brick path through the beds of perfectly tended roses. "I shouldn't say that in Beatrice's hearing, Mr. Gardiner," she warned. "She takes such matters very seriously, I think."

"But it's true. Diplomatic parties are all much the same, even those given by your lovely sister and the estimable Consul Charles St. James. The same faces, the same talk, the same food and wine. You'll see. At dinner, the khedive will talk about the opera he's commissioned, General Stuart will remind us all once again of Gordon's valiant sacrifice, a sentiment that will be roundly seconded by the horde of army officers present, and that will be followed by universal rumblings about the French sending Marchand eastward into the Sudan. I swear there hasn't been an original word uttered by any of these people for over a year."

"That sounds a bit intolerant, Mr. Gardiner," Amity suggested.

"It's not intended to be, Miss Ravenswood," he replied. "Just fair warning that Cairo is rife with ennui. If you seek even the smallest adventure, you must be prepared to take yourself from the beaten track." He smiled at her. "Or else allow a hopeful admirer the honor of offering his escort services."

Amity returned the smile, aware that it was a bit coy, but not quite sure of herself with this man. He had been introduced to her as a friend of Charles, but he seemed more than willing to criticize not only his hostess and her party but his friend as well. Society in Cairo was either more Byzantine than it had been in Boston, or she was a good deal more aware than she had been when her life was conducted under her parents' protective eyes.

"Alas, I fear I shall have to prowl the souk on my own," she replied. She flashed him another melting smile. "I have no admirer here to squire me."

Gardiner shook his head. "You underestimate the powers of your charms, Miss Ravenswood. Since the moment Charles introduced me to you three days ago, I've thought of nothing and no one else."

Amity stopped short, forcing him to turn and take a step back so that he was once again beside her. She was dumbfounded by his words. It was the last thing she expected from such a proper Englishman, and one who was a banker at that. One never expected a banker to make declarations that might in any way leave him vulnerable— at least not a prudent, successful banker. And she distinctly remembered Beatrice telling her that he was a very successful banker, a fact which Amity had come to realize vastly raised her sister's opinion of Gardiner over her rather less enthusiastic recommendations of the other unattached men who were to attend the party that evening.

She managed to gather her wits, and they continued on a bit farther in thoughtful silence until they'd come to the end of the garden and stood facing a rose-covered bower framing a small stone bench. Amity was aware of his eyes on her. When she looked up at him, he motioned toward the bench. Obediently, she sat.

Gardiner settled himself beside her, then reached out his hand to take hers. "Is something wrong, Amity?" he asked. "You haven't caught your gown on the rose prickers, have you?"

She hardly even noticed his use of her given name. Flustered, she shook her head quickly. "No, nothing's wrong," she managed to murmur.

He took her hand with his. "Then I have in some way offended you?"

Amity felt herself blush. She was glad of the dimming light so that he could not see it. "You are a perfect gentleman, Mr. Gardiner. It would be impossible for me to take offense." She considered him in silence for a moment longer. "You do surprise me, however."

He smiled at her, his handsome features growing less sharp, a bit younger with the humor that came to his eyes. "You see, I am the perfect escort. A surprise is a thing of wonder in Cairo. Among proper society, at least." He sobered and looked at her thoughtfully for a moment, then raised her hand to his lips. "Shall I surprise you once again, Amity?" he asked her softly before he pressed his lips to her hand. "Shall I tell you that I've determined to marry you?"

Amity swallowed and stared up at him uneasily. She tried to gently pull her hand away from his, but he seemed unwilling to release it, and she was too perplexed to concentrate on removing it from his grasp when other matters were filling her mind. She was not really sure she could be hearing his words correctly. She found herself dazedly bewildered as to how she had gotten herself in the position she now found herself, alone in the twilit garden with him, surrounded by the heady perfume of the roses. Why, she wondered, had Beatrice suggested this walk in the garden? And why had she so willingly obliged?

"I hardly know what to say, Mr. Gardiner," she heard herself reply, although it seemed impossible to her that the words managed to make their way past her lips. Her mouth felt suddenly as though it had become filled with cotton wool.

"You could say that you would be pleased to be my bride," he told her evenly.

Amity looked up, to the open doors to the reception

room, irrationally wishing Beatrice and Charles or some of their guests might miraculously appear and put an end to this unexpected and not entirely welcome conversation.

Gardiner laughed softly. "You have the look of a frightened rabbit caught in a trap, Amity," he said. "And I had no intention of frightening you."

"We . . . we hardly know one another, Mr. Gardiner," she stammered.

"I'm a man who makes decisions quickly, Amity. I've found that my first impressions are always the most reliable."

She shook her head slowly. "I'm flattered, Mr. Gardiner. I've never been quite so flattered. But surely you don't expect me to accept your offer?" she asked. "Surely you would not expect me to agree to marry a man I've known barely more than an afternoon?"

"An afternoon and an hour," he corrected her, then smiled. He raised her hand a bit and looked down at it, considering it, it seemed to her, with a concentration far more intense than so common an appendage deserved.

"No, I suppose I don't," he replied finally. "At least not yet. But I have little doubt but that I can convince you. I'm a very determined man. All I expect from you now is an assurance that you will consider my offer, Amity, that you will not reject it out of hand."

"I've heard it said that decisions made in haste are often repented in leisure," she told him with a smile, feeling absurdly relieved that the matter was to be concluded, for the time being at least, so easily.

"Then I think it wise I give you ample time to come to the right decision." He raised her hand once more to his lips, brushed it with his lips, and then released it. "Might I suggest that you call me Justin as a small sop to my crushed ego, Amity? And you don't object to my calling you Amity, do you?"

"Such familiarity, I think, would not be untoward, Justin," she agreed readily enough. Now that the moment of panic had passed, she was starting to feel rather pleased with herself, and more than a bit flattered that she had managed to charm such a rich and powerful man so easily, making the conquest without even knowing she was engaged in the battle until it was already concluded.

He took her hand and placed it in the crook of his arm. "Now, I think, it would be wise if we return to your sister's party. There is never enough champagne at embassy receptions. And I would hate to think I had deprived you of your fair share."

"Quite right, Cousin. Depriving a lady of champagne is an offense punishable in the Army, and quite rightly, by hanging."

Amity looked up to find that the path in front of them that had seemed so uncompromisingly empty only a few moments before was now occupied by a tall, dark-haired man garbed, as were a good number of the men at the party, in the dress uniform of the British Army. He was smiling broadly, apparently delighted at finding them there. When she turned to Justin, Amity quickly realized that the pleasure was completely one-sided.

Justin considered him a moment, apparently trying to decide if he would even bother with the effort of a reply. His manner completely bewildered Amity. She turned back to the officer.

"Surely hanging is a punishment just slightly out of proportion to the crime?" she asked him, and offered him a smile.

"I beg to differ," he told her, his expression now completely serious. "A lady, especially a beautiful lady, should be denied nothing within a man's ability to grant her." His eyes made a careful survey of her face, then returned to find hers. "For the crime of withholding a liquid as vital as champagne from a woman as beautiful as yourself, my cousin deserves to be drawn and quartered." He grinned suddenly. "It's a shame we British have grown so civilized."

Justin stirred himself, apparently resigned to the necessity of conversation with the officer. "Amity, may I introduce you to Ford Gardiner. As you no doubt heard him

14

mention, we have the dubious pleasure of being related. Ford, Miss Amity Ravenswood."

Amity smiled up at the officer, considering the neat row of stars on the collar of his immaculate white uniform, trying hopelessly to decipher their import. "Colonel Gardiner," she ventured as she held up her hand to him.

He took it firmly in his own, and bowed with sharp military precision. "Miss Ravenswood," he said as he brushed the back of her hand with his lips. "I fear you have given me an undeserved promotion. I confess to being a mere major." He grinned at her. "But if it would suit you, I'll make a great effort for a promotion."

"I thought you were on patrol," Justin commented brusquely as he and Amity stood. The three of them began to move slowly along the path back in the direction of the house.

"I will be, tomorrow dawn."

"Pity it wasn't this morning," Justin muttered.

Ford laughed. "Surely you wouldn't deny me a few hours in the presence of a lovely woman before I venture forth to possible death, all to keep you safe and all your ill-gotten gains secure, Justin?"

Justin scowled, but Amity found herself echoing Ford's laughter. He had, she decided, a far easier sense of humor than his cousin. She considered the two of them, and determined that although Ford might not be quite so starkly handsome as Justin, he probably was far more successful with women.

"Surely you don't expect to face anything so dire as death, Major Gardiner?" she asked. "Charles has made no mention of any recent violence to the south."

Ford's expression grew suddenly quite serious. "Lately one never knows what lies to the south, Miss Ravenswood," he said quietly. Then he smiled once more. "But there are far more important matters to be considered this evening. Finding you a glass of champagne to start, and then persuading you to promise me a dance after dinner."

"A soldier going off to face danger?" she asked. "How

could I in all good conscience even consider refusing?"

Amity found herself pleasantly sandwiched between the two cousins at the long dinner table. Both, it seemed, were determined to provide her with ample entertainment, as were a number of Charles's other guests. She realized she hadn't enjoyed the company of others as much since before her parents' deaths. Justin, especially, seemed to devote a great deal of effort to keeping her amused, whispering bits of just slightly deprecating gossip about the luminaries at the table with a deadpan seriousness. Each time one of his earlier predictions concerning dinnertable conversations came true, he turned to her with an arched brow and a bemused, I-told-you-so expression.

The Khedive Ismail, the evening's guest of honor, was the first to perform according to prophesy. "The libretto is going well," he said in response to the half dozen dutiful inquiries that were made to him regarding the opera he had commissioned.

He turned and looked down the table to where Amity sat, and smiled at her. She noticed that as the sole newcomer in the group, and an attractive young woman at that, he had made an obvious point of addressing himself to her as often as possible.

"I hope you will still be with us when it is completed, Miss Ravenswood. Signore Verdi assures me it will be a triumph. It is the story of a beautiful slave girl who captures the love of the pharaoh." He smiled at her pleasantly. "We easterners are enchanted with love stories."

"I think everyone is, Your Excellency," Amity replied. She considered him thoughtfully. A tall, swarthy, handsome man with a bristling, thick mustache and carefully judgmental eyes, he seemed to her far more a conqueror than the lover of music and romance he was proclaiming himself.

The khedive shook his head. "Not the British, I think," he said slowly. "They are far too interested in warfare and

16

power to waste their energy on romance." He offered her a smile. "If you are of a mind to fall in love, Miss Ravenswood, may I recommend to you to find an easterner, and above all avoid an Englishman."

Once again he smiled at her, and this time his eyes found hers with a sharply considering glance. Amity had the uncomfortable feeling he might be suggesting something more than the possibility that his countrymen made the most devoted husbands. She turned first to Justin, then to Ford Gardiner, and found them both apparently stifling their amusement.

"I'm afraid I must disagree, Your Excellency," Beatrice interjected. She waited until the khedive turned to her, then smiled at him prettily. "I must state that I have found life with an Englishman quite pleasant."

"Your unsolicited testimonial is appreciated, my dear," Charles offered, and raised his glass in toast to her.

There was a small chorus of "Here, here" from the men at the table, and a number of glasses were raised following Charles's.

The khedive, however, seemed determined. "It seems to me, my dear Mrs. St. James, that you have been unfairly influenced in that you are married to an Englishman. Had you married a Turk, you would understand what the meaning of the word romance really is." He smiled at Beatrice evenly, then turned his glance once more back to Amity.

"Surely you cannot argue that we English think of our ladies any less than you of yours, Your Excellency?" Charles asked with an amused grin.

"You may think of them, Consul St. James, but your position comes before anything in your esteem, I think. Do not misunderstand me. We admire your fortitude. It's just that we would much rather wrinkle the crease in our trousers than emulate you."

There was a moment of awkward silence at the table, and then a twitter of embarrassment from the ladies. Eager to change the subject, General Stuart gallantly broke into a short lecture on Gordon's sacrifice at Khartoum, thus proving Justin's second prediction true. Justin turned to Amity with the same slightly superior, amused glance he'd offered her when the subject of the khedive's opera was introduced. Amity found herself on the verge of giggles, and had to fight with herself not to allow them to escape. But when she turned to Ford, she saw something in his expression that completely stilled any hint of amusement she might have felt. She wondered what it was that pained him so, why he turned so suddenly completely serious.

The dinner finally ended, and the ladies retired to the sanctity of Beatrice's salon while the gentlemen indulged in their port.

"How do you find Cairo, my dear?" General Stuart's wife asked her with the air of one who had already heard any possible answer Amity might think to offer.

She leaned forward and chose a piece of candied fruit from the tray on the table in front of her, lifting it with due concern for any crystals of sugar that might drop to her skirts. She was a tall, well-endowed woman with a sharp nose and chin, dark hair and perhaps twenty less years than her husband. Amity thought she considered the piece of sweet in her heavily jeweled hand with a good deal more interest than she had shown her husband during dinner.

"Intriguing," Amity told her. "And exciting—"

"It's no wonder," broke in another woman, who Amity vaguely remembered as being introduced to her as Mary Hamilton, the wife of one of the senior officers. "You have both the Gardiner cousins vying for your attention. Not to mention the khedive." She turned to Mrs. Stuart, her expression smugly complacent. "Do you remember the feeling, Louise?" she asked. "Being the new face and the apparent recipient of every heart in the city?" She looked back at Amity, and offered her a tight little smile. "Take advantage of it, my dear. Find one worth marrying. All too soon there'll be another new face for them to flock around, and you don't want to miss your opportunity."

18

Amity felt herself cringe inside at the apparent coldness of these women, at the way they seemed to be evaluating her chances and assigning her life. "I'm here to visit my sister," she ventured softly.

Mrs. Stuart's look grew superior. "Certainly, my dear," she agreed, her tone completely dismissive, and she carefully nibbled at the piece of candied fruit. "We all come to visit a sister or an aunt or a cousin. And we all manage to find ourselves husbands. That is, after all, how it's done—"

"Amity, I'm sure, will find herself with any number of options," Beatrice broke in serenely. "As for this evening," she went on, turning to her sister and smiling, "I hope your dancing pumps are comfortable, Amity. The junior officers are always invited to the dancing, and I'm sure none of them will be content to leave without a turn."

"Are they all leaving tomorrow?" Amity asked, as anxious to change the subject as she was for an answer. "Is it really dangerous to the south?"

Mrs. Stuart's expression grew set. "That, my dear, is a question we don't voice here. We entertain them and then send them off with our best wishes. And if it becomes necessary, we accept the news of their deaths with appropriate grace and control. After all, we are British."

Beatrice stood suddenly. She had obviously heard the lecture on the role of the British wife before and found it less than stirring. "Shall we join the gentlemen?" she asked.

The other women stood, apparently ready to meet the fray.

"You dance beautifully, Major Gardiner."

Ford Gardiner smiled down at her. "The benefits of a misspent youth, I'm afraid, Miss Ravenswood," he replied, then lapsed once more into silence.

Amity realized he had been staring at her, and she found his obvious preference for silence combined with that stare rather unsettling. If he seemed content to dance with her in his arms and stare down at her, she found the proximity, the knowledgeable way he held her, as well as that evaluating stare, more than a little disconcerting.

"Have you been long in Egypt?" she ventured.

"Six years," he answered, then once more fell silent.

"Then you were here while Gordon was still alive?" she persisted.

His face lost its impassivity, and she suddenly remembered his odd expression when Gordon had been mentioned during dinner. She wondered if she had somehow said the wrong thing.

He gave her no hint. "Yes, Miss Ravenswood. I was here," he told her, but he said nothing more.

She was finally ready to admit defeat. "You really don't want to talk, do you?" she asked.

He grinned crookedly. "Sometimes dancing with a beautiful woman is occupation enough for a man," he replied.

The look somehow settled her qualms, and she allowed herself to do as he did—concentrate on the pleasant awareness of being close, on the gently flowing feeling the movement and the music imparted. It was, she realized once she had accepted the feeling, a pleasant relief after the dozen dances she'd had with strange, anxious young men, all of whom had seemed to require the same flow of pleasant, if meaningless, conversation. When the waltz ended, she found she genuinely regretted losing the respite.

Ford smiled at her. She looked up at him and smiled back.

"I know you promised me only one dance, Miss Ravenswood, but I find myself already pining for another. Could you be persuaded?"

She nodded. "I think there is a small possibility, Major Gardiner," she replied.

"Excellent," he said as he darted a glance to the group at the side of the dance floor who watched them expectantly. "I don't think I'm quite prepared to offer you up to the attentions of all those ernest, fresh-faced lieutenants. At

20

least not just yet."

It was not, however, dancing alone he had in mind. Amity found that he had soon propelled them to the far side of the dance floor, toward the large French doors that opened into the garden.

"A breath of fresh air, Miss Ravenswood?" he asked as he confidently ushered her outside without waiting for her reply. His hand to her waist, he led her away from the lights of the ballroom, to the edge of the moonlit, balustraded veranda.

Amity found herself with a pleasant feeling of expectancy. The evening, which had begun so ominously with her foolishly bursting in on Beatrice and Charles, had proved to be unexpectedly exciting. First the proposal of marriage from Justin Gardiner. And now was she about to receive another? For a young woman whose eighteenth year had been spent mourning the accidental death of her parents and then being shunted from the bleak household of one maiden aunt to the even bleaker household of another, so much attention was heady and far more intoxicating than the glass of champagne she'd drunk before dinner.

Whatever her expectations, she was not at all prepared for Ford Gardiner's words once they had settled themselves beside the garden wall.

"You don't intend to seriously consider marrying Justin, do you?" he asked.

Amity was not quite sure she'd heard him correctly. She took a step backward and stared at him curiously. "Excuse me, Major Gardiner?"

"I asked you if you intended to seriously consider becoming Justin's wife," he repeated evenly.

"What makes you think your cousin intends to ask me to marry him?" she demanded.

He caught her eyes with his own. "Because he has already proposed to you," he told her quietly.

"You were spying!"

Amity didn't know which shocked her more, the fact that he had been in the garden, eavesdropping on her conversation with Justin, or that he was so willing to casually admit to the fact.

"On the contrary, Miss Ravenswood. I was merely strolling in the garden. If circumstances conspired to allow me to overhear Justin's rather less than romantic proposal, I cannot be blamed."

His words struck her, and she realized that Justin's proposal, unexpected although it might have been, had hardly been what she'd dreamed about when she'd fantasized how a man should ask for her hand.

"How dare you?" she demanded. She felt herself shaking inside. The worst of it was the realization that he seemed to know that were he of a mind, he could probably perform her fantasy proposal perfectly, starting with the bent knee and ending with the sort of a kiss that would take her breath away.

He grinned at her once again, the same lopsided grin he'd offered her while they were dancing. "I feel I should warn you, Miss Ravenswood, that not only is my cousin a decidedly unimaginative man, I firmly believe he's not quite the forthright, upstanding pillar of society he pretends. I have no proof, but I am firmly convinced he comes by his money in a less than honest manner. But more than that, he is basically an unprincipled person, one who surely does not deserve the good fortune of you for his wife."

"I don't believe I'm standing here, listening to any of this," Amity snapped at him, and she turned away, starting back toward the doors to the ballroom.

His hand caught her arm. "More than that," he went on, as if she'd said nothing, as if she'd made no move to leave, "you deserve far better a lover."

And then somehow Amity found herself wrapped in his arms, her body pulled close to his, and his lips, warm and firm and determined, pressed to hers.

At first she felt nothing but shock, disbelief that this could actually be happening, a sort of removed, distant feeling that she must be imagining it, that it couldn't actu-

22

ally be real.

And then the feeling was lost in another, a feeling so strong it threatened to overpower her, so unexpected it completely bewildered her. She felt herself swept up on a tide of liquid fire, fire that seemed to flow through her, snaking into her arms and her legs, leaving her weak with a heated, liquid languor. She'd never before felt anything like this, never considered the possibility of the sort of rush that his touch sent through her. Whatever anger she had felt, whatever disbelief, it was all lost, swallowed by her body's questioning thirst. For a timeless moment, she wanted nothing more but for the feeling to go on and on, for it never to end.

Ford was surprised by that, by the quick, heated response her body had for him. More than that, he realized with a bit of shock just how inexperienced she must be, that a worldlier woman, under similar circumstances, would have tried to hide that response from him. For a moment he felt a stab of guilt that he was stealing something from her to which he had no right, that her innocence ought to have protected her from him. There was no place in his life for a woman who would expect more from him than the little he had to give, for a woman who might equate passion with ties. He thought to draw away from her, but the thought disappeared as quickly as it came to him. He pulled her close to him, let his tongue play over her lips, then part them to find hers. A kiss had never tasted so sweet to him, had never left his lips and tongue tasting of honey.

He pulled away from her reluctantly, and stared down at her. Her eyes opened, and she looked up at him, her expression dazed, completely lost.

"Why did you do that?" she asked him softly.

It occurred to her that he had done precisely the same thing many times before, absently pulled some woman to him, probably lit the same fire in her as she had felt when he had held her in his arms.

He smiled warily. "Because it's time someone did, Am-

23

ity," he answered. "You know it as well as I." He forced himself away from the urge to say something more, to reveal just how shaken that kiss had left him. "And I seemed a likely candidate." He smiled. "A soldier about to leave on patrol, perhaps about to encounter the bullet that will prove to him his own mortality. I'm giving you the opportunity to leave him with a memory to sustain him, to give him something to cling to when he stares into the face of death."

He was laughing at her, Amity realized. Somehow the thought that she was an object of amusement to him, more than one of passion, hurt her more than the thought that she was no different to him than any number of other women.

She drew back, pushing against him with her fists. "You are no gentleman," she fumed angrily at him.

Surprisingly, her words chased all the humor from his expression.

"No," he agreed, "I am well aware of the fact that I'm not to be considered a gentleman."

That surprised her, that a few simple words seemed able to wound him so easily. But she made no effort to consider the consequences of the power that knowledge might give her over him. She turned on her heel and started once more for the door to the ballroom.

When she reached it, she found Justin about to step outside.

"Amity?" He considered her flushed cheeks and slightly disoriented expression, then turned his glance to Ford. His stance stiffened and there was the distinct air of an animal about to defend his lair about him. "Has my cousin said anything upsetting to you Amity?" he asked her, his glance still on Ford.

Amity turned back to where Ford stood at the far side of the veranda. He was once more cool, the pained look she'd seen on his face gone, his dark blue eyes impassive. For a moment she wondered if the look had ever been there. Then she found herself wondering how many times

24

in the past he'd stood in the moonlight with a woman, how many times he'd taken a woman in his arms and pressed that strangely stirring kiss to her lips. She did not quite know why, but the thought that there were doubtless a great number of women who had shared that kiss disturbed her.

"No," she whispered as she turned back to face Justin and allowed him to take her arm. "Major Gardiner could do nothing to upset me. He is an officer and a gentleman."

Chapter Two

"I think it went quite well last evening, don't you?"

Beatrice lifted her teacup and sipped the dark liquid with the satisfied air of a woman whose place in the world is agreeably arranged and who knows her role is well executed. She stared at Amity over the rim of her cup.

"It was a lovely party," Amity replied, just as she knew Beatrice expected her to.

Charles finished cutting a bite of ham from the slab on his plate, forked it, then stared at it a moment, considering it before he raised it to his mouth. He looked up at his wife as he chewed, aware that she was awaiting his judgment and expecting a few words of praise. His glance slid away from her and to Amity before he finally spoke.

"I think we can all consider your soiree a triumph, my dear. Especially Amity." He put down his fork and lifted his coffee cup. "Or could I possibly have mistaken Justin Gardiner's solicitousness?" he asked. "I can't remember the last time I saw him hang on a woman's words. For that matter, I can't recall the last time he roused himself to come to a consulate party at all. I believe he tells people they bore him."

"Well, in my estimation he didn't seem at all bored last evening," Beatrice said with a decided note of satisfaction. Amity's success seemed almost as pleasant to her as her own might have been. "And if you mistook his interest in Amity, then so did Louise Stuart and Mary Hamilton," she

26

told her husband confidently as she considered her sister. "I shouldn't wonder if the impassive Mr. Gardiner were soon to show us all a bit of his nature we've never seen before, a decidedly romantic side."

"I do so enjoy hearing women plotting the course of their assault on the legion of man," Charles said as he tore his gaze from his contemplation of Amity and returned it to the more mundane sight of the remains of his breakfast. "It makes me realize just how incompetent we deluded, weak males are in comparison to you. I almost feel sorry for poor old Justin. I wonder if he realizes that his free, bachelor days are numbered."

"Really, Charles," Beatrice scolded him as she noticed Amity's blushing confusion. "You make what is entirely innocent sound terribly devious. If Justin Gardiner decides he wants to propose marriage to Amity, it is because he recognizes that she would make him an excellent wife, not because anyone was plotting or any other such thing."

"Not to mention the fact that a tie to my family name might prove advantageous to him if he decides to return to England, nor the fact that Amity is a very pretty young woman who comes with a goodly inheritance as a sweetener to the bargain," he told his wife dryly. He turned to Amity. "Which is not, of course, meant to cast any dispersions on your own sweet charms, my dear."

Amity felt the hot flush in her cheeks and knew they had grown even redder. "He already has," she said softly.

"Thank you, Kameel," Charles said as the white-uniformed houseboy brought him the tray holding the morning's mail. He lifted the pile and began sorting through the envelopes as Kameel bowed and left the room as silently as he had entered. "He already has what, Amity?" he asked her absently, his attention still directed to the morning's post.

Amity swallowed and looked at her sister. "He already has proposed to me," she said, as clearly as she could. For a moment she thought she might choke on the words, but once they were said, she wondered why she had bothered to utter them in the first place.

It was not as though she had accepted Justin's offer, not even as though she had thought of it much during the night before she'd finally dropped off to sleep. In fact, she realized she had thought of someone quite different, someone who apparently had no intention of offering to become her husband, someone who had suggested only that he might make her a competent lover. Was she simply gloating, she wondered, showing her beautiful older sister that she was not quite the plain, gawky child that Beatrice always managed to make her feel?

Perhaps it *was* simply gloating, she realized when she saw the amazed and quite dumbfounded expression that settled on Beatrice's face and recognized the decided feeling of satisfaction welling up inside her. She had finally managed to surprise her sister, and even if she found herself bewildered and confused about her feelings for Ford and Justin, the events of the previous evening had given her at least this small triumph to mitigate her own confused emotions.

"Justin Gardiner proposed to you?" Beatrice asked, her tone amazed, and her expression decidedly bewildered.

"Well, I suppose I could have been mistaken," Amity replied, and watched her sister's expression take on its more accustomed superior passivity. "But there was that request that I agree to become his wife," she added, her tone just a bit smug, and watched the look of dismay return. "So perhaps he really did."

"Well, haven't we grown into a sly little thing?" Beatrice said, staring at her. "I'd never have thought you the sort, Amity."

Charles had dropped the pile of letters to the table in front of him and stared at Amity with as much amazement as did his wife. "You're hardly acquainted with one another," he said sharply. "Don't you think you should take a bit of time with a decision of this sort, Amity?"

Beatrice turned to him, obviously surprised at his protest. Her eyes narrowed as she considered her husband.

28

"This is between Amity and Mr. Gardiner, Charles. I don't think it our place to stand in their way."

Charles shrugged. "It was only that I thought we might have your sister with us for a while before some eager swain stole her away from us, my dear." His words were spoken softly, but there was an odd, hard look in his eyes as he considered his wife.

Amity found herself staring at the two of them, wondering how her confidence had managed to make them seem so antagonistic with each other, wondering what minor madness ruled their lives. She really hadn't anticipated any of this, and she began to wish quite vehemently that she hadn't raised the subject in the first place.

"And what answer did you give him, Amity?" Charles demanded, turning his attention away from Beatrice and back to her. "Are you to marry Justin Gardiner?"

His vehemence startled Amity. She shook her head.

"No," she replied slowly. "I told him much the same thing you just said, that we hardly know one another."

"You didn't reject his offer altogether?"

Beatrice sounded entirely astounded that the thought might even have entered her head. Amity was conscious of a feeling of inadequacy replacing any satisfaction she had felt while she made her unexpected announcement. Beatrice had, it seemed, managed to make her feel foolish and incompetent after all.

"No," she replied. "I promised him I'd consider it."

"Well, that is one thing to be thankful for at least," Beatrice told her. "You'd be a fool not to accept him, Amity. He's the most eligible bachelor in all of Egypt — wealthy, influential, and very handsome. He knows everyone. And some day, I think, he will be important in the government. You'll never forgive yourself if you let him get away."

Amity looked down at her hands, wondering why they seemed suddenly unsteady. "I heard some things about him," she said slowly.

"Things? What things?" Charles asked.

"That he might have come by his fortune less than honestly," Amity replied.

"May I inquire who told you that?" Charles demanded.

"His cousin. Major Gardiner."

"My, you were busy last evening, weren't you?" Beatrice asked sharply.

Charles's reaction was a good deal less vehement, but equally as negative. "I think you must consider Major Gardiner's opinions of his cousin as being tainted, Amity. There seems to be a bit of bad blood between the two of them."

"They certainly didn't pretend to be fond of one another, but I can't believe Major Gardiner would lie," Amity protested.

"I'm afraid he is capable of far worse, my dear," Charles replied. "The details of the story are rather dim, but it seems the good major was involved in a small family scandal before coming here."

"Scandal?"

Beatrice nodded. "Gossip has it that he stole a valuable piece of jewelry from his grandmother's estate. As Charles said, the details are dim as there was never any public accusation, but apparently the jewel was never recovered, and Major Gardiner was forced to leave both Cambridge and England and enter the Army."

Amity shook her head in disbelief. "He seemed such a gentleman," she murmured.

Even as she spoke the words, she remembered how he had put his arms around her and pulled her to him, remembered how he had forced his kiss on her. Why, she wondered, was she defending him when her judgment of him ought only to confirm Beatrice's generally damning opinion?

"All that was a long time ago," Beatrice went on with a wave of her hand. "What's more pertinent as far as you are concerned," she said, peering sharply at Amity, "is that he has rather a reputation as a womanizer. If I were you, I wouldn't set my sights on him. Others have, and they have been sorely disappointed."

30

Amity reached for her teacup. "I'm sure I don't know what you're referring to, Beatrice," she said, just a bit testily. "I can assure you I have absolutely no interest in Major Gardiner whatsoever."

"That's just as well, Amity, because he is the sort of man who would just as soon ruin a woman as anything else," Charles told her with an air of a man who holds himself above any such things.

Amity considered his words thoughtfully for a moment, then she looked up at her brother-in-law. "If that's true, Charles, why do you entertain him in your home?" she asked him softly.

Charles considered her a moment, and then his lips curled up into a tight smile. "Unfortunately, Amity, my home is only partly mine, and only at the whim of the foreign service. And certain form must be maintained in a consulate. Without absolute proof, I am in no position to damn Major Gardiner, nor any other man."

"An admirable position, Charles," Amity told him dryly. She put her cup down, then lifted her napkin from her lap and placed it on the table. "If you'll excuse me, I have some letters to write." She turned to Beatrice. "Shall I remember you to Aunt Sophia?" she asked as she stood.

Charles stared at her a moment, then turned his attention back to the heap of the morning's mail. He took two envelopes from the pile and held them out to her. "You have some mail this morning, Amity."

Amity walked around the table to his place and took the two envelopes he held out to her. The writing on both was completely unfamiliar to her. She'd already received letters from both her aunts in Boston and had yet to answer them. She wondered who else might be writing to her.

She tore open the first, and quickly removed the sheet and read the single line it bore.

The note was short and almost cryptic: *The memory of our sweet moments together will sustain me.* There was nothing more, no salutation and no signature, but Amity knew who had written it. She could almost see Ford Gardiner's amused smile as he penned the words.

"What is it, Amity?" Beatrice asked, apparently as curious as she was.

"It's nothing," Amity said calmly, not even aware of why she chose to hide it from her sister, but finding the unaccustomed lie coming easily to her lips. "Just a word from one of the young lieutenants I met last evening, a polite thank-you for the dance we had."

Beatrice lifted her cup and sipped the now lukewarm tea. She wrinkled her nose in distaste and put the cup down again. "It's nice to know there are still some gentlemen left in this world," she pronounced. "And the second note?"

Amity slid her finger under the flap of the second envelope, and opened it with a slightly less enthusiastic gesture than she had the first. "It's from Justin Gardiner," she replied slowly as she scanned the note. "He's offered me an excursion to the souk this afternoon."

"Why would he offer to take you there?" Beatrice demanded, her tone a bit waspish. "It smells bad and it's filthy."

Amity shrugged. "Perhaps because I mentioned last evening that I would like to see it," she replied softly, then smiled. "I think I'll go and write him a note accepting his offer," she said, turning toward the door.

Charles considered her as she left, a look of disappointment edging its way onto his face. He seemed completely unaware that as he stared after Amity, Beatrice considered him thoughtfully, her own expression showing emotions that seemed far more volatile than did his.

Amity tightened the ribbons that held her hat. A wide-brimmed, straw affair that Beatrice absolutely demanded she wear when she was in the sun, it seemed determined to rebel constantly, the brim catching each waft of the hot, dry wind threatening to lift it completely from her head.

The hat finally settled, she stared curiously about the

sprawling souk. It was incredibly crowded, and although Justin attempted manfully to keep her from being jostled, he could not entirely block the mass of heavily robed bodies that brushed, oblivious, against her. Stalls displaying fruit and vegetables and tin and brass wares, little more than plank tables covered with goods and shaded by thin cotton awnings mostly, shouldered one against the next, and the mass of them against the more permanent-looking shops offering jewelry and fine rugs and silks. The air was hot and thick with dust and the scents of incense, rotting vegetation, and camel dung, as well as the noise of voices, human as well as the distinctive complaint of the camels who so negligently littered the ground. It was fascinating and exotic to Amity, even if the noise and the smells did threaten to overwhelm her.

"You're sure you want to explore, Amity? You wouldn't rather go somewhere more civilized for a ladylike cup of tea?"

Justin seemed to think that her first glimpse and whiff of the souk might be enough for her. Amity looked up at him and shook her head.

"I want to see everything. There's nothing like this in Boston," she added with a smile.

"To be sure. But then, I doubt there's anything like this anyplace even remotely civilized," he told her as he tightened his hold on her arm. "If you are determined, may I advise you not to breathe too deeply."

Amity laughed. "I thought you were unconventional, Justin—that you didn't mind a bit of an adventure?"

"Oh, I'm terribly conventional, Amity," he told her as he deftly maneuvered them through a group of hawkers selling musk melons and woven baskets. "It is only my regard for you that lures me on this mission. That, and the fear that you might actually undertake such an outing alone."

"*Shoof, ya sitt.* Look, lady. Fine, most beautiful silk for a most beautiful lady."

Amity was rather startled by the eager hawker who had bounded out to greet her face to face, waving an armful of half a dozen lengths of shimmering fabrics in lustrous, dazzling colors. She smiled at him, and shook her head regretfully, not so much at the fact that she wanted the silk and could not buy it, but that he seemed so dejected at her refusal. Justin threw him a warning look and he backed away, aware that a gentleman would not countenance any of the usual wheedling or badgering that might induce a lady to be willing to part with some coins.

Justin led her along the bustling row of stalls to finally stop in front of one heaped with fruit. The elderly man who tended it seemed to know him, for he looked up at Justin, then bowed.

"*Yom saeed,* ya sheikh Gardiner," he said, bowing once again to Justin and smiling a crooked smile that revealed his stained teeth. "A very fine day to you and the lady."

"*Yom saeed,* Abdul," Justin replied soberly.

"How may I serve you, today, ya shaikh?" the old man asked.

Justin pointed to a tray of large, dark, unblemished figs. "A few of those, I think, Abdul," he said.

The old man carefully picked out a half dozen of the largest of the fruits, then placed them on an open-weave wicker tray while he poured water over them to clean them. He held the tray out to Justin for approval, then, when Justin had nodded, offered the fruit to Amity.

"Conventional?" Amity laughed as she selected one of the figs. She bit into it gingerly, and found the grainy fruit sweet and juicy. "Delicious," she told the old man, and he smiled with pleasure.

"Abdul's fruit is the best in the souk," Justin told her as he collected the remaining figs and paid for them.

"*Khattar kherak,* ya shaikh Gardiner," the old man said, bowing as he thanked Justin for the words of praise.

"For someone who never comes to the souk, you seem to know your way around fairly well," Amity accused him as he took her arm and led her away from the stall.

"I only said I was conventional, Amity. Not that I never come here." He took a large bite of a fig.

"Beatrice says she's never set foot here," Amity noted as she took another bite of her fig, this one far less timid than her first. A bit of the sweet juice dribbled onto her chin.

"Oh, I'm sure she came once. They all come once," Justin replied. Then he grinned. "But one whiff usually suffices. I think you are an uncommon lady, Amity."

"Not uncommon," she said as she wiped away the juice from her chin, then licked it from her fingers. "Just a bit more venturesome than most." She was, she realized, enjoying herself immensely. This was what she had imagined it would be like to visit Egypt, not the carefully anglicized atmosphere that reigned at the consulate. It all pleased her inordinately—the noise, the smells, the sweet, sticky taste of the fig still in her mouth.

"Decidedly uncommon, Amity," Justin insisted. "And uncommonly beautiful."

That avowal surprised her, aware as she was of her sticky hands and chin, the straw hat pulled too tightly on her windblown curls, the dusty, gritty bite of the taste of the air making her realize that she was, most likely, as covered with a fine layer of dun-colored dust as the figs had been before Abdul washed them. She also remembered the rather distant way Justin had proposed to her, how Ford's accusation that it had been unromantic and that he was unimaginative had struck her as being a distinctly accurate description.

Before she had time to reply, their attention was drawn to a small crowd that had grown suddenly very noisy a few yards farther along the row of stalls. Their shouts were punctuated by the long, loud cry of a camel, sharper and more pained than those that had become a steady background to the noise of the souk.

"What's happening?" Amity demanded.

"I don't know," Justin said, taking her arm once more and moving forward to the scene of the excitement.

He stopped suddenly and tried to draw her back, but their path was blocked by a sudden rush of anxious men who surged forward and barred the way. Amity peered curiously toward the cluster of humanity, seeing the camel, fallen on its knees, lifting its head in angry, useless protest as the crowd pushed around it. There were loud cries, the animal's, and those of the men and boys who surrounded it. And then there was the sound of his cries grown agonized, and the splash of blood thrown against his dull tan neck.

"Don't look, Amity," Justin warned. He began to pull her back, away from the vicious circus, shouting to those around them to let them pass and finally managing to make some headway against the crowd.

"But what's happening?" Amity demanded. She darted a backward glance, saw the camel's neck and head swinging back and forth in useless, furious agony, and the dark-red splashes against his hide.

Then she saw the flash of the knives, glinting in the sunshine, and the sudden, sickening reality struck her.

"They're killing it," she gasped, appalled. The noise seemed deafening to her now, the shouts of the crowd, the loud, bellowing cries of the dying animal sharper and more horrid than anything she'd ever heard before.

"It's fallen and can't get up, Amity. They're butchering it for food."

She turned and looked up at him, amazed that he seemed so indifferent. "But it's still alive," she protested.

He pulled at her arm. "Let's get away from here," he said firmly, and forced her away from the place.

She moved mechanically, her mind still on the pitiful, dying creature, the scent of its blood seeming to overwhelm even the pungency of the souk. Men were pushing past them, eager to join the carnage, not wanting to lose the opportunity to get the fresh meat.

"Here," Justin told her, pulling her to the door of one of the more expensive-looking shops.

The door opened with the sound of a bell's tinkle. They walked inside, and Justin closed it behind them. The noise suddenly ceased, left outside, as though the souk were miles, not a few steps, away. Away from the hot glare of the sun, the interior of the shop seemed dim and almost cool in comparison to the marketplace outside.

"Sir . . . lady. May I be of service?"

The man had seemed to simply appear out of the shop's jumble to stand in front of them. He was portly, with his ample girth encased not in the flowing robes of the occupants of the souk Amity had seen until then, but in a dark suit and a white shirt that was slightly discolored and frayed at the collar and cuffs. His darting glance shifted from her to Justin, and back to her again. Amity had the feeling that he was far more surprised by her presence than he was by Justin's.

"A camel collapsed," Justin informed him. "I brought the lady here hoping to spare her the unpleasantness."

The shopkeeper nodded. "Barbaric, isn't it?" he agreed, his tone solicitous, but he could not keep his eyes from straying to the door as though he wished he might join the men with the knives outside and provide himself with some of the fresh camel meat. With a shrug of resignation, he forced his attention back to Justin. He bowed slightly. "Please come in, I would be honored if you would stay as long as you like. If it would please you to look around . . ." he ended, his tone turning a bit wheedling, as if implying they should at least take the effort to reimburse him in some small way for his hospitality. Then he looked at Amity and smiled. "Perhaps you would like some tea, lady?" he asked, once more the soul of solicitousness and concern.

Justin followed his gaze and realized Amity looked a bit pale. "Perhaps you should have a cup of tea, Amity," he suggested.

She shook her head. The fig she had just eaten seemed to be at war with her stomach, and the prospect of tea seemed to her only as if it would add another combatant to the melee. She forced herself to smile, and determined not to think of the heaving inside her.

"I'm sorry, Justin . . ." she began. "I never thought . . ."

He waved away her apology. "Nothing to be sorry about," he told her. He considered the shopkeeper for a moment, then turned back to her. "If you feel well enough, perhaps we could look about. One never knows what one might find in places of this sort."

She nodded in agreement. The shop had seemed a cluttered jumble of dingy curios to her when she'd entered, but as her stomach began to settle and as her eyes accustomed themselves to the dimness, she realized there was some sort of order, that beside the usual offerings such shops presented — odd chairs, unremarkable landscape paintings and a welter of tarnished silver teapots and toast racks — there was a shelf of earthenware figurines of a sort she'd never seen before.

She approached the shelf and stared at the small figures — surprisingly lifelike, if improbable, men with heads like dogs or hawks or rams, women-figures with bovine faces or a cat's head or with exaggeratedly rounded breasts suckling infants in their arms.

"Intriguing, aren't they?"

She turned to find that Justin was standing behind her. She nodded. "What are they?" she asked.

"Figures of deities. This sort of thing was often put in graves, to protect the dead on their long voyage."

"Then these are ancient idols?"

He shrugged. "They might be real. Grave robbing is considered a national pastime to the peasants who stumble across them. But more likely they're fakes, made especially for us British. We seem to be especially susceptible when faced with such trinkets and the Egyptians are not above a little fakery to do us out of a bit of coin."

She picked up a figure, one of a woman, this one a completely human figure, sporting an elaborate headdress and wearing a clinging gown that bared one shoulder. The folds of the fabric seemed almost transparent, the features of the female body beneath seeming only barely clothed. She was holding a tiny black cat in her arms.

"The young lady has a fine eye. That is perhaps the best

38

piece in the shop." The shopkeeper had walked up behind her and stared at the small idol in Amity's hand. "It is a figure of the goddess Bastet, miss. She is the goddess of joy. The statue is very fine, very old. It is said that those who worshipped her were blessed with riches and a very long life."

Amity fingered the tiny arms, and admired the minutiae of the minuscule cat that stood, seeming ready to spring from the idol's arms. She was amazed at the incredible detail of the tiny bright eyes, the sharp little ears, the alert stance. The small feline seemed almost to be staring at her, gazing at her with a strangely calm and knowing expression.

"Do you like it, Amity?" Justin asked her as he reached for the small figurine and took it from her.

"I've never seen anything quite like it," she replied.

"It is unusually detailed," Justin told her. "I think it might even be as old as our friend here implies."

"It is authentic, sir, I assure you," the shopkeeper intoned, his expression suggesting that Justin's doubt wounded him deeply.

"Wrap it up as a gift for the young lady," Justin told him, handing him the figurine. Then he turned to Amity. "That is, if the young lady will allow it?"

She shook her head regretfully. "I couldn't, Justin."

"Look at it as a loan if not a gift, then," he told her. "Should you ever feel disinclined to keep even so small a token from me, you can return it. I'm intrigued by the remnants of ancient Egypt. Nothing would please me more than the possibility that you might find an interest in it as well."

"I hardly know what to say, Justin," she said, wavering. She did not know why, but as she held it she had begun to feel as though the small figurine was more than merely a totem but was to become linked in some way to her life. The thought was fascinating to her, if somehow a bit frightening.

"Then say nothing," he told her.

39

He turned to the shopkeeper and attended to the matter of settling the bill while Amity browsed absently through the more mundane objects in the shop. She heard the dull drone of the men's voices behind her, and the thought occurred to her that it seemed to be taking a good deal of the expected souk bickering for them to come to a mutually acceptable price. When he rejoined her, Justin was carrying a small, securely wrapped and tied package.

"I have a friend who is quite an expert on these kind of figures, Amity. Perhaps I might bring you and the goddess round to meet him. That is, if it would amuse you?"

Amity smiled up at him. "And the goddess?" she asked.

"Oh, I have no fear but that Bastet will be more than willing to make his acquaintance. Providing, of course, you are willing to provide her escort."

"If it is the goddess's wish," she agreed easily. "I would not presume to deny a goddess."

"Excellent," Justin pronounced. "Tomorrow afternoon, I think."

He took her arm and placed it in the crook of his. They wandered out into the heat and bustle of the souk. As soon as they left the shop, a group of ragged, dirty-faced children surrounded them. They plucked at Amity's skirt and Justin's sleeves, staring up at them and speaking very quickly in Arabic. Amity thought she heard one address Justin as Shaikh Gardiner. She wondered how these street urchins could possibly know Justin by name.

Justin pulled a few coins from his pocket, tossed them at the beggar children, then spoke to them very quickly, his tone very harsh. Amity wished she could understand the words.

They seemed to hesitate for an instant, but then they scurried about in the dust for the coins he'd tossed to them. Quickly satisfied that they'd found the lot, they formed a small troop, once more calling out to Justin. He waved them aside, and they finally ran off.

"What were they saying?" Amity asked, staring after them, bewildered by the high pitched whine of their voices, the strange intensity of their pleading.

Justin shrugged. "Nothing. They were just beggars."

"But they seemed to know you," she heard herself protesting, not quite sure why she pursued the matter.

He looked away. "I come to the souk occasionally. One of them must have heard someone call me by name. They are very wily, these young thieves."

He took her arm then, and led her very quickly through the crowded lanes of the souk until they were once more at the market's edge. There, he hailed a cab, then helped her in, all the while avoiding her glance, and with it the possibility of her questions.

They rode back to the consulate in near silence. But when the cab had stopped and he'd helped her out, he seemed once more to find his tongue.

"This has been a doubly pleasant day," he said as they wandered into the marble coolness of Beatrice's parlor. "Not only have I had the opportunity to spend a few hours in your company, I also learned a good deal about you today."

"Have I given away any dire secrets?" she asked him, bewildered by his assertion.

He nodded. "Decidedly. I've learned you are a good deal more venturesome than most of my own countrywomen. And now I learn you may be induced to share one of my own favorite pastimes." He smiled at her, his expression suddenly very satisfied, very knowing, as he unwrapped the package containing the small figure of the goddess and set it on a table. "You see, we are fated to be joined, Amity," he told her evenly. "I knew it the first moment I saw you."

He put his hand to her cheek, and stared down at her a moment. Then he leaned toward her and pressed his lips to hers.

Amity stood completely still and unmoving. When his lips left hers, she drew backward, away from him.

"Am I interrupting?"

Amity turned quickly to find Beatrice standing in the

doorway. She was smiling amiably at Justin.

"I've just brought Amity home," he announced.

"Will you stay for tea, Mr. Gardiner?" Beatrice asked pleasantly as she moved into the room.

"I'm afraid that is impossible, Mrs. St. James," Justin replied. "I've business to attend to this afternoon, something I've ignored for the far more pleasant alternative of Amity's company. But I'm afraid it cannot be put off indefinitely."

Beatrice smiled, more than willing to allow him to make his escape if that was his intention. "Of course, Mr. Gardiner. Thank you so much for entertaining Amity this afternoon." She turned and looked meaningfully at her sister.

Amity stirred herself. "Yes," she murmured. "It was very kind of you to take me to the souk. It was a wonderful afternoon."

The usual words of thanks seemed to be said of their own accord. She was hardly aware she'd spoken.

Justin considered her for a moment, wondering what it was she was thinking, why she was suddenly so withdrawn. Then he smiled, took her hand in his, and raised it to his lips.

"Until tomorrow, Amity," he said, then nodded to Beatrice and strode quickly to the door.

Amity silently watched him leave. Slowly her gaze drifted to the idol. Suddenly the lure of the excitement of the afternoon seemed to have paled. As pleasant as she had found Justin's company, she found that his reference to the possibility of marriage, even his kiss, left her blankly numb when surely it ought to have set her heart racing.

Her thoughts drifted warily back to the few moments she had spent in Ford Gardiner's arms, to the realization that his kiss, his embrace, had left her feeling far differently. She pushed away the memory, telling herself that Ford was a needless complication for her emotions. If Charles and Beatrice could be believed, he was a man who cared about nothing and no one but himself, a thief, disgraced in his own family, a man she ought to avoid. Yet, despite that knowledge, she realized that even the memory of his kiss left her feeling weak and bewildered . . .

While Justin left her feeling simply indifferent. Why, she wondered, must life be so confusing? Why couldn't Justin, whom both Beatrice and Charles considered the perfect husband, inspire in her even a small amount of the feeling Ford had?

"What is this bizarre thing?"

Beatrice had lifted the small statue and was staring at it with evident distaste.

Amity forced her attention back to her sister and the statue of the goddess. As she had done in the curio shop, she considered the tiny cat's strangely knowing stare.

"It's a goddess, Bea," she replied thoughtfully. "The goddess Bastet."

Beatrice's lips pursed in displeasure. She hated being called Bea, and she knew Amity was perfectly aware of that fact. She looked up at Amity and stared at her sharply, finally deciding that her sister's expression held no malice, but seemed extremely distracted.

"Well, I think it's perfectly ugly," she said, and held it out to Amity. Then she smiled. "And I also think you are falling in love with Justin Gardiner."

Amity turned to her, surprised by the words. "Am I?" she asked vaguely as she moved to take the statue from Beatrice's hand.

Beatrice nodded complacently. "Most decidedly. And I can't think of anything that would be better for you."

Amity did not respond to her words. She was so intent on her consideration of the small goddess that she hardly even heard them. But if she had, she might have suggested otherwise to Beatrice.

Perhaps even Beatrice herself might have echoed those sentiments, especially if she had seen Justin return to the souk, to find a narrow street close to the shop where he had taken Amity that afternoon and to be once more surrounded by the same ragtag group of street children. He was more accommodating to them this time than he'd been when Amity had been in his company, allowing them to lead him to a narrow, dusty street and into a dark alley bordered by stained, crumbling walls. Within the hour Justin Gardiner would be comfortably reclining on a pillowed divan, watching as a generous sprinkling of hashish was dropped on the tobacco in the hookah that was set beside him, ready to inhale the narcotic smoke and then allow two young prostitutes to earn their keep. By then Beatrice would be happily contemplating marrying off her younger sister, putting Amity safely out of harm's way and away from Charles's wandering eye.

Chapter Three

"It's all there, in my report. I thought you might like a little firsthand observation so I had the weapons brought here."

Major Harold Strafford leaned back in his chair and waved his hand toward the table at the far side of his office. It was a rough, long trestle table, and it was covered with rifles.

Ford Gardiner rose from the straight backed wooden chair he had occupied and crossed the room. He'd been darting glances at the rifles for the previous fifteen minutes while he'd conferred with Strafford, and he was anxious to see them firsthand, to touch them, to make Strafford's unlikely story real.

He scanned the weapons on the table, letting his eyes drift quickly past the half dozen that he would have expected, and quickly found the one rifle that could not conceivably have been there, the one Strafford had mentioned so prominently in his report. He lifted it and proceeded to inspect it carefully.

"You're right," he admitted reluctantly. "It's the Meerschmidt twenty-round repeater. I've only seen one before this. The Army is supposed to get them sometime neat year." He turned and looked up at Strafford. "How the hell did Ali Kalaf's man come to have it when the British Army won't be able to get them for months?"

Strafford stood. "Damned if I know," he said, shrugging, as he crossed the room to where Ford stood. "What I do know is that if Kalaf has many of these, he'll have his hand on our throats. He'll make what happened to Gordon in Khartoum look like a picnic before he's done."

Ford lifted the rifle and sighted down it. "And no one at headquarters even knows they have them," he added ominously.

Strafford nodded. "It was purely a matter of luck that my patrol stumbled on that scouting party. If it had been the other way round, you'd be sifting the desert for our remains and we'd never know Kalaf has any of these."

"There was only this one, out of a party of eight?"

Strafford nodded. "But one could have been enough."

But Ford's thoughts were following another course. "I don't think Ali Kalaf has many of them yet," he said slowly. "I can't see him sitting idle once he's sure he can take us. That can only mean he's waiting until he can equip all his men with the rifles before he makes his move."

Strafford took the rifle from him and returned it to the table. "Maybe. But I can't see that the possibility does anything but buy us a little time even if that's true. A company of men armed with these could annihilate a whole army." His expression grew grim. "It doesn't make sitting out here and waiting very appetizing."

"And you could get nothing out of the two you captured?"

Strafford shook his head. "I've seen more accommodating rocks. The only thing I've gotten out of them is the affirmation that they consider being subjected to the immediate presence of British, a defilement to them."

"Perhaps I could see them?" Ford suggested.

"I don't see why not. You couldn't have any worse luck with them than I did." Strafford started toward the door.

46

Ford followed him out into the central compound of the small fort. The sun seemed almost to strike him, abnormally bright, reflected from the white walls surrounding the central enclosure. A company of men drilled with a weary resignation, their enthusiasm obviously long ago dissolved by the heat, perspiration leaving large dark stains on their dun-colored shirts. Ford darted a glance up, to the guard towers at the top of the wall, and observed the men pacing along the narrow walkway. If no more comfortable than their fellows drilling in the compound below, they were at least a good deal more intent as they stared out across the seemingly endless expanse of sand.

Ford followed Strafford across the compound, passing the small lean-to that sheltered the spring that was the fort's water supply. He knew that the desert was pockmarked with these unexpected sources of water, that many of them were unknown to the British and some even unknown to the Bedouin tribes that claimed the desert as their own. He also knew that sometimes they dried up unexpectedly, making life even more precarious than the heat, the hostile winds, the sandstorms, and even how Ali Kalaf had made it for Strafford and his men. He almost felt guilty knowing that he would be able to leave while the men garrisoned there would be forced to stay. It seemed almost criminal to force men to remain out in such a godforsaken place—even for the glory of Victoria's crown.

There was a guard standing by the door of the makeshift jail. Although he had relaxed his stance slightly in the long hours out in the heat, he came to immediate attention as he saw Strafford approach with Ford.

Strafford returned his salute. "Any rumblings from our guests, Carver?"

"Not a peep, sir," the private replied smartly. He allowed his glance to drift to Ford for just a second, obviously wondering what would happen now that one of

47

General Stuart's aides had appeared at the fort.

"Let's see if Major Gardiner can't convince them to change their minds," Strafford said. "Open up."

The soldier fumbled for a moment with the key, then managed to fit it into the lock and turn it. He pushed the door open and stood back to allow the officers to enter.

Ford followed Strafford inside, for a short moment blinded by the dim light after the searing brightness of the sun outside. Then his eyes adjusted, and for a moment he stood, staring, not quite believing, and realizing what he was seeing was all too sickeningly real.

The floor seemed to be soaked with blood, the air thick with the smell of it. The two men, their white robes blotched with dark stains of rust-colored blood, lay close together. One's throat was slit. The second, his hand still clenching the knife he had thrust to his own heart, had fallen just atop the man he'd killed before taking his own life.

Strafford paled visibly, then made a small gagging sound. Ford made no sign that he'd heard it. He felt more than a little queasy himself.

"Carver!" Strafford roared.

The young soldier appeared in the doorway, his expression bewildered until his gaze found the grotesque display of the bodies. He blanched, then ran outside. There was the sound of retching and ragged coughing before he returned. Strafford grimaced as Carver re-entered.

"You heard nothing of this, suspected nothing?"

Carver shook his head numbly. "No, sir. I brought their food in to them, and a jug of water. That one," he pointed briefly at the man whose throat had been slit, "swore at me and said they would eat none of the British poison. I left it and went outside. There wasn't a sound, sir. I swear I didn't hear a thing."

Ford nodded. "I believe you," he told the soldier. "I've

48

seen this sort of thing before. These men are fanatics. Their leader has promised them an afterlife in paradise and they all too willingly flee to it. Death is a gift to them, if they believe it will further their cause."

"Or keep us from hindering it," Strafford suggested.

"How did they get the knife?" Ford asked slowly.

Strafford shook his head. "I don't know. It's impossible. They were searched."

Ford moved to the side of the man who had wielded the knife so effectively, and pulled away the long robe that covered him to reveal his thigh. A thin leather strap with a knife sheath was tied just above the knee.

"But not there, I suppose?" he asked, pointing to where the weapon had been hidden.

Strafford could only stare. Visibly shaken by the sort of determination that would lead a man to silently slit his fellow's throat, then push a knife into his own heart, all without a sound that might alert the guard just outside, Strafford seemed incapable of doing anything more than staring at the gruesome tableau.

"It would seem they have expedited their travel to heaven in Ali Kalaf's service," he finally said. He put his hand to his forehead. "How could we have been such fools as to let them hide a knife that way?" he murmured, his revulsion of the grisly sight of the bodies quickly fading in the face of the crises he had now to deal with. "There's no way we can get any information about Kalaf now."

Ford stood and turned to him. "Nothing we can do about that now," he said, then looked quickly at the blood-covered bodies. "I'll leave for Cairo at daybreak," he continued thoughtfully. "Either we make sure Kalaf gets no more of those rifles or we withdraw. To do otherwise would be suicide. And Stuart will have to make his decisions quickly. I can't think Kalaf will wait a moment longer than he has to, once he knows he has the advantage."

49

Amity found she felt decidedly on edge. As soon as she and Justin had been ushered into Rahman Sareef's parlor and the old man had looked up at her, she'd become aware of the discomfort, the odd feeling his sharp-eyed inspection of her seemed to elicit. Had Justin not been there, standing beside her, she thought she might have turned and run away.

"May I present Miss Amity Ravenswood to you, Professor?" Justin said finally, breaking the near-brittle silence in the room.

The old man stirred himself. First he shook his head slowly, then he smiled and stood.

"You will excuse my lapse, please. Miss Ravenswood, was it? I'm afraid you startled me a bit." He moved out from behind his desk and strode quickly toward them, his hand extended. Then he looked at Justin and grinned. "I hardly expected you to bring such a beautiful woman with you, Justin. I'm deeply honored that you would bother to share the company of such a lovely creature with an old man." He smiled as he turned back to take Amity's hand. "Your presence in my house brightens it with a radiance it has not known for years, Miss Ravenswood."

If she'd felt uncomfortable before this unexpected little speech, Amity was quite dumbfounded when he'd completed it and lifted her hand to his lips. A tall, thin man, dressed in the western fashion, spotlessly pristine and improbably unwrinkled despite the afternoon heat, Professor Rahman Sareef was not at all what she had envisioned when Justin had told her about the Egyptian scholar. She somehow had conjured up an image of a round, swarthy man, perhaps mustachioed and definitely bearded, wearing the richly embroidered robes she'd seen worn by many well-to-do Egyptians, or perhaps the stark, black robes of the more monastic types. She certainly had not expected this gray-haired, dapper man, with his crisply articulated British accent and his clean-shaven face.

"I must admit, I thought for a moment I'd given you rather a shock, Professor," Justin told him. "I've never seen you galvanized before." He grinned. "And certainly never speechless."

Sareef shook his head. "That was rude of me, to stare as I did," he admitted. "I hope you will forgive me, Miss Ravenswood?"

Amity shook her head. "But there is nothing to forgive, Professor Sareef."

"Oh, there is, there is," Sareef protested, his manner now that of a proper British don, his head wagging and his tone decidedly professorial. "I behaved with boorish manners, but perhaps if I offer some explanation you will understand my unorthodox reaction when I looked up and saw you standing here in my parlor."

With that he started to the door with only a motion of his hand to tell them they should follow. Amity offered Justin an amused glance. He could only shrug and smile in return. Then he took her arm and the two of them followed Sareef into the next room.

The professor was waiting for them just beyond the door. "My study," he told them shortly, then stood back and watched the reaction Amity had at the first sight of it.

If the old professor considered the room his study, Amity could only compare it to a small, private museum of antiquity. The walls were lined with glass-fronted bookcases, floor to ceiling, the shelves all solidly laden with figures, most of them clay figures like the one Justin had purchased at the souk for her, but some fashioned of marble or jasper or other stone. They varied in size from the minuscule, only an inch or two tall, to some that were quite large. In the corner of the room stood one that was nearly life-sized, a coolly sleek figure

51

of a man with chiseled features holding a hawk on his outstretched arm. He stared at them with impenetrable, obsidian eyes.

The professor, however, obviously considered the prize of his collection the figure of a woman, fashioned of clay and painted in impossibly still-bright colors. It occupied a case of its own and took the place of honor in the center of the room.

At first Amity was struck by the similarity to her own statue. The stance, the proportions, the small cat nestled in the woman's arm were all very much like the idol of the goddess Bastet she and Justin had come to show to the professor. Her eyes fixed on this larger, more lifelike figure as she walked into the room to finally stop beside the case and gaze at the idol.

Amity gasped.

Sareef nodded.

"Now you see why I was so surprised when I saw you in my parlor, Miss Ravenswood," he told her as he came to stand beside her. "When I looked up, I thought that my lovely goddess Bastet had suddenly come to life. However foolish it may seem, I could not quite believe that you were real."

"The resemblance is remarkable, Professor," Justin said as he compared the finely painted features of the statue's face to Amity's own intent face. "I would not have thought it possible."

Amity could not take her eyes from the statue. "It's like looking at myself in another lifetime," she murmured.

Indeed, the statue's resemblance to her was uncanny. Her own complexion was several shades paler than the statue's painted skin, but other than that the face could have been her own. Wide, greenish-blue faience eyes peered out at her from the glass-enclosed case, eyes much the same color as hers.

"Is she not a marvel?" Sareef asked as he, too, gazed

at the statue. "She is today just as she was when she was placed in the tomb in which I found her, much as she was more than two and a half thousand years ago." He gazed at the figure lovingly. "Incredible, isn't it? Closed up in the darkness with no wind or rain to mar her beauty, she is unchanged, exactly as she looked when she was placed in the tomb. She practically breathes with life, with the life of the ancient princess whose immortal spirit she was to guide through the netherworld and into paradise."

Amity was confused by Sareef's tone, by the way he spoke of his statue and the look he wore as he gazed at it. It was almost as if he spoke of his lover, his mistress. His words, his expression, were intent and filled with restrained passion. The professor, it seemed, had centered all his emotions in his work and, through it, it seemed, in this one particular idol.

She might have been a bit more perplexed had Justin not warned her on the way to Sareef's house that the old man was a bit odd, that he lived for his research. She had dismissed his judgment, as she dismissed her own present confusion, by the observation that scholars were often thought strange, that they sometimes lived their lives through their studies. She considered Sareef's loving expression as he gazed at his statue and dismissed him as a harmless eccentric—odd, but amiable. When he looked up at her and smiled, she amended the evaluation, adding "pleasant" to the list of adjectives.

"Now that I have apologized for my lack of manners, and, I hope, been forgiven," Sareef said with a smile, "perhaps you will allow me to ply you with tea and cakes and talk to you about my love." He nodded once more toward the statue. "Justin suggested that the two of you have some questions to ask me?"

Amity nodded. "We were in the souk and we found a little shop that sold small statues like the ones you have here."

Sareef waved a hand, a gesture of dismissal. "Ah, the thieves in the souk. They sell fakes, mostly to unsuspecting British who accommodate them by paying unconscionable amounts of money for the bits of worthless clay and then carrying them back to England to treat them with reverence they certainly do not deserve." He turned to Justin. "You will forgive me, Justin. But a little bit of scholarship is a dangerous thing, I think."

Justin grinned ruefully. "I am forced to agree with you, Professor, however damning your words may be to myself and my countrymen. Wherever we travel, we swoop down on the souks and the bazaars, seeking ancient marvels to enliven our own rather staid lives." He took the small package he had been carrying under his arm and presented it to Sareef. "But I think this particular fake may prove interesting to you."

Sareef took the bundle and unwrapped it gingerly, then held out the small statue Justin had purchased the day before. His expression remained impassive for a second, but then the look slowly faded as he considered the idol. He took a pair of wire-rimmed spectacles from his pocket and put them on, adjusting them fussily until they settled themselves on his nose comfortably. Then he moved to the large window at the side of the room and held the idol up to the sunshine.

"This is quite remarkable," he muttered as he considered the statue of Bastet. "You actually found this in the souk?"

Justin nodded. "It was in one of those dim little curio shops, just sitting on a shelf with a dozen others, all obviously the fakes you so freely condemn. Amity picked it out immediately. She seemed drawn to the goddess."

Sareef nodded. "I know what it is you felt, my dear," he said to Amity. "I have felt the same power many times, when the ancients seem to reach out to us, to speak to us. And of them all, Bastet seems to choose

54

her companions and call to them the most strongly. Just as my beautiful Bastet spoke to me when I found her, just as she continues to speak to me each time I gaze at her."

Amity cocked her head and stared at the old man, surprised at the way he seemed to understand the way she had felt when she first saw the statue.

"Yes," she said softly. "That is just how it seemed, as if she spoke to me."

"Then the statue is authentic, not a fake?" Justin asked, obviously more interested in the value of his purchase than in Amity's strange kinship with the idol of the goddess.

"I can say without reservation that it is definitely authentic," Sareef told him, then returned his gaze to Amity. He put his hand to her arm and led her toward the parlor. "Come, my dear. Let me tell you about the goddess who has claimed you as one of her own."

This time, when Beatrice pressed Justin, he allowed her to convince him to stay to dinner. He made her work for her triumph, however, first vowing his abhorrence for formal consulate functions. Determined not to be done out of her chance to see firsthand how close he and Amity had become, Beatrice assured him that they were alone for the evening, just the family, an unusual occurrence at the consulate. Justin seemed a bit doubtful, but he agreed, proclaiming himself, albeit a bit uncertainly, to be delighted to be included at the family table. Amity found herself decidedly uncomfortable at the way her sister seemed to infer he belonged there, and even more so at Justin's apparent agreement.

They sat over a glass of sherry and chatted quietly about the revelations of the afternoon while they waited for Charles to be done with the last of his evening's duties in the official section of the consulate. Although her sister did not seem remotely interested in her continued fascination with the statue, Amity told her about Professor Sareef's private little museum and his declaration that the idol Justin had given her was a true antiquity. When Justin displayed his own interest in the subject, Beatrice finally managed to rouse herself to make some small show of curiosity.

Charles arrived late, looking decidedly worn and slightly disheveled. He offered no apology for either his appearance or his tardiness as he entered the room.

He walked past Justin and the two women wordlessly and made his way immediately to the liquor cabinet.

"There's been more ugliness to the south," he finally announced after he'd poured a glass of the wine for himself and quickly downed it. "That madman Ali Kalaf has roused a band of his followers to massacre a whole town near the border. There's going to be hell to pay." Thus unburdened, he turned back to the cabinet to refill his glass.

"I wondered what could be keeping you," Beatrice said. "Will there be much more for you to do this evening?" She turned and smiled at Justin. "We've the pleasure of an unexpected guest."

Charles shook his head. "I've done what can be done for now," he said as he turned and considered Justin. "Twice in less than a week . . ." he said ruminatively. "That should doubtless be considered some sort of an honor, I suppose. It couldn't be that there's some new enticement that lures you to the staid atmosphere of the consulate, is there, Justin?" He lifted the glass of wine to his mouth and quickly drained it as he had the previous one. Then he offered Justin a knowing look. "I thought you preferred to take your pleasures in the more exotic precincts of the city," he sneered as he refilled his glass.

There was a noticeable touch of hostility in his tone that surprised Amity. She'd always thought him pain-

56

fully pleasant, even when the situation called for some other response. Until that moment, she'd never seen him openly antagonistic toward anyone. She watched him as he quickly swallowed yet another glass of wine. There was no question but that he had had a strained and uneasy day. That, she told herself, doubtless explained his reaction to Justin's presence. Her thoughts on Charles, she failed to notice the fact that Justin had seemed entirely unsurprised at the news of Ali Kalaf's latest atrocity, or that his expression hardened with Charles's veiled reference to his predilection for young Egyptian whores.

Justin managed to keep himself under control. He seemed determined to ignore the open antipathy so evident in Charles's words.

"I decided that you were really not worthy of having the company of the city's two most beautiful women all to yourself, Charles," he replied as calmly as if Charles's comments had been an observation on the weather.

"I've been under the impression you've gotten more than your share of the company of one of those women of late," Charles said tersely, his eyes on Amity.

There was an odd look of proprietorship as he stared at her. Suddenly he, too, seemed to have forgotten the crises with which he'd been forced to deal during the day. He seemed to dismiss all thoughts of the horrors that had been described to him and let his thoughts be concerned with emotions that struck him closer to home.

Justin shrugged. "There are some things a man can never get enough of, Charles," he said.

Beatrice stood abruptly. "I think it time we all went in to dinner," she announced. She was staring at her husband, her eyes narrowed and knowing, but Charles seemed determined to ignore her presence.

They filed into the small family dining room, Beatrice on her husband's arm, Amity on Justin's. Beatrice

57

pointedly seated Justin beside Amity. She smiled coyly at Justin across the table.

"Isn't this delightfully cozy?" she asked as she put her napkin on her lap. "Just the four of us? What could be more comfortable?"

Charles smiled archly, turning from his wife to Justin as he spread his own napkin on his lap. "Yes, quite the little domestic group we've become, don't you think, Justin?" he asked, his tone sharp with hostility. He reached for the decanter of hock even before Beatrice had motioned for the soup to be served. "Almost as if you and Amity already shared the same bed."

At first Amity felt a surprising wave of distaste, not at Charles's words, but at the prospect of their actually becoming reality. Then she colored, not quite believing Charles could say such things, nor that she could so easily consider the possibility. It was then she noticed Charles's flushed cheeks and slightly disoriented glance. He'd been drinking, she realized, and a good deal more than the glasses of sherry in which he'd indulged before dinner. For the first time she wondered just how capable he was for the position he held, and how able to withstand the inevitable pressure it placed on him. Surely there could be no other explanation for his sudden antagonism toward Justin, or for his crude words.

Whatever Amity's reaction to Charles's remark, however, it was mild in comparison to his wife's. Beatrice stared at him with the sort of look that, in years past, might have been warranted capable of souring a nursing woman's milk or turning a virile man impotent. Historical records show more than one witch trial where the defendant was condemned for nothing more sinister than the sort of look Beatrice leveled at her husband at that moment.

"I think, Charles," she told him, her tone as cold as Arctic ice, "that you would do well to forgo the wine with dinner this evening."

58

Charles, however, seemed oblivious to his social sins. He stared at Amity, apparently quite delighted with the deep rose blush that blossomed on her cheeks and the look of confusion that filled her expression.

"Do you, my dear?" he asked Beatrice. "How odd. Because I think I would rather forgo dinner with my wine this evening." With that he leaned forward, grasped the decanter firmly, and then stood. "If you all will excuse me," he said, leaning unsteadily forward and smiling, "I think I might do well to retire. Sorry to be such a poor host, Justin. But I'm sure you'll be made more than comfortable by the ladies. After all, they do love a rich bachelor to dote on."

He straightened unsteadily, turned sharply to face the door and then made an exaggeratedly determined progress out of the room.

"Perhaps it would be better if I leave," Justin said when Charles had finally gone.

Amity turned to him hopefully, wishing that he would do just that.

But Beatrice protested. "Oh, no, please don't. He didn't mean any of those things he said. I hope you won't take offense."

Justin waved a tolerant hand. "He's obviously had a good deal with which to contend today," he said, dismissing Charles's words with the gesture.

"And a good deal to drink to salve his pains," Beatrice added sourly.

Somehow dinner progressed painfully through the soup and the roast and finally the sweet. Beatrice made an exaggerated effort to behave as though nothing unusual had happened, and only succeeded in making the situation more strained. Mercifully, the meal finally ended.

Justin stood and took his leave of Beatrice. Amity found she had no choice but to accompany him to the door when he made the request.

When they were finally alone, he took her hand in his.

"Amity, have you considered my proposal?" he asked her evenly. "Have you thought about it?"

She looked up at him, telling herself that now was the time to tell him that she could not marry him, that no amount of thought on the subject would make her feel for him what she ought to feel for the man she would wed, what she did not feel for him despite the wish that she would. She recalled her reaction to Charles's remark about Justin sharing her bed. However crude, the words had left her with a feeling of mild revulsion. If nothing else, they had served to make her realize just how impossible it would be for her to agree to become Justin's wife.

"Justin, I *have* thought about it. It must be obvious to you by now that I do esteem your friendship more than I can say, that I admire you and—"

He knew without hearing any more where her words were leading. He quickly put a finger to her lips, interrupting her before she could make the pronouncement he had no wish to hear.

"No, don't say it, Amity. I shouldn't have asked. Tonight is not the right time."

He leaned toward her and pressed a quick, dry kiss to her forehead. Then he drew away from her and stared at her silently. Amity tried to find some words, tried to draw her eyes away from his even stare, but found herself frozen, unable to either speak or move.

"Good night, Amity," he said finally. Then he turned and quickly left.

Amity watched him go with a certain feeling of regret slowly filling her. She ought to have told him, she told herself. It was foolish to go on letting him think there might be some chance, foolish for her and unfairly cruel to him.

Finally she turned away and slowly climbed the stairs

to her room. Her life seemed to be moving far too quickly for her, to be running sightlessly forward while she struggled to force her thoughts to keep up with the events in which she found herself embroiled. She entered her room with a sense of relief, as though it were a sanctuary from the world, a place where she might find the calm and leisure she needed to order her thoughts and somehow regain control of herself.

It was a relief that was shattered immediately after she stepped inside the room. Charles was sitting in the comfortable chair by the window, the now nearly empty decanter on the table beside him, a half-filled glass in his hand.

For a moment she was not quite sure he was really there.

"Charles?"

She realized her voice sounded tentative, as unsure as she herself felt.

He looked up at her and smiled complacently.

"Ah, Amity, lovely Amity."

"What are you doing here, Charles?" she demanded, suddenly feeling uneasy again, as though some part deep inside her knew something was about to happen, something decidedly unpleasant.

He licked his lips slowly before he answered.

"I've come to see you, my pretty little Amity," he replied before he swallowed the remaining wine in his glass.

"I don't think you should be here, Charles. I think you should leave."

He put his glass down on the table beside the decanter and stared up at her.

"Are you afraid, pretty little sister?" he asked her, his tone turned mocking. "Surely not of me?" He shook his head. "Ah, no, it couldn't be of me. It must be the thought of Beatrice that terrifies you. I don't blame you. Your sister has turned into a malicious harridan,

Amity. How could I have known when I met her what she would become?" His tone had become whining, complaining, as though he could justify himself by voicing his grievances. He looked away, turning his eyes toward the ceiling and his thoughts to the past. "She was so pretty then, I suppose I'd have gone on with it anyway. I wouldn't have believed how time could change her, knowing what I felt for her." He turned his eyes back to Amity then. "But I should have waited for you, beautiful Amity, waited for you to grow up. If I hadn't been a fool I'd have waited for you."

Amity shook her head. She couldn't believe what he was saying, nor could she believe that she was standing there, seemingly calm, listening to him.

"I want you to leave now, Charles."

The sound of her own voice, the tone cold and commanding, completely shocked her. She heard her own words in the air and thought they must have been spoken by someone else, someone with far greater self-assurance than she could ever hope to command.

Charles stared up at her, his expression crestfallen, as though he were a beggar on the street and she his last hope for a crumb.

"Have you no pity for me, Amity?" he asked her softly. "Will you throw yourself away on the likes of Justin Gardiner as Beatrice wants you to do without so much as looking around you to see what else you might have?"

Amity stamped her foot. "Stop it, Charles. You're my sister's husband and I won't listen to any more of this." She glared at him angrily, disgusted with his drunken pleadings. "Get out of my room."

Charles got shakily to his feet. He stood for a moment, seemingly dazed, the eyes he turned to her filled with a sodden disbelief. Then he shrugged, as though dismissing the effort as wasted time, as though he were telling himself he ought to have expected nothing else.

62

He started unsteadily forward toward the door, crossing the room with a tottering old man's gait. When he reached the foot of the bed, he wavered and then began to fall.

Amity ran forward to help him, realizing then how totally drunk he must be to find himself so unsteady. She reached him just as he started to topple, and quickly found herself being grasped by his hands, surrounded by his arms. And then she was falling with him.

Somehow she was on the bed, and Charles's hands were on her, touching her, holding her. She pushed frantically against the weight of him, but he seemed oblivious to her protests.

"Stop this, Charles," she panted as she tried to push against his neck. She could feel his warm breath close to her cheek, could smell the alcohol he'd drunk when he exhaled.

"You know you want me, Amity," he whispered hoarsely in her ear. "You know you want me as much as I want you."

"No," she cried in futile fury.

Amity felt the hot, moist pressure of lips against her cheek, the sharp press of his fingers forcing her face to turn and meet his. For a moment she could think only of screaming, of bringing the whole population of the house there to help her. But before the cry could escape her lips, she thought of Beatrice and realized how crushing it would be to her sister to learn that Charles was unfaithful to her. She garnered her strength and once again began pushing Charles from her. She told herself she must get away from him and do it silently, without causing her sister the hurt of learning her husband was trying to seduce another woman.

But then his hands were grasping hers and pinning them above her head. His lips were on hers, his tongue pressing against the wall she tried to make of them, seeking entry forcefully if she would not allow it otherwise. She could no longer even call out. She was terrified now. She had no choice. Either she must raise some alarm or else she would be faced with the alternative of letting Charles do as he wanted.

She decided she must scream, regardless the consequences, regardless the fact that Beatrice would be hurt.

She managed to turn her face from his. Gasping, she filled her lungs with air.

But she didn't have the chance to cry out.

"Whore. Ungrateful, greedy, little whore."

Charles suddenly lifted himself away from her, his expression befuddled. Amity managed to turn her head to find her sister standing in the doorway. She shuddered when she saw her.

Beatrice's eyes were blazing with undisguised hatred as she considered the two of them.

Charles staggered to his feet. He turned to face Beatrice, his expression that of a small boy who had been discovered with his hand uninvited in a box of sweets.

Amity watched him stare at his wife in silence for a long moment, then wordlessly walk past her to the door. She closed her eyes and inhaled deeply, breathing in thick, long gulps of air as a feeling of relief slowly filled her. She felt like a condemned man reprieved at the eleventh hour.

When she sat up and turned to her sister, however, the relief quickly faded. Beatrice stood, staring at her with granite determination, waiting for her to dare the first word.

"Thank goodness you came when you did, Bea," she ventured as she slipped off the bed. "He's terribly drunk . . ."

"Don't you dare speak to me, you little tramp," Beatrice shouted at her, interrupting, unable to contain the anger any longer. "After I open my home to you, how can you do this to me? Isn't Justin Gardiner enough for you? Do you have to prove that you are more desirable than I am by stealing my husband as well?"

For a moment Amity stood in openmouthed bewilderment. Surely, she told herself, Beatrice couldn't actually think that she had tried to steal Charles away from her.

Amity shook her head and began to approach Beatrice. "It wasn't like that, Bea," she murmured. Tears were biting at her eyes and her throat seemed to have filled with a great wad of cotton. She barely managed the words through her trembling lips. "He was here when I came in, it was Charles . . ."

Beatrice was unmoved. "I've seen you, the way you encouraged him," she snapped, interrupting once again. "Sweet little Amity, so accommodating to his children, so ready to laugh at his jokes, to pay him that false, wide-eyed attention that puffs him up and makes him feel as if he were the only man walking the face of the earth. Don't tell me how blameless you are, you little whore!"

She started to turn to the door.

"But Bea, please listen, you've got to listen," Amity tried once again. She ran after her sister, her hand reaching out for Beatrice's arm.

"And don't call me Bea," Beatrice screamed at her with final, unappeasable wrath. She shook off Amity's hand as though it were something distasteful that soiled her, and strode angrily to the door.

Amity stood, dazed, watching the door slam shut, listening to the silence that descended on the room after Beatrice's departure. For a few moments she remained rooted to the spot. Then the tears began to well up in her eyes and pour down her cheeks. The thickness in her throat seemed about to choke her and she gasped for air.

She lay on the bed and let herself cry, thinking of her childhood, of how she'd lain on another bed and cried a long, long time before. She'd always adored Beatrice, always been slightly in awe of her. She remembered the loss she'd felt when her beautiful older sister had married the handsome young diplomat and left Boston for far more exotic places. That loss had seemed total when Amity had been nine years old. But the pain she felt now was far greater because she realized she'd managed to lose her sister's love.

None of it was fair, a voice in her head cried irrationally. None of it had been her fault. And now, she was suddenly totally alone. After her parents had died, there had been only Beatrice left to her. There were her father's two maiden aunts, Sophia and Arlette, cold, distant, desiccated little women who'd lived their own lives so long they had no time or patience for anyone else's. The months she'd spent in their houses while she waited for her parents' estate to be settled before she'd come to Egypt had been the bleakest and most lonely of her life, made tolerable only by the knowledge that she would soon join Beatrice. Her sister and her sister's family were the only people she had left, the only people she loved. And now she found herself suddenly cut off from them, like an appendage that had been needlessly amputated. She was numb with shock and loss.

She cried until she had no more tears. Then she lay still, holding tight to her now moist pillow, telling herself it would all somehow go away, that in the morning she'd somehow make Beatrice understand. It was, she realized, the only thing she could do. Because if she didn't, she'd be completely alone, left with no one and nothing.

Beatrice had no intention of allowing her to make it that easy. It did not take long for Amity to realize that she'd become an outcast in the house, a pariah to her sister, and a cause for blushing embarrassment to

Charles, who made a great point of hastily removing himself from her presence when he walked into a room and found her there. There were no more shopping expeditions with Beatrice and her friends, no more invitations tendered from General Stuart's wife or any of the other ladies who had until then welcomed her with the unquestioned assumption that she belonged. She was pointedly told she need not bother to attend the regular consulate functions and might take her meals in her own room. Beatrice had decided on her guilt, and was determined that she pay for it, passing judgment without allowing her benefit of hearing or indication that there would be any forthcoming reprieve.

Only Justin Gardiner seemed immune to the effects of Beatrice's ire. He continued to visit her and escort her about the city, squiring her to the opera and museums and providing a knowledgeable guide on sightseeing outings. About a week after that terrible evening Charles had tried to seduce her, Justin suggested an expedition to the south, to El Giza, to see the pyramids and the sphinx.

Amity was more than willing to accept. She could only think of a day away from the consulate, away from Beatrice, as a short reprieve. Tensions had been growing ever sharper between them, despite Amity's attempts at reconciliation. She hastily accepted Justin's offer, even before he assured her that they would be suitably chaperoned by Professor Sareef.

The day proved far more pleasant to her than even the respite from Beatrice's anger promised it would be. The morning was clear and bright, as all mornings in Egypt seemed to Amity to be.

"Does it never rain here?" she asked as Justin helped her into the saddle. "In Boston a good dreary morning makes us properly thankful for our few hours of sunshine, but here one grows to expect it. It seems somehow decadent, not to be forced to be at the mercy of

67

the weather."

He stood beside her horse staring up at her. "If you miss unpleasant weather," he countered with a smile, "then you will find yourself entirely at home in England. There is more than enough rain and fog in London to satisfy even the most sun shy." He smiled then. "If it would please you, after we're married, we could spend part of the year there, reveling in the downpours and getting ourselves lost in the mists."

He gave her no time to comment on his assumption that they would eventually be married, but turned and quickly swung himself into his own saddle. Amity found she lacked the determination at that moment to disabuse him.

Despite Professor Sareef's regular lapses into a pedantically scholarly lecture at each opportunity the landscape afforded, Amity found herself overwhelmingly pleased with the outing. The ride, though hot and dusty, afforded wonderful views of the countryside that more than compensated her for the discomfort. Amity was completely stunned as they approached the sphinx, seeing the great stone beast face on, and behind him, the massive jutting mounds that were the pyramids. She could do nothing more than stare, completely awed by the ancient stone structures.

When they reached their destination, they dismounted, and she strolled at Justin's side in the shade cast by the sphinx's shadow, staring up in total awe of the great stone man-beast, realizing that as much as she had expected from books she'd read and pictures she'd seen, nothing had prepared her for the intensity of her reaction to the enormous structure, nor to the numbing mass of the great pyramids. Professor Sareef droned on as he walked at their side, but his words were totally lost on her. Like the small statue of Bastet, the great relics of Egypt's past had caught hold of her, infecting her with a sort of contagion, as though the reverence they inspired in her was bred in her blood.

They rode on, reaching the foot of largest pyramid, Cheop's great tomb. They ate their lunch from an enormous picnic hamper, their cloth spread on a huge stone at the feet of the great pyramid. When they'd finished the meal, Sareef suggested they wander on their own while he recovered from the meal.

"A euphemism for a nap?" Justin taunted him with a grin, then grasped Amity's hand and firmly tucked it in the crook of his arm. He led her to the enormous stone steps, put his hands to her waist, and lifted her onto it. They began to climb.

When they were high enough to have an unobstructed view of the river in the distance, they sat on the sand-gritted stone. Amity stared out at the distant fringe of palm trees, the tiny ribbon of blue that marked the river, the sinuous form of the sphinx and the mountains of the other pyramids around them. When she turned, she could see the vast sea of sand behind them. Two camels, with robed riders, moved with a stately swaying motion in the distance. Amity sat silent, digesting the beauty around her, letting it sink into her, savoring it like an exotic spice she would only have this single chance to taste. Justin sat beside her, silent, watching her reaction to the marvels he had brought her to see.

"This is incredible," she said finally, her words coming very slowly. "I shall hate to leave."

"Leave?" Justin turned and stared at her. "You're not serious."

She shook her head. "I don't know what else to do," she murmured. Although they had not spoken of it, she knew he was aware of what had happened between her and Beatrice and Charles. She would not have been surprised if the whole of Cairo society had heard of it. "I only know I can't stay here much longer. I can't bear seeing how much anger and hatred Beatrice bears me. I've come to the decision that I'll have to go back to

Boston."

Justin put his hand to her chin and turned her face to his. He could see the liquid in her eyes, knew how miserable she felt at the thought of leaving.

"You needn't go, you know," he told her firmly. "You could marry me and stay on here."

For a moment she told herself, yes, she could do that, marry him. He cared for her, that was plain enough. And life with a man who cared for her would be a thousand times better than returning to the cold, sterile world her aunts lived in, in Boston, the world in which she would be forced to join if she were to return there.

"I can't, Justin," she burst out, before she allowed herself to become too swayed by the easy thought of simply saying yes. "I care for you, and admire you, but I don't love you. I can't lie to you and tell you I do."

He considered her words calmly for a moment before he spoke.

"Is there someone else, Amity?" he asked her, his tone just a bit sharp.

For an instant the image of a face appeared in Amity's mind—Ford Gardiner's face. She wondered at how well she recalled it, at the detail she could remember—the exact shade of his eyes, the way his dark hair had reflected the moonlight. Mostly, though, she remembered the way his lips had tasted, the way his hands felt when they had held her. She quickly pushed the image forcefully away, telling herself that such thoughts were useless, perhaps even dangerous.

She shook her head. "No," she murmured finally. "There's no one else."

Justin took her hands in his and pressed them with his fingers. "Then marry me, Amity. If you don't love me now, you will come to. I promise you. And for the meantime, I'll bear you enough love for the both of us."

Suddenly, it all seemed so logical to her, so simple. There was no need for her to return to Boston, no need

70

to let her life become as dry and lonely as it had been that long year before coming to Egypt. He loved her, that seemed apparent enough. Perhaps, as he promised, she would come to love him. He seemed so sure. It was not as if she had lied to him, not as if she had promised him something she did not have to give.

And what did she know of love anyway? Perhaps hers was only a fancy gleaned from storybooks. Perhaps what she felt for him was all there was to feel. At the worst, it would still be a thousand times better than returning to Boston.

She looked down at his hands where they held hers in her lap. They were large and long-fingered and completely encased hers.

He seemed to be able to read her indecision. "Marry me, Amity," he whispered, pressing her while she wavered.

She looked up once more at his eyes. They were fixed on her, sharp and certain.

She nodded slowly. "Yes," she whispered.

The word seemed to be said of its own volition, but once uttered she told herself it was what she wanted, that her decision was made and for the best. She held herself stiff as he pressed a kiss to her lips.

When he released her, she smiled up at him and quickly stilled the tiny voice inside her that told her she was making a terrible mistake.

Chapter Four

Ford Gardiner looked around at the faces of the men seated at the table. He felt dirty and grimy and was quite aware that the khedive's assistant was staring at him with distinct and open distaste.

The assistant, Akim Bey by name, was a sharp-featured, long-nosed, disdainful man, entirely too impressed by his Eton and Cambridge education. Ford held an instinctive dislike for him, a dislike that had formed the first moment he had met Akim Bey and which he had been unable to dislodge since. At first he'd tried to examine the reaction in an attempt to explain the dislike, because Akim Bey had given him no outright reason for antipathy that he could think of, but eventually he had dismissed his questions, decided to accept his instincts, and kept his distance from the man whenever possible.

Keeping his distance, however, seemed to be impossible under the present circumstances. Akim Bey had been quickly summoned to the meeting as soon as it became apparent to General Stuart that the information Ford brought affected the khedive as strongly, if not more so, than it affected the interests of the British Army. In return for the favor, Akim Bey made it amply apparent by his manner that he was a good deal less than pleased with the interruption to his normal daily routine, as well as with the grimy appearance of the bearer of the tidings he had come to hear.

Had the problem been less immediate, Ford told himself he would have considered the look Akim Bey leveled at him almost justified. He had been in the saddle for days and looked and felt every hot, dirty, sand-filled moment of it. He gave his report tersely, wanting the interview to end so that he could leave Akim Bey to General Stuart's far more diplomatic attentions while he found the basic animal comforts of a bath, clean clothes, and some food. But Akim Bey seemed intent upon keeping him there, pressing him over and over about the same points as if he expected Ford to be caught up in a lie.

"You are certain that the rifle Major Stratford took from the rebel was a Meerschmidt, Major Gardiner?"

Ford restrained his immediate impulse, which was to tell Akim Bey if he did not wish to believe the report, he could take a ride out to the fort and see for himself. Made entirely too aware of the need for diplomacy with Akim Bey by General Stuart before the meeting had begun, however, Ford held his tongue. He was tired, he realized, tired and dirty and decidedly in need of a stiff drink of good single malt and a long bath. Unfortunately, neither looked to be in the offing in the immediate future . . .

All of which doubtless contributed to his consideration of just how much he would enjoy seeing Akim Bey with a bloodied nose and relieved of his seemingly irremovable superior sneer.

"You have Major Stratford's report, sir," Ford said with a studied politeness he decidedly did not feel. "And I inspected the weapon myself. It was definitely the Meerschmidt twenty-round repeating rifle."

Akim Bey leaned back in his chair, put his elbows on the arms, pursed his lips, and entwined his fingers in a studied gesture meant to convey deep thought.

"It is a pity," he said after a while, "that the two men

73

died before anything pertinent could be learned from them."

General Stuart apparently recognized the note of censure in Akim Bey's words just as Ford did, for he leaned forward and began to speak before Ford could respond.

"We all know the sort of fanatic Ali Kalaf is, and the blindly obsessive obedience he demands of his followers. Whatever precautions might have been taken, those men would have managed to make sure that they gave nothing away, one way or another."

"Still," Akim Bey pressed, "it is unfortunate that they were not deprived of the means to rid themselves of their worldly woes quite so quickly. Alive, they might have been induced to talk," he smiled grimly, "with the proper sort of incentives."

Ford considered Akim Bey's words with a grim disgust. He'd seen the inside of an Ottoman prison and knew precisely to what sort of incentives Akim Bey referred — beatings, starvation, even the slow removal of the appendages of a prisoner's body. However civilized the appearance of the khedive, his underlings still clung to a great many of the precepts of their forefathers. In Akim Bey's case, it was the method of dealing with one's enemies. Ford thought that if he were ever faced with the choice, he'd take the same route Ali Kalaf's followers had taken. Death was far more preferable than the attentions of Akim Bey's questioners.

"In any case, the two are dead, and the matter not worth debating. What must be decided is how we determine who is getting the Meerschmidts to Ali Kalaf, and then, how they can be stopped. If not, the border to the south will become meaningless, and Ali Kalaf will stand at the head of a tide we will not be able to contain." His expression grew hard as he leveled his gaze at Akim Bey. "I don't suppose I need remind you that if the British are pushed from Egypt, the khedive will fall. And

Ali Kalaf will complete what the Mahdi started in Khartoum."

Akim Bey smiled, his expression unblemished by any of the emotion Ford felt.

"Ah, Khartoum," he said tonelessly. "I believe you were with General Gordon's staff, were you not, Major Gardiner? But you left before the final rout." He smiled humorlessly at Ford. "That was quite lucky for you, wasn't it, Major? To leave before the Mahdi and his followers finally entered the city and slew every man, woman, and child unlucky enough to remain there, including the supposedly invincible Gordon." He smiled at Ford, baring a row of even, white teeth. "Or was it more than luck, Major, that allowed you to absent yourself at a most propitious moment?"

Even the dark tan on Ford's face could not completely hide the color his sudden anger ignited. "I've been on horseback for five days," he said slowly, his jaw tight, his words coldly and evenly enunciated. "I'm tired and I'm dirty, and I'm not in the mood for games. If you have something you want to say to me, I suggest you come out and say it."

"Gardiner," General Stuart hissed as he put his hand to Ford's arm.

But Akim Bey seemed unruffled by either the words or Ford's threatening stare. He continued to smile, the same knowing, humorless smile. He put his hands to the table in front of him and leaned toward Ford. "I am saying this, Major Gardiner, your escape from the end that Gordon met might be considered a simple act of benign fate. But I am not a simple man, and I rarely accept simple conclusions. I find your timely escape from Khartoum colors my judgment. When my people tell me that there have been rumors of strangers being seen in the vicinity of Tell ElAmarna, strangers who might be in the employ of Ali Kalaf, I find myself wondering. When these rumors persist, and are elaborated with hints that the strangers are there to purchase illegal weapons, I become suspicious. I consider the fact that a large tract of land near there is owned by a man named Gardiner, a man I believe is a close relation of yours, Major. As it happens, Kendrick Gardiner's estate happens to border the river, a fact which leads me to consider the possibilities—how easy it would be to smuggle illegal arms upriver and then transfer them at a place away from curious eyes. All of which, Major, leads me to be slightly suspicious of the benign fates that seem to look so kindly upon you."

Ford could barely contain his anger now. He, too, put his hands on the tabletop and leaned forward. But this time when General Stuart put his hand to his arm, he heeded the unspoken order and withdrew, slowly leaning into the back of his chair.

"Have you any proof of the allegations you're making regarding Kendrick Gardiner, Akim Bey?" Stuart asked coldly.

"If I had proof, General, I'd have Gardiner and his son in jail. Instead, I have rumors, and Kendrick Gardiner lives in ease on his estate, and his son makes a fortune trading Egyptian cotton futures." Akim Bey smiled once more. "And his nephew continues to be a trusted member of your staff."

Stuart, despite his desire to remain on good terms with the khedive, was not one to be cowed by an official, even the khedive's first assistant. Akim Bey had gone too far, and he was disposed to inform him of that fact.

"I don't suppose I need remind you that it is British arms that protect the khedive's power in Egypt, and British soldiers who keep the borders," he said thoughtfully.

"The British support us so that they may line their

own pockets," Akim Bey shot back. "You may keep your claims of altruism for someone more naive, General."

Stuart narrowed his stare and his tone grew sharp. "Whatever our reasons, without us, you are nothing. And unless you want to find yourself running back to the sultan with your tail between your legs, sir, you will do well to honor the debt you owe the empire, as well as the queen's chosen representatives here. Do I make myself completely clear?"

Akim Bey's expression turned dark. "Are you threatening me, General?" he demanded.

For the first time Stuart smiled. "I most certainly am, sir," he replied. He made no effort to hide the pleasure he felt as he spoke the words.

Akim Bey considered him for a moment in silence, then, apparently deciding a tactical withdrawal would be more advantageous than a possible rout, he abruptly changed face and pushed his chair back from the table. "I am sure Khedive Ismail will be interested in the news you have given me," he said as he stood.

"We still haven't decided just how we intend to go about tracing the Meerschmidts," Ford said. He turned to General Stuart. "I'd be more than glad to volunteer, sir, for the duty."

"That won't be necessary, Major," Akim Bey told him sharply. "Nor will it be necessary for you, General, to further waste any of your time or effort on the matter. This is an internal concern. The khedive will see to tracing this illicit trade in weapons without any additional involvement on your part."

"That's nonsense, and you know it," Stuart told him. "Before your police could find anything, we'll be overrun."

"Perhaps not, General," Akim Bey replied evenly. "Our investigation will commence immediately. And if we alone are privy to the particulars, we need have no fear that the information we learn might be conveyed to the hands of the smugglers." Once again he smiled at Ford. "Perhaps by a devoted relative."

"I personally take offense at your manner, Akim Bey," Ford said.

"Do you, Major?" Akim Bey replied, his expression more amused than anything else, his eyebrow lifted slightly and his dark eyes sharp.

"And on behalf of the military, I must object to our being excluded from the investigation of this matter," Stuart added.

"Your objection will be duly noted, General," Akim Bey told him. With that, he turned away and left with no further attempt to either placate them or smooth over the feathers he had so successfully managed to ruffle.

Ford sat in silence considering Akim Bey's words for a moment after he'd gone. Then he turned to Stuart. "Is it true, General, what he said about rumors of arms being exchanged near Tell ElAmarna?" he asked.

Stuart shrugged. "There are rumors. My agents have reported them to me just as Akim Bey's have reported them to him. But that is really all there is, idle talk, rumors. And if we could find nothing more, I have every confidence Bey's people could find even less." He stared at Ford in silence for a long moment. "You've been with me a long time, Gardiner."

"Yes, sir," Ford replied. "Nearly five years."

"I would like to think that I know enough about human nature to choose my staff well."

"Are you saying you believe Bey's insinuations?" Ford demanded. "Because if you do, I will oblige you with the resignation of my commission."

"Don't talk like a fool, Ford. You know I trust you. If I didn't, you wouldn't be here with me."

78

"Do you, sir?" Ford asked him. "Do you mean to tell me you're not the least bit doubtful that the rumors about me might not be true?"

Stuart's eyes narrowed. "Frankly, I *have* wondered. But if you were a thief, that was before you entered the service and can have no bearing on my opinion of you. There is one thing of which I am entirely convinced, and that is since you have been with me, your character, like that of Caesar's wife, is above reproach. So I would prefer not to hear any more about commissions being resigned. If there is anything with regard to your uncle, however, if you know anything at all, it would be best you tell me now."

Ford shook his head. "I can't believe my uncle could possibly have anything to do with the arms trade, sir. He's a farmer; he loves that plantation. He couldn't do anything that would endanger it or his presence there."

"And your cousin Justin?" Stuart pressed. "Are you equally sure of his innocence?"

"If you told me he'd been caught with his hand in the wrong pocket, I'd believe you," Ford replied thoughtfully. "If there was a possibility that he was involved with larceny, illegal stock manipulation, anything of the sort, I'd accept your word without question. But illegal arms trading is something else again. Not that I think he'd be morally opposed. It's just that I've always considered him constitutionally incapable of putting his hands into the mire. Dealing arms is a dirty business and, simply put, I doubt he has the stomach for it."

"Well, it's no longer in our hands in any event," Stuart said slowly. "Akim Bey wants us out, so it seems we're out."

Ford was genuinely surprised. "You don't mean to tell me that we're simply going to sit on our hands and wait for Akim Bey to find something while our men are out there getting killed?"

79

"That's precisely what I mean to say," Stuart replied. "It's out of our hands." He offered Ford a grim smile. "And I think it time you took a bit of the leave you're due."

"You can't be serious, sir!" Ford protested.

"A visit to your uncle's estate wouldn't be out of the question, I shouldn't think," Stuart mused as though he hadn't heard Ford's interruption.

"No, sir, I suppose it wouldn't," Ford agreed with a grin.

"And while you're in the vicinity, if you were to happen to do a bit of looking about, strictly on your own, of course, that would have nothing to do with Her Majesty's military adjutant."

"Of course not, sir."

Stuart smiled once more, this time with apparent pleasure. "If it would sweeten the pot for you, Major, word has it that your cousin Justin is on his way there now, with his lovely young fiancée, Miss Ravenswood."

Ford's expression lost any hint of amusement. "His fiancée? She's actually agreed to marry him?"

Stuart made a sound that seemed suspiciously like a grunt. "My sentiment precisely when I heard about it. Such a pretty little thing. She certainly deserves better than Justin Gardiner." He looked back at Ford and smiled once more. "Perhaps while you're there, you might convince her of the error of her intention."

Ford returned the smile. "Perhaps I'll do just that," he mused aloud as he pushed his chair away from the table. "Now if you'll excuse me, sir, I am sorely in need of a bath and a decent meal."

Stuart watched him stand. "Don't forget to see that your written request for leave is on my desk before you go, Gardiner. I don't want there to be any question in Akim Bey's mind that you were officially sent to Tell ElAmarna, especially after this unpleasant little meeting

80

we've had with him."

"I'll tend to it immediately, sir," Ford assured him as he started for the door.

"Have, if not a pleasant leave, Major, at least a productive one," Stuart told him.

Ford turned back to him with his hand on the doorknob. "I hope it will be, sir," he replied slowly. Then he left.

Amity was, quite simply, enchanted.

The trip downriver had been a delight for her, a kind of floating passage through a world that she would have thought had disappeared a hundred years before. She'd spent practically all of her waking hours on deck, staring out at the Bedouins in their flowing *abas* who brought flocks to the river's edge for water; at their women, heavily robed and veiled, staring out with wide, dark eyes at the unexpected sight of a western woman returning their curious looks from the deck of Justin's boat; at the dark-tanned and turbaned *fallaheen* who tended the unending rows of fields that lined the river; at the oxen who tread ceaseless circles hitched to the wheels that pulled water from the river and sent it along the irrigation canals to water the crops; at the seemingly endless parade of the felucca that plied the river. Even as dusk settled onto the Nile and the daily labors ceased, the river seemed robed in a netherworldly cloak, its surface turned to a shimmering silver by the moonlight and brightened by thousands of tiny globes of light, fireflies, diving and darting about at the water's edge and hiding in the foliage of the palm and acacia trees that lined the river and framed the piece of sky that held an unbelievably golden disc of a moon. Somehow, she mused, even the commonplace became exotic here.

Doubtless it was the fascination she had with the countryside that masked the discomfort that remained at the thought of her abrupt departure from her sister's house, the pointed hurt she'd felt at Beatrice's absence from the party who'd brought her to Justin's boat at the river. The certainty that Beatrice had intended the slight to hurt her had been almost more than she could bear, and she'd fought to maintain her composure as she'd hugged the children good-bye and exchanged a cool handshake with Charles. Had Justin not been there, his manner calmly authoritative, she knew she would have broken down in tears.

But all that was now several days in the past and buffered as much by the changing scenery as the passage of time. She'd managed to bury the hurt, to almost convince herself that it had never been there. She'd even managed to persuade herself that she'd made the right decision, that by agreeing to marry Justin Gardiner, she'd settled her life for the better course . . .

All of which conspired to make her feel all the more certain of herself, standing there beside Justin at the ship's rail as they slowly neared the dock. There was a large group at the wharf, even a dozen musicians with flutes and drums and stringed instruments, the music they played strange to her ears and a bit strident, but unerringly conveying a sense of festival.

She turned to Justin. "What is it?" she asked. "Is there some holiday?"

He put his hand to hers where it grasped the rail. "Most decidedly," he informed her, his tone completely sober. "The young master is returning home with the woman who will be his bride. The holiday is for you, Amity."

She cocked her head and stared at him, realizing that his manner had become more and more bewildering to her, that she never quite knew what to make of the things he said in his emotionless manner, or even if she ought to believe them at all.

"Nonsense," she retorted. "All these people!" She turned back to face the crowd beside the wharf, realizing there were at least three hundred people there, more than the population of many of the smaller villages they'd passed on the trip upriver. "And you speak as if they belonged to you. Young master, indeed."

Justin did not seem at all put off by her words. "They do belong to me," he told her evenly. "Me and my father."

"There's no slavery here," she told him. "No one belongs to anyone."

He cocked an eyebrow, a gesture she had come to realize over the previous few days that connoted a tolerant acceptance of her naiveté.

"It's better than slavery," he told her with conviction. "These people need us far more than we need them. We give them work and a place to live and food to eat, more than most of them have ever had before. Without us, they'd be forced to scratch out a miserable existence, raising a few wretched goats and watching their children starve. They need us, and they know it. Their lives are mine even more completely than if I owned them."

Amity realized she was shocked by the lack of emotion in his words, by his callousness with regard to the peasants who labored on his father's land. But she had little time to consider the feeling of disgust that suddenly edged into her or the way she'd automatically withdrawn her hand from beneath his. The ship had bumped softly against the wood of the wharf and half a dozen of the hands had jumped down, catching the lines that were thrown to them and making them fast.

The crowd on the dock divided to allow a man to stride through it until he was standing at its head. He was tall, with lean, sharp features, his dark hair edged

83

with gray. He looked up at the deck, letting his eyes rove until they met Justin's. Then he smiled broadly and waved.

This was Justin's father, Kendrick Gardiner, Amity thought. Even before she was introduced to him, she found she liked his smile, liked the look of delight she read in his eyes even from the distance.

Then, very quickly, the gangway was laid down and Kendrick climbed it before Justin could marshal Amity to its edge.

"You, my boy, are a far luckier bastard than you deserve to be," Kendrick said quickly, his tone jovial, by way of greeting to Justin as he offered his son a quick embrace. He then turned an evaluating glance to Amity. He smiled again, a broad, contagious smile, and held his hand to take hers. "Excuse me, my dear. But the sight of you makes even my ancient heart beat with the sort of pleasant thud I'd long ago thought never to feel again. Welcome to Gardiner's Ghenena. It is a pleasure to have you here."

Amity smiled at him and gave him her hand. "I think, Mr. Gardiner, there is nothing here nearly so ancient as you imply, except, perhaps, for the Nile," she laughed.

She was glad she'd chosen to wear her best suit, a soft moss-green linen trimmed with silver-and-black fancy braid, knowing it became her, that she had shown him her best. She was sure that she would like him and wanted very much for him to like her as well.

"None of this 'Mr. Gardiner.' I am Kendrick, even to the *fellaheen* I am Shaikh Kendrick," he told her as he took her hand, lifted it, and kissed it quickly. Then he turned to Justin and clasped his hand to his son's shoulder. "My boy, watch your step. If you ever bring even a hint of unhappiness to this woman, you shall have to answer to me." He turned back to Amity and put her hand firmly in the crook of his arm. "And lest you become too complacent," he shot back at Justin, "I may decide to give you a bit of competition for her affections between now and the wedding." He punctuated this avowal with a hint of a smile at Amity.

"I may just provide a bit of competition myself."

Both Amity and Justin turned to the gangway. To Amity's surprise, she found Ford Gardiner leaning lazily against the rail, grinning pleasantly at her. She'd neither seen nor heard him approach.

"Ford?" Justin seemed as surprised as she to find him there. "I thought you were on patrol in the south chasing after outlaws and the like." He made no effort to disguise the note of displeasure in his voice.

Ford walked up the last few steps and onto the deck beside the others. Amity had never seen him before except in his uniform. He was dressed in mufti now — khaki pants, a loose white linen shirt, and dark leather boots. His mood seemed to have changed with his clothing, relaxed and almost lazy, his walk an easy near-swagger, and the smile he offered Amity languorously lecherous. Amity found herself blushing for no reason she could discern, and hurriedly turned her eyes away from his.

"I was," Ford replied lazily to Justin's inquiry. "And now I'm taking a bit of leave as compensation for the hardships I endured." He smiled easily, at Justin this time. "A pleasure to see you, cousin." He made no mention of the fact that he'd ridden all day and all night to arrive at Tell ElAmarna before Justin's ship.

"Miss Ravenswood, this unsavory-looking fellow is my nephew, Ford Gardiner," Kendrick said to Amity, attempting to perform the role of host and provide the necessary introduction. "You would do well to ignore first impressions. He's actually quite a respectable member of Her Majesty's forces."

Ford grinned pleasantly as his eyes found Amity's

85

once again. "You needn't bother to try to deceive Miss Ravenswood on my account, Uncle," he said to Kendrick. "The young lady and I are already acquainted, and she's doubtless already formed an unshakable opinion of my worthless character."

"Not quite unshakable," Amity said with a smile as Ford reached for her hand.

There was a unsettling tingle in her hand when he touched it, a feeling that only increased as he, just as Kendrick had done, raised her hand to his lips. She could feel the warmth of them even through her thin kidskin glove, and could not help but recall the way they'd felt when he'd pressed them to hers that first evening when they'd stood in the consulate garden. He made no effort to release her hand when the formality had been completed and Amity grew painfully aware that she had begun once again to blush. This time, she found herself incapable of tearing her glance from his, however, a fact that seemed to amuse him, for his grin broadened.

"Then I may entertain some hope you've not come to subscribe to my cousin's scurrilous opinion of me, Miss Ravenswood?" he asked her without taking his eyes from hers.

"I've decided to defer judgment, Major Gardiner," she replied.

Amity wondered fleetingly why it had become suddenly so much warmer. Her hand had grown moist and sticky-feeling. She was thankful for the protection of the kidskin glove, thankful that he couldn't know how completely he managed to unsettle her simply by holding her hand in his.

"I'd not contemplated the possibility of ever having the opportunity to redeem myself in your eyes, Miss Ravenswood." His voice had grown softly intimate and his blue eyes refused to release their hold on hers.

Amity realized he was aware of just how much he affected her. She could read the certainty in his eyes, hear it in the softly stroking timbre of his voice. She finally managed to pull her hand from his and backed a step away from him.

"I hadn't realized you'd done anything while in my company for which you would need redemption, Major Gardiner," she told him, making an effort to ensure that her voice was breezy, that it suggested a lapse of memory that she certainly knew was false. "Of course, I could be mistaken. That evening at the consulate was rather hectic—so many new faces, so much champagne."

Ford cocked a brow, but said nothing. He hadn't realized it until that moment, but he grew suddenly aware of just how many times in the preceding weeks he'd thought about that night, about the way she'd felt when he held her in his arms. The thought that she retained no memory of the experience, that she had confused him with another or, even worse, simply forgotten, galled him. His ego found it hard to accept the possibility that she had made so much greater an impression on him than he had on her.

His surprise was not lost on Amity. She considered it with a secret pleasure, not quite sure why the fact that she'd managed to unsettle him seemed such a triumph to her, but savoring the feeling with relish nonetheless.

"We'll leave you to reveal your distasteful character to my fiancée some other time, Ford," Justin said as he put his hand to Amity's arm in an entirely proprietary manner and helped her climb onto the gangway. "Now, I think, she has more important matters to consider. Her first glimpse of Gardiner's Ghenena, for example." He started down the gangway to the wharf, holding her hand firmly on his arm and smiling at her, his expression demanding all her attention. "Ghenena is Arabic for garden," he went on, "and that is just what it is, a magnificent garden, as far as the eye can see. I think you will be pleased with the place where you will soon be mistress, Amity."

Amity forced her attention back to Justin, forced herself to listen to his words, to tell herself that she was delighted to be there with him. The crowd on the wharf spread itself aside as they stepped down from the gangway. There was a momentary silence as the musicians paused and a small girl, her arms laden with a bouquet almost as large as she herself, made a tentative way forward to Amity. She held out the flowers.

"Welcome, lady," she said, her words uncertain. She'd obviously learned them for the occasion and was not entirely sure she'd said them correctly.

Amity knelt and took the offered flowers. *"Khattar kherak,"* she said, her own words of thanks almost as unsure as those of the child.

The girl smiled up at her, then turned and ran as fast as her short legs could carry her back to stand behind her mother's skirts. Almost as soon as she'd hidden herself, however, she was peeping out and smiling impishly at Amity, obviously pleased with the encounter with the strange new lady. The musicians once more took up their instruments, and Justin put his hand to Amity's elbow, drawing her back up, then toward a waiting carriage.

Justin lifted her into the carriage, then settled himself on the seat beside her. His father and Ford quickly occupied the seat facing them, and the carriage started forward.

Amity turned to stare at a great stone wall they passed to their right, just downriver from where the boat was tied up to the wharf.

"What's that?" she asked.

Kendrick smiled. "Tell ElAmarna, my dear," he told her. "A booming town by local standards. Those walls

88

are over two thousand years old. They were built by the Romans when this land was part of their empire."

Amity stared at the dun-colored walls that surrounded Tell ElAmarna and wondered against what enemies they had been built.

"Egypt has had many conquerors since the days of the pharaohs, Amity," Ford said meditatively. "First Alexander the Great left his imprint, conquering them and going on to other battlefields but leaving behind a dynasty of Greek kings to rule them, then the Roman legions, and then the Persians and the Turks. Horde after endless horde, all leaving some imprint or another, forts and temples and roads, the marks of their own civilizations. But they were eventually all defeated by the desert or the ancient ghosts. And in the end, Egypt remains, as unchanging as ever, as it will be when we, too, are defeated by the shifting sands."

Amity was surprised to hear the melancholy in Ford's voice, the tone tinged with resigned defeat.

But Justin seemed to bristle at his words. "I will never leave," he said sharply. "This land is mine, and I intend to hold onto it with every breath within me."

She turned to face him, and saw him staring out at the fields the carriage had now begun to pass through— an endless expanse of green outlined by a web of irrigation canals snaking their way from the river. His expression was fixed and hard, and she suddenly realized that he was not the sort of man to give up anything he considered his own.

Her glance slipped away from Justin and met Ford's, and for the second time that day she felt an uncomfortable stirring inside her. Whatever certainty she had felt as she stood on deck beside Justin had long since crumbled and dissolved.

Ford seemed to sense her uncertainty, to read it in her eyes. He smiled at her, a smile that told her that he knew her thoughts, that they were precisely the thoughts he would have her think. She silently cursed him, wishing he had never come to Tell ElAmarna. She had made her decision, and he had, she told herself, no right to try to sway it. But a nagging voice inside her told her that if his mere presence could unsettle her so, then perhaps her decisions were not so very strongly seated as she had thought.

Chapter Five

The house completely surprised Amity.

From Justin's casual references, she'd expected a makeshift affair, a temporary shelter in the midst of being transformed into a passably comfortable home. There had even been a few joking references to Bedouin tents, but she had dismissed them, more because she knew Justin would never countenance even the suggestion that he was anything but properly British than for any other reason. Still, she expected to find the plantation house a small and muddled affair.

She was, therefore, more than a little surprised when the carriage turned away from the path bordering the river, climbed a sharp hill, and turned onto a drive through what might have been a formal English lawn had it been lined with elms or oak rather than the smooth, round, upright trunks of palms. She stared up at a nearly completed English manor house in the Palladian style with a wide, sweeping granite facade evenly pierced by pedimented windows that framed an enormous central entrance. She had expected almost anything else but this grand, pristine structure looming up out of the Egyptian countryside.

Kendrick smiled at her when he saw her expression of surprise. "I suppose Justin suggested there'd be something else?" he asked.

"There had been some mumbling about a ramshackle

farmhouse," she said, her tone a bit dazed. "And I believe there was the passing mention of tents."

"I've never before heard you utter a modest word, Justin," Ford said. "I'm surprised you didn't suggest to Miss Ravenswood that you'd had Buckingham Palace moved here, stone by stone."

He laughed at Justin's answering scowl, but Amity was only dimly aware of either of them. As the carriage drew to a stop in front of the house, she finally realized she would live in this magnificent place when she and Justin were not in the city. Until that moment, she hadn't really considered what marrying Justin Gardiner might mean to her life.

Justin seemed agreeably pleased by her surprised awe. "In a year or two, this will be the finest place in all of Egypt," he told her flatly.

Kendrick smiled again. "I hope you find it all to your liking, my dear," he added as he helped her down from the carriage. Once more he offered her his arm, then, with her hand firmly settled on it, led her inside.

The interior of the house, Amity found, was equally as impressive as the facade. Kendrick led her through the parlors and dining rooms, elegantly proportioned rooms made light and airy by tall windows, cleanly uncluttered furnishings, and many antiques, all apparently imported from England and all of the very finest workmanship.

"I fear the solarium is still a rubble," Kendrick told her as he showed her the last room at the far side of the house. "Things go slowly here, it seems. I think it has something to do with a land that has monuments thousands of years old. Somehow, no one seems to find the passage of a few years of any great importance." He grinned at her as though feeling it necessary to apologize. "I have, however, managed to see that your rooms are ready for you, my dear. I hope you find them to your liking."

And she did. He showed her to a huge bedroom with tall windows overlooking a magnificent garden, splendidly furnished with a tall canopy bed swathed with sheer white, lacy netting, an inlaid satinwood dressing table, and a wonderfully inviting-looking chaise covered with a heap of white, lace-covered pillows. There was also a small dressing room and a meticulously appointed bath. Amity thought she'd somehow wandered into heaven, sure that nothing could be more luxurious or more pleasing to look at.

"It's wonderful," she breathed when she'd made a first, quick inspection and turned back to find Kendrick anxiously waiting for her reaction. "Are you sure you haven't spirited us all to some castle in the English countryside?"

He seemed pleased at the response. "Would that I had," he said with a small sigh. "But with a woman's hand to civilize us here—your hand, my dear—perhaps the possibility will one day exist for us to feel as though we'd done just that."

When he'd gone, leaving her to bathe and rest from the trip, Amity stood for a few moments, staring out at the formal gardens that backed the house. None of it seemed quite real to her, especially when she noticed the gardeners at work—young Egyptians, clad in white *thobes,* the typical ankle-length shirt of the peasantry, over loose pants. Somehow the sight of them, laboring over the rows of rosebushes, made her realize how very alien she, as well as Justin and his family, were in Egypt.

Perhaps Ford had been right, she mused, perhaps Kendrick and Justin were only making what all those other outsiders had made throughout the ages, an attempt to change Egypt to their own liking, to make it an image of their own lands. Perhaps their attempt, like all those that had gone before, would meet with ultimate failure. All those rosebushes, with their intimations of formal English gardens, could not possibly live long in the endless Egyptian heat. Surely, in trying to turn this place into an image of the world he had left behind, Kendrick was saying more about what he had lost than what he had gained.

The thought unsettled her, and left her feeling more than a little sad.

She bathed, relishing the luxury of the huge tub, but when she was done, found herself unable to take the nap that Justin had advised. She was, she realized, far too anxious to explore, to simply laze about in her room. Instead, she dressed in riding clothes, then descended the long marble stairs to the parlor, hoping to find either Justin or Kendrick willing to show her around.

The parlor, however, was empty, save for the tall, dark steward who had been introduced to her as Naseem. He bowed to her.

"May I be of some service, mistress?" he then asked her in very precise English.

For a moment the term of address shocked Amity. It was hard for her to believe that she would soon be mistress in this magnificent house.

"I was hoping to persuade Mr. Gardiner to take me for a ride," she admitted when she'd managed to collect herself, her voice showing a bit of disappointment at finding her expectations for the afternoon apparently dashed.

Naseem shook his head sadly. "Shaikh Kendrick and Shaikh Justin have gone to oversee the unloading of the ship, mistress," he told her.

Amity reminded herself that Justin's boat was not a pleasure craft, but used in the family business to transport the cotton produced on the plantation to Cairo for export, and then to return with supplies for the plantation as well as goods to be sold in Tell ElAmarna.

"Of course," she replied dully. "They must have a

great deal to do." She felt a stab of disappointment as she realized she would be forced to spend the afternoon in quiet solitude despite her inclination.

"You might still find Shaikh Ford has not yet gone. He went out to the stables only a few moments ago," Naseem offered.

Amity brightened. "Excellent," she pronounced, then looked around, a bit bewildered. No one had shown her any stables when she'd arrived.

Naseem grinned at her good-naturedly, then showed her to a side entrance to the house. He stood by the door and pointed to a long, low building a hundred feet along the drive.

"There," he pointed. "Shall I accompany you, mistress?"

Amity quickly shook her head. She could see Ford leaving the stable, leading a sleek white Arabian into the yard beside the building.

"No thank you, Naseem," she replied, and then ran off, determined to catch Ford before the stable boy saddled the horse and he could leave.

"Don't go off and leave me, or I shall be condemned to an afternoon of unrelieved boredom all alone."

Ford turned. Amity thought his expression showed surprise and even a bit of displeasure to find her there. She pushed away the thought. After all, she told herself, he had no reason to be displeased with her. And she was aware that she felt a decided pleasure at the prospect of spending some time with him.

"I thought you were resting," he said.

"I can't," she told him. "I'm not the sort who can laze about all afternoon and then appear at the dinner table and pretend the effort had been taxing."

He considered her a moment, then nodded. "No, I suppose you're not, are you?"

"Will you give me a bit of a tour?" she asked.

"I don't think Justin would like that," he said abruptly.

He turned back to his consideration of the horse, grasping the saddle cinch and checking to see that it had been pulled sufficiently tight.

"I can't see any reason why he'd mind," Amity insisted.

Despite her words, she realized she could think of a good many reasons, starting with the memory of Ford's kiss. Even after the passage of so many days, just the thought of it left her with a pleasant stirring, an odd liquid heat that began to pulse through her.

He turned back to face her. "Can't you?" he asked her shortly when his eyes found hers.

"No, of course not," she replied.

She had spoken just a shade too quickly for her words to sound sincere, and she knew it. She pulled her eyes from his and turned them instead to the horse for lack of a better object for her attention.

"He can't expect to go off and leave me with nothing to do with myself and then object to whatever means I find to occupy my time," she added, this time with a touch of defiance. She was not quite sure why she felt the need for it.

He considered her silently for a moment, then handed his horse's reins to her. "Here," he said, dropping them into her hand and starting back into the stables, the boy trailing along, bewildered, behind him. "I won't be long."

Amity considered the fact that to all appearances he'd lost the playful lechery that had been in his manner when he'd met her at the wharf. She told herself that she ought to be relieved, that she didn't want to have her life made any more complicated than it already was, but she didn't quite manage to convince herself. Perhaps, she thought, all that had been just for Justin, just

96

a way to return a bit of the antagonism his cousin seemed intent to show him. Perhaps he had no thoughts for her at all. She found she was pained at the speculation despite the fact that she told herself she ought to feel otherwise.

Ford returned in a few moments with another Arabian, this one a bit smaller, with a rust-colored blaze on her face and a full, long mane. He saddled her quickly, not offering Amity so much as a word until he was done.

"Ready?" he asked as he checked to see he'd properly tightened the cinch.

When she nodded, he brought the horse up beside her, then turned to her. "You *can* ride?" he asked, as an afterthought. "Perhaps I should get you an animal with a more placid nature than these Arabians?"

Amity smiled a bit smugly. "I'll manage," she told him.

She let him give her a hand up, then swung herself into the saddle with an ease that obviously surprised him. He grinned up at her, then turned to his own horse and mounted.

"What will you show me first?" she demanded.

He looked suddenly serious and very thoughtful. "Why don't we go down to the river?" he suggested. "We can start from there."

There was something in the tone of his voice that made Amity think he'd been bound there in the first place, and that he had his own reasons for going there, reasons beyond merely admiring the scenery.

He turned his horse slowly, then peered round to assure himself that she was following. Amity obediently turned her own mount, and walked her forward until she was beside Ford's.

"Which way?" she asked.

He pointed, then made a sweeping gesture with his hand, inviting her to take the lead. She smiled in response, and cocked her head. Then she leaned forward, took up the slack in the reins, and kicked the horse's flanks. The Arabian started off at an easy gallop, obviously pleased with the opportunity for a run.

She glanced back quickly, just enough to read the surprise on Ford's face, before she leaned into the horse's neck and urged her on. She heard Ford's laughter as he started after her.

Ford called to her to draw up her horse when they'd reached a short bluff overlooking the Nile. Amity did as he directed, then slipped from the saddle to stand and stare down at the dark water, watching as it moved with a turgid sweep downriver, carrying with it a good number of small craft. Other boats, canvas unfurled to catch every last wisp of the wind on the water, labored in the opposite direction. Even this sight was peculiarly foreign in her eyes, the feluccas and dhows seeming inordinately exotic to her compared to the packets that she remembered filling Boston Harbor.

She turned to Ford and was surprised to see his attention not on the movement of the vessels on the water but on a thin file of *fellaheen* who tramped along a narrow cart path at the water's edge guiding a half dozen ox-drawn carts loaded with wooden crates. His gaze grew sharp as he watched the carts come to a halt near a small wooden structure not far from the water's edge and the *fellaheen* began to unload the crates.

"What's that?" she asked.

"Freight from your fiancé's boat, I should think," Ford returned, his tone terse. "The young financial wizard is no doubt in the midst of earning his next fortune."

Amity considered the distaste she heard in his voice. "You sound jealous," she accused him.

He turned to her finally, and she found his expression

when he stared at her was contemplative and sharp.

"Do I?" he asked. Then he shrugged. "Perhaps I am. But not of Justin's money. I earn all I need for my wants."

Amity ought to have turned away, and certainly not pursued the subject. She knew that well enough by the expression she'd seen on his face, the sharpness in his eyes. But something inside her goaded her, and she heard the words with a tinge of surprise even as she spoke them.

"Then of what?" she demanded.

He hesitated only a second before he replied. His response, however, was not an answer but a question of his own.

"Why have you agreed to marry him?" he demanded abruptly. "You don't love him."

She turned away from him, afraid of what he might see in her eyes were she to let him.

"You have no right to say that. You know nothing of me."

He put his hand to her arm and pulled her back to face him. "I do know. I knew it that first night, at the consulate. And you knew it, too."

"Stop it," she said, pulling her arm free. "I knew nothing that night—nothing." She looked up at him, and felt a surge of anger—with him, with herself, with the way circumstances had led her to a position she could not quite convince herself was right. "And you were just playing games with the foolish little American," she spat out, her tone suddenly bitter. "Don't try to lie to me and tell me otherwise."

He tightened his hold on her arm, then waited until she'd realized she could not free herself and quieted.

"I meant what I wrote to you," he told her softly. "I did think of you. All the time I was gone, I thought of you."

Once he'd said the words aloud, he realized how true

they were and just how many times he'd thought about the way she'd felt in his arms that night, the way her lips had tasted against his. It had seemed a joke to him at the time, but he'd been haunted by the memory of her and it did no good for him to tell himself otherwise.

He put his other hand to her free arm and drew her close to him, holding her tight even though he realized she was no longer making any effort to free herself from him.

He lowered his lips to hers, firm and warm and seeking, letting the first nectared taste fill him. Her lips were like honey on his, sweet and supple and filled with promise.

He released his hold of her arms and wrapped his own around her, holding her close to him, feeling the sharp beat of her heart, the heady throb that echoed his own. He knew at that moment that the same fire that burned within him was in her as well.

He was right. Amity knew it as surely as he did. Somehow his lips managed to touch her in a way that bewildered her, that caused a liquid heat inside her that melted her. Justin's kiss had not done this to her, had not left her feeling breathless and weak and yearning only for another. Somehow her arms lifted themselves, for surely she had not directed them, and her hands felt the hard, tense muscles of his shoulders, then found the dark curls at the back of his neck.

When he kissed her again, she welcomed the probe of his tongue, surprised at how the contact of it to her own made her tremble, how it made rivulets of sweet fire throb through her. She could not understand what it was he did to her, but she knew she did not want it to stop. Whatever magic his lips held, she wished she could drink in enough of it to sate herself of it, enough for a lifetime. She felt bereft when his lips finally left hers.

"And you thought of me, too," he told her firmly, his words knowing and sure. "I've haunted you just as you've haunted me."

His words startled her. Not so much that they were true, for they *were* true and she knew she had no thought to deny them to herself any longer, but the way he said them, so certain of himself, so contained, as though she were a prize he'd won, as though there was no question in his mind that she was his.

She forced herself to push away from him. "Stop this. I will not be treated this way." She balled her hands into fists and beat them against his chest.

He released her, surprised that she no longer welcomed his touch, wondering what had angered her. He watched her step back from him, saw the flush in her cheeks, and wondered if it had been caused by her anger or his kiss.

"How would you have me treat you?" he demanded sharply. "As Justin does, with politely superior restraint? Do you think that once he has you, he'll still be such the proper British gentleman?"

"That's no concern of yours," she snapped back at him.

She stood for a moment, not quite understanding why, but wishing he would say that it was his concern, that what happened to her meant something to him, that he would not have her marry Justin because he wanted her.

He didn't. She told herself she was a fool to think he cared about her, that he thought of her as anything more than a prize he might be able to take before his cousin did. She told herself she hated him.

"You don't love him," he said finally, as though that were explanation enough.

"I do," she countered. "And I'm going to marry him."

He took a step toward her, stopping only when he saw she backed away from him at his approach.

"Is it him you love, or the idea of being mistress here, of being a rich man's wife?"

He realized he only said it to hurt her, to repay her for the blow she'd so easily dealt his ego. But he was far from prepared for the look of hurt he saw in her expression and wished he could call the words back.

"You are despicable," she sneered.

Then she grabbed her horse's reins and climbed deftly into the saddle. She looked down at him when she was mounted, a look of anger and hurt and disdain that made him want to cry out to her that it had all been a mistake, that he wanted to begin the afternoon with her again and proceed differently.

He didn't. Instead, he stood in silence and watched her turn the Arabian and then deliver a sharp blow to the animal's flank, sending it galloping off back toward his uncle's house.

He hesitated for a moment, wanting to follow her, wondering if he could somehow make peace with her. But then he turned away and brought his glance back to the small structure at the foot of the scarp where the *fellaheen* had by now finished storing the crates and had turned the ox carts back along the path toward the wharf.

He'd come to Tell ElAmarna with a purpose, he told himself. He could not afford to let his feeling for Amity Ravenswood interfere with what he knew he must do. He found it unpleasant to consider, but he realized that if she was so determined to marry Justin, then perhaps she deserved him.

In any case, he was in no position to stop her. Her anger with him made that more than apparent to him. And that, he realized, was probably the most painful thought of all.

Amity found as she rode away from Ford that her anger with him, despite his certainty that it was deep-seated and unshakable, was soon overshadowed by her curiosity. She had realized immediately when she'd confronted him at the stables and demanded to be taken for a ride that he was not merely in search of fresh air and a view of the countryside. And when he'd stared down at the *fellaheen* as they unloaded the carts from the boat, he'd seemed especially intrigued.

Something was going on, she realized, something he was curious about. And his curiosity piqued her own. She found she could not simply ride back to the house and dismiss the events of the afternoon to an unfortunate lack of judgment on her part. He'd been far too willing to let her leave for her to think he had no interest in their ride other than to spend an hour in her company and steal a kiss. He was looking for something, and she suddenly decided she might look for it as well.

She turned the horse and returned to the spot where she'd left Ford, only to find it vacant. She realized that part of her had expected that, had known he'd set about doing whatever it was her presence had prevented him from doing at the start.

She stared down curiously at the shed where the *fellaheen* had stored the crates, remembering that he'd seemed to show a special interest in the disposal of the cargo from Justin's boat. The shed was tiny with the distance and quieter now, the *fellaheen* having finished their task and gone. The figure approaching it on foot and with apparent stealth seemed even tinier. Still, she was sure it was Ford.

She did not quite know why, but it struck her that he would not be pleased were he to turn and see her watching him. She dismounted, and drew the horse back, far enough from the edge of the hillside so that it could not be seen from below, and found a bush on which to tie the reins. Then she crept forward to the edge of the slope and stared down at him.

She had been right in her caution. As he neared the shed, he turned and looked around carefully, obviously assuring himself that no one was watching him. Amity dropped down to her knees, obscuring herself in the tall grasses, wondering even as she hid herself why she did not want him to know she was there.

Finally deciding he was alone, Ford moved to the door of the shed, tested the latch, and seemed entirely unsurprised to find it securely locked. Then he moved to the side, to a shuttered window, and carefully pried it open, stopping from time to time to look around and assure himself no one was near. When he'd provided himself with access, he slipped inside.

He was not there long, only a few moments, but while he was within, Amity found herself growing more and more curious, and, for some reason she could not quite understand, more and more concerned. Why didn't he merely ask Justin or Kendrick what was in the shed if he was so determined to know, she wondered. Why would he steal about, acting the part of the spy? Everything that had before seemed so pleasantly benign—the river, the laboring *fellaheen* with their ox carts, the bright afternoon sunshine glinting off the water, all of it suddenly seemed sinister to her. She found she didn't like the change.

When finally he emerged, climbing out through the same window by which he'd entered, she expected him to simply mount his horse and ride off quickly. Instead, he carefully replaced the shutter, obscuring any evidence of his entry. And this, too, Amity found decidedly sinister.

His task obviously accomplished, he darted a last quick look around. And for the first time, Amity felt afraid, for his glance seemed to stop as he considered the top of the scarp where she knelt in the grass. She thought for a moment he'd seen her. Although she had no reason to think he was aware of her presence, or if even he was, that his knowledge might prove dangerous to her, still she realized she was afraid.

Ford seemed satisfied he had not been observed, however, and he turned away and remounted his horse. Amity kept herself still for a moment, kneeling in the grass and watching the thin trail of dust the animal's hooves kicked up as he rode along the path by the river. Then she stood and turned to find her own horse, realizing she had found nothing to satisfy her curiosity. Instead, what she'd seen had only made it more nagging.

Something was decidedly wrong, she realized, and she had no idea what it might be. She tried to recall what Charles and Beatrice had told her of Ford's past, of the incident that had caused his ruin in England, the event that had precipitated his entry into the Army and his forced abandonment of England for the rigors of colonial Egypt.

It had been a matter of missing jewels, she remembered, jewels that Ford had purportedly stolen. For the first time she seriously wondered if the story might be true, if he really was a thief. She realized she had dismissed the story as gossip until that moment, doing so simply because she could not believe what she'd been told of him. But now, after what she'd seen with her own eyes, she found she was no longer quite so sure in her belief.

If Ford *was* a thief, she mused, perhaps he was considering some portion of the contents of the shed as his next target. The goods stored there were Justin's. There was certainly no love lost between the two cousins. It pained her to think it possible, but she could not dismiss the possibility that Ford might choose to steal something from Justin simply as an act of maliciousness.

Her thoughts were muddied as she mounted her horse and turned him in the direction of the house. Her images of Beatrice and Charles had been shattered since she had come to Egypt. And now, it seemed, the expectations she'd held of Ford Gardiner were crumbling as well. She wondered if she would ever learn to see people as they were and not as she would have them be.

Far more painful was the contemplation of what other images she held might prove as false as those she had already watched falter and fall.

There had been the appropriate compliments from Kendrick when she'd entered the parlor, and the tersely appraising look from Ford. Now, as she settled herself on the silk-covered sofa and accepted a glass of sherry from Justin, Amity found herself at a loss as to just what words she had for him. She would soon share this man's bed, she told herself firmly, and she forced herself to smile up at him, to offer him her cheek for a chaste kiss.

She had spent a good deal of time considering just what she would tell him of that afternoon's adventure, and yet she had been unable to come to any decision. Part of her told herself quite firmly that as Justin's future wife, she owed it to him to tell him what she'd seen Ford do that afternoon. But there was another voice inside her, one equally as strong, that told her she had really seen nothing at all, nothing truly damning at any rate; she had nothing beyond her own suspicions, and baring such tales could only reinforce the animosity between the two men. And that, the voice told her with unswerving logic, would serve no purpose whatsoever.

She would have accepted the second voice's advice easily enough except that she realized it came from the same part of her that had relished Ford's kiss, that part of her that, despite her strong admonitions to the contrary, longed still to repeat the experience. Her conscience, she found, nagged at her with an unmerciful persistence, countering the voice that prompted silence with the question of whether it was Ford she wished to protect from Justin's anger or herself.

"I thought you intended to rest this afternoon. But Naseem tells me you roused yourself to take a ride with Ford."

Was there a hint of suspicion in Justin's tone, Amity wondered, or was it only her own guilty conscience? She sipped the sherry before she replied.

"I couldn't sleep," she told him with what she hoped was a disarming smile. "And you were off somewhere. I'm afraid I forced Major Gardiner to accompany me on a short ride so that I could admire the scenery."

It seemed apparent to her as she heard her own words that she had made her decision to remain silent about Ford's entry into the shed. She did not remember having made a conscious decision in the matter, but there she was, smiling at Justin and pretending nothing untoward had happened so it would seem her decision was, somehow, made. She hoped it was the right one, and made for the right reasons.

Justin had turned away, moving back to the side table that held the liquor chest, and proceeded to prepare a whiskey and soda for himself. Amity stared at the back of his perfectly-tailored jacket and considered the stiff, upright shoulders beneath it. Unbending and inflexible, she thought. She stared, wondering where the words had come from, why they had popped into her mind. And then she realized they were true. Justin's back *was* unbending and inflexible. Just like the rest of him.

"Naseem also mentioned that you returned alone," Justin went on mildly, as though he had no pressing desire for her answer, just a passing curiosity.

And Naseem plays the spy for you, Amity suddenly thought with a touch of bitterness. She found herself growing suspicious of him and not sure why. Ford's search of the storage shed had made her suddenly unsure of everything—of Justin, of Ford, even of herself. She found she hated the feeling.

She shrugged, and once again sipped the sherry. "I

found the ride more taxing than I had expected. Perhaps I ought to have stayed in and rested as you suggested. In any event, Ford put me on the path leading back to the house, then went on with his own ride. Apparently he was prepared for a bit more exercise than I was this afternoon."

Once again she found herself wondering why she was so evasive, why she made no mention of what had actually happened that afternoon. She tried to still the accusing voice inside her by telling herself that she had no need to foster further trouble between the already antagonistic cousins. She dared a glance at Ford, and found he was carefully ignoring her. She returned her attention to Justin, who, having prepared his whiskey and soda, once again turned to face her.

"And just what did Ford deign to show you on your tour?"

She tossed her head. "Oh, a glimpse of the river and the boats, a ride through some of the fields," she replied, once again aware that she was being evasive and feeling Justin's eyes on her, questioning her, even doubting her. "I couldn't stop staring at the *fellaheen* working with the oxen," she went on, hoping to dispel her discomfort with a flood of words. "At home one sees tractors and reapers and threshers. But there is none of that here. It all seems so, well . . . so ancient."

Kendrick smiled at her. "It is, my dear. Nothing has changed here in hundreds of years."

"But wouldn't modern machinery make the plantation more profitable?" she asked, curious now.

Justin answered before Kendrick had the chance. "Human labor is cheaper here than machines," he said deliberately.

"And the *fellaheen* don't require the care or maintenance that a thresher or reaper might," Ford said, his e sharply bitter.

istin turned to Ford. "And you, where did you go

108

this afternoon?" he demanded abruptly, refusing to rise to the bait and apparently still unwilling to abandon the subject.

Ford smiled a crooked smile. "Oh, you know how it is, Cousin. We soldiers need to be in the saddle a few hours each day or we feel out of sorts. A good ride keeps the evil humors at bay."

"And calluses in all the right places," Kendrick added.

Ford laughed at that, and Amity could not help but smile.

Justin, however, seemed disinclined to humor at the moment. He seemed about to say something, but Kendrick held up a hand.

"If the two of you continue to behave like bickering children, I'll be forced to send you to your rooms without supper."

Ford smiled broadly. "A fate too awful to be contemplated, Uncle," he said with a laugh. He stood and walked toward Justin. "Shall we make our peace, Justin?" he asked, offering his hand. "After all, I've only a few days' leave. We could pretend we were boys again, pretend we liked each other."

Justin stared at him steadily, with none of the humor Ford showed in his expression.

"We never liked each other," he said simply. "You were always getting me into trouble."

Ford laughed again. "And you were always so damned determined to stay out of trouble," he said. "You made such a tempting target. Do you remember the time I lured you away from the garden party at Grandmother's for a swim in the stream, then stole your clothes and left you to come back with nothing but a few handfuls of leaves to protect your sins against modesty?"

Amity burst into laughter, and with it, she realized, came the dismissal of her tense and unsure mood.

"You didn't?" she giggled.

"He most certainly did," Kendrick affirmed with a

smile.

"But the best part was that Justin chose poison ivy as his protection. A few hours later he was screaming from the rash," Ford added with another laugh.

"And you weren't quite silent, I recall," Justin noted.

Ford nodded. "My father made sure I couldn't sit for a week," he agreed. "But it was worth it, just to see you appear out of the woods, holding those leaves in front of you, blushing like a child bride."

"I suppose it must have seemed rather amusing at the time," Justin admitted, then finally smiled.

Kendrick stood. "If you two have made your much overdue peace, may I suggest we go in to dinner?" He held out an arm to Amity.

She stood quickly and put her arm through the crook his made. "I think you are right, Kendrick. I think we should send these two off their rooms to contemplate their childish manners," she said, flashing a smile at Ford and Justin.

"And ban them until they learn to behave," Kendrick suggested as he led her toward the large mahogany doors that opened into the dining room. "And in the meantime, we'll be forced to drink all the champagne in the house ourselves."

"Bravo," Amity agreed. "Remind me to offer a toast to your suggestion."

Ford grinned at Justin. "Shall we?" he asked as he put his glass down and rose to follow Amity and Kendrick.

Justin grimaced, then turned and, ignoring Ford, started toward the dining room.

Ford stood where he was and considered his cousin for a moment, his expression losing all hint of the amusement that it had displayed moments before. He'd learned something that afternoon, something disturbing, and no amount of taunting Justin could mitigate the distress that knowledge brought him.

110

Amity had felt a bit of trepidation when she entered the dining room on Kendrick's arm, but that was all quickly dispelled. Both Ford and Justin, who trailed in behind her and Kendrick, seated themselves and made a show of maintaining their humor throughout the meal. She wasn't quite sure if the apparent bonhomie was for her benefit, Kendrick's, or simply caused by the healthy quantity of champagne that was served to celebrate her arrival. Whatever the reason, she was grateful for it, and thoroughly enjoyed the meal.

"I'm well enough brought up to know that it is the habit of gentlemen to require a period of respite from the presence of ladies at the conclusion of dinner," she said with a smile as she put her napkin on the table and stood.

"A habit that would be gladly broken, Amity," Kendrick objected as he, as well as Ford and Justin, stood. "Especially on this evening."

She shook her head. "Actually, this evening I would appreciate it if you would hold to that particular practice," she replied with a smile. "It has been a very long day, and I must admit to a certain undeniable weariness. If I may, I think I will borrow a book from your library, Kendrick, one that is especially boring so I won't be particularly disappointed when I nod off after a page or two."

"Certainly, my dear," Kendrick replied.

"Then I will leave you gentlemen to your brandy and whatever nefarious activities you choose to pursue," she told them with a grin.

"Rest well," Justin told her as he stepped forward and took her hand.

He pressed it slightly. Amity wondered why all she felt at the contact was the awareness that his hands were warm, and very moist. It was not a pleasant thought.

"Good night," she told him, then turned and left.

When she'd gone, the three men resettled themselves. Ford was the first to reach for the decanter of brandy Naseem had set on the table. He poured a healthy measure into a tumbler and added a touch of water.

"To nefarious pursuits," he said affably as he raised the glass in toast, then brought it to his lips.

Kendrick raised a brow. But it was Justin who seemed put off by his words.

"Just what is that supposed to mean, Cousin?" he demanded, all trace of the amiability that had prevailed during the meal suddenly vanished.

Ford shrugged, then took a healthy swallow. He leveled his glance on Justin.

"It means nothing, Cousin," he replied simply. "The word was Miss Ravenswood's." He grinned, apparently enjoying Justin's obviously ruffled feathers.

Justin considered him in steely silence for a long moment, then leaned across the table toward him.

"Precisely why are you here, Ford?" he demanded, his tone sharp.

Ford shrugged. "A rest," he said as he considered the contents of his glass. Then he turned to Justin and smiled. "To be held to the loving bosom of my family and find comfort there after the hardships a soldier's life imposes upon me," he added with a slightly wicked gleam in his eyes.

Justin's jaw hardened. "If it's a loving family you're seeking, perhaps you ought to look elsewhere," he said sharply. "Perhaps back in England."

"Justin!"

But Kendrick's interruption came too late. Ford's face colored sharply with anger and embarrassment. And Justin, seeing that and obviously satisfied, went on.

"Or don't you think you'll find a warm welcome there, either, Cousin?" he taunted.

"That was uncalled for, Justin," Kendrick said angrily. "Ford is always welcome in this house."

112

Ford emptied his glass quickly, then set it down on the table before turning back to face Justin. He realized his cousin had ignored his father's words, that he sat and stared at him with pleasure in his expression that said only too plainly to Ford how much hurt his own held.

"Under the circumstances, I think it would be wise were I to be gracious enough to remove myself from your presence, Justin, knowing that is the one way I might bring you any pleasure," he said as he stood. "Uncle," he said, nodding to Kendrick and offering him a grim smile.

"Ford, there's no need . . ."

Ford ignored his words. He turned and quickly left the room. When he'd gone, Kendrick turned his glance to Justin, to find his son's expression apparently quite pleased.

"There was no need for any of that," he said sharply. "He's been through more than enough over that damned necklace."

Justin offered him a crooked grin and shrugged. Then he reached for the brandy and refilled his glass.

"Found anything interesting?"

Amity turned from the bookshelf to find Ford standing just behind her. She wondered how he had entered the room so quietly. She had not heard a sound.

"I thought you were drinking brandy with Kendrick and Justin," she said, turning her back to him, pretending interest in the contents of the bookshelf.

"The thought of you drew me away," he said softly, and put his hand to her shoulder.

She shrugged sharply and drew away from him. "How dare you?" she hissed at him under her breath. "Is there no end to this game of yours?"

"It's not a game," he said evenly, and this time when

113

he put his hand to her shoulder, he grasped it firmly so that she could not evade him, and turned her to face him. He stared down at her, his blue eyes sharp and knowing as they found hers. "And it's not a game to you, either. If it were, you wouldn't have lied to Justin about what happened between us this afternoon."

"I didn't lie," she protested, but her words sounded weak and unconvincing even in her own ears.

He smiled at her slyly. "No, you simply didn't tell the truth," he said. "And we both know why. You lied to him because it's me you're in love with, not Justin."

"You?" she asked with a humorless little laugh. "What sort of woman would fall in love with you? You're a womanizer, a . . . a . . ." She stopped. For some reason the word refused to be said.

"A what?" he asked, his tone icy now. "Could the word you're searching for be *thief?* Do you want to ask me what sort of woman falls in love with a thief?"

She was shocked by the bitterness she heard in his tone, shocked that he could seem so hurt by the unspoken accusation.

"No," she murmured, surprised at the regret she felt at what she'd heard in his voice and wishing to protest her innocence despite the fact that what he'd said was true. She managed only the one word. Any further protests were smothered by his lips pressing hers.

He was right and she knew it. She knew it before his lips touched hers, but once they had, she realized there was no use in trying to convince herself otherwise. She felt the molten fire ignite within her, sweeping through her. She knew she had said nothing to Justin because she had wanted to feel his lips against hers, at least this one more time. Because even as she felt herself begin to melt inside, she told herself this must be the last time, there must never again be so much as this simple contact between them ever again. For if there were, she knew, it could only lead to her own ruin.

She let the sensation fill her, and told herself she had no need for thought; for just this one moment, she would let it lie unbidden and unrecognized. For this last time, she promised herself as she let him draw her close, this time and never again.

But although she might try to deny rationality, it would not be so easily dismissed. This man was virtually a stranger to her, and yet he'd forced upon her greater intimacy than she'd ever allowed anyone. He'd made no suggestion that he might offer her marriage as Justin had, no suggestion that she was more to him than a woman he would like to take himself, as he had undoubtedly taken many others. If that weren't condemnation enough, he was a thief, a strident voice within her told her sharply, a thief and perhaps worse. Reality struck her like cold water thrown on flames.

She pushed angrily against his chest until he released her.

"Don't you ever so much as touch me again," she hissed at him, her voice low and angry. It seemed almost as though her fury constricted her throat and kept her words to a hoarse, angry whisper.

"Was there something you needed, Amity?"

She looked up, surprised to hear Justin's voice and aware of the hot flush that crept to her cheeks.

He was standing in the doorway to the library, his tumbler of brandy in his hand, his eyes icy blue and sharp. She felt afraid for a moment, wondering what he had seen. But then he smiled at her and walked into the room to join them and her fear melted away.

"As you seemed to have no need for my presence," Ford told him deliberately. "I thought I'd offer my advise to Miss Ravenswood with regard to appropriate bedtime literature."

Justin smiled at him humorlessly, then pointedly put his hand to Amity's waist.

"A kindness you need not bother to complete,

Cousin," he said. "I am here and will be more than happy to provide *my fiancée* whatever help she might require."

There was no mistaking the tone of proprietorship in Justin's words, or in his gesture as he put his hand on her. Amity shivered slightly as she heard the words, and then again as she felt the heat and pressure of his grasp.

She darted a quick look back to the bookshelf. "I think I'll forgo the book this evening," she managed to murmur, "I really am too tired to read, after all."

Justin turned to smile at her. "As you like, my dear. Then we shall bid you a fond good night."

She smiled wanly, then backed away a step. "Good night," she said, then quickly fled from the room.

Justin watched her go, and a determined expression settled on his face. Contrary to her supposition, Justin had seen Ford embrace her, had watched as she murmured something, something he had been unable to hear. And as she left the room and he stared after her, he made a vow to himself: He wanted her and he would have her. Before he'd give her up to Ford, he would see them both dead.

Chapter Six

Amity awoke with a start. It took her several seconds to realize where she was and to recognize the lovely gauze draped bed and the beautiful room which Kendrick had shown her the day before. Once she'd reoriented herself, however, she settled herself back into the heap of pillows with a comfortable, contented sigh.

There was a tentative knock at the door, not very loud but enough to have roused her, she realized. It must have been preceded by another, and that which had caused her to wake so suddenly.

She answered the uncertain knock with an equally tentative call to enter. The response to this was the entrance into her room of a very small, gray-haired woman dressed in immaculate and crisp white and carrying an impressive-looking tray which she proceeded to place on the table beside Amity's bed.

Amity offered a drowsy "Good morning" as her white-clad visitor smiled warily at her, then scurried off to tend to drawing a bath. Amity was struck with the impression that the woman was more than a touch wary of what demands the prospective mistress of the house might make and was determined to see that she made no move that might prove offensive.

A careful inspection of the tray showed her that it contained a small pot of fine Worcester porcelain, a matching cup, saucer, creamer, and sugar pot. A very proper, very British early-morning tea, Amity realized as she sat up and poured out a cupful of the surprisingly dark liquid. Her first few sips of the strong tea were enough to chase away the last vestiges of drowsiness. She finished the cup, rose, and made her way to the bath. A look toward the window was more than enough to tell her the sun was already bright and it was well into morning.

"*Ya sitt,*" the servant murmured with a small smile, addressing Amity as lady and pointing to the filled and sweetly scented tub. Then she bobbed a quick bow and disappeared.

Amity wondered how long it would take her to learn enough Arabic to speak to the inhabitants of Tell ElAmarna without causing them to treat her like a visiting deity, one who might bring about total and absolute destruction if they did not show proper respect. She was not at all sure she enjoyed the abject reverence the maid had shown her.

She bathed and dressed quickly, anxious to begin her first full day at Gardiner's Ghenena. It surprised her to realize she had lost the feeling of trepidation and uncertainty that had plagued her the evening before. She'd been certain, after that horrible moment with Justin and Ford in the library, she'd get no sleep whatever during the night. But the quantity of champagne she'd drunk with dinner, combined with the exertions of the day, had managed to outweigh the uncomfortable memory, and she'd fallen off immediately, completely undisturbed by thoughts, disquieting or otherwise, of what had happened.

With morning came the determination to simply forget the events of the previous day—both Ford's strange activities, the embrace and kiss that preceded them, and the unfortunate scene in the library. It was best for all concerned, she told herself firmly, and then simply pushed the matter completely from her mind.

She thought herself quite frugal in the expenditure of time she spent on her morning toilette, slipping quickly into a pale dimity morning dress and merely pulling her brush through her hair and tying it back with a thick grosgrain ribbon. But despite her attempt at haste, she found Justin alone at the cleared breakfast table, already finished with his meal and obviously awaiting her arrival.

"Good morning," she ventured as she slipped into the room and made her way to the one place remaining at the table. She looked at him a bit sheepishly. "Is it terribly late?" she asked as she seated herself and reached for her napkin.

Justin stood and moved around the table to her place, then bent to offer her a quick kiss on the cheek.

"Past ten," he told her with a slightly deprecating smile as he straightened up and moved to the sideboard to refill his coffee cup.

"I'm sorry. I had no idea," Amity murmured. She wished she'd taken the effort to look at the small clock that adorned the mantel over the entirely unnecessary fireplace in her bedroom. Not that knowing that the hour was late would have in any way changed the matter, she decided as she addressed herself to the small bowl of figs in thick cream Naseem silently placed in front of her. "I hope I haven't inconvenienced you," she said as she swallowed the first sweet-rich bite.

Justin shrugged. "No matter," he told her. "Today I am entirely at your disposal. I'd decided to spend the day giving you a *proper* tour."

From the less than pleasant way he pronounced the word, Amity realized he was comparing his proposed excursion with the one she'd spent with Ford the day before. She chewed ruminatively on another bite of fig, wondering if he was censuring her or simply lapsing back to his animosity toward his cousin. It seemed the feeling of fellowship Kendrick had managed to kindle

119

between the two the night before had already grown thin. She wondered how much the scene in the library had had to do with that.

Amity finished the last of the figs quickly, then raised her napkin to her lips and wiped them firmly.

"With so appealing a prospect, it is entirely rude of me to keep you waiting," she told Justin with a smile.

"No need to hurry," he replied with a wave of his hand. "Finish your breakfast."

She shook her head. "The food is entirely too good in your father's house," she told him. "If I spend much time here, I fear I will grow fat."

Justin's face showed the hint of an unpleasant scowl, as if the prospect was entirely distasteful to him, far too distasteful even for contemplation.

"Well then," he said as he put his coffee cup down on the table, "I suppose we should be off." He offered her his arm and led her out to the front courtyard and a waiting carriage, then ceremoniously handed her up to the seat before climbing up beside her. There was, she found, a fancy parasol on the leather seat, set there, apparently, for her use.

Justin lifted it and handed it to her. "It wouldn't do for you to let yourself grow dark from the sun," he told her firmly.

Amity opened the parasol obediently and positioned it so that it provided shade for her face and shoulders. It seemed Justin thought it necessary to maintain the distinction between her and the local women, the paleness of her skin apparently raising her well above the status of the Egyptian women. She wondered why the same did not seem to apply to men. All three—Justin, Kendrick, and Ford—were darkly tanned from the Egyptian sun.

Justin played the part of guide with a decided relish. He took her first to the town of Tell ElAmarna, showing her the ancient Roman walls she'd glimpsed the day before, then the small marketplace with its handful of stalls selling everything from fruits and vegetables to live poultry, tinware, and a scattering of small, dust-coated prayer rugs. Despite the fact that the air was equally as thick with the scents of camel dung and incense, compared to the souk in Cairo, it seemed a paltry affair.

They proceeded through the narrow streets of the town, their passage gathering a good number of intrigued glances. Amity noticed that the townspeople seemed to treat Justin with deference, bowing to him and calling out greetings to ya shaikh Gardiner. She wondered just how dependent the economy of the town was on the trade and goods Justin and his father brought to Tell ElAmarna.

The town itself she found intriguing. Obviously old, the buildings all seemed to have sprung from the desert sand at some point in the distant past. There was a mosque, its entrance and small minaret trimmed with blue-and-white tiles, and she tried to peer inside, curious to see what lay within. Justin didn't stop, however, although when he noticed her interest, he did promise to return with her at some time in the future if she desired. They passed a small school—which Justin told her with some measure of smug proprietorship was built by him and his father, who also paid the teacher—a handful of stores, and a few dozen houses where old men wearing striped robes and white *kaffiyehs* were gathered on the front stoops, sitting cross-legged on blankets sipping their thick coffee, gossiping, and playing a game Justin told her was called *shesbesh*.

They left the town behind, and Amity quickly realized the desert encroached quite close to the city precincts.

"Why does it become barren here, so close to the river?" she asked, intrigued. "Your father's land extends much farther from the Nile, and yet it is lush and green."

Justin smiled a slightly superior smile. *"Our* land,

121

Amity," he corrected her quickly. "My father's and mine. Soon yours as well. And some day our children's."

She didn't know why, but his words startled her. Until that moment, she had not even considered the possibility of children, even less the act that would eventually bring them into existence. She found, when she pondered the matter, she could imagine herself in Ford's arms, but picturing herself lying naked with Justin simply seemed beyond her powers of creativity.

She returned his smile, but weakly, finding the prospect of marriage to him suddenly not quite as appealing in her mind as it had been only a day before. He seemed not to notice the uncertainty in her expression.

"To answer your question, though, the estate utilizes an extensive system of dikes and canals to provide irrigation. And my father was forced to heavily fertilize the acres farthest from the river."

"So many acres," Amity mused softly.

Justin nodded. "It was a costly effort," he told her. "My father went deeply into debt, very nearly lost everything. But he proved the desert, given the proper incentive, could be made to bear fruit. Since the work was completed, the crops here are the finest outside the delta. And it will grow even better as time goes on. Mine will be the finest plantation in the country before I'm done."

Amity watched him as he spoke, his jaw jutting out and setting hard and so terribly certain as he spoke of what was his—what would one day be his. She realized with a start that his expression made her shudder inwardly. She wondered if he thought of her in the same way he thought of his acres.

She turned away from him and they rode on in silence for what seemed to her a very long time. The scenery grew slightly monotonous, the deep gold of the encroaching desert sand on one side of them that seemed to stretch on endlessly and to the other side a thin ribbon of green edging a ribbon of blue, the green, the cultivated land that ran at the edge of the Nile.

Eventually Justin turned the carriage so that their backs were to the river. To Amity's eye, it seemed they were heading into the nothingness of the desert. She wondered how he had found a path when it all seemed very much the same to her.

Justin cast an amused glance at her and smiled. "Wait," he told her as he saw her puzzled expression. "It's not much farther."

"What isn't?" she demanded, and looked up from under the protection of the parasol. She was now glad he'd brought it for her. It had grown hot as the afternoon passed, and she began to feel as though they were riding through an oven.

"You'll see," he said, then made it apparent he had no intention of saying more.

Amity refused to give him the satisfaction of begging for another word, and looked around, wondering where he could possibly be taking her.

It seemed the massive rock outcrop appeared magically out of the sand, but Amity soon realized it was the a matter of the light and monotony of the landscape's color. The dunes ran up to the edge of the outcrop, making the rock seem, from the distance, to appear a continuation of the sand. It was only when they drew close that she could discern the difference.

Justin drew the carriage up alongside the edge of the huge mound of stone, then drew it to a halt. He climbed down and offered her his hand. Amity took it, and let him help her down, not at all sure what it was he intended to show her.

"What . . . ?" she began.

He only shook his head. "Come," he told her, putting her hand to the crook of his arm and drawing her around to the edge of the stone.

She could not keep a small gasp from escaping her

lips. It was not a large temple, but it was beautifully carved, the pillars that supported an overhanging roof having bases in the shape of large doglike animals sitting up on their hind legs, the pillars themselves like tall, ornate crowns that rose from their heads, the capitals adorned with lotus leaves and flowers. It was all carved from the stone of the outcrop, and the rooms of the temple behind, too, were carved out of the living rock.

"It's beautiful," she whispered, somehow unable to raise her voice and disturb the silence of the place. It seemed to her that to do so would be almost a sacrilege.

"It was once a temple to Anubis, the jackal god of the underworld. There are many temples to him along the river, but few remain as pristine. We are a bit remote here."

Amity moved forward, putting her hand to the pillars, shocked to see the tiny vestiges of paint that remained coloring the jackal carvings and on the capitals, somehow still preserved despite the passage of more than three thousand years. The stone felt warm and soft beneath her fingers.

She turned back to face Justin. "May we go inside?"

He seemed amused by her question, and smiled back at her.

"There has been no priest of Anubis here for a very long time, Amity. No one to tell you a woman is not allowed inside the holy precincts."

She blushed, feeling more than a little foolish, then wandered forward, past the jackal columns and into the temple proper. It contained two rooms, the outer one, the larger of the two, with walls decorated with paintings of the god surveying his domain of the underworld, and the smaller room beyond, bare except for a niche in the far wall.

She returned to the larger front room to find Justin behind her. "What would have been inside?" she asked.

"What happened here"

He shrugged. "I don't think anyone knows for sure," he said. "The niche might have held an image of the god, and there was probably some table on which sacrifices to the god were left. Beyond that, there is little information. As far as I know, ceremonies were secret, mysteries only for the priests usually, and not documented."

Amity wandered around the room, staring at the scenes on the walls. "It's strange, isn't it, to think there were people here, touching this very wall, all those hundreds and hundreds of years ago?"

"I think it stranger, Amity, to think we are here, alone, and yet we concern ourselves with other peoples, other times, when we should have no concern but for ourselves."

She felt his hand on her arm, and she turned to face him, to find his eyes, expectant and hard, searching hers. She wondered what it was he was looking for, what he expected to see in her glance. Could it be guilt, she wondered, the admission that she had let Ford kiss her?

And then his hand fell to her waist and he was drawing her to him. When his lips found hers, she found herself oddly uninvolved, as though she were not there with him, but outside and staring in. There was no passion, no heat in his embrace, and none of the liquid fire that Ford had somehow ignited in her. That seemed strange to her, that he could not rouse in her what Ford so easily called up. But she pushed away the thought of Ford, telling herself that she had been mad to allow him so much, and madder still to allow herself to feel anything at all when he'd held her.

She was, she told herself firmly, going to marry Justin. The matter was determined and no longer open to discussion, not even a discussion she might have with herself.

Justin released her finally, and she simply stood staring up at him, wondering if he felt as little as she did, wondering, and not for the first time, why it was he had asked her to marry him.

"I think, Amity," he said slowly as he gazed down at her, "that it is time we fixed a date. I want us to be married as quickly as possible."

She had not expected that. In fact, she realized she really had very little idea at all as to what she ought to expect from him.

She looked down, away from his eyes, not at all sure she could say the words with him staring at her with that searching glance.

"As you like, Justin," she murmured. "I have only Beatrice and Charles—"

"Good," he interrupted before she could say anything more, his tone firmly decisive. "I will tend to whatever arrangements need be made. There is no need to disrupt the embassy or your sister with the matter. In fact, we could invite them here and have a small ceremony at Gardiner's Ghenena. That way, we could be married within the fortnight. Later, if you like, we can have a formal reception in Cairo."

She heard his words as though from a distance; they sounded muffled and almost indistinct in her ears. It seemed to her suddenly that decisions were being made for her, that her life was being arranged, willy nilly, without her opinions being sought or considered. But then she told herself it was best so, that once she and Justin were married, she would at least know where her life was leading, that the questions Ford's presence had led her to ask herself about her feelings for Justin were not matters that needed to be considered.

"As you think best, Justin," she replied, her words sounding less than enthusiastic, even to her own ears.

He reached out to her once more, but she turned away, ignoring the implied request. He started to move

126

forward after her, but then decided it better to let the matter lie. In a few days, he told himself, he would have the right, and she would have no reason to deny him.

Until then, he would bide his time.

Amity considered the house with a critical eye as they drove up along the long drive, and, as she had the day before when seeing it for the first time, was struck with its beauty, and with the odd sensation that she would soon be the mistress of Gardiner's Ghenena. That was what she wanted, she told herself firmly, to be the mistress of her own home, to live her own life as something more than an odd appendage to Beatrice's life, or as an unsought nuisance in some aunt's house.

"I'm glad we've decided to marry soon."

She was quite surprised to hear the words, hardly realizing she had spoken. But Justin turned to her and smiled, and so she realized she'd said the words, intended only to enforce her decision in her own mind, aloud.

"As am I, my dear," he told her firmly. His words sounded oddly final, as though once he had said them, the act was cast in stone.

He drew the carriage to a halt, jumped down, and then helped Amity out. They wandered into the house. Amity felt oddly separate, as though she were taking part in a play, saying her lines with proper intonation and gesture, but without having any real understanding of the basic import of the underlying plot.

As they entered the front hall, Kendrick was just exiting from his office, a white-clad workman trailing along behind him. His expression showed decided exasperation.

"Is something wrong?" Amity asked.

He turned to her and smiled.

"A small matter, my dear. Nothing with which you need concern yourself." He looked up at Justin. "It seems Abdul has found some damage done to the irrigation system on the southernmost acres. I'll have to ride out there and oversee the repairs."

Justin scowled. "How did it happen?" he demanded, his gaze wandering to the now worried looking Abdul.

"It is not known, ya shaikh," the workman replied. "The channels were in perfect repair yesterday. But today my *fellaheen* found them broken. It must have happened in the night."

"Broken?" Justin snarled. "How are metal pipes broken unless someone decides to do the breaking?"

The man lowered his head and shook it. "I do not know, ya shaikh," he protested, well aware of the implication Justin made—that he, or some of his men, were to blame.

"I will know who is responsible for this," Justin hissed.

"I'll tend to it, Justin," Kendrick said, his tone placating. "I'm sure I'll be back before dinnertime."

"No," Justin said flatly. "You have another matter to see to this afternoon. I'll tend to this." He turned to Amity. "I'm sure you'll want to bathe and rest after the ride in the desert," he told her, his words as much a command as a suggestion.

She nodded, acquiescent. "Yes," she agreed.

She watched as Justin motioned to Abdul, then strode out with the decidedly intimidated-looking workman following.

When she turned back to Kendrick, she found he was staring at her with a thoughtful expression. But he roused himself quickly.

"You will excuse me, won't you, my dear?" he asked her with a smile. "As Justin mentioned, I do have a matter to which I must tend this afternoon. I'll see you at teatime."

"Certainly," she replied as she started toward the stairs. "It was a dusty ride out to the temple. A bath would be pleasant."

Kendrick's expression grew suddenly sharp. "Justin took you to the Anubis temple?" he asked.

She turned back to face him, surprised at the change in his manner. "Yes," she replied. "He knows I'm interested in antiquities. Is there any reason why he shouldn't have taken me there?"

He recovered quickly. "Of course not," he replied quickly. "Just as long as you've returned early. It wouldn't do to be caught out in the desert after dark."

"Oh," she murmured, not able to think of anything better.

"I won't keep you any longer," Kendrick said.

She nodded, and climbed the stairs to her room.

Amity ordered a bath, then stood by her window as the servant tended to drawing it, staring out at the lovely rose garden and the stables just visible to the side. It didn't surprise her to see Kendrick striding to the stables a few moments after she had left him, mount, and then ride off. After all, he had told her he had some business to which he must tend. What did surprise her was the sight of Ford arriving at the stables a few moments after Kendrick had left. He motioned to the stable boy, who quickly brought out a saddled horse for him, mounted, and left, apparently following after Kendrick . . .

All of which roused the curiosity that had been piqued by Ford's search of the shed the day before. As she had when she'd watched Ford slip inside the shed, she grew aware of an uncomfortable feeling that something was happening, something of which people seemed intent upon keeping her ignorant. The realization bit at her until she found herself determined to find out just what it was that she wasn't supposed to know.

She ran down and made her way to the stables, calling out to the boy to bring her a horse quickly. He stared at her stupidly for a moment, and she realized she was hardly dressed for a ride. But when she ordered him firmly to do as she had bid him, he ran obediently into the stables. When he returned, he was leading the same animal she'd ridden the afternoon before. Amity stared out across the field, aware she could just make out Ford as a small dot on the horizon. She mounted quickly, and set out after him, determined not to allow herself to lose sight of him.

He rode across the fields, and then, at their end, into the desert. She kept a fair distance behind him, aware that he seemed to be doing the same thing with Kendrick, following at a great enough distance so that he wouldn't be noticed. She was so intent upon him that she hardly noticed that it was growing slowly darker, that the sky had dulled to an even gray-blue and the horizon had filled with color where the sun lowered to meet it. Nor did she realize until she saw him dismount and climb to the top of a dune that she had allowed herself to draw close to him. She slowed her mount, falling back, and waited until he had disappeared over the top of the dune before she started forward again, wondering what it was he'd found.

She tied her horse to the tether on which he'd left his, then started to climb through the sand after him. She was hardly dressed for this sort of outing, she realized, and sorely wished she'd taken the time to change into a riding outfit and boots. Her petticoats dragged in the sand, and her shoes were soon filled with it. Still, she refused to give up.

Once at the top of the dune, she fell to her knees, breathless with the effort of the climb, and found herself staring down, with decided surprise, at the small temple to which Justin had taken her that afternoon. Kendrick was standing in front of it, looking around with apparent displeasure. It seemed obvious he had expected to meet someone there, and he was not pleased at being forced to remain waiting.

Of Ford, she could find no trace.

And then her attention was drawn to the sound of horses approaching. She turned to see a group of horsemen, heavily robed and with their faces obscured by white *kaffiyehs*. What held her attention, however, was not the exotic character of their clothing; it was the fact that they all held rifles in their hands. They neared from the far side of the stone outcrop, and thus were blocked from Kendrick's view.

She remembered then the things she'd heard at the embassy, the talk of a man who seemed determined to fulfill the promise of the Mahdi who had wrested Khartoum from Gordon, a man called Ali Kalaf who intended to push the English as well as the khedive from Egypt and the Sudan. These tribesmen riding toward the temple seemed ferocious in appearance. And it occurred to her that Kendrick, unaware of who it was who approached, might be in danger.

She started to stand, intending to call out to Kendrick, to warn him of the men and possible danger that neared him.

But even as she stood, she felt a heavy weight being thrust against her and she was pushed back down and into the sand. She struggled uselessly, then tried to scream. Before the sound escaped her, however, it was choked back as a hand was clamped firmly to her mouth.

Chapter Seven

"You will not make another sound, do you understand?"

The words were hissed close to Amity's ear, and the heavy weight of the man's body pinned her in the sand, her face against it, the taste of grit in her mouth. She was completely terrified.

She barely managed to nod her head in acquiescence, scratching her cheek against the sharp grit as she moved. It hardly mattered that she was agreeing to his demand for silence, she realized, for she was far too frightened to cry out.

The hand loosened its hold and then released it completely. She realized as the terror ebbed slightly that in its wake the hand left a numb feeling in her jaw from the intensity of the pressure the fingers had exerted.

She turned her head slightly, just enough to see who it was who lay beside her, holding her firmly now by the shoulders and keeping her low against the dune.

"Ford!" she gasped.

The hand was immediately returned to her mouth. "I don't want to hurt you, Amity," he whispered. "But I can't have you warning them that we're here." He seemed satisfied that his explanation was enough to ensure her silence, for he again removed his hand from her mouth.

He was wrong.

"Warning who?" she asked in a terrified whisper.

She wondered where he had come from, how he had hidden himself and then crept up on her. It occurred to her that he was not surprised at her presence, that he acted as though he expected her to be there.

Once again Amity found his hand covering her mouth, and, she realized, he seemed far too worried to make any effort to keep it from hurting her.

"Damn it, be quiet," he hissed at her, apparently quite angry now.

He stared at her and watched as she nodded, wide-eyed, agreeing to his demand. For a moment he seemed to hesitate, but then finally decided to release her. She only nodded again when he had, and that seemed enough to satisfy him.

Apparently satisfied that she would behave circumspectly, he crawled forward to stare over the edge of the dune. Once she realized what he was doing, Amity followed him. Below them, the group of horsemen had rounded the rock outcrop. The first to arrive had already begun to dismount. Kendrick stood by the temple portal, watching the tribesmen with apparent impatience.

"What's happening?" Amity whispered to Ford.

She could think of no reason why her future father-in-law might be meeting with such men as these, even less as to why the encounter took place in so remote a spot.

The first of the tribesmen to dismount turned to look up at the dune, squinting his eyes into the growing darkness even as Kendrick motioned to him impatiently to join him. The man was swarthy and tall, with a lean, bearded face, a long, hooked nose, and dark eyes that Amity felt could almost bore into her. Even from the distance, and despite the dimming of the light, she had

133

the feeling that he could see her plainly.

Ford pulled her back down sharply, below the top of the dune.

"I didn't have time to go back and keep you from following me, Amity," he told her in a hushed tone that still managed to impart a measure of command. "Nor do I have time now to discuss the matter. You will stay here, keep still, and make no noise. Do you understand?" He stared at her, his blue eyes sharp and suddenly cold enough to make her shiver. "If you don't do as I say, you may very well get us both killed," he added by way of inducement to her to obey him.

His words had the effect he wanted. She nodded mutely, and mouthed the words, "I promise."

"Good," he replied.

And then he was gone, moving silently off across the dune and into the growing shadows. Amity watched him leave her. When she could no longer see him moving, when there seemed to be nothing but the sand and darkness surrounding her, she felt a dull feeling of dread at being left alone. She inched her way carefully to the top of the dune, reaching it in time to see the last of the tribesmen move into the small temple, apparently following Kendrick inside.

Ford's words echoed inside her head. He'd realized she had followed him, and yet what he was doing, he felt, was more important than turning her away. And now, it was important enough for him to risk death. That was what he told her, that discovery might mean their deaths. And yet, she wondered, by whose hand? Surely not Kendrick's. Those tribesmen had appeared ferocious enough to kill and yet they were meeting with Kendrick, and so could not possibly be in any way tied to the man Ali Kalaf. But why would Kendrick meet in secret with them? And why would he go so far away from both his own land and Tell ElAmarna? Her questions seemed to multiply, and there were, as far as she could see, no answers for any of them.

As she peered carefully down at the entrance of the temple, she saw Ford appear from behind the dark shadows of the dunes to the north and move carefully forward, then disappear once more in the darkness behind the row of pillars. She could feel her heart begin to pound. She believed him, she realized. She didn't know why, but she accepted what little he had told her. There was no longer any question in her mind that the men within were dangerous. She had no concrete reason to think they might do violence, and yet, she knew they would. If they found Ford spying on them, they would certainly kill him.

She could hear noise. Even from the distance she could discern the sound of voices raised in argument, even though she could not make out any of the words that were being shouted. Whatever was happening inside the temple, someone there was angry, decidedly angry. And she found herself filled with the fear that Ford had been discovered.

It seemed forever before anyone reappeared. By then the sun had completely set, and there was only a dull gray haze, the light that precedes the total darkness just after sunset.

The tribesmen appeared first, sweeping out with their robes swirling as they moved with the speed of their anger. Their leader, the one who had searched the lip of the dune before entering the temple, now repeated the procedure, searching along the line of sand for his enemies. His stare seemed to linger at the point where Amity lay, trembling, against the sand. Once again she had the feeling he could see her.

Behind him, Kendrick reappeared, a lamp held high, his pace slower but no less determined than the tribesman who had preceded him. He strode directly to where

135

the leader stood, put his hand to the man's robed arm, and said something that was muffled with the distance. The tribesman turned to him angrily, shaking off Kendrick's hand. Then he quickly mounted the horse one of his men held for him.

Amity stared down, searching for some trace of Ford, but could find nothing.

Kendrick stood and watched as the remaining tribesmen remounted their horses, then stood back as they kicked the animals into motion. Then he, too, untied his horse, mounted and rode into the darkness of the desert.

Amity found herself shivering. The night had turned suddenly chilly as the sun had set, but not cold enough to account for the way she trembled. She was afraid, she realized. She was alone in the darkness, and had no idea what had happened to Ford. She stood up finally, unable to think of anything to do but make her way to the temple. She'd seen him go inside. There was no choice for her but to think he was still there, although she could not understand how or why he could be unless he'd been discovered, unless he was hurt, or worse. She found herself trembling again, and this time she realized it was not from the cold at all.

She almost stumbled, then caught herself and began to climb down the far side of the dune slowly. She tried to call out to Ford, to shout his name, anything just to hear her own voice, to convince herself that she was not alone. But her throat was too constricted, and her mouth felt as though it was filled with cotton. She found she couldn't utter a sound.

If being suddenly aware that she was alone in the darkness was frightening to her, the sound of approaching horses was terrifying. She held herself rigid, and forced herself to listen until she could gauge the direction and the distance from which the noise came. And when she realized the horses were approaching from the rear, from where she had left her horse tethered along with Ford's, she became certain the tribesmen had found him in the temple and now were looking for her.

She had an image of him, lying against the cold stone wall of the temple, hurt and bleeding. Those men had beaten him, perhaps worse, and he needed help, he needed her. For a single instant the possibility that he might be dead haunted her, but she pushed it away, refusing to believe, finding it far too painful to accept.

She started to run again. Only this time her movement was blind, for she could no longer see even a shadow that would indicate the temple entrance to her. Fear clutched at her throat and constricted it. She felt as if she could not breathe. All she knew was that she had to find Ford, somehow find him and get him away from this place.

The contact of the hand to her arm was a nightmare thing, like a ghost coming out of the darkness, reaching up out of the sand to clutch at her. She tried to jerk away, to pull herself free, but it kept its hold firm. And then there was movement at the top of the dune behind them, and whatever it was that held her arm pushed her forward. She was falling, tumbling through the sand into darkness, and all the time she was aware that she was being held, that there was another body tumbling through the sand with hers.

When the tumbling stopped, she had no time to try to escape, no time even to think. The hand was pulling her upright, then forcing her forward.

She realized he'd taken her to the temple when she felt herself pressed against one of the columns, sandwiched between the stone and his body. She caught her breath until finally she'd calmed herself and realized that now

137

was the time for her to fight back if she had any hope of getting away. She balled up her fists and pommeled them against his chest.

"Ugh."

It was the sound of his breath suddenly and sharply exhaled. She felt some satisfaction at that, that she'd managed to hurt him enough to force his breath from him that sharply. Now, she thought, while he still seemed unsettled from her attack, was the time to break away from him.

"For God's sake, Amity, stop it. It's me," he hissed.

"Ford?"

She realized she hadn't even considered it might be him. Somehow she'd accepted the image of him lying somewhere in the temple, hurt and bleeding, and this very whole, obviously unhurt man standing beside her did not for a moment seem real to her.

"Shh," he cautioned, and pressed her close to the pillar.

And then, from the top of the dune, came a light as several of the tribesmen climbed to the lip and held lit torches aloft. They were searching, she realized, searching for her and Ford.

Two horses rounded the stone outcrop and once again drew to a halt in the front of the temple. Amity pressed herself close to the pillar, too frightened now to think of anything save what might happen to her and Ford should the two dismount and return to the temple interior. The horses had passed close enough to them for her to reach out and touch them. And now they stood only a few feet in the distance.

She held her breath, hoping that the pounding in her heart was not audible to their ears. The sound of it seemed to fill her own.

"I told you, no one followed me."

That was Kendrick's voice, she realized. One of the

horsemen was Kendrick.

"I find it grows harder and harder to believe anything you tell me, Englishman," the second answered. "I find I do not like the games you play."

"There are no games," Kendrick replied. "If you want to buy the rifles, I will see them delivered to you. But first, I will have the gold, the full amount agreed upon."

"You demand my trust, yet offer none in return," the tribesman told him sharply.

"I have the rifles," Kendrick said evenly. "I have no need to be trusting. You, on the other hand, if you want the rifles, will do as I say."

"What is to prevent me from getting word to the khedive that you are illegally dealing in arms?" the other sneered. "Perhaps I hold the key to your trust after all."

Kendrick shrugged. "Then we both lose, and you, I think, would lose the most. Without arms, your cause will fail. If you lose that, you lose your place in paradise as well. So you see, my friend, if anyone holds keys, it is I."

"We are not friends, Englishman. And I am not at all pleased with the way you have altered the bargain we made. I may decide to see that you lose more than the khedive could take from you."

With that, the tribesman turned his horse sharply and called out to his men as he started off into the desert. The torchlight quickly disappeared, and the sound of hooves followed, fading into the distance. Kendrick stayed where he was for a moment longer, until there seemed to be nothing but silence in the desert. Then he turned his horse and rode off into the darkness as well.

It was several seconds before Amity felt her heart slow to a more natural beat, and several seconds more before she realized that Ford was still standing pressed against her. It came as a shock to her to realize that at some point in the preceding moments she had put her arms around his shoulders and pressed herself to him as though by being close they might escape detection.

She quickly dropped her arms. "I'm sorry," she murmured.

"No need," he replied. She could see his eyes glittering in the growing moonlight, and almost feel his grin. "It was the only part of this little adventure that even came close to being pleasurable."

She found herself suddenly filled with the desire to slap him. "How can you make jokes?" she demanded as she tried to back away from him, only to find her way blocked by the pillar.

"I don't know," he replied softly. "There's little enough that's even remotely amusing about the situation. Right now I wish to God I hadn't followed Kendrick. I wish I hadn't seen or heard any of it."

She was surprised at the anguish in his tone, at the realization that he felt pain because of what he had learned. It hadn't occurred to her that there was anything about the preceding moments that was capable of dealing him hurt, that he might not consider everything with the same absent amusement with which he seemed so determined to consider her.

She stared up at him. "What did you learn?" she demanded.

He considered her challenging expression in silence a moment before he spoke. He wondered why they always seemed to be at odds with each other, why they seemed to choose exactly the wrong words to say to each other. He'd never in his life felt himself incapable of proving himself at least amusing to a woman, and often a good deal more. Yet he found when he was alone with her he seemed driven to say words he knew ought best be left unsaid. He wondered at his own clumsiness with her, and then at why it mattered so much to him.

"I learned that your sterling fiancé's father is selling rifles to a fanatic madman named Ali Kalaf," he told her bluntly, "and that those men were here tonight to arrange for delivery, but Kendrick backed down because he wants the full price in gold paid before delivery."

She shook her head slowly. "I can't believe any of it."

"What reason would I have to lie?" he demanded sharply. Then he sighed. "None of it pleases me, either."

"But why would Kendrick do such a thing?" she persisted.

He shook his head. "I don't know. When I found the rifles, I hoped it was Justin, not Kendrick. But none of that seems to matter much now." He backed away from her, then put his hand to her arm. "I'll take you back to the house."

She looked toward the dune, in the direction of the place where they had left their horses.

"They must have found the horses. They rode there."

He shook his head. "I moved them," he said. "And if you had stayed where I left you, we wouldn't have been forced to behave like nursery-rhyme characters to avoid being seen." He made no effort to disguise the note of censure in his tone. "Now shall we go?"

She didn't move. "What are you going to do?" she demanded.

"I don't have much choice," he replied.

"You're going to have him arrested, aren't you?" she demanded. "You aren't even going to ask him to explain."

"Damn it, there are no explanations," he returned sharply.

"I can't believe you would condemn him without giving him the chance to defend himself," she told him angrily. "He's your uncle. He's given you the hospitality of his home."

"He's given me more than that," he said, returning her anger with his own. "He's been as close to a father as I've had since my own died. And he was the only one to defend me . . ." His anger seemed to drift off with his words, and he turned away.

"Defend you?" she asked, putting her hand to his arm.

He only shook his head. "It doesn't matter. It all happened a long time ago." It was apparent he wouldn't say more of the matter. But she didn't need him to tell her that he'd referred to the incident that had forced him to leave England, the matter of the stolen necklace.

"All the more reason for you to give him a chance to explain," she told him.

He turned back to face her. "Damn it, I heard what he said to those men. Do you think I've made it up? Do you think I like the prospect of turning him over to a military tribunal?"

"But surely there must be some other way to right matters," she insisted. "Think what will happen to him. To Justin."

She stopped abruptly as she saw his expression change at the mention of Justin's name.

"You needn't worry," he assured her, his words filled with scorn. "Your precious Justin won't be involved. You'll still be able to become Mrs. Justin Gardiner. In fact, you and Justin should thank me. You'll come into the house and the estate quite a good deal sooner that you might otherwise." His eyes narrowed as he glared at her with a sudden anger he was hard put to explain. "I don't suppose a bit of scandal in the family is enough to turn you away from Justin's loving embrace."

His words filled her with a dull hurt. Was she really as shallow as he seemed to think her? Did she care only for what marriage to Justin would bring to her—money, position, a place in the world? She filled with anger toward him. The more she fought against the thoughts his words had roused, the more she denied them to herself, the stronger, the more biting, seemed the taunt.

He had no right to say these things to her, she told herself, no right to question her or to make her question herself. This time, when the urge struck her to slap him, she didn't fight it. Her hand flew out and came in contact with his cheek with a loud, sharp sound.

"I should think you know more about family scandal than I," she snapped.

He obviously hadn't expected the attack. He raised his hand to his cheek for a second, as though he weren't quite certain what she'd done. Then he caught her hands in his and pulled her arms sharply behind her. He stood close to her, staring down at her, and as her eyes found his, Amity realized that her heart was once more beating fast and hard, just as it had been when she thought they might be discovered hiding behind the pillar.

Then he was pulling her close to him, and his arms were around her, and when his lips touched hers, they were angry and hungry and hard.

She ought to fight against him, she told herself. She had sworn to herself she would not let this happen again. And still, despite the promise she had made, still she knew she would not.

"You're not going to marry Justin," he said sharply. "Say it. You're not going to marry Justin."

"I won't marry Justin," she murmured, not quite sure where the words were coming from, not sure why he demanded them from her.

But once she had spoken them, she knew they were true, that she couldn't marry Justin, not knowing how she felt about Ford. The recognition of that fact was like a weight being lifted from her.

Ford, too, felt relief, and once she'd uttered those four words, the anger he'd felt drained from him. He dropped his grasp of her hands, letting his arms snake around her and pull her close to him. He gazed down at her, at the glow the newly risen moon imparted to the silk of her hair, at the questioning stare he saw in her eyes. He wondered why it had mattered so much to him, why it mattered at all. And yet it did, he realized. Nothing, it seemed, had ever mattered so much to him before in his life.

"You don't love him," he murmured as he pressed his lips against her neck and felt the sharp response of her pulse beneath the soft flesh. "You love me."

Amity closed her eyes and let herself be swept up by the feeling of his lips and his arms and the press of his body close to hers. It was like a drug to her, a narcotic that filled her with a strange and potent euphoria.

His lips had left her neck, and his hands cupped her face now. She opened her eyes to stare up at him, to see his face framed by the moonlight, his blue eyes searching hers, demanding the truth of her, leaving her no choice but to admit it to herself.

"You don't love Justin," he repeated. "You love me."

She nodded slowly in agreement. It was as though he had mesmerized her, somehow forced her will to his. Only deep down, she knew it was her will as well, and if he forced her to do anything, it was to face the truth.

"I love you," she whispered.

And then he was kissing her, and she him, the taste of his lips on her tongue as heady as wine. The sand, when they knelt to it, was still warm beneath her, holding the heat of the afternoon sun, and overhead, the stars, filling the sky now, as brilliant as diamonds and far more luminous against the total blackness of the dry desert night.

There were no thoughts, no consideration of what it was she was doing, no concept of how she might come to regret these moments when they were past. There was

144

only the feel of his hands and lips and tongue against her flesh, and the mysterious fire that wound through her veins like a luminous snake, awakening her, revealing to her the ancient mystery of promised life within her. If, earlier that day, she had considered the act of conceiving a child with Justin with faint distaste, she had no such thoughts now. All she knew was that Ford's touch was wondrous to her, and that she never wanted the moment to end.

She made no protest when his hands, obviously well practiced in the intricacies of women's buttons, swept aside the wrinkled dimity dress. Nor did she feel any sense of embarrassment at being seen by a man in only her shift, a fact which quite bewildered her. It seemed, suddenly, a game to her, like the unwrapping of gifts on Christmas morning. She reached out to his shirt, deciding to take a part in the game as well, and carefully, with a good deal more difficulty than he had encountered, began to release them.

Ford felt her fingers against his chest with a growing excitement that astonished him. He reminded himself of one occasion when he'd sat idle on a velvet-covered chair in one of Cairo's best and most expensive bordellos while a very attentive whore had quite expertly helped him to undress. Somehow that whore, with all her expertise, had not come close to equaling the feelings Amity's trembling fingers roused in him as she unfastened the buttons of his shirt. Her touch was a sweet, slow torture to him, setting a fire inside him unlike any he had ever known before.

Finally he brought his hands to hers and helped her with her task, then shrugged out of his shirt before he lowered himself to her. He stared down at her a moment, and realized that there was a fleeting hint of fear in her eyes. It made him hesitate, made him realize that what he was doing was wrong, taking her there in the sand, that he ought to have given her more, offered her more. He'd demanded an admission from her that he had never made to her, one he'd told himself he would never allow himself to make to any woman. And yet, if he had not said the words, he knew he could not escape the feeling. What had begun as a game to him had suddenly become serious, far too serious and far too strong for him to simply walk away and leave behind.

But the fear ebbed quickly from her eyes. When she reached her hand out to him, there was no doubt in him that they had already traveled too far to turn back. He lowered himself to her, tasting her lips and tongue, finding them sweet and reminiscent of honey. He could feel the sharp beat of her heart beneath his lips when he touched them to her breasts. He knew it echoed his own.

Amity closed her eyes, shutting out even the majesty of the stars above them, and lost herself to the feel of his hands and lips on her breasts and belly and thighs. She had no idea what had happened to her shift, no idea how he had managed to remove it and shed the last of his own clothing. She knew only that she felt his body, his flesh, naked and hard and lean, touching hers, and that it radiated the same mysterious heat that filled her.

He entered her like a shaft of pure, sweet fire. She had never anticipated this wonder, never thought her body could feel as it did. And she started to move as his hands urged her, almost as though some part of her had long ago learned the dance and let the knowledge lie dormant inside her until he came to release it to her. It seemed to her almost as though there were some foreign creature, knowledgeable and sure, hidden deep inside her, waiting for this moment to be wakened and roused.

She was floating, adrift on a alien sea with only Ford's arms to hold her, only his body to which she might cling. She pressed herself to him, letting the waves lift her and hold her, each one carrying her higher and higher until she was dizzy and breathless and lost. All there was for her was the feel of him deep within her and the teasing touch of his lips and his hands and his tongue. He seemed to know all the secrets she had never known about herself, to know those places where the fires might be banked or released to leap upward in a mad race for the stars. She gave herself up to him, letting him take her to those places he deemed it fit she go.

Ford held himself back, knowing only that he wanted to show her pleasure, to teach her the sweet magic that lay within her. He had never felt this way before, never wanted so much to please another or ever felt the need as sharply within himself. It was only when he felt her arch her body to his, when he heard her surprised moan of pleasure, that he let himself follow her to the precipice. Then he gathered her close in his arms and held her until the trembling ceased.

Ford stared up at the stars wondering what it was that had happened to him, wondering why this one act seemed so unique to him, why the release had seemed so crushingly complete. He'd certainly wanted women before, but always the having had cured the longing. Yet even as he pressed his lips to her forehead, her eyelids, her lips, he felt the longing return to him, and with it the hunger. This taste, he realized, was but a preamble to the real hunger, and he doubted that it would ever be completely sated.

Amity lifted her face to his, and found him staring down at her, his eyes probing and keen.

"What have we done?" she asked in a confused whisper.

He smiled at the innocence in her expression, at the naiveté of her question.

"We've made love, Amity," he told her softly.

"Yes," she said thoughtfully. She seemed almost surprised at the realization. Her expression grew contemplative and a bit puzzled.

He leaned forward to kiss her, softly, on the eyes and then the lips. She lay still, accepting the small offering but little more. When he lowered himself to the sand beside her, she turned away, bewildered suddenly by the thoughts that had fallen on her, a thick, dark curtain of unpleasant thoughts to plague her.

She was ruined, she realized. There was no longer any possibility that she could marry Justin, nor, she knew, did she want to. If only Ford had once said he loved her, if only there was the remotest possibility that he thought of her as more than a means to a few moments' pleasure. But he had never suggested he felt anything more than desire for her. And she knew she had no right to expect anything more.

The jackals at the base of the stone columns at the temple entry stood still and considering, their sightless eyes seeming to condemn her, their superior expressions without a hint of sympathy. Her petty thoughts, they seemed to be telling her, were nothing compared to the tragedies they had witnessed through the ages. She was a fool to think her life was more than a mote in the great fabric of history that they'd seen move relentlessly past them.

She pulled herself from Ford's arms, surprised at how cold she felt once she was free of them and sat, her back to him, naked on the sand.

He, too, sat up.

"Amity, what is it?" he asked.

She shook her head and pretended to cast about in the sand for her clothing, not daring to turn and face him.

"Nothing," she replied. "It's grown late. There'll be

148

questions to answer if we're not back by dinnertime."

The mundaneness of her words seemed suddenly to overwhelm her. Ford was planning to expose Kendrick as an arms trafficker, and her own life lay in tatters around her. And yet she clung to the simple worry of being late for dinner.

She found her shift and choked back a sob as she lifted it. Ford stared at her, bewildered, for a moment, then reached out to her, putting his hand to her shoulder.

"Amity . . ."

"No," she said, pulling away from him. "I let it happen. It was my own fault. You needn't worry that I'll make any demands of you. I expect nothing from you. There's nothing I want."

He was struck by the sudden bitterness in her words. And then by the way she seemed so completely able to dismiss him. She was right, he told himself. He had nothing to offer her, nothing that she might want. After all, he reminded himself, he was still a thief to her, and there was no way he could prove to her that he was anything else. And Justin, lest he forget, was still a rich man and her fiancé.

"So be it," he said, his tone sharp now, as he determined to be as cool as she.

He turned to find his own clothing. He pulled on his trousers and boots with an angry haste, then picked up the rest.

"I'll get the horses," he said tonelessly as he thrust his hands through the sleeves of his shirt. He kept himself purposely from staring at her, from watching the way her hands moved as they fastened the buttons of her dress. "Don't stray. I don't want to have to hunt for you."

She nodded, not bothering to look up at him, pretending indifference as he turned away and walked off to

149

the side of the temple. What's done can't be changed, she told herself firmly, concentrating her attention on her buttons. She certainly wouldn't beg him for anything he wouldn't offer. Nor would she let him see that inside she was crumbling and her heart was breaking.

Chapter Eight

As much as she had dreaded it, Amity knew she had anticipated the knock at her door.

She rose and crossed the room quickly, putting her hand to the knob with a willful determination and forcing herself to pull it open.

"Is something wrong Amity? Naseem said you asked for your dinner in your room."

Justin's expression, she thought, seemed more perturbed than concerned at the thought that she might be ill. Or was her reaction to him shaded now, she wondered, with what she expected to see in him rather than simply in what was there?

"No, I'm just tired, Justin," she told him, then took her hand from the doorknob and turned away, moving back into the room.

It was a lie and she knew it. Had it been otherwise, she would not have turned away from him, would not have had the feeling he could see the truth in her eyes. The fact was, she simply did not have the nerve to face both him and Kendrick at the dinner table after what had happened that afternoon. She had betrayed Justin, and no amount of rationalizing could change that immutable fact.

151

She suddenly found herself wondering what Ford was doing, wondering if he was in the front parlor with Kendrick, drinking Kendrick's whiskey and laughing with him, all the while knowing what he intended to do. If she was a traitor, he was one twice over—to Justin by making love to her, and to Kendrick by intending to expose his uncle to the authorities. It seemed the only thing he seemed capable of espousing wholeheartedly was his duty to the Army.

"There seems to be a bit of that going around." Justin interrupted her musings with a considering glance. "Ford, as it happens, is keeping to his room as well. It appears he must leave early in the morning."

"Oh?"

She didn't turn back to face Justin. She could hardly admit to him that she wasn't surprised to hear that Ford was leaving or tell him that his cousin was doubtless on his way to the authorities in Cairo to report what he'd learned about Kendrick and the rifles he was selling illegally to the insurrectionists.

"I don't suppose he discussed that with you while you were riding with him this afternoon?" Justin pressed.

"Justin, please, can't we leave this until the morning?" she begged.

He'd followed her into the room and stood, now, close to her.

"Look at me, Amity!"

She hesitated, but the bite of his fingers to her shoulder and the cold authority in his tone could not be ignored. She turned to face him.

"Naseem said you went out shortly after I left this afternoon. And that you came back with Ford." He was breathing hard now, and his eyes had grown sharp with his anger. "Where did you go with him?" he demanded.

She shook her head slowly. "You can't bully me, Justin," she told him flatly. "But since you are determined

152

to pursue the subject now, I have little choice but to discuss it with you. I'd hoped to have some time to think of the proper way to tell you, to try to make you understand." The anger she saw in his eyes was sharper now. She could almost feel it radiating from him. "What I did this afternoon is really of little consequence," she went on slowly. "What does matter is that I realize now I can't accept your proposal of marriage."

His eyes narrowed. "You already have, Amity."

"I was wrong," she said. "You deserve someone who loves you, Justin. As much as I might want to be that person, I cannot force myself to feel something that I don't feel. I don't love you, and I can't marry you."

It seemed a harsh, abrupt way to say it, but once the words were spoken, Amity realized there was simply no kind, painless way to phrase something he must, of necessity, find unpleasant to hear. It didn't please her to watch his expression change to one of shocked surprise, but she knew nonetheless that she had done the right thing. She felt a wave of relief, as though a weight were being lifted from her shoulders.

"I'll leave immediately, of course," she went on, her tone quiet now, and gentle. "I have no desire to cause you any more hurt than I already have brought you."

"There's no necessity for that, Amity," he replied.

His words were subdued, those of a man who had received a blow for which he had not been properly braced. She found herself feeling guilty, wishing she had never been so great a fool as to allow herself to become mired in a situation that she had known from the very outset was impossible.

He seemed to recover himself quickly, however. His expression resettled itself.

"I think we should talk about this later, when we've both had some time to think." He stared at her coolly, as though he were evaluating the advantage the passage of a few days time might bring him.

"It won't change matters, Justin," she told him. "You can't believe I haven't thought about this. It was all my fault for having let myself accept your urgings as reason enough, for letting difficulties with my sister and my desire to stay here in Egypt color my judgment. But I've come to realize that those are not sufficient reasons to form the basis of a marriage. I'm only glad I've realized my mistake before things got to a point where they couldn't be remedied. Justin, please believe me. I'm sure this is better for both of us."

"Amity, I realize I pushed you this afternoon, that you're not quite ready to set a date. You're tired. And I'm forced to admit I've behaved boorishly these last few days. Ford's unexpected presence unsettles me. And I made the mistake of leaving you too much alone at a time when you were forming your first opinions of what your life here would be like."

"It's none of that, Justin," she objected, but he raised a hand, stilling her protest.

"I can understand your growing disenchantment, and I appreciate your caution," he told her. "But those things can be remedied. Tomorrow, matters will look less bleak and far more propitious, I promise you. Get a good night's rest, and we'll talk in the morning. I'll show you that you're wrong, that we need each other, that we're right for each other."

"Justin, please . . ." she began.

He shook his head. "Tomorrow, Amity. There will be more than enough time to talk tomorrow."

She had no choice but to let him leave still harboring hopes she knew were groundless.

Naseem nearly dropped the tray he'd just lifted. Although his hands were shaking, he managed to regain his wits, and quickly lowered the tray to the long counter from which he'd taken it. He darted a quick look around the kitchen, then moved quickly to the door and secured it before turning once more to the dark robed figure that had appeared so unexpectedly.

He bowed formally, and brought his right hand first to his forehead, then to his lips, and finally his heart. *"Salaam aleychum, ya shaikh,"* he murmured respectfully.

"Aleychum salaam." The response was returned quickly.

Naseem considered his unexpected guest with a shade of bewilderment. His presence, the servant knew, was a danger to them both. Discovery could prove to have unpleasant consequences.

"You told me, ya shaikh, you would never to come here," he said tentatively.

Naseem realized that there was a small ball of anger growing inside him. Although he lacked the courage to openly show it, it ired him to realize this man considered him so meanly as to needlessly imperil him by suddenly appearing as he had.

His uninvited guest was tall and lean, with dark hair and eyes, a long, hooked nose and narrow, bearded face. He considered the servant coldly, sensing the emotions that churned within him but gave no overt sign of recognizing him. He seemed entirely unconcerned with Naseem's anger, as well as his obvious fear of discovery. Instead, he stared at the servant with dark, distant eyes—eyes that seemed to see deep inside. Naseem found himself growing uncomfortable with the inspection.

"I would not have come here were the need not great," the robed man said finally, breaking the uncomfortable silence. "Be assured, I have no desire to place myself in Gardiner's hands. I do not trust him."

"It is more dangerous than you think," Naseem told

him, his voice now lowered to a hoarse whisper. "There is a British officer here as well—Kendrick's nephew."

"Then it is best I conclude my business and leave as quickly as possible."

Naseem nodded, more than willing to agree to this sentiment.

"What is it you would have me do, ya shaikh?" he asked.

The other man ignored his question, asking instead one of his own.

"The woman who was to arrive with Gardiner. She is here?"

Naseem nodded. "She came upriver with Shaikh Justin."

The other scowled. *"Shaikh Justin.* We let these foreigners make themselves lords over us without so much as a murmur."

Naseem lowered his head. "It is the part I play, ya shaikh. The part you bade me play."

The second man nodded. "It is not your fault, Naseem. And your presence in this house has proved useful to me."

"What is it you will have me do, ya shaikh?" Naseem asked a second time, this time a bit more forcefully.

"Gardiner is proving difficult. I need some means to force him to deal with me in a more amenable fashion, to accept my terms." His eyes narrowed, and he seemed to be searching the other man's face, looking for some sign of weakness, of unwillingness to do the task he was to be asked to perform. "The woman," he said finally, "will provide that means."

Naseem inwardly shuddered. He was deeply convinced of the righteousness of the jihad begun by the Mahdi and now being furthered by Ali Kalaf, but still he could not quite accept the idea of involving a woman in war, especially a holy war. He would certainly do as he was

156

ordered, but still he could not help the feeling of revulsion growing within him, or keep from himself the thought that a woman's blood could only defile what ought to be kept clean and holy.

"What must I do, ya shaikh?" he murmured, wondering if his loyalty was to be tested by an act that might end in death.

Amity looked up from the letter she was writing as Naseem entered her room bearing a large dinner tray. She watched as he silently crossed to the table by the window and set out her meal. When he was done and seemed about to leave, she stood and faced the servant. "Naseem, is there any way to return to Cairo from Tell ElAmarna?" she asked him.

He seemed bewildered by her question. "Certainly, ya sitt," he replied. "Shaikh Justin's ship—"

"Any *other* way?" she asked, interrupting him.

He considered her question for a moment, then turned dark, unblinking eyes to hers.

"A steamer comes each fortnight with the mail. It takes passengers, if there are any, back downriver."

Once a fortnight, Amity thought. If Justin refused to send her back to Cairo on his ship, she might be forced to remain for as long as two weeks more. The thought was far from pleasant.

"When does the steamer next come?" she asked.

"Tomorrow morning, ya sitt," Naseem replied without hesitation. "It will arrive tomorrow morning at dawn."

Amity started. Somehow, as unpleasant as she found the thought of remaining on with Justin at Gardiner's Ghenena for a fortnight, she was not quite prepared to leave before dawn the next morning. But she quickly decided it might be better to depart quickly, before she and Justin became embroiled in arguments neither of

157

them could win. Anything she had still to say to him could be said in a letter. She made her decision quickly.

"Would it be possible for you to see me to Tell ElA-marna in time to meet the steamer, Naseem?" she asked.

He stared at her thoughtfully for a second. "If you so desire, ya sitt," he replied finally. "Am I to assume you would rather I not so inform Shaikh Justin until you have gone?"

Amity was rather startled by his offer. But she found herself inclined to accept it without undue suspicion, as it greatly simplified matters.

"Yes, Naseem," she agreed. "I would very much appreciate your silence until I've gone."

He nodded. "As you wish, ya sitt," he murmured, and once more started for the door.

Amity stood for a moment after he'd gone, considering her decisions and determining that they were for the best. Then she turned back to the desk, picked up the letter she had begun to Beatrice, and crumpled it in her hands. She would have more than enough time to consider what she would say to her sister when it became necessary to face her. In the meantime, she had to compose a letter to Justin, and one to Kendrick, explaining her departure. That task, she decided, would be more than difficult enough, knowing, as she did, that her broken promise to Justin was only the first of a series of blows that would soon fall on Gardiner's Ghenena.

"Why have you not brought her?"

Naseem was startled by the sharp anger in the tone, and frightened by it. It took him a moment to gather his wits about him enough so that he could reply.

"If it please you, ya shaikh, there is no need to take her by force. We have but to wait a few hours, and she will leave the house willingly, will even take care to rouse no one as she leaves."

He then proceeded to quickly relate the conversation he'd had with Amity, proudly mentioning his invention of the fictitious mail steamer. As he did, his visitor nodded and finally smiled.

"You have done well, Naseem."

Naseem preened in the praise, feeling much as he had when he'd been a boy and earned a rare compliment from his hard to please father.

"I have brought you food, ya shaikh," he said then, producing the linen-wrapped bundle he carried. He pulled back the material to reveal several small, flat, round loaves, some goat cheese and olives. "It will be several hours until you will again have the opportunity to eat," he added practically.

The other man nodded his acceptance and grinned. Then he seated himself on a bundle of hay while Naseem pushed another forward to provide him with a makeshift table.

"It has been many years since I have eaten in a stable," he said.

Naseem took the words as censure, although none had been intended.

"It is the only place where I am sure you will be safe, ya shaikh," he said, trying to hide the diffidence he felt at the reproof.

His guest shook his head. "I am comfortable here," he said. "Even the English cannot humble the majesty of these handsome beasts." He looked around at the dozen horses ensconced in Kendrick's stable and nodded with contentment. "Will you join me?"

Naseem shook his head regretfully. "I fear I must return to my duties, ya shaikh."

The other man nodded. "Perhaps that is best. Go with Allah," he murmured as he reached forward to pick up one of the small loaves of bread. "I will wait here

159

patiently for you to bring to me the prize I need to pry my rifles from Gardiner's grasp."

It was still well before dawn and the sky was dark, the blackness relieved only by the golden orb of the setting moon. Still, Amity was dressed and ready to leave when Naseem knocked at her door.

She had made no attempt to sleep, for the night had been almost exhausted by the time she'd finished with her letters. Instead, she'd splashed cold water on her face, dressed, and packed a small valise of her belongings to take with her. The rest, she decided, could be sent for later, once she was back in Cairo with Beatrice.

"You are ready, ya sitt?" Naseem asked in a hushed whisper when she opened the door to admit him. He appeared wraithlike, she thought, his narrow, lined face almost ghostly in the light of the single candle he held in his hand.

"Yes," she replied, and let him take the bag as she slipped her arms into the sleeves of her jacket. She felt almost like a thief, leaving this way, stealing off in the darkness. Still, she realized she hadn't the heart to stay on any longer, that the sooner she got away, the better for both her and Justin.

She slipped out of the room, following Naseem noiselessly along the carpeted hall and down the stairs to the front door.

"It will be quieter, ya sitt, if we leave by the rear," he whispered to her.

Amity nodded again, and followed him through the darkened rooms to the rear of the house, then out onto the dimly moonlit path to the stables. When she darted a quick look back at the house, it appeared completely still. And beautiful. A small stab of regret filled her. She could have come to love this place, she thought. If

160

only she could have come to love Justin as well, it would have been a wonderful place to live.

For a moment, she felt a stab of bitterness and anger towards Ford, but it quickly faded. As much as she might want to blame him for what had happened, she realized it had been her fault as much as his — perhaps more. Her only hope, she realized, was to get away from *all* the Gardiner men, and as quickly as possible.

"This way, ya sitt."

She hadn't realized she'd slowed her pace until she heard Naseem's words. She turned away from the house and hurried forward, telling herself she had no right to mourn the loss of something to which she held no claim.

He opened the door to the stable and stood back to let her pass. It was dark inside, with only the dim light of a single lantern far to the rear. She did not know why, but she felt an odd disinclination to enter.

"Perhaps I should wait here while you bring the carriage," she suggested.

"You might be seen, ya sitt," Naseem told her firmly.

"No one is awake to see me," she insisted.

He seemed surprised at her sudden inclination to argue. His expression changed from one of subservient helpfulness to one of disgust.

"There is no time to discuss the matter," he told her as he took her arm and pulled her sharply forward, into the stable.

Amity hadn't the time to balk. At first she was simply surprised that he would put his hand on her, and then shocked at the way he pulled her rudely into the low, dark stables. By the time the surprise had worn thin enough to allow her to think that something was wrong, she was inside and the door swung shut behind her.

"Take your hand off me," she hissed angrily. "How dare you treat me this way?"

161

"Because I ordered him to do so."

The words were spoken with a quiet calm that ought to have been soothing, and yet was anything but. Amity shrugged herself out of Naseem's grasp and turned to find the speaker, the man who had shut the stable door and stood now, staring at her with an absent amusement.

"I demand that you . . ."

The words died on her lips as she recognized the robed man as the one who had led the party of tribesmen who had met with Kendrick the day before at the temple. His dark eyes, searing and hard, found hers and held them. She had the disquieting thought that he knew that she recognized him, that he had, after all, seen her hiding in the sand with Ford.

"You are in no position to demand anything," he said with a harsh smile as he moved forward to her.

She backed away a step, bewildered but frightened enough to know that she was in danger.

"What do you want of me?" she asked, her tone wavering now and entirely without the sure anger that had prompted her previous words.

He smiled at her, but she thought there was no humor behind the smile.

"That depends on Kendrick Gardiner," he told her deliberately. Then he reached out his hand toward her.

Amity had no idea what he intended, but she had little doubt it would prove pleasant. She backed away a step more, then turned on her heel and began to run down the long central alley of the stable. Her flight was fruitless, as both Naseem and the robed tribesman immediately set after her, their hands reaching out for her, grasping her arms and her shoulders. And when the thought came to her that she ought to scream, that, as well, was too late. A hand was quickly clamped to her mouth. It was soon followed by a thick gag.

162

Before she realized what had happened, she found herself on a horse, her hands bound together and tied to the saddle's pommel, her face obscured by the heavy robe that had been thrown over her.

The tribesman led her horse forward to the stable door, to where Naseem waited with a second animal.

"You have served me well, Naseem," he told the servant.

Naseem bowed slightly. "I would only that there were more, ya shaikh."

The second man smiled. "There is one more thing," he said slowly.

Again Naseem lowered his head. "You have but to name it, ya shaikh."

"You will bring my message to Gardiner," he said, putting his hand to the belt he wore beneath his robe and withdrawing a piece of thick paper.

"As you wish, ya shaikh," Naseem replied and reached for the letter.

The tribesman's right hand pulled sharply back, and then, as Naseem's attention was directed to the folded paper in his left hand, forward once again. The blade it carried was buried deep in Naseem's chest.

Naseem stared down at the blood that crept slowly onto his shirt, a brilliant red flower against the white of the linen. There was a look of shocked surprise on his face as he realized what had happened.

"Why?" he whispered, looking up to the other man with disbelief. Then he fell to the floor.

The tribesman stared down at him, his expression betraying no hint of emotion.

"Because you are now useless to me, because Gardiner will know you were in my employ. You can, however, do me one final service," he added as Naseem's eyes grew glazed and sightless, "and show Gardiner that I am not afraid to spill blood."

Amity watched this scene with growing horror. The scream that rose in her throat when she saw the bright red fingers of blood soaking into Naseem's shirt died there, muffled by the gag. And although she pulled furiously against the ropes that bound her hands, they remained firmly secure.

She was in the hands of a merciless murderer, and she was powerless to do anything, she realized. She filled with a cold and deadening terror.

The tribesman pulled open the stable door and then swung himself into the saddle. He was oblivious to both her horror and her fear. He grasped his own reins and those of her horse, and set out into the quiet, thick darkness that was still untouched by the first light of dawn.

Ford wished Kendrick had not risen to bid him farewell. He felt awkward with his uncle now, and wanted only to get away, to make his report to General Stuart and try to forget everything that had happened in the previous days.

Part of him, he realized, wished he could forget completely before he returned to Cairo, the part of him that still bore his uncle the love he had always felt for him. But he knew that was impossible, knew that if Kendrick were allowed to continue selling rifles to Ali Kalaf, hundreds of men would die as payment for his weakness. As much as he might dislike the fact, he was to be forced to be the hand that brought Kendrick to justice. He felt a dull emptiness inside himself, an emptiness that was only made harder to bear by the knowledge that Amity was lost to him as well.

Kendrick looked up to the lightening sky. Dawn was filling it with the rosy, golden glow that never ceased to please him.

"A good morning for a long ride," he offered warily. He was slowly becoming aware of Ford's uneasiness, and not sure what had caused it or how it might be dispelled.

"Every morning is a good morning for a ride in Egypt," Ford replied dryly. "It almost makes one yearn for a dawn filled with fog and the luxury of the need to shiver occasionally."

"A yearning I've managed to avoid," Kendrick replied, then gave out with a mutter of surprise as he looked toward the stable and saw the door open. "What's this? That damned boy has gone and left the stable unbarred. If he's left any of my ponies out of their stalls and free to wander out, I'll have his skin."

But his anger was quickly displaced by disbelief as they wandered into stable and nearly stumbled over Naseem's body.

"My God!"

Kendrick seemed in a state of complete shock. The bloody puddle on the bare wood floor surrounding Naseem reflected up at him, dully rust-colored, grimly final. In the center of it, Naseem lay still and silent, his sightless eyes staring up at Kendrick with an unblinking, accusing stare. There was the thick buzz of flies, greedily busying themselves with the gore.

Ford dropped the duffel he had been carrying, knelt, and put his hand to Naseem's neck, searching for a pulse despite the fact that he knew the procedure was useless. He had seen enough corpses to recognize a dead man's face.

"He's dead?" Kendrick asked, although he, too, by now realized that Naseem's pale-gray features no longer held even the final ghost of life within them.

Ford nodded. "Dead." It was then he noticed the folded paper held grasped in Naseem's hand.

"But who?" Kendrick muttered, bewildered. "Why?"

165

"Perhaps this will tell us," Ford said as he withdrew the blood-spattered letter from Naseem's stiff fingers.

He unfolded it and stared at the few lines that were neatly lettered on the page:

I have taken the woman. If you wish to see her again whole and alive, you will deliver the rifles as you originally agreed. You will receive instructions tomorrow. Follow them. If you refuse, the woman will be returned to you in a condition you might consider unpleasant. Do not mistake my words for idle threats.

The words set a thick rage welling up inside Ford. It was bad enough that Kendrick was selling rifles that would eventually be be turned against British soldiers, but now his dealings with Ali Kalaf's men had also put Amity in terrible danger.

He turned to look up at Kendrick, and his expression filled with disgust.

"What is it?" Kendrick asked, but there was a reticence in his voice, almost as though he already knew.

"Do you have any idea what you've done?" Ford asked him coldly as he held the letter out to him.

Kendrick took the page and read it quickly, then turned his eyes to Ford's and observed the disgust in them.

"I never thought . . ." he began, and turned his eyes away from Ford's, unable to meet them any longer.

"Why?" Ford demanded sharply, aware now that he had no longer any need to keep his knowledge of Kendrick's actions to himself. The questions that had burned him since he'd first discovered the rifles vented themselves. "How could you allow yourself to become involved with this?"

Kendrick shrugged. "Debt," he muttered through tight

166

lips. "You must understand, Ford. I could have lost everything. I could have had Gardiner's Ghenena taken from me. After everything I've done to hold on to it, I could have lost it all."

"And so you give this madman rifles to kill your countrymen?" Ford spat out at him. "Is that the way you save your precious land?"

Kendrick shook his head slowly, as though trying to force his thoughts to order themselves.

"I never thought . . ." His words trailed off into silence.

Ford found he suddenly had no pity for him, that with the knowledge of Amity's abduction, all sympathy he had felt for his uncle had fled.

"How many people know the rifles are stored in the shed by the river?" he demanded sharply.

Kendrick's head turned sharply. "How did you know?"

"How many?" Ford demanded, ignoring his question.

"Only me and Justin," he murmured. Then, as he slowly came to realize that was not quite true, he added, "And you."

"Justin!" Ford hissed in disgust.

"It wasn't his fault," Kendrick protested, thinking now to protect his son. "If there is fault, it's mine."

"The hell with fault," Ford retorted as he strode to a stall and led a horse out of it. He turned and methodically began to saddle the animal.

"Where are you going?" Kendrick asked.

"After him, to get her back," Ford replied coldly. "Or do you have some other suggestion?"

"I'll come with you," Kendrick said, and started to move toward a stall.

"You've done enough," Ford told him sharply.

Kendrick turned back to face his anger.

"You can't expect me to stay here, doing nothing, knowing what kind of danger I've put her in?" he asked.

"You won't be doing nothing," Ford directed him sharply as he pulled the saddle girth tight. "You'll wait for his instructions, and then give every indication that you intend to follow them. Stall however you can. But whatever you do, don't hand over the rifles."

"But he gives me no choice," Kendrick objected, and pointed to the note. "You can't expect me to risk Amity's life?"

Ford turned to stare at him with cold disgust. "Do you really think this madman will let you or her live once he has everything you promised to give him? Are you so great a fool as that?"

Kendrick only stood, mute with his own guilt.

Ford removed his pistol from its holster, checked to see it was properly loaded, and then returned it. Then he knelt to his dropped duffel, removed his rifle from it, and secured its harness to the saddle.

"Where is his camp?" he demanded when his preparations were completed.

Kendrick shook his head slowly. He seemed stunned, almost as though he were not quite awake.

"To the southwest, somewhere near the Abar el Masash Oasis. I don't know precisely where."

Ford nodded, then swung himself into the saddle.

"Remember . . ." he said. "Give them every expectation that you'll cooperate and do as they tell you. But don't, under any circumstances, let them know where the rifles are hidden. Hopefully, I'll be back with Amity before they realize what you're doing."

Ford's expression was grim as he spoke. By leaving the rifles in Kendrick's hands, he was risking the possibility that Ali Kalaf still might gain possession of them. Equally unpleasant was the knowledge that he had little chance of getting into Ali Kalaf's camp alone and then getting Amity away without being discovered. But he had no choice. It would take far too long to send to

Cairo for help. To do so would be condemning Amity to certain death.

Whatever chance she had, he knew, rested entirely in his hands.

Chapter Nine

Amity's terror was slowly dulled by simple weariness. Her captor had ridden without stopping for what had seemed to her endless hours, either oblivious or simply uncaring that a rest and a drink of water would have been a welcome kindness to her. The heavy cloak he'd thrown over her had kept what little breeze there was from providing any comfort to her, and the midday heat was stifling, leaving her feeling dizzy and weak and her clothing soaked with perspiration. She could scent her own fear in it, a sour, acrid odor she thought very much like that of an animal. It sickened her to realize it was her own.

The gag chafed her cheeks and left a stale, bitter taste in her mouth. Her tongue seemed like something alien, thick and dry. And she was thirsty, thirstier than she had ever been in her life.

As the day wore on, her fear, her curiosity as to who her captor was, why he had taken her and what he intended for her, even the horrific memory of watching Naseem die, all faded. Eventually all she could think of, when she managed to gather the strength for concerted thought, was how much she wanted a long cool drink of water.

When finally her captor drew their horses to a stop, the sun had already begun to lower itself in the sky. Amity found herself staring at what appeared to be a small gathering of nomad tents. Her vision was obscured by the deep hood of the cloak, and although she shook her head, trying to shake it back, it remained firmly settled. She was forced to content herself with the sight of her captor dismounting. He handed the reins of their horses to a young man who sprang forward to take them from him and then stood staring up curiously at her.

Her captor moved to the side of her mount and pulled a knife from the hilt he wore at his belt. Amity stared down at it dully. She was exhausted, weak from thirst and dizzy from the heat. She had to force herself to concentrate on the sight of the blade, to wonder dispassionately for a moment why this man had bothered to bring her so far if he intended to kill her. It took a moment for the thought to register, to realize that the knife held danger, and for the fear to flow slowly through her and settle in an aching, thick, dull ball in the pit of her stomach.

He looked up at her and smiled, apparently deriving pleasure from the fear he saw slowly kindled in her eyes. He brandished the knife, letting the dying daylight play on its shining blade, letting her eyes follow the deadly metal and remember how it had been plunged into Naseem's chest, to notice the few dried coppery flecks of blood that he had not wiped away. Then he put it quickly to the ropes that bound her wrists to the saddle pommel and deftly severed them.

He put his hand to her arm and pulled her roughly from the saddle, not even allowing her the dignity of dismounting. Had he not held her arm, she would have fallen to the ground at his feet. Her legs were numb from the hours riding and she stumbled as he half dragged her forward to the entrance of the nearest tent. He pulled aside the flap, then pushed her inside. She landed on her hands and knees while he walked past her, indifferent to her fall.

171

He stood for a moment, considering her, before he returned to her side, knelt toward her and pulled away the thick cloak. It was almost like release to her, the relief from the heat of the thing, and she sat as she was and simply breathed deeply for a moment, inhaling the comparatively cool air before she finally raised her hands to the nape of her neck where the gag was tied.

He let her struggle, her hands still numb from the ropes that had bound them to the saddle. After a moment, though, he seemed to lose whatever amusement he had found in watching her frustration as her stiff fingers struggled. He pushed her hands away, and removed the gag, letting it fall beside the discarded cloak. Then he grasped her wrist and held it, his fingers biting into the flesh that was just beginning to regain the circulation the ropes had denied it. She turned terrified eyes to his.

"Your cries will bring you nothing here and will only rouse my anger," he told her. "Do you understand?" he asked as his fingers bit deeper into her flesh.

Amity let a small sound escape her lips. She nodded.

That seemed to satisfy him. He stood then, and wandered forward, into the interior of the tent. Amity stared after him, surprised to find how large the space was, and how luxuriously appointed. She was, she realized, sitting on one of the dozen or more colorful rugs that covered the ground, and there were several low tables, chairs, and a pillow-covered divan. Brass lamps hung from the canvas ceiling.

His back was to her, she realized, and she darted a quick glance to the entrance, wondering how long it would take her to reach it, wondering what she would find waiting for her outside were she to make the attempt.

He seemed to read her mind.

"You would not get fifty paces," he said calmly, "before my men would take you." He turned back then, to face her. "And that, too, would anger me."

172

She felt herself cringe before his dark, knowing glance. Even his words, his threats, were too potent to be dismissed. They held power in them, and the promise of danger.

She watched as he clapped his hands and two women appeared from a curtained-off place to the rear of the tent and bowed before him. They were darkly robed and completely silent as they carefully removed his sandy robe and brought him water with which to wash. There was reverence in their manner as they brought him a thin silken robe to replace the one he'd cast off, sliding it onto his arms and lifting it to his shoulders while he stood, still and unmoving. It seemed almost as though they considered it an honor to be allowed to serve him. Amity felt her terror slowly ebbing, to be replaced by a wave of disgust for their servility and his obvious attitude that it was due him.

As he sat on the divan and the women brought him food and drink, he turned to Amity, his glance seeming to tell her that she should learn from his women's actions, that they behaved as a female ought, silent and subservient.

They brought him water and he drank, thirsty from the long ride, apparently not quite as oblivious to physical needs as he had seemed to Amity. But as she watched him drain a cup, she found her own thirst was raging. It had seemed days since she'd had a drink, and watching him empty the cup, feeling the thirst in sight of water, only served to make it overpowering.

"May I have some water?"

She was surprised to hear her own words, and knew she would not have dared speak to him were the need less. He glanced at her, a sharp, angry look as though he were insulted by the sound of her voice. But he seemed to reconsider his anger, for he turned to one of his women and pointed at Amity.

"Mayya," he said.

The woman nodded, then silently filled a cup and brought it to her.

Amity took the cup from her hand and brought it to her lips, gulping the water greedily, draining it quickly and spilling some in the process. The woman frowned at that, her brow wrinkling above dark eyes, as though the waste of a few drops were a grievous sin. But when Amity held the cup out to her, she silently refilled it, without voicing whatever reprimand had been in her glance. Amity once again emptied the cup. The lukewarm water tasted better to her than anything she'd ever drunk before.

It seemed to give her some courage, and the ability to back away from her fear and think. If this man had not hurt her yet, she told herself, he had some need for her, some purpose in having taken her. She held the cup up to be filled a third time. This time she sipped the water the woman poured into it and stared contemplatively at the tribesman.

He was, she found, gazing at her with the same emotionless expression with which he had considered Naseem's dying body.

"Why have you brought me here?" she asked finally.

She found herself surprised at how cool her voice sounded. Could this person who sat here and calmly eyed the man who had kidnapped her, she wondered, possibly be the same one who had only a few weeks before quivered at the thought that she might in some way displease her own sister? Surely not.

"What do you intend to do with me?"

She watched his eyes, noticing the momentary hint of surprise they betrayed that she would be so bold as to question him.

"I will consider your lack of decent respect due to your British upbringing," he returned, "and so will ignore the fact that you have spoken without being addressed as no decent woman would."

174

Amity pulled herself upright, her back and shoulders straightening and her chin jutting forward in a small show of defiance as she returned his stare.

"I am American, not British. And my government does not ignore such insults done to its citizens as you have done to me. You will come to regret the actions you have taken, I assure you."

He smiled at that, apparently amused now by this unexpected show of defiance from her.

"Your government be damned along with the British," he told her without apparent concern. "Do you really think anyone, either British or American, can touch me in my own land, among my own people?"

"They will send troops to find me," she countered firmly, despite the fact that she was not in the least certain any attempt at all would be made on her behalf. Even if anyone could learn what had become of her, a single woman, and one of no great import at that, would hardly be worth a military incursion into a country already plagued by a highly unstable political environment.

He shrugged at the suggestion, displaying a total lack of concern.

"If they do, they will find you dead," he told her, still with no apparent emotion.

He turned back to the food the women had brought for him, lifted a piece of bread and took a bite, chewing it with apparent relish as he considered her reaction to his assertion.

She stared at him silence for a moment, wondering if he was merely trying to frighten her or if he was serious, if he really would kill her. She could not keep the vision of Naseem's death from returning to her, the sight of the man's chest as the bright stain of blood flowered on his shirt. No, she decided, this man did not make idle threats nor did he shrink at the thought of killing, even killing a woman, especially a woman.

175

It was she who finally broke the silence.

"Why have you brought me here?" she asked him again, only this time softly. "What do you intend to do with me?"

He put down the plate from which he'd been eating, stood, and crossed to her. For a moment he stood beside her, staring down at her where she sat on the rug at his feet. Then he knelt to her, grasped her face with his hand, letting his fingers bite into her cheeks.

"Were you one of my women," he said evenly, "I would beat you to teach you some manners, so that you might learn when a woman speaks and when she should be silent."

She told herself that if she were to let him frighten her, cow her to the sort of subservience he expected from his own women, she would be lost.

"Why have you brought me here?" she asked again, this time forcing herself to keep her eyes levelled on his, not to cringe away as he seemed to want her to do.

For a moment there was rage in his eyes; then it was replaced with a distant hint of amusement.

"I brought you here to convince Gardiner of the error of his ways," he told her.

Then he smiled and let his hand slip to the nape of her neck, catching up a handful of her hair. He pulled it tight, jerking her head back sharply, and brought his face close to hers.

"But perhaps I will not trade you for my rifles, after all. Perhaps I will simply take them, and you."

Amity brought her hand to his chin and pushed it away. He released his hold of her hair, slapped her on the cheek, not hard but hard enough to make her feel the sting. She drew back and put her hand to the red mark that blossomed quickly on her skin.

He straightened up to stand staring down at her and smiled again, a humorless, unpleasant smile.

"Perhaps," he said levelly, "when I am done with you,

Gardiner will not want you back."

"You're an animal," she spat out at him.

He shook his head. "No," he said simply. "I am one of Allah's most blessed, chosen to lead his holy jihad."

"Ali Kalaf," Amity whispered, wondering now why she hadn't realized it all along.

His lips formed themselves into a tight, crooked grin, obviously pleased that she knew of him, that his reputation had grown great enough so that he was spoken of in the pampered society from which she had obviously come.

"And when I have done dealing with Gardiner," he finished dispassionately, his eyes like black fires as he considered her prone on the floor at his feet, "I will show you the power of one of Allah's chosen."

Ford dismounted and stared across the dunes. There was the dim light of campfires in the distance, and he could just make out small dark shadows moving near them. They were Ali Kalaf's men, he knew. The Abar et Masash Oasis was not far, and these men would have no other reason to be camped out in the desert except if they were there to guard the camp's perimeter.

He realized he had ridden this far without really planning what it was he was going to do. His thoughts had been on Amity, on what a ruthless man like Ali Kalaf might do to her. The more he had thought of it, the more desperate he had been to get her away before it was too late.

But being desperate to free her from Ali Kalaf's hands was not the safest frame of mind for him, he realized. If there was to be any chance for him to get in and out of Ali Kalaf's camp, he would need to keep his mind clear. The emotions that were churning around within him were hardly going to help him do that.

One thing was certain and that was that he could

hardly expect to simply walk into Ali Kalaf's camp and demand that Amity be handed over to him. And he certainly had little chance of convincing anyone that he was a disinterested stranger, just happening by. He found himself staring around in the growing darkness of the desert, picturing in his mind the possibility of finding a camel herder who might be convinced to stampede his animals through Ali Kalaf's camp and provide a diversion for him to steal Amity away. That was all nonsense, he knew. Still, the picture was a pleasant one to contemplate, however absurd, especially as he knew it would be a good deal more difficult to divert Ali Kalaf and his men than by merely setting a few dozen animals to running through the encampment, and he could not keep from wishing that there actually was a herd of camels trudging through the dunes silhouetted against the darkening sky.

After a moment, though, he forced himself to more constructive thought. He'd have his best opportunity, he realized, if he could pass himself off as a convert to Ali Kalaf's cause. Dressed properly, he decided, he might be able to pass. Thanks to the amount of time he'd spent in the saddle during the previous weeks, his face was certainly tanned dark enough so that he would not rouse undue suspicion. And although they were hardly common, blue eyed Arabs were not unknown, a lasting memento bequeathed by the ancestors of his own countrymen during the Crusades, men who had apparently not considered a bit of rape inconsistent with their holy cause.

He considered for a moment his knowledge of Arabic. During the years he'd been in Egypt he'd become fluent enough, he knew, but he wondered if his accent would manage to fool a native. Perhaps, he mused, if he were circumspect.

As the sun set and plunged the desert into darkness around him, he decided he had little options open to

178

him. He would have to find himself a *kaffiyeh* and an *aba* to disguise himself, and then he would simply have to enter the camp and see what happened. Although it hardly seemed very much of a plan to him, he couldn't think of anything that might prove better.

He started to creep forward, toward the campfires the guards had lit. Sooner or later one of them would leave the group and go off into the darkness to relieve himself. And when he did, Ford would be ready.

Ford pulled the guard's still body farther back behind the dunes. The man's limp body was heavy, and he found himself breathing hard from the exertion.

He forced himself to silence and then stood, listening for the sound of men coming, something that might mean the struggle, however short-lived, had been heard. The night was still, though, and the only sounds were the murmurings of the other guards as they sat around their fire and talked, their voices low and muffled with the distance. Ford breathed a quick, deep breath of relief that he'd managed not to alarm the other guards, then set himself quickly to work.

This one had been easy enough to take, he thought as he removed the man's clothing and threw it in a heap on the sand. He'd been full of the dinner he'd consumed as he'd sat beside the fire with his fellows, and sleepy from the boredom of spending his hours staring out at a still and quiet desert. Although he'd taken his weapon with him when he'd ventured out into the dunes to relieve himself, he'd taken no special effort at watchfulness, a situation that Ford had been quick to use to his advantage.

Ford eyed the rifle as he carefully tied the guard's hands behind his back and then to his feet. It was a Meerschmidt twenty-round repeating rifle, all right, just like the ones that Kendrick had stored away in the storehouse by the river.

The fact that he had managed to capture a guard who was armed with one of these particular weapons seemed a good omen to Ford. Not that he was one to put much faith in omens. Still, for the first time since he'd set out after Amity, he began to think there might actually be a chance to get her and himself away from Ali Kalaf alive. The fact that he was now in possession of one of the Meerschmidts had given him an idea.

Ford checked the ropes one last time, assuring himself that the guard wouldn't be able to escape them. Then he forced a gag into the man's mouth and tied it securely so that when he awoke, he would be unable to give an alarm. With any luck at all, this particular guard wouldn't be missed until well after dawn. There was little chance it would take very long after that for the others to find him. Still, if he hadn't located Amity by then and gotten her away, Ford told himself grimly, then it wouldn't matter if the guard was found or not, if he could identify who had attacked him or not. If he hadn't gotten Amity away by morning, Ford knew he would probably be dead.

He pulled on the *aba* quickly, then wrapped the *kaffiyeh* around his head, taking care to do it properly, as would a *fellaheen*. Then he lifted the guard's rifle and considered it, wishing he had the luxury of some light to work by. He shrugged. If he couldn't do what he had to do with only the dim moonlight, then he should resign his commission.

His face set with determination, he seated himself in the sand and carefully began to break down the rifle.

Less than an hour later, Ford was standing at the guard post at the opposite side of the encampment. His hands were clasped together and resting on his head, the rifle he had stolen from the guard was lying on the sand

180

near his feet, and a half dozen weapons were pointed at various parts of his body. He had the distinct feeling that the men who held them were deep in consideration as to which might be the most painful places to put a bullet before they killed him.

"Ali Kalaf," he said slowly. "You must take me to see Ali Kalaf."

One of the rifles was drawn back, turned, then the butt end delivered with considerable force to his belly. He dropped his hands and doubled over with the pain.

"What do you know of Ali Kalaf?" asked the guard who had delivered the blow.

Ford breathed hard, his hands to his belly, and let the pain wash over him. Finally it began to abate.

"I must see Ali Kalaf," he repeated, his voice ragged with the hurt. "I must warn him."

"Warn him?"

The rifle butt was raised threateningly, but this time the blow was not immediately administered.

"The rifles," Ford muttered in reply. "Gardiner's rifles."

These words, at least, had enough effect on the guard to induce him to lower his own rifle. He motioned to one of the others to pick up and bring along the Meerschmidt that Ford had allowed them to induce him to surrender.

"You will have the honor of Ali Kalaf's attention before you die," he told Ford indifferently.

Then he turned to lead the way to the encampment.

The woman seemed reluctant to give her the plate of food, but Ali Kalaf's sharp words had been enough to convince her. Amity took it from her and considered the stewed vegetables and olives and flat bread with relish. She was hungry, and now that food was within reach, her stomach reminded her that even fear must give ground to the body's need for fuel.

Her stomach growled as she picked up the piece of bread and used it to scoop some of the vegetables to her mouth. Her mouth was still full when she looked up and saw the woman standing in front of her, unmoving, staring at her with distaste.

"Yallah ruh," Ali Kalaf said harshly, ordering the woman to leave.

The woman turned to him, bowed her head obediently, and then left silently, darting only a last, disgusted glance at Amity.

Amity swallowed as she watched her leave.

"She does not like foreigners?" she asked as she took a bite of the bread.

She realized she was trying to pretend all this was normal, that she found the circumstances of this strange meal no different from a dinner party back in her sister's house.

"A woman doesn't eat in the presence of a man," Ali Kalaf replied. His tone was dull and flat, as though he were voicing some obvious truth that she should not need to be told.

"You ate in her presence," Amity countered. "And mine."

He shrugged. "Certainly. A woman serves. A man is to be served."

Amity considered his words in silence as she ate. The food was surprisingly good, she thought as she chewed contentedly on a bite of the vegetables. And, much to her surprise, she realized she had lost her fear. Perhaps it was simply the fact that she'd had enough to drink, and now was easing her hunger cramps. Or it may have been the fact that she had managed to convince herself that Ali Kalaf's threats were, for the time being at least, baseless. He seemed to think she would get him the rifles he needed. That made her, she realized, far too valuable to him to waste himself in mere pique. The more she considered her situation, the surer she became that he would most certainly not hurt her, at least not until he had what he wanted from Kendrick Gardiner.

As though to reinforce her impression, she realized he had left off objecting to her speaking to him, and even seemed willing to answer her questions, if not effusively, at least with some measure of civility. And she noticed that he now stared at her with a certain interest. It occurred to her that a woman with her coloring—pale skin, green-blue eyes, and mostly the fine chestnut hair—must seem exotic to him. She wondered if she might not somehow be able to use his interest to her own advantage, somehow beguile him to a carelessness that might allow her to get away.

She squelched the thought as quickly as it occurred to her. This man was violent and convinced of his own righteousness. She'd be a fool to think she could manipulate him with a smile or a word, even if she were far more adept than she actually was in an art she had never considered worthy of cultivating.

"Then why don't you send me to your women's quarters so that you need not be offended by the sight of so base a thing as a woman consuming food?" she asked offhandedly as she took another bite of the vegetables. She stared up at him with wide eyed curiosity. The women, she thought, might prove a bit less formidable, easier to outwit.

He gazed fixedly at her a moment, and leaned forward to the table near where he sat, putting his plate down on it. Then he rose and stepped around the table, crossing to where she sat on the floor. He knelt beside her and took her plate from her hands and put it down as well.

He put his hand to her hair, pulling free that little of it that still remained caught up in its pins. He raised a handful of it, staring at its luster in the dim light cast by the lamp and then letting it drift through his fingers to fall free to her shoulders.

"Perhaps," he said slowly, "I prefer to keep you with me because I have decided that the sight of you is not entirely offensive to me. Perhaps I do not send you to my women because I have decided I will see more of you this night."

Amity's hunger disappeared. She had been right when she had seen interest in his eyes, but she suddenly realized that this interest was not quite the same as that of the British or American men she had known. Ali Kalaf would not content himself with nothing more than an hour's conversation with a woman, and this was most certainly not a dinner party at her sister's house after all.

She pulled back, shaking her hair from his hand.

"I would sooner suffer the company of your women," she told him sharply.

He put his hand to her shoulder and held her, ignoring the way she struggled against his grasp.

"Your preference matters little," he told her.

He began to pull her to him.

Chapter Ten

"Keep your hands on your head and walk."

Ford did as he was told, trying not to think of the rifle barrel that was digging uncomfortably against his ribs. From all indications, he was not exactly in a position to protest his treatment.

He looked around surreptitiously as he was led into the camp. It was not large, he realized. Perhaps four or five hundred men. Not a negligible force, certainly, but not so great that a division of British troops could not deal with them. They were, he knew, only a small portion of Ali Kalaf's troops, most of whom would be waiting somewhere in a permanent hidden camp to the south. But leaderless, even a large force was nothing. If Ali Kalaf and this group could somehow be captured, the uprising might be completely suppressed before it went any further.

Not that there was any chance a division of British soldiers might simply happen along, he mused. Unfortunately, things were never quite that simple.

"Igri shwaya!"

Ford had to stop and think. He realized he had been thinking in English again, and the Arabic words sounded strange to him. That, he knew, could prove dangerous. He forced himself to reorient his thoughts, to concentrate on his Arabic.

Igri shwaya. Go faster.

The order did more than make Ford quicken his pace.

His actions were being watched, he realized, and the fact that he had ventured to glance around at the camp had not gone unnoticed. He wondered if his curiosity was considered suspicious by these men or if it could be taken as nothing more than the natural awe of a village oaf who was seeing a large number of armed troops for the first time.

"Iywa, ya shaikh," he replied quickly as he hurried himself in response to the command.

He saw the look of amusement on the faces of the guards at his use of the formally deferential term of address. *Good,* he thought. *They'll remember that I treated them with respect, calling them "sir," men who are used only to showing respect to others. That will overshadow the fact that I might have shown a bit too much interest in the makeup of their camp, and just might make them believe I've never been outside a small village like Tell ElAmarna.*

"Stanna," the guard who had struck him back at the guard outpost told him gruffly as they neared a tent in the center of the encampment.

Ford stopped immediately at the order, nodded his head amiably and smiled, hoping he appeared merely good-humored and anxious to please, not as dimwitted as he found himself feeling. He darted a quick look around as the guard turned and entered the tent.

It seemed to Ford that this tent was the largest of those in the camp. The thought gave him a spurt of hope that the guards had actually brought him to Ali Kalaf after all, and not to some middle-ranking officer assigned to keep his leader free of unnecessary bother. He knew that eventually he would be brought to the rebel leader—at least he would if they believed his story had even a remote chance of being true. But the longer it took, the longer Amity would be left in the madman's hands, and that thought was more than a little unsettling to him.

The guard reappeared, and stared at Ford for a moment, his dark eyes unpleasant, distrustful, glittering bright in the light of the campfires. He motioned to the others to stand aside.

"Taala!" he said sharply, ordering Ford to come.

Ford hesitated for a moment, then motioned to the Meerschmidt they had taken from him, now in the hands of one of the other guards. The leader grimaced, but his glance, too, fell on the weapon in a manner that conveyed the fact that he understood its import. He brushed past Ford, and took the rifle. Then he turned back to Ford.

"Taala," he said once again, and pushed Ford forward, to the entrance to the tent.

The light within was hardly brighter than that cast by the campfires outside, but it was reflected off rich surfaces here, brass tables and fine carpets. None of that interested Ford, however. His eyes were riveted on Amity.

She sat on a heap of pillows beside a divan at the far side of the tent. She was rumpled, her hair was disarrayed, and she was staring up at him, wide-eyed with terror. He looked away quickly, hoping she hadn't recognized him, hoping, if she had, she still possessed the presence of mind not to give him away.

Ford turned his attention to the man who was settling himself on the divan near where she sat. It was obvious he had not been there when the guard had entered, that he, too, had occupied the place on the floor where the pillows were piled. There was still the hint of anger in his eyes, the look that said he was not pleased at the interruption.

He was tall and dark, his long face bearded and his dark eyes cold, sharply piercing, treacherous and knowing. Ford recognized him immediately. The man who had been at the temple with Kendrick. Ali Kalaf.

Amity had been thankful for the reprieve, however short it might prove to be, that the guard's entry had allowed her. Now she stared with absolute disbelief at the newcomer the guard had brought into the tent with him. It was impossible, she told herself, but still she was sure it was Ford.

Her first inclination was to run to him, to throw herself into his arms, but something held her back. She could only

187

wonder what he was doing there, how he had managed to find her. She felt a long stab of regret, knowing that his effort was useless, that he was as much a prisoner of Ali Kalaf as was she.

The guard who had escorted him inside pushed Ford a second time, catching him unawares. As he stumbled forward, the man put out his foot and caught Ford's shin, a simple expedient move to get Ford to his knees.

"Bow before your betters, cur," he hissed.

Ford accepted the treatment as would one who was used to it, making no effort to rise from his knees or object. Instead, he bowed his head.

"*Ya shaikh,*" he murmured as he dared another look at Amity and realized by the shock in her expression that she had recognized him. He darted her a warning glance, then once again lowered his gaze.

Kalaf stared at him with those cold, strangely knowing eyes.

"You know this woman?" he demanded sharply.

Ford nodded. "*Iywa.* Yes, ya shaikh. She came with the younger Gardiner in his boat. She is to be his wife." He turned and made a motion as if he were about to spit, then caught himself. "We were all ordered to the pier to greet her, the new mistress."

Kalaf seemed pleased at the disgust Ford's few words had managed to convey. He smiled.

"You come to me with a story of rifles?" he then asked, his voice low, purring almost, as if there was nothing he might be told of which he was not already aware.

"Yes, ya shaikh," Ford replied hastily. "To warn you about the rifles."

He looked up, into Kalaf's eyes, and saw the doubt in them, the suspicions. He realized the man was staring at his own eyes; he could almost hear his thoughts, the question that Kalaf asked himself—if he could trust any words from a man with blue eyes.

"Your mother was a whore for the infidels?" Kalaf

188

asked, his words without rancor, but not without disdain.

Ford quickly lowered his eyes, and pulled back the *kaffiyeh*, hoping his dark hair and tanned skin might somehow mitigate the sin of his fair eyes.

"No, ya shaikh," he replied quickly, hoping he sounded like one used to the slur. "It is a curse one of them laid upon my family fifty generations past, one Allah has seen fit to let us carry since."

"A curse is Allah's payment for sins," Kalaf told him.

Ford looked back up at him, knowing that he would have but one chance, that if he were not convincing now, Kalaf would have him killed.

"Then I pray that in coming to you, I have atoned for the sins of my ancestors, ya shaikh," he said. "I have come to warn you, that your holy cause might not be harmed."

Amity listened to the words intently although they meant nothing to her. Any thought that Ford had come to save her slowly vanished. A prisoner did not carry on conversation of this sort with his captors, she told herself. She was filled with the sickening thought that he had managed to fool her all along, that it was Ford who dealt with the rebel tribesman, that he was somehow a part of Kendrick's dealings with the rifles and Ali Kalaf.

The talk went on, and there was no way she could not recognize the sharp, questioning stare Kalaf leveled at Ford.

"Who are you?" Kalaf asked him. He leaned forward, his hand to his knee, and stared down at Ford. "Where do you come from?"

"My name is Rasheed, ya shaikh. My family has farmed the land near Tell ElAmarna for generations," Ford replied.

"You give your labor to an infidel?" Kalaf hissed.

"A man must eat," Ford countered. "He must find food for his woman, his children."

"If you are content to befoul your soul by contact with the Englishman, then why do you come to me?" Kalaf demanded.

189

"To save it, ya shaikh. To warn you that Gardiner has tampered with the rifles. To beg to be allowed to join you in your holy cause."

"What is this talk of rifles?"

"They were on the boat, ya shaikh. I helped to offload them, to take them to the storehouse."

"Even if what you say is true, what has that to do with me?"

"There is talk, ya shaikh. Gardiner thinks us all fools, but we have eyes to see and ears to hear."

Kalaf sat back then, apparently amused by Ford's words, perhaps even a little pleased.

Ford could see that some of the suspicion seemed to have gone from his eyes. He breathed an inner sigh of relief.

"Why do you say you have come to warn me about Gardiner's rifles?" Kalaf asked softly.

"He intends to sabotage them, ya shaikh. To alter the firing mechanism so that they will explode."

Kalaf put his hands to his knees and began to rise, a look of real alarm in his eyes.

"How do you know this?" he demanded.

"I saw, ya shaikh. He went to the storehouse, and I looked in and saw him. I brought one of the rifles he has altered, to show you." He motioned to the rifle the guard still held in his hand.

"Show me," Kalaf ordered.

Ford looked up to the guard, then rose and took the rifle from his hands. Then he got back on his knees, and, with a studied hesitancy so that he would not seem to know too much of arms for a *fellaheen,* he slowly broke down the rifle.

He felt a small thrill of satisfaction, seeing how well he had worked despite the darkness and the desert sand. The rifle was immaculate, without mark of having been fired or odor of cordite. It looked new, without any evidence of ever having been used.

"I saw him do this, ya shaikh," Ford said, showing Kalaf

the filed firing chamber. The wall was obviously far too thin to stand the pressure of the small explosion that pushed the bullet through the barrel. It was more than apparent that after one or two firings, it would simply explode.

Kalaf stared at the rifle, an expression of sharp anger spreading across his face.

"Then Gardiner has ruined them all?" he demanded.

Ford shook his head. "No, ya shaikh. There are many rifles, and he works slowly, and alone. It will take him many hours, perhaps days, to do this to all those crates of rifles in the storehouse."

"Where is this storehouse?" Kalaf asked sharply.

"Gardiner's Ghenena, ya shaikh. Not too far from the river."

"You can direct my men to it?"

Ford nodded. "Certainly, ya shaikh."

"Then we will leave at dawn. I will have these rifles before Gardiner destroys them, and you will lead me to them."

"It will be as you say, ya shaikh."

Amity could not understand the words, but she could see the look of satisfaction on Kalaf's face, and knew that whatever Ford said, it pleased him. It had to do with the rifles, she told herself. Ford was offering to take him to the rifles.

The realization sickened her. The thought that she had let this man deceive her, let him take her, left her with a numbing sense of revulsion. She did not know which disgusted her more, the fact that he had lied to her, betrayed her, or that he was betraying his honor and his fellows.

She scrambled to her feet and flung herself toward him. "You bastard," she screamed at him.

Her hands flailed with rage, and she seemed intent upon ripping out his eyes with her nails.

Ford caught her, his hands grabbing hers, then pulling her down to him as he forced her arms behind her back. He

191

tried to warn her with his eyes, to hope that she would understand, but she refused to look at him. He jerked her arms sharply, knowing he hurt her, but at least silencing her before she could say anything more.

Kalaf rose and went to Ford, clasping him on the shoulder. "It would seem the new mistress of Gardiner's Ghenena is not pleased with her servant," he said.

Ford smiled at him in agreement, then rose, pulling Amity to her feet with him. Kalaf put his hand to Amity's arm, taking her from Ford's hold. Ford released her, but let his hands slide along her hip and thigh as Kalaf pulled her back.

"If our venture tomorrow is successful, Allah will reward you," Kalaf said with a smile. "And so will I."

Ford nodded, apparently pleased, and darted another look at Amity, which Kalaf did not miss.

"This woman pleases you?" Kalaf asked him.

"As well as any," Ford replied, his eyes finding Amity's, seeing the disgust in them, the anger.

"Then when I have done with her, she is yours."

Ford offered him a smile that said clearly he could not believe the luck that Allah had seen fit to allow to befall him.

"Until the morning, ya shaikh," Ford said.

Kalaf clasped him once more on the shoulder. "Until the morning, my friend."

Kalaf waved to the guard. "Find this man food and a bed. Tomorrow he comes with us. We return to Gardiner's Ghenena."

The guard nodded, then took Ford's arm and led him away.

Amity watched them go, realizing as they disappeared out into the night that she felt leaden inside, completely bereft. Even Kalaf's threats had not left her so empty, so completely without hope.

Kalaf's fingers tightened their hold on her arm. "Do you know what that man has offered me?" he asked her. There

192

MORE PASSION AND ADVENTURE AWAIT... YOUR TRIP TO A BIG ADVENTUROUS WORLD BEGINS WHEN YOU ACCEPT YOUR FIRST 4 NOVELS ABSOLUTELY *FREE* (AN $18.00 VALUE)

Accept your Free gift and start to experience more of the passion and adventure you like in a historical romance novel. Each Zebra novel is filled with proud men, spirited women and tempestuous love that you'll remember long after you turn the last page.

Zebra Historical Romances are the finest novels of their kind. They are written by authors who really know how to weave tales of romance and adventure in the historical settings you love. You'll feel like you've actually gone back in time with the thrilling stories that each Zebra novel offers.

GET YOUR FREE GIFT WITH THE START OF YOUR HOME SUBSCRIPTION

Our readers tell us that these books sell out very fast in book stores and often they miss the newest titles. So Zebra has made arrangements for you to receive the four newest novels published each month.

You'll be guaranteed that you'll never miss a title, and home delivery is so convenient. And to show you just how easy it is to get Zebra Historical Romances, we'll send you your first 4 books absolutely FREE! Our gift to you just for trying our home subscription service.

BIG SAVINGS AND FREE HOME DELIVERY

Each month, you'll receive the four newest titles as soon as they are published. You'll probably receive them even before the bookstores do. What's more, you may preview these exciting novels free for 10 days. If you like them as much as we think you will, just pay the low preferred subscriber's price of just $3.75 each. *You'll save $3.00 each month off the publisher's price.* AND, your savings are even greater because there are never any shipping, handling or other hidden charges—FREE Home Delivery. Of course you can return any shipment within 10 days for full credit, no questions asked. There is no minimum number of books you must buy.

4 FREE BOOKS

TO GET YOUR 4 FREE BOOKS WORTH $18.00 — MAIL IN THE FREE BOOK CERTIFICATE T O D A Y

Fill in the Free Book Certificate below, and we'll send your FREE BOOKS to you as soon as we receive it.

If the certificate is missing below, write to: Zebra Home Subscription Service, Inc., P.O. Box 5214, 120 Brighton Road, Clifton, New Jersey 07015-5214.

FREE BOOK CERTIFICATE

4 FREE BOOKS

ZEBRA HOME SUBSCRIPTION SERVICE, INC.

YES! Please start my subscription to Zebra Historical Romances and send me my first 4 books absolutely FREE. I understand that each month I may preview four new Zebra Historical Romances free for 10 days. If I'm not satisfied with them, I may return the four books within 10 days and owe nothing. Otherwise, I will pay the low preferred subscriber's price of just $3.75 each; a total of $15.00, *a savings off the publisher's price of $3.00.* I may return any shipment and I may cancel this subscription at any time. There is no obligation to buy any shipment and there are no shipping, handling or other hidden charges. Regardless of what I decide, the four free books are mine to keep.

NAME

ADDRESS _____ APT _____

CITY _____ STATE ___ ZIP _____

TELEPHONE

(   )

SIGNATURE _____ (if under 18, parent or guardian must sign)

Terms, offer and prices subject to change without notice. Subscription subject to acceptance by Zebra Books. Zebra Books reserves the right to reject any order or cancel any subscription.

129002

GET
FOUR
FREE
BOOKS
(AN $18.00 VALUE)

ZEBRA HOME SUBSCRIPTION
SERVICE, INC.
P.O. Box 5214
120 BRIGHTON ROAD
CLIFTON, NEW JERSEY 07015-5214

was pleasure in his eyes as he gazed at her, the distinct knowledge of victory.

"Your damned rifles," she spat out. "That's apparent enough."

He smiled at her. "Precisely," he said. "It would seem I no longer require you as an object with which to bargain."

Amity had no need for him to tell her what he intended now. She found herself suddenly unable to breathe, gasping for air as though she were being smothered. He pulled her back to the heap of pillows, then pushed her roughly so that she fell to them. A small cry escaped her as she landed on her hands and knees. Then she turned to look up at him, to see him coming toward her.

The remaining guards had been dismissed to return to their duty on the camp's perimeter, and Ford walked amiably at the side of the one who had witnessed his interview with Ali Kalaf. The change in the man's manner was quite apparent. There was a sudden acceptance, even a tentative attempt at friendliness, about him. Kalaf's approval, Ford thought wryly, brought some unexpected benefits.

He was brought to one of the soldiers' campfires, and his guide introduced him as a new recruit. He was greeted amiably enough, and offered food which he rejected, pleading exhaustion after the long trip from Tell ElAmarna. He wrapped himself in the blanket he was given, and found himself a place by the fire where other soldiers sat over their meals or made themselves comfortable for the night. Soon his guide left him to return to his post, and Ford found himself benignly ignored, no longer a matter of interest, but simply another of Ali Kalaf's followers.

A few moments later he was moving stealthily away from the fire, offering the excuse that he needed to relieve himself to the single man who turned to him questioningly as he rose. Once away from the group of men surrounding the fire, he found he could walk through the camp without notice as though he had long been a member of the cadre.

He was weaponless, a matter which left him less than pleased. Still, he realized, he could hardly hope to steal a weapon without rousing suspicions. His best chance, he knew, was to appear to be just another of Ali Kalaf's troops, to pretend that he belonged. That would not be easy, he realized, once he had left the soldiers' precincts of the encampment and returned to its center, toward Kalaf's tent.

At least the moon had not yet risen, he told himself, and the night was dark. It seemed a very slim asset, and yet it was something in his favor.

He moved forward, his head down, feeling as conspicuous as if he were a freak, something with two heads or three arms. He expected at any moment to find fingers to be pointed at him, someone to cry out in alarm that there was an enemy in the camp.

Yet, despite his fear, Ford seemed to move through the camp like a ghost. No one seemed aware of his presence. He might have been invisible for all the attention he roused.

Finally he found himself in the circle of tents at the center of the encampment. It took him only a moment to orient himself, to spot Ali Kalaf's tent. In front of it a guard stood at attention, one of the deadly Meerschmidts in his hands. There was no way, Ford knew, he could simply walk past this man and enter Ali Kalaf's private domain. Yet he knew he had little choice. Amity was in there. And there was little doubt in his mind what Ali Kalaf intended for her.

He moved into a shadow beside one of the tents, hoping to hide himself as much as he could as he sidled closer to Ali Kalaf's tent. His hand reached out of habit for the service revolver that was no longer at his waist, the pistol he had left in the desert. A British service revolver on his person would have condemned him to death by the perimeter guards before he had even gotten into the camp. But now its absence was an irreplaceable loss.

194

"You! Halt!"

Ford peered out of the shadow into the circle of light that surrounded the guard. He saw the Meerschmidt being lowered, pointed toward him. He'd been seen, and there was no way he could turn away or try to flee.

Resigned, he lifted his hands into the air and stepped slowly forward.

It was a nightmare. The feel of Kalaf's hands, groping at her breasts, pushing against her, pushing her back until she was pinned and unable to move. This was what he'd intended when the guard had interrupted, bringing Ford to talk to him. Only this time there was no guard at the entrance begging his pardon, telling him there was an urgent matter about the rifles. Ford had solved his problem, promised to bring him his weapons. There was nothing more that could possibly stop him from doing what he wanted, taking what he wanted.

She reached up to his face with her hands, trying first to push him away, then to dig her nails into the skin of his cheek, but both efforts were futile. As soon as he felt the bite of her nail against his flesh he raised his hand and slapped her, hard, then pulled her hand away and held it over her head.

He lowered his face to hers, and Amity turned away, closing her eyes, telling herself this was delusion, this could not be happening.

"Why do you fight me?" he demanded. "You only bring yourself hurt."

She turned back to face him, to stare up at his cold, dark eyes, searching them, hoping to see some spark of humanity, of pity. There was none.

She raised herself to him and spat.

For a moment he hesitated. He seemed shocked at the affront, as though the possibility that she could truly want to deny him had not occurred to him, as though he had

195

thought the fight she offered him nothing more than a game. And then his cheeks darkened with his anger. He brought her two hands together and held them with one of his own, then raised his free hand and wiped away the spittle from his cheek.

He held his hand near her face, seemingly undecided as to whether he would strike her again, then changed his mind and brought it instead to the front of her crumpled dress, tearing it away with one quick, angry movement. His hands followed, roughly kneading the soft flesh of her exposed breast, then groping downward, tearing at the skirt, seeking the warmth of her body while she writhed in useless agony, attempting vainly to wrest herself from his grasp.

Amity was in an agony of fear. This could not be happening, she told herself, none of this could possibly be happening to her. Rape was a far off, meaningless word to her, one barely even whispered in Boston, never uttered in the very proper world in which she had been reared.

And yet it was happening, and happening to her, despite her disbelief. She could feel his groping hands and the heat of his body pressed against hers, could smell the odor of his flesh and that of his breath, could sense the arrogance and the determination that was a part of him, that told him he had the right to do with her whatever he wished.

She felt his hand moving against the soft flesh on her inner thigh and heard a scream. With a shock she realized it was her own voice she heard, crying out in hopeless protest. It seemed impossible to her to think that she had been the source of so wild, so primitive a sound.

She saw his eyes staring down at her, and knew he enjoyed this, realized he relished her pain and her terror, realized that it was of itself a pleasure to him.

She forced a measure of calm, telling herself that what he touched was a shell, what he took was of no value, that he could not truly hurt her if she did not let him. She forced herself inward, hiding herself in a small dark part, a place she could shut away and keep safe from his touch. No

196

matter what he did to her, she told herself, he could not touch this part of her if she chose not to admit him.

But still she could not completely distance herself from the feel of his hands, from the force of his legs pushing against her legs, forcing them apart. Once again she heard the scream, only this time it seemed very far away.

Chapter Eleven

Ford moved forward, into the circle of light in front of the tent.

It took the guard a moment, but eventually he recognized Ford as the *fellaheen* who had been brought to see Ali Kalaf only an hour or so before, the latest recruit who had come to join the cause. He lowered his rifle.

"You shouldn't be here," he said, his tone bluff, but he was smiling and his expression was easy, without blame or challenge.

Ford flashed him the same dull-witted smile he'd offered the guards at the outpost.

"So many are here," he said with a hint of awe in his words. "I had no idea there were so many."

"This is but a small part of Ali Kalaf's followers," the guard told him with obvious pride. "There are enough of us to burn away even the memory of both the British and the khedive. Soon this land will once again be ours."

"With the blessing of Allah," Ford murmured, and piously bowed his head.

"With the blessing of Allah," the guard repeated.

He seemed to accept Ford as one of his fellows now rather than a threat. It was apparent he was inclined to let his attention return to where it had been before he had spotted Ford in the darkness, to the sounds that were coming from within the tent. His curiosity of what occurred there, it seemed, outweighed even his devotion to his duty. Ford moved a bit closer to him, and he nodded, apparently not averse to share the entertainment.

Ford heard a short, terrified scream from inside the tent. That was Amity, he realized. He felt a knot of rage within him.

The guard turned to him, and grinned. "Tonight Ali Kalaf fights a different sort of war," he whispered. Then he made an obscene gesture and broke into a short spasm of laughter.

Ford smiled at him in return.

"The Englishwoman does not recognize the honor being given her, eh?" he said, and smiled lewdly.

The man nodded in response and repeated the gesture. "She should praise Allah," he said with a leer. "By Allah's blessing, Ali Kalaf has the strength of ten. He will teach her things an Englishman could not."

Ford nodded, disguising his revulsion at the thought in a mask of amiable, lewd camaraderie. He leaned toward the tent entrance, pretending to listen for more, and waited for the guard to do the same.

Ford used the side of his hand quickly, bringing it down on the back of the guard's neck as he turned away.

There was the short, hard sound of the contact, the feeling of bone moving beneath his hand and the sudden sharp exhalation of the guard's breath. Then the man fell, and Ford quickly pulled him back into the shadows and out of the circle of light cast by the nearby fires.

Ford was disgusted by what he saw. Kalaf was on top of Amity, his hands roughly kneading her breasts, his knees forcefully parting hers. She struggled uselessly, her hands flailing, her panic dictating her movements, which were now simply frenzied motion with no direction.

There was a dull ball of sheer animal rage within

Ford, something he'd never felt before, something that filled him quite simply with the urge to kill. He ran forward, a cry of primitive anger escaping him despite his conscious knowledge that silence was the wisest course. Kalaf turned at the sound, his eyes glazed with want but clear enough still to see the danger that approached him. He rolled off Amity, leaving her to draw up her knees, to fold herself into a ball, oblivious to what was happening, aware only that the weight on top of her was gone and that she was no longer held, no longer being forced to admit entry to the angry, vicious invader.

Kalaf reached for his knife, thrown off with his clothing, lying nearby on the elegantly patterned carpet. But despite his speed, Ford was faster, racing forward and kicking away the blade just before Kalaf's hand found it, then delivering a second blow, vicious with his anger, to the Arab's stomach. Kalaf drew himself up in pain, and Ford fell to his knees beside him, his anger ruling him now as he delivered blow after blow, unaware when Kalaf ceased to struggle to prevent them, thinking only of what he had seen when he'd entered and determined to repay the agony he had seen in Amity's terrified eyes.

Ford might have gone on, beating Kalaf to death, had he not heard Amity's moan of terrified misery. The sound seemed to bring him to his senses. He rose and turned to her, letting Kalaf fall senseless and bloodied to his feet, forgetting the moment of maddened bloodlust and seeing only her.

He went to her, pulling her into his arms despite her blind protest. "It's all right, Amity," he whispered, letting her feebly pound her fists against his chest, knowing it was not him she thought she struck, but Kalaf.

Slowly her vision seemed to clear, and the frenzied panic leaked away from her eyes. She looked up at him as though she were staring at a ghost. And then her eyes drifted to Ali Kalaf's still body, his face covered with blood.

"He . . ."

Her voice caught then and she sobbed, as though the thought were too painful, the words beyond her ability to utter.

Ford put his fingers to her lips. "I know," he told her softly. "I know."

He put his hand to her head, gently stroking her hair, holding her close to him. He wanted to say more, to hold her and comfort her and make the fear that lingered in her eyes disappear completely. But there was no time for that, no time for the words that might help her bear the pain and chase away the terror. He pushed her gently from him.

"We have to get out of here, Amity," he said slowly, his eyes on hers, watching to see if she understood.

She nodded, and dutifully began to gather her torn dress around her, holding the torn strips to her naked breasts. It was a useless gesture, but the effort seemed to steady her.

"Wait here," Ford told her.

Again she nodded, and stared up at him as he rose and moved to the entrance to the tent. He disappeared out into the night, and for a moment she was filled with complete terror, as great as that she'd felt when Kalaf's hands had been on her, that he had deserted her. She stared blankly at Kalaf, expecting his eyes to open, expecting him to stand and come at her yet again.

But Kalaf lay unmoving, and Ford reappeared quickly, bearing an *aba* he had removed from the senseless guard he'd hidden outside in the shadows. He held it out to her as he approached, as though it were an offering of peace.

She let him help her to her feet, then cover her with the robe. The rough fabric scratched against her skin and smelled of the sweat of the guard who had worn it, but still it gave her a bit of a sense of control that she'd lacked when she'd pulled uselessly at the torn shreds of her dress.

"Thank you," she murmured, the acknowledgment sounding much like that of a polite child who had been given a sweet. It seemed she had told herself she must not allow herself to think of what had happened, must act as if all this were normal or else she would succumb to the hysteria that reached out to claim her.

"We have to leave here, Amity," Ford whispered to her, talking calmly, as though to a frightened child.

He pulled off his *kaffiyeh* and tied it around her head and face, covering her hair and much of her pale skin. Still, two green-blue eyes, wide and terror-filled, stared back at him. The disguise would not fool anyone for long.

"You must do as I say," he told her.

She nodded. "I will," she murmured, a child still, promising to behave. She stepped unsteadily forward.

He stooped and retrieved Kalaf's knife, tucking it carefully into his belt.

"Keep your head down," he whispered as he took her arm and led her to the entry of the tent. "Don't look at anyone."

He pulled the flap back and stared out at the dark quiet of the night, amazed to find that there had been no alarm. He darted a quick glance at the place where he had left the unconscious guard, his eyes just managing to discern the form amidst the shadows. The man lay still, sprawled on the ground, just as Ford had left him.

He put his hand to Amity's arm and led her silently out, guiding her forward in the dim light to where he'd hidden the guard's rifle and retrieving it. Then, keeping to the shadows and stopping whenever there was the sound of someone moving nearby, they made their way to the edge of the encampment to where the horses were confined.

"Can you ride?" he asked her.

202

"Yes," she told him quickly, but there was uncertainty in her tone, even more in her expression.

He looked around quickly in the darkness, soon discovering there were no saddles left with the horses. They would have to ride bareback. There was no question in his mind that Amity was fit to handle a horse without a saddle, especially in her still shaky condition.

He chose what appeared to be a strong, spirited animal, lifted Amity onto its back, then swung himself up behind her. Riding double would doubtless slow them down, but with any luck they would be far enough away by the time their escape was discovered that the lead would be sufficient. Hopefully the sands would have shifted in the meantime, obscuring their tracks. In any event, he doubted that the rebels would bother with them until after they'd done what Ali Kalaf had intended for them to do—retrieve the rifles. They would set out for Gardiner's Ghenena in the morning, saving their revenge for him and Amity until they'd taken their arms.

Once he had mounted behind her, Amity seemed to shrink, falling back against him. He could feel her trembling, and knew he had made the correct decision. She could not have handled a horse by herself. He put his arm around her, holding her close.

"Just a few hours more, and you'll be able to forget any of this ever happened," he told her, hoping he sounded more confident than he felt.

Just for a moment he allowed himself to think how good he felt with her in his arms, how right it seemed for her to be there. It surprised him to realize how contented he felt knowing she was safe, knowing he held her close to him. He drew himself up quickly, however, and told himself that those thoughts could lead nowhere.

He looked up into the sky, searching for the north star to fix his direction, then turned the horse to the

203

east, toward the Nile.

There was just the faintest hint of dawn nibbling into the darkness of the sky when Ford sighted the ribbon of green-edged blue in the distance that told him they were nearing the Nile. It was none too soon, he thought. He'd driven the horse hard, and the animal was close to collapse.

Amity had dozed fitfully in his arms, but it seemed to him she had gotten little rest. She had been, he realized, plagued by her dreams. They caused her to whimper in her sleep and wake with a start, then turn to stare up at him, to assure herself that she was safe and in his arms, and no longer held by Ali Kalaf's. He had no doubt as to the cause of her nightmares. Nor did he doubt that had she been less exhausted, she would not have surrendered herself to such painful dreams. He realized that each time she woke, she fought to keep herself from falling back to their haunting terrors.

The strip of green along the river was narrow here, the pale, sandy soil that reached almost to the river's edge nearly bare, offering little vegetation. Ford was not surprised to find the handful of huts huddled by the river long ago abandoned, their occupants trading the independence of working their own barren plots for the security of laboring for others on the far richer lands to the north.

Ford stopped the horse at the river's edge, then handed Amity down and helped her to the water so that she might drink. As Amity knelt, bringing handfuls of water to her lips and sipping thankfully, Ford led the horse a bit downstream from her, letting the animal gratefully take his fill.

Amity eyed the horse with an evaluating glance. It was not beyond her spotty knowledge of animal husbandry to realize that he would not take them much farther without a rest.

"What do we do now?" Amity asked.

"I'm not quite sure," Ford told her before he sank to his knees, wet his face and hair, then brought his cupped hands, filled with water, to his lips.

Amity peered across the river, watching the sky slowly begin to fill with color and lighten. It seemed nothing less than mad to her that she was kneeling in the mud at the water's edge, that the nightmare of the previous night seemed to tug at the edge of her conscience like a deep veil of darkness despite the fact that she was staring at the rising sun, letting its light burn her eyes. Ford had gotten them this far, she told herself. She had no reason to question him, to think he would not get them safely back to Tell ElAmarna.

But when she turned to him, she seemed to see her own fears mirrored in Ford's face. And then he looked away abruptly, as though he found the weight of her glance painful to bear.

He stared along the water's edge for what seemed an unending moment, and then he stood abruptly.

"Stay here," he told her as he started to slog through the muddy river's edge.

"What is it?" she called after him.

"Just stay here," he called back.

She watched his back with dull concentration for a moment, then let her own gaze drift farther upriver toward a dark object that floated at the river's edge. She watched it slowly bob as the water pushed against it, but it was unmoving, apparently caught in a thick stand of reeds and the roots of a large acacia tree that edged the water at that point.

She stood and scrambled up the bank, then began to follow after Ford, quickly realizing that what he had found was a boat. When she reached the place where he worked freeing the small dhow from the vegetation, she started down to the water to help him.

205

"No, stay there!" he shouted at her.

Slightly cowed, she did as he directed, squatting in the dun-colored soil and watching as he cut away the reeds that held the small boat trapped.

It didn't take him long. He pulled the dhow free of the roots and reeds, then pushed it a bit downriver, to a place clear of growth, and forced it forward onto the shallows until the hull scraped bottom and settled in the mud.

Amity stood and made her way down to the water's edge to watch him sit, roll up his pants legs, and carefully begin pulling away the leeches that had attached themselves to his skin.

"Don't look," he told her as he turned and found her staring, transfixed with revulsion, at the slimy, slowly growing things on his legs.

He returned to the task of removing them, scraping them away with the knife he'd taken from Ali Kalaf. Amity looked up, away from the horrible things, realizing now why he had ordered her to remain on the riverbank. She wondered how he could bear to touch them.

"How did the boat get there?" she asked.

"Probably blown free from someplace upriver by the floods early in the year," he replied. "Incredibly, the mast appears serviceable, even if it is covered with mold. I'd say it's an unbelievable stroke of luck." He smiled grimly. "Perhaps Allah is smiling on us after all."

"Do you really think it will get us downriver?" she asked, ignoring his last words and staring at the dhow. She was not at all sure as she eyed the grayed, sun-bleached wood of the open hull, that it would even hold the two of them.

"Let's hope so," he replied as he flicked the last of the leeches from his calf and began to roll down his pants legs.

"What about the horse?" she asked.

He looked up to where the horse had climbed the

bank, and was now nosing at the tough grass, reluctantly eating what it could find for lack of more appetizing fare.

"He should be able to find enough to eat until someone comes along and finds him," Ford told her as he got to his feet.

She nodded, then looked away. She felt suddenly extraordinarily foolish. It was only too obvious to her that lives hung in the balance, that if they did not reach Tell ElAmarna before Ali Kalaf's men did, if Ford did not somehow manage to secure the rifles from the insurgents, there would soon be acts of terrible violence all through the area north of the Sudan. Yet there she stood, worrying about the fate of one lone horse.

Ford smiled at her, then put his hand to her chin and lifted her face until she was staring up at him. He moved his thumbs against the blush-warmed circle on her cheeks.

"Sometimes it's simply easier to think of what's standing in front of you, for fear of what your thoughts might tell you of other matters," he told her softly.

His words surprised her, the sudden realization that he seemed to know what it was she thought, what it was she felt. She leaned toward him, wanting to feel the solidity of his body close to her, needing to feel his strength, to know it was great enough for them both.

He put his hand to her back and held her close for a long moment, as content to hold her in his arms as she seemed to be to be there.

"We have to go, Amity," he murmured, aware of the reluctance he heard in his own voice.

She nodded, and pulled slowly away. Then he held out his hand to her and helped her into the dhow.

He pushed the vessel free of the shallows, then pulled himself into the small boat beside her. For the next few moments he busied himself unfurling the single tattered and mold-spotted sail, setting it into the wind and maneuvering the dhow into the center of the river where it would catch the current. Then he removed the *aba* he had stolen before he'd approached Ali Kalaf's guards. He spread it out on the dry and splintering planks in the stern to make a place for Amity to sit.

"My lady's bower awaits her," he told her with a wry smile.

"As elegant as Cleopatra's barge," she agreed as she settled herself on the makeshift cushion.

She looked up at him, at his now bared chest, tanned and muscled, his skin glowing in the first clear rays of the morning sunlight. She watched the muscles move beneath his skin as he adjusted the line, letting the sail out a bit so that it did not strain too hard against the stiff morning breeze. It struck her that his body was a marvel to her, more beautiful certainly than any marble statue she'd ever seen in a museum. She could not keep herself from remembering how it felt to be held by those arms, how it felt to be so close to his body that she might have been a part of it.

"Will my lord join me?" she asked. She edged over a bit, making a place for him beside her in the dhow's stern.

He secured the line, standing for a moment and watching to see that the dhow moved in the path he had set for it, down the center of this wide and empty portion of the river. Then he settled himself beside her, putting his arms around her shoulders.

"You could sleep a bit, Amity," he invited.

She shook her head sharply, rejecting the offer. The thought of returning to the sort of dreams that had plagued her during the night she found not the least appetizing.

"I'd rather talk," she replied.

"Very well," he agreed, more than willing to be amiable. He turned to face her and his gaze grew gently comforting. "What shall we talk about?" he asked softly, wondering what he could say to her if she chose to talk about Ali Kalaf, about what had happened to her the previous night.

But her thoughts were on a different matter altogether.

"We could discuss the apology I owe you," she told him softly. "I could beg your pardon for having thought what I did of you last night."

"And having tried to scratch my eyes out," he added with a short laugh.

She offered him a weak smile. "And for that, too. I don't know how I could have believed you would help him, how I could have thought you would give him the rifles." She stared up at him. "That was what he told me, that you had come to him, to lead him to the rifles."

He nodded. "It was the only thing I could think of to say that would get me to him, that would get me to you."

"I understand now. But last night . . ." She hesitated, searching for the words that would tell him what she'd felt, what she'd thought. "When I saw you brought in to him, I thought they had captured you, and that they would kill you. I thought my heart would break at the realization that you had come after me, only to lose your life for the act. And then there was all that talk, talk that meant nothing to me. But finally I understood something, the pleased look he gave you, as though you had brought him some great gift. And I then I told myself you hadn't come to save me after all, but to sell him his damned rifles."

"It's all past, Amity," he told her gently. "I accept your apology."

"No," she insisted. "There's more. I hated you, Ford. I told myself I hated you more than I have ever hated anyone. And when he told me you would lead him to the rifles, I wished you dead."

He sat in silence for a moment, considering her words. Perhaps she was right, he thought. Perhaps honor should be considered before passion. But he found the concept hard to accept. Maybe it was because he wanted so much to know that she loved him, despite the possibility that he had done wrong. For there was one thing of which he was completely certain, and that was there was no way he could ever prove himself innocent of the charges that had first brought him to Egypt. Or perhaps it was simply because he'd been denied the luxury of claiming a right to honor for so long that he had somehow lost the value of it.

Finally he turned back to face her, to consider her wide eyes, liquid now and filled with tears of remorse. Rumpled and dirty, he thought, and still she's beautiful.

"All his talk was not of rifles," he told her, grinning with playful lechery. "He told me that as my reward, when he was done with you, he'd give you to me."

She managed a smile at that, and put the heel of her hand to her cheek, forcing away the tears that wanted to be shed. Then she looked up at him.

"It would seem he's done with me now," she said softly, wondering that she dared the words.

He gazed at her a moment, and felt the longing begin to throb through him. But he could not go on, he told himself, lying to himself, letting himself believe there was any hope that he might one day be anything more than he was at that moment, or have anything more than he had at that moment, most certainly not her.

"Amity . . ." he began, his tone sharply serious now, "you know about my past, the fact that my family has disowned me."

She stared at him, searching for some answer in his eyes. Finally she voiced the question.

"Is it true, Ford? Were you a thief?"

"If I told you I am innocent, would you believe me?" he asked.

210

She nodded. "Yes," she said softly. "I would believe you."

"I am not a thief," he said quietly. "I've never stolen anything in my life."

"I believe you," she replied.

He shook his head. "You don't understand. There's no way I could prove my innocence eight years ago. There's even less way now. I will always have this stain on me."

She put her hand to his lips. "That doesn't matter to me, Ford. That was all a long time ago."

He put his hand to hers, and pulled it aside. "It does matter. It means I have nothing, nothing but the brand of thief. It is not something I could ever give to another, nor is it something I will ever bequeath to a son."

For a moment he stared at her in silence. She stared back, wondering what it was he thought of her, if all this was simply an excuse, a way to tell her had no desire to tie himself to her.

"I'm not asking for any pledges, Ford," she said finally, her voice a hoarse whisper, strained and hard. "I don't want them. Not now. Not ever."

She wondered that she had the strength to say such words, wondered what it was she felt growing so sharply inside herself. But when his arms surrounded her and he pulled her close to him, her questions fled. She knew what it was she felt. She could not help but recognize the even, growing throb of her own heart beating in her chest.

His lips found hers, at first a soft, gently probing question, and then, as he grew aware of her answer, with greater, far more urgent ardor. There was no question in his mind as to why he had set out after her with such a fired need, nor why he had felt such murderous rage at the sight of Ali Kalaf forcing himself upon her.

For some reason he did not quite understand, he had let himself become tied to this woman, had left himself

211

open and vulnerable to the need for her in a way he had never before allowed himself to be. He knew that eventually this feeling he had for her would only serve to bring him pain, that eventually she would think about the matter and realize she had no desire to tie herself to a man who had been branded a thief by his own family. Nor would he blame her. He himself had sworn years before that he would bear this brand alone, never allow himself to grow so weak that he would ask another to bear it with him, or, even worse, to leave it as his legacy to a son.

But for now, he realized, more than anything else, he wanted this, to be close to her, to hold her in his arms, to make love to her. Even if he knew this was to be the last time, still he knew he needed her as much as he needed air to breathe.

He brought his hand to her hair, pushing it back, away from her cheek, letting it pass like ribbons of silk through his fingers, marveling at how soft it felt to him. Then he slowly pressed his lips to her eyelids and her cheeks and then to the lobe of her ear and her neck. He wondered if it was the heat of the newly risen sun warming her skin that he felt when he touched her or the heat of something else, something he woke within her.

Amity reached up to him, putting her arms to his neck, feeling the thick, dark curls at the nape of his neck and the hard muscles of his shoulders beneath her fingers. She let herself float for a moment on the sensation of his lips against her eyelids, her cheeks, and her neck. It seemed to her that they were teasing her, raising this strange fire within her, letting it smolder until it broke fiercely forth, until she could stand it no more. She pulled him abruptly to her, finding his lips with her own, wanting to burn away the memories of Ali Kalaf with this strange fire that he could so easily ignite, this pulsing, liquid heat that so suddenly coursed within her.

212

He leaned back against the stern of the dhow, then pulled her onto his lap, smiling up at her as he lifted away the *aba,* and then the tattered remains of her dress. His smile disappeared as he saw the darkly bruised marks on her breasts, angry reminders of Ali Kalaf's attentions. He raised his hand gently to the bruises.

"I should have killed him!"

It seemed incredible to him, the wealth of anger that surged up within him, and once again he felt the rage, the wish to see another man's death. It was not until that moment that he realized he had left the Arab lying senseless in his tent, that he had not given him a second thought as he had hurried Amity away. For a moment he wondered if he had indeed killed Ali Kalaf after all, if in his rage he had beaten the man to his death.

But his thoughts were quickly distracted as Amity leaned forward to him, inviting his hands to caress, his lips to taste and touch her naked breasts. And then she lowered her lips to his, and he took them, watching the shadow that fell as her long chestnut hair made an undulating curtain around them, muting the brightness of the early-morning sun.

Amity could only wonder at the magic that made her feel as she did when she was in his arms, when she tasted the sweet, potent magic of his lips. She craved the growing heat that coursed through her body, wanting it to sear away the memory of the horrors of everything that had happened since the moment she had entered the stable at Gardiner's Ghenena, since she had turned to see Ali Kalaf waiting for her in the shadows. Until that instant she had never really considered the possibility of violence touching her life. And yet since the previous morning she'd seen a man murdered, had known the terror of having a man reach for her with the intent of rape. *Love,* she thought. Ford's love and nothing else, only that could ever enable her to look at the world

213

with eyes that were willing to see beauty and innocence around her and not be haunted by the specter of blood and violence.

She pressed herself to him, drinking in the sensation of his touch like wine, heady and sweet to her tongue. Then she leaned forward to him and kissed him as he had kissed her, kissed his eyelids and lips and neck, and then the thick, wiry curls on his chest, savoring the taste and the salty heat of his body.

She found herself fumbling with his belt, and then, finally managing to free the buckle, she started at the buttons of his trousers. He was smiling at her with an absently tolerant expression, she realized, but she refused to allow herself to accept the thought that he might be laughing at her. She worked diligently at the buttons, savoring the feel of the hard muscles of his stomach beneath her fingers, and even more the obvious evidence of his arousal as the last of the buttons was released.

And then somehow he'd shed the last of his clothing and he was pulling her down to him. She felt him inside her, and the hot, sweet magic was filling her, buoying her, tearing away everything that had gone before, separating it from her and diminishing it until none of it mattered, until nothing mattered but that moment and the way she felt, the way he made her feel.

She was floating in his arms, awash with the feeling of him inside her. She was filling with a rising tide, the heated, swollen press of her own body's rushing throb. There was a cadence and beauty to the dance that nearly overwhelmed her as the subtly insistent pulse grew in intensity, as it increased its speed until she felt as though she might burst from the beautiful agony of it.

She collapsed against him, her breath ragged and her body trembling. He enfolded her in his arms, cradling her close as though she were a child. She looked up, staring beyond their tiny vessel, out at the water of the river around them, shimmering and golden in the now-bright morning sunlight, at the ragged patches of greenery that clung to the river's edge, at the wealth of creatures who had come there to drink and now stood staring at the spectacle of naked humans lying entwined as they floated along on the river. It was as though they were alone in the world, as though civilization had lost itself and left only them to admire what man had left untouched behind him in his passing. And everything, everywhere she looked, seemed unutterably beautiful to her.

She turned to him and found him staring at her with a startled yet pleased look in his eyes.

"I think it was like this at the beginning," she whispered. "I think Eden must have felt this empty, this beautiful."

"Perhaps," he replied and smiled, a bit warily, for he shared her wonder with the heated passion they shared, but had not been quite as ready to reject the presence of the world that would press all too close and soon upon them. He put his hand to her eyelids and gently closed them. "Sleep now," he whispered as he caressed her shoulders, her thighs.

She nodded, willing now, sure her dreams would no longer bear any terror, and closed her eyes.

He held her in his arms, felt the silken weight of her hair across his chest, the stir of her breath and the heat of the sun against his skin. He stared at her, imprinting the sight of her naked body on his mind, letting his fingers drink in the feel of her skin, the fine shimmer of her hair. He told himself that he would remember, that there would at least be that for him, the memory of how she felt in his arms, the shattering magnificence of how it had felt to make love to her. He wondered idly if the memories would ease the loss of her when it came, or make it only the more painful.

As she drifted off to sleep, he stared up at a brilliant, unblemished sky. He was a fool, he told himself, to think only of his own unhappiness. It was in his hands to stop a madman's war. For he knew that if Ali Kalaf's jihad were to succeed, it would mean the end of not only the British presence in Egypt, but the very basis of civilization there.

The sky seemed so clear to him, so sharply blue and unstained. He found himself silently praying to a God he long ago had decided had abandoned him, that it would not soon be stained by the smoke and stench of Ali Kalaf's mad war.

Chapter Twelve

After a few hours' sailing, the brisk wind on the river had managed to shred the rotted and mold-encrusted sail of the dhow. By then, however, Ford was able to recognize the countryside bordering the river and realized they were fairly close to Tell ElAmarna. He managed to maneuver the dhow close to the bank, then, when the sail became completely useless, slid into the water and guided it close enough to the side to enable Amity to swim the remaining distance.

Amity was not entirely pleased with the excursion. They had seen crocodiles lazing in the mud at the river's edge as they'd sailed downriver. Despite Ford's assurances that he had seen none of the beasts for several miles and that the presence of a small herd of gazelle nearby meant there were no predators in the vicinity, still she was not completely convinced. She watched him drop over the side of the dhow into the water, expecting at any moment to watch him gasp with pain as an unseen monster rose up from the riverbed to grasp him in its powerful jaws and pull him downward.

They rested for a few moments at the water's edge, and let the sunshine warm them. Then they climbed up to the road that ran along the embankment. It wasn't long before Ford managed to stop a farm wagon laden with melons for market. The driver gave them a suspicious inspection, not surprising Amity thought, considering their appearance. But having obviously decided they were harmless if a bit bizarre in appearance, the driver invited them to share the bed of the wagon with the melons. The ride proved to be bumpy, but not entirely unpleasant given the circumstances.

Amity was almost surprised to realize the wagon had come to a halt. She had to force herself to turn around and look at the fields and the gardens and the house. It seemed odd to her that everything was entirely familiar to her, that Gardiner's Ghenena had remained entirely unchanged when she felt herself completely different. The events of the preceding hours had made a stranger of her. It seemed only natural to her that everything else ought to have changed as well.

Ford lifted her out of the farm cart, then, as he set her on the ground beside the stone steps, called out a thank-you to the *fellaheen* who had given them the ride.

Amity stared up at the handsome facade of Kendrick Gardiner's house. It seemed impossible to her to think that she was actually there, that the house, the perfectly tended flower beds, the surrounding fields, all of it looked so normal, so completely unchanged. After the events of the previous two days, she would have thought everything would appear different to her—muted, tinged somehow by the unpleasant knowledge she had gained. But it was all as she had left it, beautiful and peaceful.

And now they'd returned to Gardiner's Ghenena, and the house glowed a pale mellow sepia color in the brilliant afternoon sunshine, and it seemed to Amity as though they'd fled one world and managed to enter another.

"Amity? Is that you?"

Justin was dressed in his shirt-sleeves, an odd breach of propriety, Amity thought, for it was well past noon. Still, there he was, the door left open behind him as he ran down the steps, pausing only for a second to offer a glance to the farm cart that was now lumbering slowly

218

down the long drive. It was a slightly perturbed glance, she thought, as though he were wondering how such a poor, rough thing dared venture on Gardiner land.

He quickly turned his glance to her. She found herself expecting the same disapproving stare considering her state, the fact that she herself was decidely less than pristine, that she wore the *aba* Ford had stolen from Ali Kalaf's guard, dirty and stained and uncontestably rank, surely not appropriate attire for the future mistress of Gardiner's Ghenena, the future wife of Justin Gardiner.

She drew back as he approached her, and told herself she would never be either of those things, neither mistress in this great house nor wife of this man who seemed now intent to enfold her in his arms. It startled her to realize that the thought of neither loss generated any great sense of deprivation within her.

"Yes, it's me, Justin," she replied evenly. She stepped back once more, away from him, from his approaching arms and his evaluating glance.

He stopped when he realized she had purposely avoided his touch. For a moment he hesitated as he stared at her. Then he abruptly dropped the arms he held out to her.

"You weren't harmed, were you, Amity?" he asked her, his voice low and solicitous now, and a bit hurt. "I've been so worried since Father told me what had happened. I can't believe it. I can't believe any of it."

She found herself filling with an unexpected rage toward him. She wanted to scream at him, to say that she had been most grievously harmed, that she'd seen a man murdered, been abducted, nearly raped. How could he think she was anything but hurt? And how could he stand there and stare at her with such innocence in his eyes? How could he tell her he couldn't believe?

"Believe, Justin."

Ford's tone was harsh and his eyes steely as he glared at his cousin. But when he moved to Amity's side, the

219

hand he put to her waist was gentle. It was odd, she thought, how safe his touch made her feel. It was oddly seductive, that feeling of safety, the assurance that nothing could happen to her as long as he was near to her.

She darted a glance at him, and realized his eyes were on Justin, just as his thoughts were. She was stricken with the possibility that she might be nothing more than a tool to him, a way of getting back at his cousin. That was why he had made those excuses while they were on the dhow, why he had let her understand he had no intention of offering her marriage. She felt herself grow suddenly dead inside.

She pulled away from him, telling herself she could never again allow herself to be seduced by what she felt, by what she wanted him to feel. If she were strong enough to realize she could not marry Justin, she must be strong enough to accept the fact that Ford, too, was not what she had believed him to be. It was not, after all, as though she had not been warned about him. Before all the madness had begun, both Beatrice and Charles had warned her about Ford Gardiner. She'd simply been too obstinate to listen.

Ford's eyes were still on Justin, still as sharply unforgiving. It seemed he hadn't even noticed when Amity pulled away from him. She realized with a sickening dread that he was returning her, the stolen goods, to her fiancé. No matter that the goods were a bit worn now. He had done his duty as a good soldier, and could dismiss his obligation once he'd returned her to her rightful owner.

"Where's Kendrick?" Ford demanded.

"Here."

Kendrick's voice was low and pained, but there was no way he could disguise the emotion he felt as he stared at Amity. He quickly descended the steps and moved toward them.

"Thank God you're both safe," he said, not taking his

eyes off Amity, as though he couldn't believe she was actually there. "All this has been my fault, my dear," he murmured as he took her hand, tentatively waiting to see if she would reject his embrace as she had rejected his son's. "I can't tell you how I regret everything you've suffered."

There was pain in him, she saw, real regret. And somehow she could not back away from his arms, somehow they felt welcoming to her despite the fact that she knew what he had done. As abandoned as she felt at that moment, Kendrick's embrace at least gave her some small amount of comfort.

When Kendrick released her, Ford put his hand to her arm and began to move her toward the house.

"I think we should let Amity go to her room," he said. "She undoubtedly would appreciate a long soak and some sleep." He turned steely eyes to Kendrick. "And we have serious matters to discuss, you and I."

Kendrick tore his eyes away from Amity's, and a hint of color tinged his tanned cheeks.

"I've done precisely as you directed," he said. "The instructions I received are to prepare the exchange to be made at the temple, tomorrow at sunset. I've indicated that I'll cooperate."

Justin cleared his throat and turned to Amity. "I think Ford is correct," he said. "I think Amity should retire. There's no need for her to be distressed any further."

She flashed him an angry glance. "I know what is going on, Justin," she said sharply. "That fanatic made no effort to hide the fact that he was buying arms from your father. So there's no need to think you must keep me from being 'distressed further.' The only thing I don't know is your part in all of this."

Justin's eyes turned cold in the face of her anger. But Kendrick put his hand to her arm, forcing her attention away and to him.

"It was all my doing, Amity," Kendrick told her. "You

mustn't put any blame on Justin that rightly is mine."

She stared at him in silence for a moment, then slowly shook her head. She had never felt quite so confused, or so alone.

"It doesn't really matter, does it?" she asked softly.

"It pains me to agree with Justin, Amity," Ford interjected, offering her a hint of a smile, "but you might as well get some sleep. The three of us have a bit of work to do."

He turned his glance to Kendrick then, and his expression grew completely serious. He had dismissed her, she thought, and returned to those matters that really interested him.

"They won't wait until sunset tomorrow," he told Kendrick. "We have to destroy the rifles now, before they get here—"

"That's insane," Justin interrupted, his expression as much of an objection as his words. "Those rifles are worth more than a hundred thousand pounds. We can make them secure, make sure Ali Kalaf doesn't get his hands on them."

Ford turned to him. "And then what do you intend to do with them?" he asked. "Offer them at auction to the highest bidder?"

"Of course not," Justin spat out at him. "But the British Army could certainly make good use of them. There is no reason to destroy my father's investment."

"Ever the perfect banker, aren't you, Justin?" Ford sneered. "Always trying to manipulate, to make a good investment out of a losing position."

"That's enough," Kendrick shouted, quieting the two of them, despite everything, still the patriarch, the peacemaker. "I don't need the money. Gardiner's Ghenena is safe for the time being." He turned his glance to Amity, hoping to make her understand, to see why he had done what he had done. "There were so many debts," he told her, his eyes holding hers, "and no matter how good the crops, they never seemed quite good enough to clear all the money I owed. The past ten years I've been haunted with the possibility that despite all the work, I'd lose this land. After everything I put into it, it would go to someone else's hands."

"That's why you sold Kalaf guns?" she asked him softly.

He nodded. "I did it the first time to pay off this year's portion of the debt. It seemed so easy, a way to finally see things begin to become settled, to start to see Gardiner's Ghenena actually becoming mine and not the property of some faceless, soulless bank." He shook his head, obviously pained at his own thoughts. "But such things are too seductive, too easy to fall back upon, to have said only I'd do it just once more." He turned back to Justin, and his expression grew set and determined. "This last time it was greed, not necessity. We destroy the rifles as Ford says. And then I turn myself over to the authorities. I've lived with all this long enough." His eyes grew cold. "Too long."

"None of that is necessary," Justin countered, refusing to be silenced. "We can load the rifles onto the clipper and take them downriver, to Cairo, where we can sell them to the Army. And that's the end of it. No one need know about the arrangement with Kalaf. Your going to prison serves no purpose." He turned to Ford, and his eyes grew hard and his expression sharp. "Or do you intend to put the only person who ever believed in you in prison for no other reason than as a balm to your injured sense of justice?"

His words were an accusation, one he knew Ford could not accept. He stared at Ford, his look challenging.

"Well, does your debt to the damned Army outweigh your debt to my father?" he demanded.

Ford seemed to ignore Justin's words. He turned away from him, his eyes seeking Kendrick's as though he could find the answer to the questions his conscience asked him in them. It surprised to find that his uncle looked suddenly old to him, that his shoulders stooped and his face looked wan, as though the last twenty-four hours had aged him in a way the years alone never had seemed capable of doing.

As much as he hated Justin, Ford told himself, he could not deny that what he had said was true. Kendrick had been the only one who had ever believed him innocent of the theft the rest of his own family had determined he'd committed, the only one who had stood beside him when it seemed the world had turned its back on him. Sending him to prison would satisfy nothing — not justice, certainly, and not the personal debt Ford owed him.

Although nothing could remove the first shipment of rifles from Ali Kalaf's hands, with Meerschmidts of their own to fight the insurgents, the Army certainly had a fair chance. And except for his own admission, there was nothing linking Kendrick to that first shipment of rifles. There remained only this second shipment, the rifles Justin was suggesting he offer to the British Army. Surely giving the arms to the Army would satisfy morality, Ford told himself. Surely that was far more important than the strict letter of the law.

He turned to Amity, and he could see it in her eyes, that her thoughts mirrored his own, that Kendrick did not need the punishment of prison to impress upon him the knowledge of what he had done. It occurred to him that she had come to love Kendrick just as he did, even in the short time she'd known him, that she had willingly offered up to him the affection and loyalty that had had no home since her own father's death the previous year. For a second he wondered what it was about his uncle that so quickly inspired trust and regard, but then dismissed the question. After all, he felt just as Amity did, only perhaps a good deal more strongly. He realized that he needed very little more to spur his own inclination to mercy.

"Get together a dozen workmen," he ordered Justin. "Send them down to the storehouse with some carts."

Justin didn't like his tone, that was obvious from the rush of ire in his expression. But he held his tongue, saying nothing as he turned away to do as Ford had directed.

Kendrick put his hand to Ford's arm. "I don't know what to say, my boy," he said softly. "I'll never be able to thank you."

Ford waved off his words. "I won't be able to protect you again, Uncle," he replied.

There was a sharpness in his words that he knew was unintentional, that stemmed more from the fact that he realized by agreeing to do this for Kendrick, he was entering into the conspiracy; by agreeing to keep his silence, he was in fact now as guilty as Kendrick and as liable for the responsibility of the results if matters did not go as they expected.

"There won't be need, Ford," Kendrick said. "I swear to you. On my honor."

Honor. It seemed to Ford that there had been a great deal of talk about honor that morning, first from Amity, now from Kendrick. He wondered why the thought of honor made him feel so uncomfortable. Could it really be that he had lost all caring for his own lost honor, or simply that he cared too much to bring his feelings out to be examined? It was not a subject he had either the leisure or the inclination to explore at that moment, but he knew the time would come when it would be necessary, and he would not be able to simply push the thought aside because it did not please him.

Amity watched the play of emotion on his face, and wondered what it was that seemed to cause him so much hurt. For all his strength, he was as vulnerable as she, she realized with a dull surprise. Somehow that fact

225

made him far more human to her, and her feelings far more confused. She wished she could understand him, understand what it was that he really thought, really wanted. The only thing she knew for certain was that he didn't want *her*.

He turned abruptly, starting away from the house.

"We've a lot to do. Let's hope Kalaf gives us the time to do it," he said. Then he looked back to see Amity following. "You'd best stay here," he told her.

"You can't expect me to stay in this house alone, Ford," she replied, suddenly terrified at the thought that he might demand that she do just that. "I couldn't."

He stared at her a moment, recognizing the fear in her eyes. Despite the strength she'd shown in the previous hours, she was far from recovered from what had happened, he realized. There was no question but that he would allow her to do as she wanted.

"Very well," he told her. "You can board the clipper. You should be safe enough there."

He would leave her on board the clipper, she thought miserably, where she would be safe, where he wouldn't be forced to think about her. He'd done his duty as a soldier, saving her from Ali Kalaf, and then, however reluctantly, claiming the reward she had offered him. Now, it seemed, he was willing to dismiss her.

For just a fleeting moment, she wondered if it might not have been kinder of him if he had left her to Ali Kalaf's less than gentle hands.

Amity found it incredibly difficult to simply stand on deck and watch the men work. She was filled with undirected energy, an energy that was in no way appeased by the sight of the laborers leading the ox-drawn carts along the riverbank toward the storehouse, to then disappear in the distance.

She pictured the place in her mind. It was easy for

her to close her eyes and see it, a fringe of palm trees at the river's edge; beside it the ramshackle storehouse, quiet and deceptively unassuming in the afternoon sun, like an ancient dowager, belying the wealth of jewels she wore beneath the slightly worn disguise of an old shawl.

It wasn't her fault, she told herself by way of excuse, if she found herself incapable of standing idly by, waiting. With the laborers gone back to refill their carts, she didn't even have the luxury of watching others work. She felt as if she had to move.

Her thoughts were unpleasant, no matter where she directed them. Justin she could think of with only mild antipathy, tinged with the guilt of the wrong she'd done by accepting his proposal when she knew she did not love him. Ford she could think of only with a gut-wrenching misery. And she found she hated herself for the accusations that entered her mind when she thought of Kendrick. She felt that if she stayed there with only her thoughts, she would soon be mired in her own misery.

She tried to clear her mind, to rid it of the matters that only served to unsettle her, to make her realize how completely mistaken she had been about everything she'd done and everyone with whom she'd come into contact since coming to Egypt. But standing about on deck, staring off to the south and waiting, she found, was almost as unsettling. She found she expected to see a horde of horsemen with Ali Kalaf at their head bearing down upon her at any moment. That image, she realized, was more wearing than any physical labor she could remember ever having performed. She had to get away, even if it was only to have herself eventually sent back to the relative safety of the boat's deck.

She wandered down to the wharf and then started up to the roadway. She would burn off some of her excess energy walking to the storehouse, she told herself. And the exercise would keep her from thinking. Then, if Ford ordered her back, at least she would have the return walk to occupy her.

The roadway was still and quiet in the late-afternoon sunshine. She could just make out the sounds of the laborers' voices as they urged along the oxen, dim and muted with the distance. The sound seemed to punctuate the drone of the insects in the low growth by the river's edge and the cries of the birds that rested from the heat in the branches of the palms and acacias that grew thick and verdant in the moist soil there. It seemed almost like a springtime walk in the park, she thought, the sort she'd taken when she was a child, stopping along the way to pluck a handful of dandelions.

The thought amused her, enough so that she was distracted from the urgency of the situation, and she knelt to pluck a handful of wildflowers, small daisy-shaped blooms tinged blue and yellow.

She stood suddenly, ashamed at the frivolity that seemed to have gripped her, and started forward again, this time with a quickened pace. The noises around her, she thought, had somehow changed in content, and as she walked, she tried to determine just what it was that seemed different to her.

The drone of the insects was still there, as was the occasional bird cry, but she could no longer hear the *fellaheen* calling to the oxen. Perhaps, she told herself, they were already at the storehouse, already begun loading the crates of rifles. But still there was something else, something faint and yet undeniably present now that she set her mind to listen for it. Surely that underlying sound had not been there before, she told herself. Surely if it had she would have noticed it.

There was nothing that ought to alarm her, she told herself. The day was still unchanged, as warm and still as it had been. The dull noise, however, a sound like muted thunder far in the distance, seemed louder, more pressing. It had become incredibly disturbing to her. She

228

turned to the scarp, and hurriedly began to climb up it.

Something was wrong, she realized, and she meant to find out what it was.

There was a small, dark cloud clinging to the horizon at the edge of the flat landscape that held the fields of Gardiner's Ghenena. When Amity had scrambled up the side of the scarp, her eyes were immediately drawn to it. She stood staring at it, first wondering what could have caused it and then with dulled awareness. This cloud held an aura of misfortune about it, and the sight of it filled her with regret.

This could be no storm cloud, she knew. It was too small, and it hovered too close to the ground. In a land where there are no storms, she realized, dark clouds could not be harbingers of rain; they could only be evidence of fire.

Even as she watched, the cloud began to slowly rise, a dark, wisp-fingered spiral, reaching up to the heavens. And as she watched, she realized she knew there was only one thing in that direction that could burn with such ferocity, only one thing that could send such great plumes of smoke rising. It could only be Kendrick's house.

For a moment she was stunned at the thought of that beautiful house, and with it Kendrick's dreams, all being turned to ash.

Regret seeped into her, filling her, rooting her to the spot where she stood. All Kendrick's work, all the wrong that had begun by his trading rifles to Ali Kalaf, all of it was equal now, made the same by the whim of the flames. The product of honest work and dishonest alike, it all had met the same fate.

Perhaps she would have stood there, immobilized by shock and regret, had not there been another cloud on the horizon. This one was dun-colored, the shade of the soil, and it was, she soon realized, slowly growing larger. At first she was too frozen to think, to realize what this second cloud of dust could mean. But then it struck her, and the awareness filled her with terror.

That cloud of dust could only be kicked up by horses, many of them, and the fact that it was growing larger could only mean that those horses were approaching. Ford had been right, she realized. Ali Kalaf had come after his rifles just as Ford had said he would. But before he collected them, he had decided to show Kendrick just how dangerous it was to play with him. He had set fire to Kendrick's house as a demonstration of his power, to show Kendrick just how fruitless it was to try to outmaneuver him. Now, his ruthless message delivered, he was coming to take what he considered to be his.

She had to warn Ford, she realized, that Kalaf and his men were bearing down upon him. If the insurgents were to come upon him without warning, they would kill him and the others. Then they would take what they wanted. There was no thought in her mind that Kalaf might suddenly have developed a sense of pity or compassion for the Englishmen he considered his enemies. This was a holy war to him, a jihad, and in his mind a holy war absolved him from morality where it concerned those who opposed him or stood in his way.

Spurred by her terror, she turned and began to run. Somewhere along the edge of this rise, she knew, was the place where she had stood at Ford's side, where they had quarreled, where she had hidden to watch him break into the storehouse and search for the rifles. It seemed as though that had been years before, a lifetime before. She was a different person from the one she'd been that afternoon when she'd spied on Ford. Everything she had held to be secure and certain in her life that day had crumbled in the few days since. Everything she had believed, she realized, everything she had accepted as true she knew now to be as unstable and as shifting as the desert sand which edged Gardiner's Ghenena.

There was only one thing of which she knew she could be totally certain. If Ali Kalaf reached Ford before she did, Ford, Kendrick, and Justin would all be dead men.

The thought ate at her, seeming to echo in her mind as the sound of her own footfalls came to her ears: dead men, dead men, dead men. No matter that she knew Ford didn't want her, that she realized she would never share his life, still the thought that she might exist in a world where he no longer lived was inconceivable to her.

She ran, spurred by the thought that if she failed, the man she loved would die.

Amity ran. Her legs were aching and her heart had begun to feel as though it wanted to break free of her chest, thumping angrily against the wall of her ribs like a prisoner demanding to be released. The sound of it filled her ears so that even the gasping breath she drew did not drown out the sound of it. And still she ran.

She knew she was nearing the place where she had stood at Ford's side and stared down at the storehouse. She could see the tops of the stand of trees that surrounded the small building, just peeking up to the top of the scarp, and recognized the clump of bushes where she'd tied her horse before she'd watched Ford make his careful entrance to find the rifles he somehow had known would be hidden there. All that seemed a lifetime ago, but her memories were precise and clear. Only a few feet more, she told her thumping heart and her protesting thighs, only a few feet more and then she would be at the narrow path that led down the scarp and to the storehouse.

But something was wrong, she realized. The noises she

231

heard were far too loud to be caused only by the thick pounding of the blood in her veins, and the rumble that shook her seemed also to make the very ground beneath her feet tremble. Surely this was far too strong to be caused by the thudding beat of her heart.

She darted a glance behind her, and it was as though a nightmare had come to life. There were horses, everywhere, it seemed, filling her vision, huge, frothing horses bearing down upon her, their robed riders bent forward, urging the animals forward, eyes filled with a ferocity like none she had ever seen before.

She had no idea how they had gotten so close, how she had not heard them, or why she had not felt the pounding earth beneath her feet until that moment. But they were close, so close she could feel the heat the lathered animals generated, thick in the air. And leading them, bearing down upon her, his eyes intent on her, his bruised face contorted with his fury, was Ali Kalaf.

For a second Amity froze in terror. She knew immediately what Kalaf intended for Kendrick in return for the duplicity with which he had dealt with the matter of the rifles, and what he intended for Ford and her in payment for the injury and insult they had given him the night before.

And then his eyes found hers and she saw him smile, sure he had won.

His smile was pure evil. She could think of no other word to describe the expression, nothing else that could come close to conveying what she saw in his eyes. The sight of it finally managed to move her rooted feet. She turned and ran to the edge of the scarp, screaming a warning to Ford, wondering if he could hear her above the din the laborers made as they loaded the carts with the crates of rifles.

She felt movement behind her, and she willed herself to fall forward, over the edge of the scarp, sure the fall could not do her so great a harm as would Ali Kalaf if

232

he were to take her a second time. For a second she seemed suspended in the air, the inertia of her body fighting the tug of gravity that pulled her forward and down. And then she felt the flow of air pressing upward against her face as she began to fall.

But the movement ended quickly, punctuated by a sharp jerk as something caught her arm. The shock seemed to travel upward, to her shoulder, the pain following a moment later and stilling her cry before it had the chance to be uttered. Through the hurt she dully realized she was being lifted, that he had halted his mount just at the edge of the scarp and caught her before she could escape him.

There was the heat of horses around her, the scent of their sweat in her nostrils, the sharp contact of their hooves only inches away from where she was held suspended just above the ground. But mostly there was the blinding ache in her shoulder and the bite of his viselike grip where it held her. And there was the chilling sound of his laughter.

He pulled her up finally, perhaps deciding he had let her see enough of the terror the prospect of her own death beneath the horses' hooves generated, sure the prospect of being trampled made a sufficiently strong impression on her mind to keep her from fighting him. He deposited her facedown across the horse's back in front of him, letting his hand fall from her shoulder down her arm until he grasped her hand and held it at her back.

Amity found her face pressed against the horse's side, the rough hair biting into the skin of her cheek, the wet and stink of the animal's sweat almost gagging her. She tried to push herself away from it, but when she struggled, Kalaf pulled her arm sharply upward. Pain filled her arm and shoulder until she heard herself cry out.

233

Unable to fight him, she lay still and silent, gasping for breath as he lowered her arm and the pain slowly ebbed.

Satisfied she would be submissive, he lifted her to let her sit in front of him. Then he grasped her hair and pulled it, forcing her to face him.

His cheeks were swollen and bruised she saw, and there was a cut above his left eye, jagged and lined with the dark-rust color of dried blood. She realized this was the result of the pummeling Ford had given him just as she knew it was not nearly the measure of the real injury he had sustained, the blow to his ego and his confidence, his self-esteem.

"I owe you a debt, woman," he hissed at her through a tight jaw, his tone like the promise of a painful death. "First I pay your companions, and then I will deal with you."

He raised his arm.

"Hinak," he shouted to his men, pointing to the storehouse huddled in the grove of trees below.

Obediently, they urged their horses to the edge of the scarp, and then slowly downward. Like an angry wave, they started down the hillside in search of death.

Chapter Thirteen

Ford was not *really* sure he had heard anything. But it seemed to him there had been a sound like a woman's cry, and he could not dismiss it. Probably just a bird, he told himself even as he started toward the storehouse door and his thoughts suddenly filled with the image of Amity in Kalaf's less than kind hands.

This is foolish, he told himself. After all, Amity was safely tucked up on Justin's boat and there was no need to worry about her. But the sound was repeated, and he found he could not keep himself from leaving the storehouse and looking up to the scarp.

What he saw shattered him.

First there was the vision of Amity, standing at the edge of the scarp and shouting, waving her arms wildly. Then it seemed as if she were about to fling herself over the steep incline. He started forward, uselessly he knew, but unable to keep himself from running forward to reach her, as if he could somehow lift his arms up and catch her.

But she did not fall.

Instead, he saw the white-robed horseman draw up beside her and reach forward to grasp her. And Ford knew then what it was she was fleeing, of what it was her cry had been intended to warn him. Although he could not see the face of the robed man who pulled her back and away from the slope, he knew it could only be Ali Kalaf.

He shouted out to Justin and Kendrick, and started to run forward, scrambling up the incline, thinking only that he had to get to Amity, that he must somehow get her away from Kalaf. Then he saw the horses as they drew up to the edge of the scarp, a long line of them, more than he could count. They urged the horses forward, over the edge, slowly making their way downward. There were enough of them to force some measure of sanity on him. He turned and ran back to the storehouse.

If he'd had time to think of anything save Amity, to see anything except for the image of Amity being pulled up onto Kalaf's horse, he would have noticed that the laborers had dropped the crates they had been carrying, letting them fall open on the ground in their fright; he would have seen them run off as though pursued by devils, fully aware of who it was who approached, and what it was he intended. They scattered like leaves in the fall, disappearing into the undergrowth.

But Ford had other matters to occupy him. He darted into the storehouse, grabbing up one of the fallen rifles as he entered.

Kendrick looked up at him, startled.

"What is it?" he asked.

"Your friend Kalaf is out there," Ford told him as he used the butt of the rifle to break open the cover of a crate of ammunition. "And somehow he got his hands on Amity."

Kendrick darted a disbelieving glance at Justin, then turned back to Ford.

"But how? Why?"

"Why do you think?" Ford shouted back at him, impatient, in no mood to answer questions. "He's come for his damned rifles." He scooped up a handful of the bullets and began loading the rifle. "And to get back at me for having stolen Amity away from him, right under his nose." He turned steely eyes to Kendrick. "I don't think he'll be in the mood to talk."

"What do we do?" Kendrick demanded.

Ford shook his head, thinking there was little any of them could do save keep the rifles from Kalaf's hands. "You two can try to get out of here. I intend to make sure he doesn't get his hands on these rifles," he replied.

The rifle he'd appropriated was loaded now, and he set it down beside the broken crate. He set about pulling the other crates of ammunition to the center of the room, pushing them together in a large heap. He paid no attention to the movement at the door, assuming Kendrick and Justin were doing as he had told them, making an attempt to get away.

When he had pulled the crates of ammunition together, he pulled off his shirt and placed it on the crate he had broken open. It would make a fuse of sorts, perhaps allow him enough time to get out of the storehouse and make an attempt to save Amity. He silently cursed Justin and Kendrick, at that moment hating them both for having brought her there, for having placed her in danger that was of their making.

He was reaching for the lantern that had been left near the door when he realized that Kendrick was still there. He hesitated for a moment.

"If you don't get out of here now, there won't be another chance," he told his uncle.

Kendrick ignored his words. "You're going to set it on fire, aren't you?" he asked Ford as he watched him grope for the box of matches left near the lantern. "You're going to blow it all up."

"Can you think of any other way?" Ford asked him angrily.

Kendrick shook his head. "No, I can't."

237

"Get out of here," Ford told him, his tone sharp. "There's no need for both of us to blow ourselves to kingdom come."

"No, there isn't." Kendrick spoke softly now, listening for the noises outside, the cries and sounds of horses' hooves which were close now, and coming even closer. "Which means you had better get out of here before it's too late."

Ford shook his head. "This is my responsibility," he replied.

Kendrick reached out his hand to grasp Ford's arm. "No, it's not," he replied. "I started all this. At least let me redeem myself by finishing it honorably." He stared at Ford, his eyes searching his nephew's, punctuating his words with the cold, level stare that attested to the certainty of his logic. "Besides, you have to get Amity away from him somehow. You know what he'll do to her." The stare melted now, and turned pleading. "Don't let me die with that on my conscience as well, Ford."

For a moment Ford hesitated. Then, realizing the older man had his reasons, and they had as much value as his own, he nodded. He reached for another handful of bullets, then for the rifle he'd set on the ground.

"Pour the oil from the lantern on the shirt and then set fire to it," he instructed. "It should buy you a few moments to try to get out if you can. Not long, though, so run like hell. That heap will go up with a bang the devil would admire once it gets hot enough."

He waited until Kendrick had nodded, indicating he understood. Then he started to the door.

The horsemen were only a few hundred feet from the storehouse now. Ford leaped from the doorway, racing to the cover of the underbrush and then jumping and rolling as he landed. All around him he heard the sharp

238

report of bullets, saw the cascades of dirt they lifted around him.

Kalaf's men seemed less interested in him, however, than they were in the rifles they'd come to collect. By the time Ford had managed to find some shelter in the undergrowth, the shooting ceased. The horsemen seemed to have turned their attention to more pressing matters, letting him disappear amidst the dense growth.

Ford peered out carefully and saw Kalaf raise a hand to the men behind him. The Arab leader's followers assembled themselves into some sort of unruly order at his sign, moving forward slowly now, toward the quiet storehouse.

With his free hand, Kalaf held tight to Amity. He stared at the broken crates littering the area in front of the storehouse and at the carts that had been in the process of being loaded with the rifles.

"Gardiner!" he shouted, obviously having decided Kendrick was still nearby. "Gardiner, I have your woman. If you don't want to watch me slit her throat here and now, show yourself."

His hand moved to his belt, retrieving the knife that was sheathed there, and brought it to the side of Amity's neck. She tried to pull back, trembling with fear as she felt the heat of the metal near her skin, but he held her firmly, keeping her close to him.

"Let her be, Kalaf," Ford shouted from the cover of the undergrowth. "I have a rifle aimed at your head. Harm her and you're a dead man."

Kalaf smiled humorlessly. "I think that is the voice of my blue-eyed convert come to lead me to my rifles," he said. "You lied to me. You meant only to steal from me. But I have decided to forgive you your transgression, because you did lead me to my rifles after all. My mercy is limited, however. Have you come to steal from me once again? What lies do you have to tell me now?"

239

As he spoke, Kalaf peered into the undergrowth, searching for movement, for something that would show him where Ford was hidden.

"No lies," Ford replied. "Your rifles are here. You can take them and be damned. Just set the woman free."

Ford realized he was wondering how much time he had, whether Kendrick had already set the fire that would cause the ammunition to explode. He had to fight to keep the sense of urgency he felt from becoming apparent in his tone, afraid he might warn Kalaf away and yet, in a way, hoping he would if that were the only way to keep Amity safe.

"I think I do not trust a man who tells me he points a rifle at my heart when he speaks," Kalaf told him slowly. "Under the circumstances, I think even you could not blame me."

"Between your eyes, Kalaf," Ford responded. "You have no heart. And I do not trust a man who uses a woman's life to blackmail another man. Let her go and I will give you whatever proof you need."

"My men could cut you down. I have but to give them the word," Kalaf hissed at him.

"Not before I put one bullet between your eyes," Ford said without sign of emotion. "Give the order to fire and I will most happily place a bullet of my own where not even Allah's protection can keep you from the grave."

Ford had Kalaf at an impasse and he knew it. His finger grew tight on the rifle's trigger. He was not about to lose his advantage.

"Where is Gardiner?" Kalaf demanded suddenly, as though he had momentarily forgotten about Kendrick's existence and only then reminded himself of it. "It is with Gardiner that I have my business."

"Here I am, Kalaf," Kendrick answered before Ford had a chance to reply. He opened the storehouse door

240

and slowly moved forward. "Your rifles are there," he said, motioning behind him. He held his hands in tight fists as if he were afraid to release them lest they betray him. "Now release my son's bride."

Ford felt a sick wave of disappointment fill him. What a fool he'd been to trust Kendrick's word, to believe he would destroy the arms. Not that he could blame him entirely. The rifles were the only coin Kendrick had to trade for Amity's life. Ford was not sure he would not have done the same thing given the circumstances. Still, he could not free himself of the suspicion that Kalaf fully intended to kill them all once he had what he wanted, and the rifles, in turn, would be used to take countless more English lives.

"Perhaps I should see for myself, Englishman," Kalaf told him. "I have learned to doubt your word."

"It is no worse than yours," Kendrick told him. "You sneak like a thief into my house, kill my servant, steal a woman to use as hostage. You call these acts honorable?"

Kalaf sneered. "Naseem was not your servant, Englishman, but mine. And he died for my cause, for the glory of Allah. He will find his reward in paradise."

Kalaf seemed to be pleased by the dismay Kendrick showed at this revelation, that Naseem had been a spy in his home. The Arab smiled once again, this time with some show of enjoyment. He did, however, withdraw the blade from where he had been holding it near Amity's throat. Then he lowered her to the ground and pushed her toward the place where Kendrick stood.

"You may have her for now, Englishman. Know that if it pleases me, I can take her from you whenever I choose." There was something about his expression that seemed to imply he intended to do just that when he had tended to other, more pressing, matters.

Kalaf slid from his mount as Amity ran to Kendrick's

241

arms. He motioned to one of his men, and told him to keep watch on the two of them. Obedient, the man moved his rifle from where he'd held it aimed at the place in the undergrowth where Ford had disappeared, repositioning it so that it was pointed toward Amity and Kendrick.

But Kendrick ignored the threat, turning his back on the rifle and pulling Amity so that he blocked her from it.

"Run," he whispered to her, his tone sharp with urgency as he watched Kalaf approach the storehouse door.

She didn't understand. She shook her head. "What . . ."

"Do it," he told her, and pushed her forward, toward the undergrowth where Ford had hidden himself.

She ran, too frightened to stop even when she heard the rifle shot. She threw herself into the undergrowth, landing roughly, scraping her hands and cutting her cheek on the rough edges of the fronds. All she could do was scramble forward, aware of the noise behind her, of Kendrick's cry and Kalaf's men starting forward after her.

Suddenly there was a hand on her arm, Ford's hand, pulling her roughly forward and up the scarp.

And then the earth seemed to give way beneath her, and the air was filled with searing heat and a deafening noise.

She found herself thrown on the ground, and there was a heavy weight on her. Momentarily dazed, she didn't realize it was Ford, didn't realize he had placed himself between her and the blast and so taken the brunt of the impact. All she knew was that the air around her seemed to burn, and each breath she drew

242

seared her lungs.

"Up, Amity."

Ford had rolled off her and was standing now, pulling her to her feet. She felt herself tottering unsteadily, felt his hands as he half carried, half dragged her farther up the scarp. He didn't stop until they had escaped the heat of the fire that raged below.

Amity fell to the ground when he released her arm, sitting clumsily. She felt as though she would never be able to fill her lungs with enough air, never be able to breathe without feeling the burning deep inside her chest. But slowly the hurt began to ease.

She looked up at Ford. There was a long, ugly gash on his temple, above his right eye. He absently wiped his arm at it, pushing away the warm seep of richly red blood before it could reach his eye. The blood caught on his naked arm, coating the skin and the hairs there, an ugly, long crimson smear. But Ford seemed unconcerned with the injury or with the grisly sight of his own blood. Instead, he was staring downward.

Below, there was havoc. Flames were shooting upward from the remains of the storehouse, and bodies, both human and equine, littered the ground. Those few of Kalaf's men who had not been seriously hurt were taking flight, moving south on the path by the river.

"Stay here," he ordered her, and started to move away.

She reached up to him and grasped his hand.

"You're not going back down there?" she demanded. She tightened her hold on him, realizing that that was precisely what he intended to do.

"I can't just leave Kendrick down there. I have to know if he's alive or not," Ford told her as he gently pried her fingers loose from his.

She sat, totally numb with shock, and watched him make his way back down the scarp. Then she stood and started after him, not really sure what it was she was doing, only knowing that she could not sit idly and watch him.

She wasn't walking into a fire, she knew she would not draw that close, but still her senses told her otherwise. The air pressed against her skin, and it felt as though she were wading through boiling oil. She put her arm to cover her mouth and nose, trying vainly to keep the burning heat outside her, terrified to feel herself once again drawing the heat into her lungs. The air shimmered around her. Nothing seemed real.

She tried to keep her eyes firmly set on Ford's back, not wanting to allow herself to glimpse the horror of burned and thrashing men and animals that gave the scene the aura of hell. But the sound of terrified cries drew her attention as much as she fought to control them. And she filled with revulsion at what she saw.

She had nearly reached the place where she and Ford had fallen. The undergrowth was crushed there, but not burned, and there were a few scattered drops of red — blood from her scratches and the gash on Ford's temple. She paused and stared at the red droplets, watched them as they were turned a dull rust color by the heat of the fire below.

When she looked back to find Ford, she found him starting once more up the incline. She felt almost grateful to know that she need not force herself farther toward the heat of the fire, until she saw the limp and burnt thing he pulled along with him.

It was Kendrick, she knew, and still the realization came as a shock to her, to see, even from the distance, the charred skin on the side of his face, the way his arms and legs hung limp and useless in Ford's arms, the dark-red blood that seeped from the bullet hole in his chest.

She fought against the sickening feeling that filled her, and forced herself forward to meet Ford, to help him pull Kendrick up the incline and away from the fire.

It was torturous going. Kendrick moaned with pain, but the sounds seemed to Amity's ears more those of a wounded animal than of a man. She recalled the camel she had seen the day Justin had taken her to the souk, remembered the sounds the animal had made, its agonized cries as it was butchered while it was still alive. She heard the same anguish in Kendrick's cries of pain.

When finally Ford decided they were far enough from the blaze, he laid Kendrick on the ground as gently as he could. Amity knelt at his side, not quite knowing what it was she felt at that moment. She was filled with pity for Kendrick, and yet she was forced to fight her revulsion for the sight and smell of his burnt flesh.

She looked up at Ford.

"What shall we do?" she asked him. "A doctor . . ."

Ford shook his head. "There's no doctor close enough," he told her softly. "Even if there were, I doubt anything could be done."

She forced herself to stare at Kendrick, grateful that despite the moans, he seemed senseless, still, and with his eyes closed. The gratitude vanished when she saw his hand move.

"Ford?"

Kendrick's voice sounded like that of a ghost, parched and agonized as though he had already entered hell. Amity gasped when she heard it, realizing that he had been aware through the torture of being moved, that his eyes remained closed only because the charred eyelids refused to be moved.

"I'm here, Uncle," Ford whispered. He moved himself closer, lowering his head to Kendrick's lips to hear.

"Amity?" Kendrick asked. "Did you get her away?"

He tried to reach up, to grasp Ford in the urgency of his need to know she was safe. His movement was too much for him. He gasped in pain, and fell back.

"I'm safe," Amity murmured, then cringed as she heard him groan once again in agony.

Kendrick's lips moved slightly, into a rictus of a smile. "Thank God," he breathed, and then groaned in pain again, as though the effort of those two words had cost him dearly.

Amity started to reach for his hand, then drew back, her own hands shaking, afraid the contact would only hurt him more.

"Don't move," she pleaded. "Don't talk."

"Nothing left to save," he told her with sudden force. For a moment he rested, and Amity heard the rattle of his inhalation followed by a painful gasp as the breath was expelled. After several breaths, though, he seemed to have reclaimed some measure of strength, or perhaps it was simply willpower, the will of the dying. He tried to push himself forward.

"Take care of Justin," he said slowly. "He needs someone."

Justin. Amity realized she hadn't so much as given him a thought since the horror had begun. She leaned forward to Kendrick.

"I will," she murmured.

She was weeping, she realized, weeping silent, remorse-filled tears knowing that what he asked of her was impossible, that in trying to comfort him she was forced to lie.

"Ford?"

"Lie still, Uncle."

But Kendrick would not. "The necklace, Ford," he rasped, his voice rising in his determination. "I beg you." Once again there was the rattle of painfully drawn breath. "Forgive me."

Amity turned to stare at Ford's tortured face. Somehow she knew what it was Kendrick was trying to say. Somehow she knew that Ford did, too.

"There is no need, Uncle," he replied gently.

"*I* stole it," Kendrick insisted, his words coming singly now, each produced with obvious pain, each preceded by a single painful gasp of breath. "I never meant to hurt you."

"It doesn't matter any more, Uncle," Ford told him, his voice tight with emotion.

"I regret . . ."

Kendrick never finished the sentence. His words trailed off into the rattle of another breath, a rattle that grew louder, then, suddenly, ceased.

Amity gasped, uselessly fighting back the tears. Ford put his arm around her and pulled her close to his chest.

"He knew he would be shot. When he pushed you into the undergrowth toward me, he knew they would kill him. And he knew the explosion was coming to finish what Kalaf's men would do to him. It was almost as if he wanted to die."

Amity heard Ford's words as a deep rumble from inside his chest. They were hardly comforting to her. Despite her own guilty relief in having somehow survived, it still brought her pain to know that Kendrick had traded his life for hers. She tried to block out the words, to keep herself from listening, but they droned mercilessly on.

"He must have rigged a fuse somehow, to give us time. It was almost as if he willed Kalaf forward, into the storehouse, knowing the explosion would kill him. And he seemed satisfied with that, with his own death, as long as I got us both away."

She pulled away from him, turning her face up to his, her expression wild.

"Stop it," she cried. "He's dead. Isn't that enough?"

He put his hand to her cheek, and stared into her eyes. She realized he could see the guilt in her, and that

247

seemed almost as painful to her as the knowledge that Kendrick had died for her.

"You hate it, that he died, that he chose your life over his," he told her softly.

She nodded, and tried to turn away, but his hand drew her cheek back until she was once more staring into his eyes.

"Listen to me, Amity," he said evenly. "You have to learn to accept this now, or it will haunt you for the rest of your life. Believe me, I know. I was with Gordon at Khartoum. Two weeks before the final assault I was sent downriver with a boatload of civilians, women and children mostly. The Mahdi had given them safe passage, but as soon as we were away from the protection of the guns mounted on the city walls, his men opened fire on us from the riverbank. We managed to get away, but there were deaths—six of the women and two children. And I was wounded, too badly wounded to go back to Khartoum once I had gotten the survivors to Cairo."

"You wanted to go?" she asked. "Even knowing there would be no reinforcements for Gordon?"

He nodded. "I felt as though I had been singled out to live, when the men I had served with for the previous three years seemed certain to die. And they did. Every one of them was slaughtered along with Gordon. That seemed impossibly unfair to me, that they should all die and yet I was still alive. I was certainly no more worthy than the rest of them. I felt as you do now for a long, long time, ashamed to be glad I was still alive, angry with the providence that had spared me. I think there's no greater guilt than that, knowing you were simply lucky enough to survive."

Amity swallowed, and her eyes darted to Kendrick's still body. Then she turned back to face Ford, and shook her head, as though she were rejecting everything he had told her.

"It wasn't simply luck," she whispered.

"No," Ford agreed. "But Ali Kalaf did this, not you. If you must place guilt, at least place it where it belongs, with Kalaf."

The mention of Kalaf brought a shudder from Amity. She forced back the tears.

"Kalaf's dead?" she asked.

He nodded. "I saw what was left of him down there," he said. "He was one of the luckier ones. There's no possibility he survived the explosion long enough to have felt the fire before he died."

She turned to stare downward, to the fire that was starting to wane now, burning itself out, and the charred and blackened remains of Kalaf and his men. The sight brought back the sense of revulsion, the sick feeling in her stomach.

Nothing, she told herself, nothing in her life would ever compete with the events of the previous hour for sheer horror. She tried to look away, not to think of what had happened, but even the dry heaving of her empty stomach could not force her eyes away. This is what hell is like, she thought, staring at the charred things that once had been human beings, aware of the thick odor of the burnt flesh filling her nostrils.

Still, despite the horror and the revulsion, she realized the feeling of guilt was easing now. Perhaps Ford was right. Perhaps there was nothing wrong in being glad to have survived.

They sat in silence for a while, staring into the flames, not yet ready to return their attention to Kendrick's dead body. But finally Ford put his hand to Amity's arm.

She turned, finally, to face him. "Do you hate him?" she asked him softly.

He seemed puzzled by her question. "Hate him?"

"For what he did to you. For letting you suffer for the

249

theft he committed."

All those years, she thought, Ford had been branded a thief. And Kendrick, hiding his guilt behind a curtain of kindness, of warmth, had allowed another man to bear the painful fruit of his crime. Despite it all, she could not shake the desire she felt to think of Kendrick as a good man. Somehow she knew he had suffered for the pain he had caused Ford. If only he had been strong enough to take the responsibility of his own actions. If only he had loved his nephew a little more than he had loved his land.

Ford shook his head. "He had his reasons. I've managed to survive. And I will continue to survive."

"But it's over now," she said, surprised at the sound of resignation she heard in his voice. "You can go back to England."

He shook his head. "Words don't mean much, Amity. Especially when the man who spoke them is dead."

"But I heard him. We both heard him. He cleared your name."

"And none of it matters. Without concrete proof, I'm still a thief."

"I don't understand," she murmured, wanting to, wanting him to finally tell her what had happened to him, to tell her everything he had held away from her, to explain about the theft that had caused him to flee to Egypt an outcast.

He only shook his head once more. "My father's dead now, and my grandmother. And now it would seem Kendrick has taken my only chance at redeeming my honor with him to his grave," he said. His tone had turned bitter. He stared down at the still body. "Funny, I never thought it was him. Justin, perhaps. But not Kendrick."

There was bitterness in his words, and when her eyes found his, he turned away as though he could not bear to see the compassion in them.

"We'd better find Justin," he told her dully.

She nodded, and stood when he did, then watched him lift Kendrick's body in his arms.

Justin was sitting on the ground, staring at the ashes of what had once been his father's house. He seemed numb, as though he could not believe what had happened to him, as though it were inconceivable to him to accept the fact that he could have suffered such a loss.

He didn't turn when he heard Ford and Amity on the road behind him, didn't even move until Amity put her hand to his shoulder.

"Justin, I'm sorry."

The words seemed empty and meaningless to her, but he raised his head to her, showing her eyes filled with misery. Then he turned and stared for a moment at the spot where Ford placed his father's body on the grass beside him.

His body seemed to stiffen and then collapse as he realized that Kendrick was dead. Then he lurched forward to Amity, reaching his hands out to her. When she made no move, neither one of welcome nor rejection, he put his arms around her legs and buried his face against the rough fabric of the *aba* she still wore.

"It's gone, Amity," he moaned. "Everything is gone. I have only you now."

His words, the way he clung to her, it all chased away the surge of pity she had felt for him when she'd come up and seen him sitting staring numbly at the ruins of his father's house. If he had turned to Kendrick's body and showed some sign of pain at his father's death, the pity, she knew, would return. But he didn't. Instead, he clung to her to like a disappointed child, bemoaning all those things Kalaf's fire had taken from him, as though she might have the power to turn the ashes back into that beautiful house, as though she could restore to him the hundred thousand pounds the loss of the rifles and ammunition had caused him to suffer.

Quite simply, his self-pity disgusted her.

But still she was unable to pull herself away from him. This weakness of his, it was a trap to her, just as Kendrick's request that she stay with him had been a trap. She'd lied to Kendrick to ease his death; even now she realized she was more than prepared to face the specter of his ghost should it choose to reprove her for that lie. But what lie could she tell Justin, she wondered, what assurances could she give him, when she knew he would try to hold her to her word? She looked up at Ford, her eyes silently beseeching him to come to her aid.

"We can't just sit here, Justin," Ford said finally. "We have to send for the authorities at Tell ElAmarna. It's a charnel house down by the river."

Justin looked up at him for a moment and a smile edged at the corners of his lips.

"Authorities?" he asked. "My father and I are the authorities at Tell ElAmarna."

"You're a fool," Ford hissed at him. "The khedive's spies have sent him word that Ali Kalaf was nearby, that he was buying arms from someone nearby. He has sent his people here to investigate. Don't you understand? Kendrick would have been found out sooner or later. It would be better if you went to them now rather than waiting for them to come to you. Besides, the bodies of Ali Kalaf and his men are down there. They will have to be dealt with."

Justin nodded. Ford's words seemed to come as no surprise to him.

"Kendrick must be buried," Ford continued, his words heavy now with the reluctance he so obviously felt. "And then you have some decisions to make, you and

252

Amity."

Amity could only stare at him, shocked by his words, by the way he could so easily link her life to Justin's. Somehow everything that had happened in the previous days had made her feel a part of him. Despite the fact that she had told herself she was resigned to his abandonment, the realization had not really hit her until that moment, not until she had heard him tie her to Justin with a few simple words.

Before Kalaf had taken her, she had decided to leave Justin and Gardiner's Ghenena. Her flight had begun a series of events that left her numb with horror. She was no longer sure she had the strength to try to do it again.

She was, she realized, lost. And there was no one to whom she could turn to help her find her way.

Chapter Fourteen

It pained Amity that the boat ride to Cairo provided her with little opportunity to be alone. It would have been much easier for her, she thought, if she could simply have avoided both Justin and Ford completely on the journey downriver. Although Ford seemed willing enough to leave her to her own company, in fact avoiding her whenever possible to a point just short of rudeness, Justin was far less obliging.

He must have ensconced himself by her cabin door, she decided, aware that she must eventually show herself. When the afternoon heat drove her from the confines of her cabin, he was standing there, waiting for her, staring at her with the same mournful eyes with which he'd considered the ashes of what had once been his home, with which he'd stared at the hastily prepared grave in which they'd been forced by the heat to bury Kendrick.

The look made her feel guilty, as though her desertion of him were a final blow he did not deserve to be dealt. She almost wished he'd return to the sort of imperious manner with which he'd treated her when they first arrived at Gardiner's Ghenena. At least that way she could have consoled her feelings of guilt by telling herself he was immune to hurt. Instead, faced with his misery, she found herself pitying and despising him all at the same time, feelings that were only made worse by the knowledge that she'd gotten herself in the situation by accepting his proposal in the first place.

"Amity, please, can we talk?"

He reached out for her, his long fingers suddenly unsteady as they grasped her arm.

She nodded and bowed her head in lieu of an answer, letting him lead her to where a bench had been placed along the boat's stern. She moved to his side silently, dreading the prospect more than she could have thought possible, knowing what it was he intended to say to her.

As she settled herself on the bench where he pointed and waited patiently while he sat beside her, she told herself she must be strong or she would be lost to him and the sudden needs she knew he would press upon her. She searched within herself, hoping to find her courage.

"When you were missing, I found your note . . ." he began slowly. "The one saying you were leaving, that you wrote before Kalaf kidnapped you."

There was a lump in her throat now. She wondered why it had been so much easier to write the words, why she had felt so much more certain of herself when she had not been forced to face him. Now she would have to say them to him, face-to-face, knowing how much he'd lost in those past few days. She felt like an impossible shrew and, even more, a coward. Why couldn't he rail at her, she wondered? Why did he have to sit there and stare at her with that lost, hurt expression in his eyes?

"It wasn't easy, Justin," she murmured, "writing it. But it was right." She grew a bit more determined. "It was right for both of us."

"I was hoping you'd changed your mind," he told her as he reached for her hand. She let him take it, let it lie limply in his. "So much has happened since then. We both need some time to think. Even Ford said as much, that we have decisions to make."

She looked up, tearing her glance from his. She was determined to hold herself apart and not give in to the pity she could not help feeling for him. By mentioning Ford, he was as much as telling her that she need not expect any intervention from him, as though they had already decided the matter between them. She wondered if it was intentional cruelty on his part, hoping to hurt her before she had the chance to hurt him, or if he was simply trying to tell her, if she was not already aware of the fact, that he was her only alternative.

Damn them both, she thought.

She saw Ford standing on the far side of the deck, leaning over the rail and staring at the riverbank. She let her eyes settle and rest on his lank form, wishing she could be like him, wishing she could lead her life with the same cold determination with which he seemed to pursue his.

"More talk won't change anything, Justin," she replied finally. "And dragging things on will only make it worse later. I regret the hurt I've given you, I honestly do. But I can't change it much as I might want to."

He followed her glance to where it rested on Ford.

"It's because of him, isn't it?" he asked, suddenly intent. "You've fallen in love with him?"

She felt a knot in her stomach as she heard the words and knew they were the truth. She *was* in love with Ford, and a useless, painful love it was proving to be, one that would lead nowhere, that would only serve to poison whatever chance she might have had for happiness for the rest of her life.

She looked down to where her hand was sandwiched between his, then to her lap, to the flowered dimity of the clean frock in which she'd dressed herself. It had seemed so good to her, the luxury of a long bath and clean clothes, as though she had been denied those things for months, not days. She wondered why the feeling of being scrubbed and fresh had suddenly faded. Justin's accusation made her feel dirty.

"He has nothing to do with it," she said softly, wishing her words were true.

"Did you lie with him?" Justin demanded sharply. "Did you thank him for his daring rescue by giving him the freedom of your precious body?"

His tone had turned mean, an angry hiss, and he leaned forward to her until his face was close to hers. She could smell his breath, the scent of his body, acrid and bitter with his anger and with the intensity of his jealousy.

His fingers were pressing on her hand now, holding it with enough firmness to make her fingers begin to grow numb. She tried to pull it away, but he refused to release her.

"Stop it, Justin," she cried softly, finally returning her glance to meet his. "You're hurting me."

He was, she realized, hurting her more than he knew, his words more painful than the bite of his fingers into hers. She put her free hand to his, trying to pry his fingers from hers, wanting only for him to release her and let her flee from him, from his demands for her pity. She felt the sting of tears in her eyes.

And he saw them. It was only then, when he realized there was liquid edging her eyes, that he seemed to realize his fingers were biting into hers. He released his hold of her hand.

"I'm sorry, Amity," he told her, raising his hand to her cheek, intending to wipe away the drops should they spill. "I don't know what I'm doing. The last thing I ever wanted is to hurt you."

She pulled her hand away, then jerked her head back from his touch. His fingers seemed to burn her, as if they dripped acid onto her skin.

"If that's true, Justin," she cried, "then let me go. Don't make it harder."

She stood. Without turning to offer him another glance, she fled from him.

He watched as she ran along the deck toward her cabin. Then he looked down to his hands and remembered the feel of her skin, soft against his fingertips.

"I won't lose you, too," he whispered aloud, as though she were still sitting there beside him. "I won't let go so easily as that." His expression grew determined, and when he looked up and once again saw Ford leaning against the rail, his eyes filled with hatred. "If not me," he finished with sudden determination, "no one will have you."

Ford was the first to disembark when they reached Cairo. He left as soon as the boat was tied up to the pier.

"I think I should report to General Stuart as soon as possible," he told her just before he left. "The news of Ali Kalaf's death should not be unwelcome to him. It should herald some easing of tensions to the south."

"Then you must be quite pleased with yourself," she replied, and offered him a prim, mirthless smile. "You will, no doubt, be decorated for a job well done."

She was bitter, she realized, bitter that all he seemed to care about was meeting his expectations of what he considered was his duty, pleasing his military masters. He had done his job, and done it well. Going after her, that had been nothing more than his duty, all the same with destroying the storehouse and its precious contents of rifles. And now, with Ali Kalaf dead, the uprising would soon peter out, its momentum lost without its leader. The fact that Kendrick was also dead and Justin had been ruined must be nothing more than justifiable losses in his eyes, especially in view of that greater good, justifiable, at least to Ford and the Army.

"I'll visit you soon," he offered as though he were seeking to mitigate his defection, the fact that he was leaving her to Justin.

"Certainly," she agreed without enthusiasm. "It's only fitting that we say a formal good-bye before I leave Egypt."

His expression showed surprise at that revelation, but he said nothing, just nodded to Justin and turned away to make his way down the gangway and to the pier.

Justin, however, was certainly interested in this sudden revelation of her intentions.

"You can't mean it," he told her. "You don't really intend to leave Egypt?"

"I don't see that I have many alternatives," she told him.

"You could stay here, with me," he said, his tone forceful, more so than she had heard it since before Kendrick's death.

She fought the temptation to anger. "I thought we'd been over all that, Justin," she told him.

"I'll try, Amity," he told her. He put his hand to her shoulders and turned her to face him, despite the reluctance she showed in complying. "I won't ever bring up the subject of you and Ford, I'll never ask you again. I only know I'm not prepared to lose you, not now, not after I've lost everything else."

She could only close her eyes and force away the image of his, the pleading she could not ignore in them, the pained, furtively needy way his eyes held hers. She shook her head slowly.

"Please don't ask, Justin. You just make it harder."

He held her a moment longer, but when she refused to open her eyes again, when she made it apparent to him that she would not do as he seemed to want her to do, even if it was only pity that forced her, he finally released his hold on her.

Amity had only the haziest recollection of the events that led her from the piers to her sister's house. She had no memory whatsoever of leaving the boat or moving along the pier. The carriage ride was only a blurred image of houses and storefronts moving past her window.

It was only when she stood at the door to the embassy that she allowed herself to focus sharply on her surroundings. It would not be easy for her here, either, she knew. As much as she might want to find a comfortable shoulder on which to shed some tears and release the painful tension that had been building within her since she'd left Gardiner's Ghenena, she knew none would be forthcoming in this house. Both Beatrice and Charles had made her realize in their own way that she could never afford to be anything less than wary in their home.

Traps seemed to have been placed in her path, and at every step she ventured, she felt threatened that she might be swallowed by one.

Beatrice took no pains to hide the fact that she was not at all pleased to see her sister once more in her parlor. She was even less pleased at the news of the broken engagement.

"It would seem the chickens have come home to roost," she said sharply when Amity had finished with her revelation. "I'm afraid you'll be disappointed, however. The rooster is off in Alexandria, meeting with his chief resident."

Amity colored at her tone and the implication of her words, in her sister's expectation that she would be willing to seduce Charles. She found herself staring at Beatrice with different eyes than those that had seen her in the past, eyes suddenly jaded with lost innocence. For the first time she could see crow's-feet edging Beatrice's eyes and wrinkles at the corners of her mouth; for the first time she noticed the dissatisfied way her sister pursed her lips and her greedily appraising glance. She found herself puzzled and surprised by the sudden clarity of her observations, but still she could not help but wonder why the sister she had once idolized no longer seemed so perfectly beautiful to her.

"I don't intend to impose upon your hospitality very long, Beatrice. As soon as arrangements can be made, I intend to return to Boston." She smiled grimly. "And as for Charles, you may certainly consider yourself free of any threat from me. I have not now, nor have I ever had any designs on your husband."

Now it was Beatrice's turn to be surprised. She raised an arched brow. "I would have thought, now that you've lost your chance with Justin Gardiner, Charles would be more, not less, interesting to you," she said, her hand reaching to the glass on the table beside her chair and lifting it. "After all," she added, her tone thick with sarcasm, "he certainly isn't immune to your sweet young charms."

She kept her eyes on Amity as she drank, a healthy swallow. It was only then that Amity realized the contents of the glass were dark amber in color. She moved close enough to Beatrice to catch the scent of the liquor.

Amity wondered why she felt so shocked. After all, it was no longer a surprise to her to realize Beatrice's marriage was not the perfect union she had once considered it. But Beatrice drinking—that seemed so, well . . . so unladylike, an unthinkable lapse in a woman who was as caught up in appearances as Beatrice had always seemed to be.

She felt herself fill with regret. She moved forward, to

kneel beside Beatrice's chair. This was the last thing she wanted, to be at odds with her sister. And the knowledge that Beatrice's unhappiness had led her to seek solace from a bottle only brought home Amity's desire to cling to her, to find once more the feeling between them that had somehow been lost.

"Please, Bea," she begged softly. "Let's not argue. Can't we be friends again? I need a friend just now, and I think you might, too."

But Beatrice pushed her offered hand aside, standing and leaving Amity kneeling beside an empty chair. She crossed the room, then turned on her heel to glare at Amity.

"You'll have to find whatever it is you need elsewhere," she snarled. "As for me, I don't need anything, certainly nothing you can give me. If you'd wanted to be my friend, my loving sister, you never would have tried to seduce my husband."

Faced by Beatrice's anger, Amity felt herself returned to that night, found herself staring up at her sister and protesting just as she had done so uselessly that night.

"I didn't. I swear to you, Bea . . ."

Her protestation fell a second time on deaf ears.

"Liar," Beatrice screamed, stilling Amity's words.

The two faced each other in silence for a long moment, both seemingly shocked by the word. Beatrice was the first to collect herself.

"You will, of course, remain here until arrangements can be made for you to return to Boston," she said. "I won't have all Cairo buzzing about how I forced my sister from my house." She looked down at Amity and her eyes grew hard. "Not that there would be any doubt as to the reason why," she sneered. "But while you are here, you will have the decency to stay out of my way, and out of my sight. Do you understand?"

Amity, numb, nodded in agreement.

"And you will stay away from my children. I will not have them infected by your lack of moral character."

"Bea," Amity cried in anguish.

Beatrice, however, ignored her, apparently unconcerned for anyone's hurt save her own. She threw back her head, regally dismissing her sister. Then she turned and stalked from the room, leaving Amity kneeling on the floor, clinging to the chair she'd vacated and wondering how a sane and ordered world had been so completely shattered.

Amity stood by the window, but it wasn't the garden at which she stared. Instead, her glance was transfixed, held by the small statue she held in her hand. It was the statue of Bastet that Justin had bought for her that day in the souk. It all seemed so long ago to her now, as though ages had passed since that day. This small piece of Egypt, she thought, this piece she held in her hand, this and her memories would be all she would take back to Boston to remind her of what had happened to her. Little enough, she mused, to exchange for a broken heart.

When the maid knocked at her door, Amity assumed she had brought a dinner tray. She had thought it wisest, considering Beatrice's current opinion of her, to stay as much as possible to her room, even taking her meals there. So she simply called out, "Come," without bothering to turn away from the window.

"Excuse, ya sitt."

The tentatively murmured words surprised her. She turned to find the maid, embarrassed at being forced to demand her attention, blushing and staring down at the floor.

"Yes?" she asked, puzzled to find no dinner tray, wondering what message the girl could possibly have for her.

"A visitor, ya sitt," the girl muttered. "Shaikh Gardiner."

Justin, Amity thought. Why did he persist? She was tempted to say she was unwell, that she couldn't see anyone and have him sent away. But that, she realized, would be unfair of her. She certainly owed him a few moments of her time. She put the statue down on her dressing table and turned.

She nodded. "Very well. Is he in the parlor?"

The girl nodded, too, and blushed. As she passed her, Amity smiled at her, offering her a bit of courage even as she searched vainly for her own. It refused to be rallied. On the short trip down the stairs and into the parlor, she found herself feeling painfully exposed.

The room was dim when she entered, for only one lamp had been lit and the last of the daylight that entered the long row of windows was diffused with the pale gold of Egyptian twilight. Still, she had no trouble recognizing that it was not Justin but Ford who stood by the windows and stared out at the garden. If she saw only the outline of him, she thought, she would know him by his stance, the way he held his shoulders, the strong profile of his jaw. Those were things she knew she would never allow herself to forget.

She stood silent, simply staring at him and wondering why speech seemed beyond her at that moment. Then he turned, as though he had felt her presence near him, and looked at her. Still, she remained silent, waiting for him. She found herself reaching for a last shred of hope and wondering if he had come to her finally to ask her to stay.

Although she couldn't know it, that was precisely what Ford wanted to do, to hold his arms out to her, to watch her run into them and then enfold her in them, to hold her close to him. It amazed him to realize that he had set out to seduce her simply to keep her from Justin. She had somehow managed to awaken a wealth of feeling within him, roused things inside him he had never thought to know. Only now, now that the damage had been done, did he realize how much better it would have been for the both of them if none of it had ever happened.

He offered her a weak smile. "A man of my word, I've come to say good-bye," he said.

She felt as if her life were draining out of her, as if it was lying, a weak and useless puddle, on the floor at her feet.

She felt her jaw grow tight. She had to pry it apart to whisper, "Well then, good-bye."

They stood and stared at each other in painful silence for a long moment. Finally, when Amity thought she could stand it no longer, she spoke.

"If we've nothing else to say to one another, Ford, perhaps you should go," she murmured.

His eyes on hers, he crossed the room until he was standing close to her.

"Not yet," he told her softly.

She wondered why it was she could feel his eyes peering inside her, why she felt as though he could read her thoughts, could see the hurt she felt now that she had been forced to accept the fact that there was no hope for her love for him. She found herself growing angry with him, hating him for doing this, making her feel this way. And she hated herself as well for letting him see her pain.

"Why have you come here, Ford?" she demanded weakly. "What good will it do?"

His hand rose, coming close to her cheek as if he wanted to touch it, but he wouldn't let it. It hovered for a moment, suspended near her face before he forced it down to his side.

"I had to explain to you, Amity, to make you understand," he told her, his voice low and ragged as though he were forcing the words unwilling from his lips. "I couldn't just let you leave thinking I want it this way."

"Then what do you want?" she demanded, letting the anger take her again, not caring now that he could see it as well.

"To tell you I love you," he replied.

Suddenly the anger was gone and her heart was pounding until the sound of it filled her ears. This was what she wanted, nothing more, just those simple words. She moved closer to him, raising her face to his, expecting him to reach for her, to take her in his arms, to hold her and kiss her.

Instead he stepped back.

She felt as if she'd been slapped.

"Why are you doing this?" she asked him, beyond anger now, knowing she had never felt quite so miserable in her life.

"Understand, Amity. If things were otherwise, if I had anything to offer you, I'd ask you to marry me," he told her.

"And just what do you think you must have in your possession before you make such an offer?" she demanded. "What do you lack that's so important?"

"My honor," he told her. "My good name. Do you think I could ask you to marry a man who has been branded a thief by his own family? Do you think I could give that legacy to a son?"

At first she couldn't believe what she heard. It seemed ridiculous to her, like a child's rhyme, words strung together with no more reason save their cadence and sound.

"But Kendrick confessed before he died," she protested. "You've done nothing wrong."

He shook his head. "I told you, Amity. Kendrick took his confession with him to the grave. I've no way to prove my innocence now."

"Surely you can tell them. It's your family, Ford. Surely they'll believe you."

He took her hand and pulled her toward the sofa. She sat, staring up at him as he settled himself beside her, waiting.

"Listen to me, Amity . . ." he began, obviously searching for the words, not at all liking the necessity to talk about a subject that he would much rather have avoided. "I was a bit wild when I was young," he said, speaking with a quiet determination, as though it were someone else he were discussing. "I gambled, ran with a rowdy group. I make no excuses. That was who I was, and perhaps what happened was my own fault. When I was eighteen I came into a small fortune that my mother left to me, and I proceeded to lose it, every cent, gambling. But I didn't stop there. I kept on, thinking I might win it back. I don't know." He shrugged. "I was finally forced to go to my father, to ask him for the money I owed and couldn't pay. He refused."

"All that was a long time ago," she replied. She almost smiled, thinking his fears suddenly charming, those of a small boy, cowed by the knowledge he'd done wrong, ashamed to face his parent and confess his sin. "Surely he's forgiven you by now."

He put his hand to her cheek, touching it fleetingly, then pulled it away.

"He's dead now, Amity," he told her. "And he never forgave me."

Her spurt of humor disappeared, and she remembered his words as they knelt by Kendrick's body, the bitter way he'd told her his father was dead. She felt like a fool to have forgotten.

"But what has that to do with the theft?" she asked.

"Shortly after I went to him to beg him to buy my way out of debt, a piece of my grandmother's jewelry disappeared. An incredibly valuable emerald necklace, a piece she had received as a wedding gift from my grandfather. She was crushed at the loss. She came to me and begged me to return it. A proud old woman, and she cried, begging me to return it to her."

"But why would they think it was you?" Amity demanded. "It could have been anyone."

"Because nothing else was disturbed. There was no sign that someone had broken into the house. And nothing else was taken. Just the necklace."

"Because it was Kendrick," she countered. "Why didn't they suspect Kendrick?"

"Because it wasn't Kendrick's gambling debts that were paid two days later. It wasn't his markers that were returned to him."

He remembered it all as if it had been the previous day, all of them seated at the breakfast table when the servant delivered the letter to him, the markers falling out of the envelope when he opened it. He remembered their eyes on him, his grandmother's, Justin's, Kendrick's, but mostly his father's, mostly he remembered the look of accusation in those dark-blue, knowing eyes.

Amity could see the look of hurt, and knew he showed only a bit of what he felt, knew he was tortured by the memory of his family's condemnation.

"It doesn't matter," she whispered. "None of it matters."

He shook his head. "Don't you see, Amity? I was disowned, disinherited. I have nothing but what the Army gives me, no home to offer you, no future."

"People survive on less," she told him. "Besides, I'm not penniless."

He drew back from her and stood. "I won't live off a woman," he told her sharply.

She stared up at him. "What difference does it make?" she demanded.

"If I've nothing else, at least I have some pride."

"You said you loved me," she countered. Why, she wondered, didn't that mean as much to him as it meant to her? Why couldn't he see that nothing else mattered but that?

"I do."

He said the words defensively, as though they were painful for him to utter.

"But you'd give me up because of pride?" she asked.

He turned away from her. "I haven't any choice."

She stood, angry again, angry that he could be so blind to what was truely important, angry that he seemed to be so willing to throw her love aside. She stamped her foot in frustration.

He turned to face her once more, surprised at her anger.

"Damn your pride," she hissed at him. "Damn your pride and damn you!"

For an instant she saw hurt in his eyes, and regret. For that instant she thought he might come to her, but he didn't. Instead, he stared at her, his glance growing slowly colder until it felt like ice to her. She turned her back to him, suddenly unable to bear the sight of him.

"You've said good-bye," she told him coldly. "Leave now."

He put his hand to her shoulder and it seemed to her that it might burn her. But she refused to turn to face him, and he quickly gave up the effort.

"Good-bye, Amity," he whispered.

Then he dropped his hand, and carefully skirted around her as he passed her, taking pains to ensure that he did not touch her. He moved to the door, and paused for a moment as though leaving were painful for him. He turned to her, but her back was still to him, and he found he had nothing that seemed worth being said. He turned away again, and left.

It was then that she turned, in time to see him walk through the door, leaving her life forever.

She fled, running back to her room before she gave in to the crumbling feeling inside her. After everything that had happened between them, she couldn't allow Beatrice to see her misery.

She slammed the door behind her and stood leaning against it, her eyes closed, and listened to her heart beating. She realized that nothing had changed in her life, that everything was exactly as it had been before Ford had come. Still, she felt shattered now. Whatever hopes she might have secretly harbored within herself were gone. And somehow having heard him tell her that he loved her made it all the more painful to know that he did not think love enough.

She told herself she hated him, that if he'd cared for her at all he never would have come to her, never told her that he loved her, that he should have known he was only making her decision to leave more painful. Her life seemed to stretch out before her, endlessly long, empty and bleak, and as unpromising as a sentence of imprisonment. She felt the loneliness settle around her, as if it were something palpable, something she could touch. The feeling frightened her.

When finally she opened her eyes and saw Justin sitting in the flowered chair by the window at the far side of the room, she was startled. Later, she would wonder why she hadn't been afraid, why his appearance, as though he'd been conjured up by some magician's trick, hadn't sent her running from the room. But at that moment, she felt too numb inside to feel anything more than a mild irritation and to wonder how he'd gotten there.

He smiled at her, stood, and quickly crossed the room

to her.

"How did you get in here, Justin?" she asked crossly. He smiled with secret amusement.

"Charles has a few private tastes he would prefer your sister would not discover," he told her with a certain amount of glee at the revelation. "Over the years I've enjoyed them with him, then helped him back here through an unpublicized entry." Once again the smile, only now it seemed sinister to Amity. "Sort of the consul's private little pathway to safety."

She stepped back, away from him as he neared her. He put his hand to her arm before she could get too far away, and held firmly onto it, stopping her retreat.

"Why did you come here?" she demanded.

"First I came to see if one last attempt might convince you to change your mind, Amity," he told her, his tone conversational, lightly-pleasant. "But as I approached the consulate, I saw Ford enter."

His expression changed suddenly, growing angry and flushed. And it was at that moment, watching the change settle over him, that Amity began to feel the first twinge of fear. She tried to pull her arm from his grasp, but he tightened his hold until his fingers bit into her flesh.

"I give you one last chance, Amity," he said. "Will you marry me?"

She shook her head, beginning to feel the fear within her grow, but guileless still, knowing no other path but the truth.

"I told you from the first that I didn't love you, Justin," she replied.

"And I told you that would come with time."

She shook her head. "No, no it won't. I believed you when you said it, but now I know it won't happen, not ever."

"It would have," he said. He pulled on her arm, forcing her close to him. "If you hadn't fallen in love with Ford, it would have." He put his hand to her chin, his fingers hard against her cheek, forcing her face upward until her eyes met his. "Tell me you don't love him, Amity," he hissed. "Tell me you haven't lied to me."

His eyes had become suddenly wild, like an animal's, and his fingers bit into her cheeks, into the flesh of her arm. She filled with panic, realizing, finally, that he would not be content to leave her with his anger unanswered.

"You're hurting me, Justin," she whimpered.

He pushed her head back, pressing his fingers into her cheeks until they were rimmed with dark splotches of red.

"Tell me you don't love him," he repeated. "Tell me you didn't give yourself to him."

"I don't love him," she cried.

"Liar," he shouted at her.

He took his hand from her cheek and slapped her, hard. Then he released his hold on her arm, pushing her forward, toward her bed. She stumbled, her legs coming into painful contact with the dressing table, and then she was falling, sending her brushes, a scattering of tiny bottles, and the statue of Bastet all flying as she tumbled to the floor.

It took her a moment to catch her breath, to steady herself. But when she turned, Justin was coming toward her again. Her eyes settled on the white cloth he held in his hand. This was wrong, she thought, not knowing why, but sure. She scrambled to her feet, trying to run, trying to scream but finding her throat too tight to emit much sound and hearing only a faint, useless cry in the air around her.

And then she felt his hand on her arm again, pulling her back, pulling her close to him. This time the cry rose to her lips, full and ripe, only to be cut off by his hand and the cloth he pressed close to her nose and lips.

The smell was sharp and burning and she tried not to breathe, not to let the fumes into her lungs. Despite herself, she couldn't keep it out. The stuff seemed to seep into her nostrils, filling them. As it did, it cut off the thought of fleeing, of crying out.

She felt herself grow limp, felt her legs begin to bend beneath her, no longer capable of supporting her weight. She was falling, falling endlessly, and the only solidity was Justin's arms, snaking around her, and Justin's chest, a hard wall she fell against.

And then there was nothing but blackness.

Chapter Fifteen

Amity opened her eyes to the night. Never had darkness seemed so complete to her, so totally unrelieved. For a second she thought she might still be asleep and this was a dream.

She quickly realized, however, that she could not be dreaming. It seemed unlikely to her that a dream would come to her complete with a stomach heaving with nausea and a throbbing head. Besides, she was conscious of the distinct feeling of movement, and that, she thought, was something too immediate to accept as being merely imagination.

She stirred, and tried to sit up. The movement spurred the pain in her head, leaving her feeling dizzy and disoriented. Determined, she forced herself to sit and found herself on the floor of a carriage. She pulled herself up to the leather seat and stared out through the narrow window.

Despite the throbbing in her head and the queasiness she felt in her stomach, she couldn't ignore the splendor of what she saw, the intensity of endless blackness of the desert sky with its brilliant punctuations of light. Stars, she told herself firmly, even as she admired the beauty of it, the incredible contrasts of a night sky with stars over the desert.

She wasn't dreaming. It was a desert night as beautiful as the sky had been when Ford had made love to her that first time. The memory gave her a painful start and she pushed the thought away, telling herself it would do her no good to remember. But the hurt served to settle her, to convince her that indeed she was not dreaming.

It was only then that the memory returned to her, the memory of Justin coming after her, holding her, thrusting the cloth to her face and then the dulling, acrid fumes. She hadn't been simply asleep, she told herself. She'd been drugged. And now Justin, probably assuming the effects of the drug would last longer and she was still unconscious, was taking her someplace in the desert. She felt the panic return. Whatever he was planning for her, she somehow knew it would not be pleasant.

She slid along the leather to the carriage door, put her hand to the latch, and pushed down on it. It surprised her to find it moved easily beneath her hand, giving way and the door falling ajar. Had she not kept her hand to the latch, the door would have swung completely open. She quickly pulled it back shut.

She sat then for a moment, considering her alternatives. Whatever Justin's intentions for her, she wanted no part of it. If she could get out of the carriage without him noticing, perhaps she could get away from him in the darkness. She would not let herself think that the desert could be dangerous. Instead she told herself that if he was driving a carriage, then he was keeping to an established road. She told herself calmly that she could follow that road back to Cairo.

She hesitated for a moment. She would have to jump down from the moving carriage if she were to get away, and then try to find some shelter where she might conceal herself. She stared out into the darkness, searching rock outcrop, anything that might provide her a to hide. She could see nothing but the open expanse of sand and beyond that only shadows and a deep, lightless void.

She could wait, she thought, wait until there was some feature on the landscape. But she had no idea how long she had, how long before Justin would realize the drug had worn off and think to look in on her. She would have to jump out and then press herself to the ground, hoping the darkness alone would conceal her from him should he chance to turn back. She braced herself for the fall, pushed the door open, and threw herself forward.

She landed on her hands and knees with enough force to press the breath out of her lungs and scrape her skin. Still, she managed to keep herself from making any loud noise as the sand bit into her palms and shins. She resettled her skirt quickly so it would lie flat and then pressed herself down into the sand.

It seemed forever to her as she lay there, barely daring to look up to see the carriage moving away from her, sliding into the darkness, the open door swaying with the carriage's movement, the bright beacon of the lantern by the driver's place growing smaller and dimmer with the distance. But finally she allowed herself a sigh of relief and let her taut muscles relax. She told herself she had escaped undetected. She pushed herself up to her knees . . .

And immediately threw herself back down to the sand. The carriage had been drawn to a sudden halt. Justin jumped down, reached for the lantern, and carried it to the side of the carriage. He looked quickly inside, then to the rear, and then, holding the lantern high, to the circle of sand illuminated by the lamp's glimmer.

"Amity!" he screamed into the night.

Amity could feel her heart beating with fear inside her, and knew she was trembling. She closed her eyes tight, not wanting to watch as he climbed back into the carriage and turned it around. But she could feel the pounding of the horses' hooves against the ground and knew he was coming closer. She forced her eyes open, forced herself to realize the circle of light thrown by the lantern was nearing the place where she lay in the sand.

She was frozen, unable to move until the light touched her and he called out again, angrily, "Amity."

It was then the fear released its hold on her. She scrambled to her feet, and began to run.

She heard Justin slap the reins to hurry the horses, and she heard the contact of their hooves quicken. She ran faster, moving forward into the darkness, less afraid of whatever unknowns might lie in front of her than she was of what pursued her.

She felt the pounding in her chest grow harder. Common sense told her she stood no chance of outrunning the carriage, and still she ran, refusing to stand uselessly rooted by fear, refusing to do nothing as she had done nothing when Ali Kalaf had taken her from Gardiner's Ghenena. But soon her breath was coming in ragged gasps and her legs were filled with cramping pain. Just as she was deciding it was impossible for her to run another step farther, she realized the horses had drawn up beside her.

She screamed, and veered off the roadway into the deeper sand. But behind her Justin drew the carriage to a halt and jumped down after her, racing with the speed of untired muscles as she pulled herself, exhausted now, through the sand.

When he fell on her, pushing her beneath him onto

the sand, she felt as though she were too weary to fight him any longer. His body was heavy, an enormous, ungiving weight on hers.

"Why are you doing this, Justin?" she cried.

She looked up at him and realized with a sickening lurch that a stranger stared back at her from his eyes, a stranger whose eyes were as cold and as malicious as a viper's.

He grasped her hands and then pulled them together, holding them above her head. With his free hand he fumbled, searching for something in his pocket, finally drawing out a small glass vial.

"I gave you every opportunity," he hissed at her. "I even begged you. And you turned me away."

The vial shook in his hand. In his anger he grasped it so tightly then that it burst. He seemed not to care. He pressed the sleeve of his jacket to the sand where the liquid had fallen, letting it soak up some of the liquid that had seeped into the sand, then moved his arm toward her face. She recognized the odor of the cloth he had held to her face back in her room in the consulate, could feel the bite of the fumes even before he moved his arm close to her face.

She tried to pull away, shaking her head wildly as he moved his sleeve toward her.

"No, Justin. Don't do this. I'll do whatever you want. Don't . . ."

Her cries were muffled and then silenced as he pressed his forearm to her cheek, pinning her head motionless in the sand, and the fumes began to work again, sending her back into the darkness.

This time when she awoke it was because he was shaking her. She had been quite content with her dreams, dreams of her childhood, of her life as it had been when her parents were still alive, of the house in Boston where she was the petted and indulged little sister. Part of her had no desire to leave that place and she protested the intrusion, dazedly pushing at the hand he had put her to shoulder. He seemed intent upon having her attention, however, for he shook her even harder.

"Amity, wake up."

She forced her eyes open with reluctance, unable to ignore the command. Her dreams nipped at the edge of her consciousness, leaving her feeling lost. She felt only confusion when she looked up at him.

"Justin?" she asked hazily as he pulled her up until she was sitting facing him. "Where are we?"

She looked about with a distant interest, half expecting to see the house in Boston with its austere clapboard facade when she looked out the carriage window, and finding only the darkness of the desert night.

It was then that the feeling of nausea struck her, and she gagged, her empty stomach heaving. She remembered the drug, could faintly smell the acrid scent of it that lingered still in the fabric of his jacket sleeve as she turned to push uselessly against the hand that held firmly to her shoulder. The smell brought back the memory of the rest of it, each detail that returned to her worse than the one that preceded it.

He waited only long enough to let her stomach settle and the gagging to stop. Then he backed out of the carriage, pulling her along with him and ignoring her weak struggle to free herself from his grasp.

Once outside the carriage, she ceased struggling against the arm he'd placed around her waist. The last thing she expected to see was the ancient temple, looming out of the darkness. He let her stand for a moment, staring up at it, letting her listen to the sound of chanting that edged its way to the outside, along with the soft glimmer of torchlight.

"What is this?" she asked, her voice muted by awe and a finger of uncomprehending fear.

He smiled down at her with grim pleasure.

"This is your fate," he told her.

Then, without allowing her time to speak, he began to walk forward to the pillared entrance, pulling her roughly with him.

At first the torchlight blinded Amity after the darkness of the desert night. She closed her eyes against it as he pulled her past the columned portico and then inside. She moved blindly at his side, too weak still from the drug to protest the rough way he handled her, too shocked by this sudden turn of events to find any meaning in what was happening to her.

She stumbled as her foot hit the base of a column, and emitted a small sharp cry of hurt. He seemed not to notice, or not to care, and he continued to pull her along as though she were a beast or simply a sack of grain.

There was a wave of warmth that enveloped them as they entered the temple, and sounds, louder now, much louder, the sounds of voices raised in monotonous chant. There was a thickness to the air, the scent of incense and human sweat, the mixture sharp and biting in her nostrils. She opened her eyes slowly, admitting the light, finally able to focus.

She stood for a moment, dazed, unable to believe what she saw.

Justin stood beside her, staring at her, smiling now with a sort of malicious pleasure as he read the disbelief he saw in her expression. He let her stand and stare, letting her drink it all in.

"Time, I think, for you to learn a bit about the Egypt that is not always seen by the visitor," he whispered to her, putting his lips close to her ear so that she might hear without his having to speak above the sound of the chanting. "You have so much to learn before you leave us."

She hardly heard his words, hardly even noticed that he was pulling her once again along the pillared side isle of the temple. Her attention was lost amidst the men who filled the center of the temple proper, milling about, their voices rising now, then falling with the cadence of the chant. Their bare chests glowed softly in the flickering torchlight, the same light that glinted off the thick collars of colored beads they wore about their necks. They moved silently, on sandaled feet, seeming to draw closer to the raised dais at the far end of the temple, to where robed priests stood in front of a fire that burned in a huge brass brazier and behind that, an enormous statue that seemed very much like the tiny statue of Bastet she had held in her hands only hours before.

This was some insane fantasy, she told herself, some bizarre dream of ancient Egypt brought on by a desire to escape from an all too painful reality. Surely she would waken and find herself in her bed in the consulate, surrounded by lace and pillows, uneasy in the luxury, unable to find comfort with the knowledge that soon she must leave Egypt and Ford behind.

But the noise and the heat of so many bodies and the scents all assailed her, filling her senses in a way that seemed impossible for a dream. And Justin's hand, pulling her roughly forward, was all too unpleasantly real.

"Look, Amity," he hissed.

His lips were so close to her ear she could feel the heat of his breath against her neck when he exhaled, but she had no thought for that, no thought even to disobey him. They had skirted the side of the temple, and were close to the dais, near enough to feel the warmth of the fire burning in front of the great statue of the goddess. The statue seemed to peer out at her worshippers, her stone expression one of peaceful serenity, the cat in her arms lazily staring out, too, at the crowd with a knowing, superior glance.

Amity realized that she and Justin were not alone in this part of the temple, that others had drawn back to let them pass. But this awareness was quickly drowned out by other, more pressing observations. There was the sensation of movement, a sort of scurrying, close by, underfoot. Her first thought was that the temple was infested with rats. She stared down with horror into the relative darkness of this side aisle where she stood with Justin, terrified she might see one of the beasts.

It was then she noticed the cats, even heard the soft sounds of their mewling, a dull undertone that tinged the chanting with a kind of netherworldly eeriness, as though their voices were an integral part of the song. There seemed to be hundreds of them, roaming freely through the crowd, somehow managing to keep themselves from being trampled underfoot, serene creatures at home with the havoc that surrounded them.

And then her attention was drawn to the priests, those who moved before the goddess's statue. They seemed to be performing an intricate sort of dance, weaving together, then drawing apart, their dark robes swaying around them as they moved in time to the cadence of the chant. Their shaved heads seemed almost unattached, like pale, glowing globes rising out of the

282

dark cones of fabric that covered them.

In their center, standing in complete stillness, stood the high priest. He was tall, taller than those who surrounded him, and his robe was of golden fabric, with an irregular pattern of dark reddish-brown spots. In his hand he held a scepter, long and narrow and embellished with a swirling pattern of dark-blue and gold. On his head he wore a headdress of gold and feathers and bright jewels that glittered in the torchlight, all of it making his long, thin face seem like a caricature, or even a death mask. He seemed so still he might have been another statue, like the carved figure of the goddess behind him, except for the darting stare of his dark eyes and the occasional movements he made, turning to the brazier behind him and throwing bits of incense into it. They sputtered as they hit the flames, and sent up small clouds of thick, heavily scented smoke.

Amity gazed at him, somehow sure he was familiar to her, but bewildered by the feeling and unable to place him.

"What is this?" she murmured to Justin, turning to him as the only person with whom she might claim any kinship. She was filled with a sense of disbelief, the only sure knowledge she could claim the certainty that what she saw could not possibly be real.

He yanked on her arm, hard, pulling it behind her until it hurt.

"Be quiet," he hissed in her ear. "Look, that you might learn."

Terrified, Amity did as he directed her, staring into the mass of humanity. The hurt in her arm served to focus her thoughts, to make her realize that everything she saw was all too real despite the fact that her mind told her it couldn't possibly be. The air was heavy, thick with the incense and hot from the fire that burned in the brazier before the goddess.

She felt dizzy, felt as though the warm air she breathed held some sort of a drug just as had the fumed soaked cloth Justin had held to her face. Only this drug didn't send her to the oblivion of sleep; this drug seemed to make her lose herself. It seeped into her with every breath and filled her with the cadence of the chant and of the swaying bodies of the men who surrounded her. She felt as though she were floating, as if she were far away, staring down at herself and the bizarre scene that surrounded her. Even the pain from Justin's hold on her arm, although he had not loosened it, seemed to be slowly fading until it was merely a distant throb.

The chanting suddenly ceased. Amity had to force her attention to the fact, for the sound of it had seemed to become a part of her, and its loss now felt like an omission somewhere inside her. She turned toward the dais, to where the dark-robed priests had arranged themselves in a line behind their chief and now stood as still and unmoving as did he while the worshippers ceased their movement and, with a hushed expectancy, stared forward, anxiously watching.

From some place to the rear a dark-robed priest moved forward, passing the others, leading a beautiful white ram to where the high priest waited. The animal's fleece had been washed and groomed, the thick folds of wool dazzling white and glowing in the torchlight, completely unblemished. It moved docilely at the side of the priest who led it, staring curiously at the worshippers and the temple, but without making a sound.

When the ram was brought near to him, the high priest moved aside, revealing a thick slab of stone behind the place where he'd stood, a large rectangle, about waist-high, darkly mottled and streaked. Amity grew sick as she watched four of the priests move forward to tie the ram's feet, then grasp it and lift it to the top of the block where they held it firmly. The stone, she realized, was a place of sacrifice, and the dark mottlings which colored its surface were stains of shed blood.

The ram, too, seemed finally to understand what was about to happen to it. It had lost its serenity now, and it bleated out its helplessness, shaking its head, its large dark eyes staring out, seeking compassion. One of the priests hurried forward and put his hands to the animal's head, holding it down firmly as the high priest reached out to the top of the scepter he held and drew from it a long, thin blade.

In the silence, Amity could hear the crackle of the fire in the brazier, the voice of the high priest who had begun to murmur words of prayer, strange and meaningless to her, as he raised the knife over his head and stared down at the life he was about to take. She felt the cry of revulsion rise in her throat and Justin's hand clamp firmly over her mouth to smother it as the blade was brought down with a sharp, abrupt movement. She tried to turn away, but his hand held her head firmly, forcing her to watch.

Amity could taste the bile rising in her throat and felt her body tense with the desire to heave. As much as she wanted to, she found herself incapable of closing her eyes. Justin finally removed his hand from her mouth and she gasped for air, trying to settle herself. She prayed he would take her away now that the gruesome sacrifice was over. Whatever Justin's reasons for bringing her to this place, for forcing her to witness this spectacle, she only knew she felt relief that it was done.

Her senses dulled by the violence, she watched as the

priests lifted the ram's carcass from the stone and carried it away. She turned her face to Justin.

"Please, will you take me away from here now?" she begged.

Justin smiled as he shook his head. "But there is much more for you to learn, Amity," he told her, his tone pedantic, that of a teacher instructing an unruly student. "The real lesson of the evening is only just about to begin."

He nodded toward the dais, to where a woman was being led forward by two of the dark robed priests.

She was young, Amity realized, hardly more than a girl although her body was well developed, with full breasts and rounded hips, all amply visible beneath the thin drape of the fine gauze dress she wore. Like the ram, she had been carefully groomed, her dark hair arranged in many tiny braids, each one embellished with gold beads that shimmered with her movement. Her face, fine featured and pleasant, had been painted so that her cheeks were unnaturally bright and her eyes were elaborately enhanced, dark kohl encircling them and a thick shimmer of color on the lids. Gold rings shone from her fingers and bracelets encircled her wrists and upper arms.

Although her eyes were wide and bright, it seemed to Amity that she walked between the two men who guided her unsteadily, as though she were dazed. When the high priest moved forward to her, she smiled at first absently at him, and then her painted lips formed themselves into the caricature of a smile, a harlot's smile of invitation. He remained aloof, his expression unchanged, but he raised his still-bloody hands to her cheeks and her forehead, leaving a bright red smear in their wake where he touched her.

One of the priests came forward, bearing a golden

286

cup, and this the high priest took and handed to the girl. She took it from him with a strange eagerness, as though she were well acquainted with the drink it contained and coveted it. She raised the cup to her lips and drank, quickly emptying the contents, letting a few drops fall to her chin in her eager greediness to swallow. When she'd done, she lowered her hands and let her eyes drift closed. She swayed, and the priests at her side held her firmly, keeping her upright. Had the high priest not taken the cup from her hands it would have fallen.

The high priest then lifted her in his arms, and carried her to the great statue of Bastet, turning to face the goddess, as though to display the girl, to show her beauty. His voice once again began slowly to fill the temple, the strange words rumbling louder and louder until the sound of it was taken up as a low hum by the others. Then he turned and laid the girl on the bloody sacrificial stone, her limp legs dangling down the side.

Then the high priest opened his robe, revealing his nakedness. Amity gasped, surprised, not quite believing what she was seeing happen nor the hushed expectancy of the men who filled the temple. But once again Justin put his hand to her chin, forcing her head forward, forcing her to watch as the priest pushed aside the thin gauze of the girl's skirt and thrust himself into her.

It was then that the girl opened her eyes, her blood-smeared face grotesque as she reached up to the priest, pulling him to her, drawing him into her with the same greedy thirst with which she had swallowed the liquid in the cup. Amity shut her eyes, trying to force away the image, but it remained there in her mind, inescapable. The sound of voices began to fill the temple, rising slowly as the act was performed, until it seemed to shake the very walls. And then it suddenly stopped.

Amity felt Justin's hand tighten its grasp and felt the heat of him, the warmth of his breath close to her neck. She dared to dart a look at him and realized that he was as caught up with the rite as were the other worshippers, his attention riveted, his body taut as he leaned forward to watch.

Now the priest moved away to stand by the girl's head. She lay limp on the stone, her eyes staring up blindly at the goddess's face, her expression passive and rapt, almost as though she were entranced by the sight of Bastet's calm stone features. Even when the priest brought out his scepter, even when he pulled the blade from it, she made no move, gave no sign she saw anything, felt anything, but the ecstasy of being one with the goddess. The chanting started again, a low murmur that slowly swelled.

The priest's movements were swift and efficient. The girl's death, like the ram's, was quick and clean.

Amity screamed. This time Justin's hand wasn't fast enough to completely muffle the sound, and the cry seemed to suspend all movement in the temple, temporarily freezing the priests and the worshippers, stilling the chanting, turning the scene into a grotesque *tableau vivant*. The high priest was the first to recover, then the chanting started again, filling the void of quiet until it seemed as if it had never been interrupted.

Locked in Justin's arms and unable to move, his hand firmly clamped over her mouth, Amity felt herself retreat within herself.

She hardly realized when Justin began to move forward, half dragging her, half carrying her along with him. There were vague impressions, distantly imposed on the chaos of her mind, of stone steps, and a dim, flickering light, and a growing stillness to the air.

Somehow she found herself standing in a sparse white room facing the high priest, watching as one of the dark-robed priests helped him to remove the blood-spotted golden robe and the ornate headdress. The sight of seemingly mundane matters, the bowl of water brought to the priest so that he might wash the stain of red from his hands, the pale silk robe that was brought and held out for him, these things finally returned her to herself. The high priest shrugged into the thin robe, tied it to cover his lanky, naked body, then turned to her.

"My dear, Amity," he said softly, and offered her the benignant smile of the scholar.

It was only after he'd uttered her name that she realized why he had seemed familiar to her.

"Professor Sareef," she muttered with disbelief. And then, with dull shock, she screamed out, "No."

Her eyes darted around the blank stone walls of the room, staring at the uninterrupted white. She was below ground, she realized, and the room seemed to close in on her, to entomb her. She felt a dull, sick feeling inside herself as she realized it had been the professor who had drawn the knife along the girl's throat, taking life with such practiced, knowing ease. Surely this man could not be the same one who had seemed to her so westernized, who had fit so well the image of the dedicated scholar. Surely that man could not have performed the murder she had just witnessed.

Sareef remained serene, as though she'd made no sound whatsoever, as though he could not see the look of complete shock with which she regarded him.

"I knew you'd come," he told her. "I knew from the first moment, the goddess was calling out to you, pulling you to her, bringing you here so that you might become one with her."

Amity shook her had. "No," she gasped, her mind filling with the image of the girl, the blank, drugged way she'd stared, the way she'd seemed to welcome the knife.

Sareef moved close to her, putting his hand to her chin and staring into her eyes.

"Tomorrow is the full moon, a night sacred to Bastet," he went on. "Tomorrow night you will be honored, an earthly goddess who will embrace the otherworld."

He spoke calmly, as though he could think only that she was accepting and grateful for this fate.

"Professor, you can't do this!" she cried.

But he was already turning away from her, apparently unconscious of her protest, motioning to Justin to follow. He led them from the room and down a narrow passage, then drew open a thick wooden door and turned to watch Justin drag Amity, her wrists firmly encircled in his grasp, to its entrance.

She turned to Justin, her eyes filling with desperate tears.

"Justin, please," she begged.

His eyes glistened, bright and sharp, as he stared at her.

"You could beg me, Amity."

"I am, Justin," she cried. "I'm begging you."

"Tell me you love me, Amity," he hissed.

The words stuck in her throat, but she forced them out, knowing only that she must not let him leave her there, that if he did she would die.

"I . . . I love you," she gasped.

But as soon as she had uttered the words, she regretted them, regretted she had given him the satisfaction of them. He was smiling at her, his expression filling with pleasure.

"Liar," he snarled between clenched teeth. "Whore. I offered you my name, but instead you gave yourself to my cousin. This is where you belong, whore, this is the fate you deserve." He offered her a malicious smile. "Spend the night in repentance for your sins," he told her. "Cleanse yourself for the goddess." He seemed pleased that she would have the intervening hours to be tortured by thoughts of what would happen to her. "Tomorrow you become one with Bastet."

He pushed her forward, into the room, waiting only to watch her fall to her knees before he turned away and swung the door closed behind him. The bolt fell with a loud thud, the noise echoing in her mind with the finality of the grave.

Chapter Sixteen

Ford lifted his glass to his lips. He seemed surprised to find it yielded nothing despite the fact that he tipped it far back. He raised it, squinting his eyes so that he could peer into it. Deciding reluctantly that he really had already drained its contents, he leaned over the side of his chair and grasped the bottle he'd left there on the floor. He uncorked it, lifted it to refill the glass, then thought better of the idea. He dropped the glass and lifted the bottle to his lips instead.

It occurred to him that he had been drinking for a very long time, and still it seemed not enough. He wanted to be drunk, so drunk he could not think, so drunk that he was cleansed of the aching hurt inside him. But no matter how much liquor he swallowed, he seemed unable to achieve that goal.

He pushed himself to his feet and began to move around the room, his room, the front room of his home. He stared at everything carefully, looking at each object with the eyes of a stranger, and what he saw disturbed him.

The room was sparse, furnished only with necessities, one comfortable chair, one that was decidedly less welcoming, a table, a lamp. Through the years he had told himself it was better to live this way, keeping his home uncluttered, just as he kept his life uncluttered, everything unencumbered and stark. At that moment, however, he saw his surroundings differently, saw that they were bleakly empty just as was his life, saw his lack of material objects as an outward evidence of his own fear of allowing himself to acquire other, more meaningful ties.

He stared at the room and realized that the man who lived in it was a stranger and wished to remain a stranger, from himself as well as from everything and everyone else. The realization was not completely pleasant to him.

He closed his eyes and imagined how the room might feel if it were home to another, imagined what it would be like to share the emptiness and fill it with another presence, a woman's presence. No, he amended, not just any woman, but Amity. It surprised him to realize how clearly he could imagine her there, how easy it was to think of her as part of his life, a permanent part.

He put the bottle down on a table and walked through the three remaining rooms, seeing them as they might be if she shared them with him, filling the emptiness with the warmth of feminine clutter. He stopped finally in his bedroom and imagined a woman's dressing table occupying the far, empty corner, its top a disordered array of small, delicate bottles, the air lightly scented with her perfume. He imagined the windows sheathed with lace curtains, the chair cushioned and inviting, lace-covered pillows on the bed. A bedroom, after all, ultimately belonged to the woman who occupied it, who gave birth to her children in it. He was surprised to find he could imagine the transformation easily, even with pleasure.

It shocked him to find how much the mere thought of her there, in that room, aroused him. Although he had shared his bed with other women in the past, he found he could not remember even one of them. All he could see was Amity, lying on his bed, welcoming him. Her image was so real, he reached out to it. But when he approached the bed, she suddenly disappeared.

He returned to the front room, and reluctantly admitted to himself that his head ached but that it was completely clear. The liquor had done him no good, he decided. Nothing, he realized, would ease the hurt he felt inside. Nothing, that was, except seeing her again, holding her in his arms.

He made one last survey of the room, and told himself he had no right to ask her to share this small house with him. Four rooms, hardly regal quarters by British terms, relative poverty compared to the life she was accustomed to leading, compared to the life she would have led had she agreed to marry Justin. Still, she had refused Justin. Perhaps it was poverty of the soul of the sort his cousin had that seemed ugly to her. Perhaps she did not place as much importance on lack of material goods as did so much of the society amongst whom he'd always lived. All he knew at that moment was that it was not a matter he had the right to decide for her. And more than anything else, he knew he wanted her.

He went to the door, pulled it open, and stared out into the night. Here, by the river on the very outskirts of Cairo, one might even forget the city, one might lose oneself in the beauty of the river and the land and the sky.

The sun was just beginning to rise. Ford watched the eastern sky slowly fill with color and light. It would be day soon. He would go to her, admit to her that he had been wrong and convince her to return with him. After all, he loved her. Perhaps that was riches enough.

Funny, he thought, that he suddenly felt such a sense of well-being. Despite the fact that he had not slept the night before, that he'd spent the hours drinking, he felt clear-headed and sure. For the first time in more years than he cared to count he was going to take steps to make a life for himself, a real life.

If she would have him, he would ask for nothing more.

It would be, he decided, a beautiful day.

The sun began its daily ascent outside the temple walls, but closed up within her cell, Amity had no idea of the hour nor the fact that a new day had begun. In her stone prison the only light she saw was unchanging, the light admitted by the barred window in the door, that given off by the torches that lined the corridor outside. The lack of the natural change of light began to torment her. It reminded her that there was no daylight in a tomb.

She was completely exhausted, and yet she was afraid to sleep. At first she had pounded at the door, crying out, hoping someone might hear her and come to free her. But as the hours passed she came to realize that even that slight hope was misplaced. She gave up the effort, having been rewarded with only bruised, aching hands and a hoarse throat for her pains.

The temple seemed completely empty now, the only sound the occasional soft mew of a sleepy cat. She walked the length of her cell, afraid that if she allowed herself to sit on the small bed that stood against the wall she would fall asleep, afraid that if she slept, she might never waken.

Her throat, dry and scratchy, made her feel her thirst more keenly. She could not keep her eyes from straying to the pitcher of water set on a table by the door. This, too, she was afraid to touch. She found she could not get the image of the girl who had been brought to the altar out of her mind. She pictured the way the girl had walked, as though she had been dazed, drugged. Amity stared at the pitcher of water, and wondered if it might contain the drug that had so dulled the girl's senses she had not even protested her own death.

She paced, but with each step she grew wearier, and as the moments passed, her thirst grew until it was intolerable, until the thought of a drink of water became more and more insistent. Her eyes kept straying to the pitcher. She wanted to pick it up and drain it, and still she was afraid, always afraid.

Her thirst eventually dominated, and she crossed the room to where the table stood. At first she simply stood for a moment, and stared into the still contents of the pitcher. It seemed perfectly normal, completely clear, colorless. Finally she lifted the pitcher and sniffed. She found nothing, no odor whatsoever, certainly nothing to remind her of the sharp, acrid fumes of the cloth Justin had held to her face, nothing at all to make her think the water had been tainted.

She turned and looked around her cell. There was nothing there she had not already stared at during the preceding hours, but still she surveyed the small room. Blank, uninterrupted stone walls. The only way in or out was through the heavy door. But it was firmly bolted, of that she was absolutely sure. There was no escape for her here.

Her thoughts strayed to Ford. He'd turned her away, telling her he had no life to offer her. It was an excuse, she told herself, an excuse so that he could leave her without qualm. The simple truth was that he didn't want her. He'd tasted the fruit and found it not to his liking after all.

She shook her head, and told herself her thoughts were wandering. Then she stared down at the pitcher in her hands. What would it matter if it was drugged? she asked herself. There was no escape for her. Would it not be better to face her death with unseeing eyes than to watch the knife and know what it would bring her? And why did she so fear an endless sleep? She had nothing, no one. Death would be at least a relief from the hopelessness, from the misery of knowing she was in love with a man who felt nothing for her.

The more she considered it, the more acceptable the thought seemed to her. She would simply resign herself to her dreams, let herself drift back to her childhood, to her memories, and stay with them forever. The more she considered it, the more attractive the prospect seemed to her.

She lifted the pitcher, brought it to her lips, and drank.

She stood for a moment waiting for something to happen, some change to come over her. When nothing seemed to happen, when she felt no different, she became aware of a feeling akin to regret. The thought of returning to the dreams had seemed so seductive, and she was so terribly tired.

She raised the pitcher again to her lips and drank, thinking now only to alleviate her thirst. It started very quickly then, the numb sensation in her arms and legs. She saw the pitcher fall from her suddenly clumsy hands, watched it tumble ever so slowly to the floor, strike it and send out a beautifully supple spray that arched with a languid, serpentine grace. The droplets fell, meeting the floor leisurely, spreading out slowly into tiny puddles of dampness. And then her legs seemed to collapse and she was falling, ever so slowly, down through an endless hole that had somehow opened up beneath her.

The light seemed to flicker, and darkness filled the space around her. She never felt herself land.

"Major Gardiner," Beatrice said as she slowly lowered

her cup to the saucer on the table before her. She pushed her chair back slightly so that she could look up at him without lifting her head too far back. She attempted a halfheartedly coquettish smile, but let it disappear when he made no effort to respond.

Ford stared at her, suddenly disgusted. He considered her glazed and thick-lidded stare, and realized she was not quite sober.

"I've come to see Amity," he said, his words clipped and short.

She returned her attention to her cup and the stack of mail she had been slowly working her way through when he'd suddenly appeared in her breakfast room.

"I'm not my sister's keeper," she said, matching her tone to his. "If you have business with Amity, the maid can fetch her for you."

"The maid has been up to her room. The door is locked and she doesn't answer," he told her.

Beatrice shrugged. "Is this information supposed to interest me?" she asked.

Ford moved forward, putting his hands to the table and leaning toward her. "Damn it, something's wrong. Either you unlock the door to her room for me, or I'll break it in."

Beatrice started up into his intent eyes and smiled at him. "You, Major, can go to hell," she said in a tone that dripped honey. She leaned forward to the decanter in the center of the table and quite blatantly poured a tot into her morning coffee. "And you can take my thankless snip of a sister with you."

Ford stared at her a moment and then made a dismissive movement, turning away and returning to the hallway. The maid who had reluctantly admitted him stood waiting, not sure of herself but slightly cowed by his manner.

He started for the stairs without so much as looking

at her.

"Show me which room is Miss Ravenswood's," he called back to her as he started to climb, taking the stairs two at a time.

She hung back, staring at him, then darting a worried look in the direction of the breakfast room. She was obviously afraid Beatrice might appear, might disapprove of this strange man storming through the house, afraid she might be blamed.

She had good reason. Ford had climbed half the flight when Beatrice appeared. Her cheeks were unnaturally bright, flushed with anger.

"Major Gardiner, you will leave this house immediately!" Beatrice screamed up at him, her voice turning shrill and sharp in her anger.

Ford stopped and turned to look down at her. "Not until I've seen Amity," he replied.

"Go, fetch Hassan," Beatrice shouted to the maid as she started up the stairs after Ford.

"Iywa, ya sitt," the maid replied, fleeing, glad she was not being blamed for having admitted Ford into the house and conveying to him the information that the mistress's sister refused to answer her call.

Ford turned away, starting again up the stairs, taking the last of them quickly. He found himself in a long corridor, flanked by a half dozen identical doors. He began to move forward, stopping to open door after door as he progressed.

"What do you think you're doing?" Beatrice shouted up after him.

"Looking for Amity," he replied. He was completely calm now, and determined. No matter that he was roaming uninvited through the consul's house. Something had happened to Amity, and he had no intention of allowing himself to be turned away.

The first room was obviously shared by Beatrice and

Charles. A maid in the midst of straightening it looked up when he opened the door, surprised at the sight of a strange man.

"Which room is Miss Ravenswood's?" Ford demanded.

The maid crossed to the door, and pointed. *"Hinak, ya shaikh,"* she replied, pointing to the door at the far end of hall.

Beatrice had by now reached the corridor. She darted a glance at the maid, then started after Ford who was running along the corridor.

"You have no right to be here," she shouted as she ran after Ford, growing more and more angry now that he seemed to be so completely unaware of her, that he seemed to have dismissed her with no more effort than he would a slightly bothersome but unimportant insect.

Ford ignored her. He had reached the door to Amity's room and he knocked sharply. "Amity? Amity can you hear me?"

There was no answer, and he tried the door. The lock held firm.

He turned to Beatrice. "Either you open it or I'll break it down," he said.

"I've sent for a guard," she told him, apparently hoping that would persuade him to leave.

He shrugged his dismissal of her, turned back to the door, raised his foot to just below the knob, and kicked once and then again. The wood cried out in protest, then parted with a dull shattering sound. The door fell open.

He realized he wasn't surprised by the disarray. The bed was still made, untouched, but the rest of the room was a shambles. A chair lay on its side, and the rug was pushed toward the door, bunched up. The dressing table had been overturned and its contents lay broken and scattered, strewn across the floor. He knelt and retrieved a small, carved figure, the idol Justin had bought for

Amity at the souk. He considered it curiously for a moment, then dropped it as his eyes found a crumpled white cloth among the objects on the floor. He lifted it, and sniffed it. It still reeked of the drug in which Justin had soaked it.

If Ford had seemed to expect to find the disarray, Beatrice certainly had not. She had been convinced Amity was simply playing some game with her, trying to get back at her for their argument. But one look at the room convinced her it was no game. Something had happened there, something violent. She stood staring dully at the havoc, slowly shaking her head.

"What could have happened?" she asked, her voice weak now, no longer strident, no longer certain.

Ford had moved to the window and was staring out. He turned back to face her, and only then realized that she knew nothing of this, that she was genuinely shocked.

"She was drugged and taken out of here," Ford told her, his tone harsh, knowing he would have to bully her if he expected to get any information from her. "But there's no sign anything was disturbed down there." He motioned toward the window, to the garden beds that lay, neatly tended, below the window. "Whoever it was didn't take her that way." He crossed the room and stared down at her with steely eyes. "Perhaps you might have some thoughts on the matter."

She shook her head. "I don't believe it," she whispered, and seated herself on the bed, her hands clasping the bedpost as though she needed it for support.

Ford put the cloth close to her face. She started at the acrid odor and drew her head back.

"Is there any other way into this room?" he demanded, pointing to the door he had been forced to break open.

She swallowed, then nodded, unable to speak.

301

Ford put his hands to her shoulders, grasping her, letting his fingers bite into her. He ignored her wince of pain.

"Where?"

She pointed to the paneling on the far side of the room. "There's a passage," she told him softly. "A passage to the street."

She seemed unable to bear his stare any longer, for she looked back down to the cloth he'd let fall on the bed beside the place where she sat.

Ford crossed the room and gingerly felt the edges of the paneling. The wall seemed entirely solid. He turned back to Beatrice.

"Where?" he demanded.

She didn't look up. "To the left," she murmured. "Near the corner of the last panel."

Ford put his hand where she had indicated, running it along the edge of the raised panel. About halfway down he found a small metal lever. He pulled it, and the panel fell forward, revealing a narrow passage.

He crossed the room, back to where Beatrice still clung to the bedpost. Once again he put his hands to her shoulders, and this time he shook her, forcing her attention back to him.

"Who knows about this passage?" he demanded.

She bit her lip. "Charles," she said softly. She shuddered. "Charles uses it when he's been off to someplace horrible, one of those houses, when he doesn't want to be seen leaving and entering at odd hours." Her expression grew pensive, and then, suddenly relieved. "But he's away, in Alexandria, with Ebaring, the chief resident. It couldn't have been Charles," she asserted firmly, as though she were trying to convince herself. She seemed pleased at her deduction.

Ford told himself he had no time for her to work out her suspicions of her husband. Amity had been taken from this room, obviously against her will.

He pressed his hands to Beatrice's shoulders and shook her again, this time a bit less roughly. He would have pitied her had he not been so afraid for Amity.

"Who else?" he demanded. "Who else might know about it?"

She shook her head, her expression blank. Then she pointed to the rumpled cloth that lay beside her on the bed. It was a large linen handkerchief, and in the corner were embroidered two letters: JK.

"Justin might," she whispered. "He might have brought Charles home that way." She forced back a small sob. "On one of *those* nights."

Ford released his hold of her shoulders and snatched up the cloth, holding it so that he could see the initials, white embroidered on white, but distinct to him now that she had pointed them out to him.

"Justin," he murmured.

"He wants to marry her," Beatrice protested. She looked up at Ford now, for the first time seriously considering what might have happened to Amity. There were always stories of women disappearing, sold into white slavery. She shuddered. Whatever anger she had felt for Amity, she realized at that moment that they were still sisters, that she still loved her. "He wouldn't hurt her," she said, addressing Ford but really speaking to herself, convincing herself. "He would never allow her to be harmed."

She turned to follow Ford with her eyes as he strode to the door. His way, she saw, was blocked by three uniformed men. Hassan, she realized, Hassan and two others. She'd sent for him. She wasn't quite sure why now, but she remembered she had sent for him.

"Out of my way," Ford hissed at them. There was something about his stance that said he was ready to fight the three of them if need be.

303

Hassan looked to Beatrice. "Ya sitt?"

Beatrice was staring at Ford, wondering why there was such a look of determined desperation in his expression. She waved her hand, a brusque, dismissive motion, toward Hassan, wishing he had not disturbed her thoughts. He stepped aside, allowing Ford room to move past him.

"He would never hurt her," she said again, this time loud, forcefully.

Ford turned to face her. His glance was derisive, as good as telling her he thought she was a fool. Then he turned away, and brushed past the guards.

It was only after she'd watched him leave that Beatrice realized Ford was in love with Amity. She wondered what her own life might have been like if Charles had felt even half as much for her.

"Ever the conscientious banker. I would have thought you might have taken a day or two to mourn for your father. But then, it seems I was mistaken."

Ford closed the door behind him and crossed the dark expanse of Justin's office, an English banker's office, a rich English banker's office. The room was sheathed in mahogany paneling, the floor swathed in thick Oriental rugs, the furniture Chippendale, finely carved and perfectly proportioned. Everything was solid, muted, exuding an air of perfect respectability. Ford inhaled, wondering what it was that seemed strange about the air in this room. It took him a few seconds, but he decided that it was money, the air was rich with the smell and taste of money.

Justin looked up at him and scowled in distaste.

"Who let you in here?" he demanded. "I pay people to keep out the riffraff."

"I didn't ask to be admitted," Ford told him amiably.

304

"It's amazing how much leeway people will allow you if you act as though you had the right to do something." His tone turned suddenly harsh. "But you know all about that, about abusing your power, don't you?"

Not that he hadn't done his own bit of abusing others that morning, Ford realized. He'd bullied his way into Beatrice's house, and then Justin's, storming through the rooms, snapping out questions at bewildered servants as though he had the right to interrogate them. And all for nothing, nothing save learning that Justin had gone to his office that morning. There had been absolutely no sign of Amity. And each minute that passed pained him as though it were drawing her further and further away from him.

Justin pushed himself back from his desk and stared up at Ford, apparently resigning himself to the interview.

"What do you want, Ford?" he asked mildly.

"I want Amity."

Justin's lips formed themselves into a humorless grin.

"A sentiment I will reluctantly admit I share with you. Unfortunately, it's done me no good whatsoever. And I can say with perfect candor that I wish you even less success."

Ford crossed the room and skirted the desk. He approached Justin, leaning forward to put his hands on the arms of Justin's chair.

"I'm in no mood for this, Justin. Where is she? What have you done with her?"

Justin looked up at him with innocent eyes and smiled at him.

"How would I know where she is?" he asked. "If anyone ought to be privy to personal information about her, it's you. I'm just the man whose proposal she accepted and then refused to marry. Not the one who managed to doff her. Not you, Cousin."

Ford filled with burning rage at Justin's manner, at

the casual way he referred to Amity. He sickened at the thought that Justin could speak that way about her, that he had protested his love for her once and now referred to her with no more respect than he would a whore. He wanted to beat Justin, to feel the impact of his fist against Justin's chin, to sense the rupture of flesh and bone. Only once before had he felt such rage, when he'd pulled Ali Kalaf away from Amity. And now he felt it again, an animal rage that would only be satisfied with the taste of blood, Justin's blood.

Justin seemed to sense it, to see it in Ford's eyes. For a moment a spark of panic worked its way into his expression. Then he leaned back in the chair and kicked, aiming for Ford's groin.

Ford sensed Justin's movement just in time. He moved to the side as Justin's foot rose and found only air instead of the target it had been intended to meet. He retaliated quickly and brutally, slamming his hand into Justin's chin and then his stomach. He felt a reluctant but undeniable sense of pleasure as a thin line of red trickled from Justin's cut lip.

"Where is she?" he demanded once again as he raised his hand in unquestionable threat.

Justin stared up at him. There was fear in his eyes, but there was still a spark of defiance.

"I don't know where she is," he spat out. "And I don't care."

Ford pulled out the handkerchief with Justin's initials on it and pressed it to Justin's nose.

"Perhaps this will remind you," he said. "You made a mistake. You left it behind."

Justin pulled his head back at the sharp whiff of fumes, then took the handkerchief and used it to wipe away the line of blood on his chin. Then he turned away, his expression set.

"Go to hell," he said.

Ford put his hand to Justin's throat.

"I've no more time for games, Cousin," he hissed angrily. "Tell me where she is or I'll choke the life out of you before I leave to find her." He pressed his hand against Justin's larynx.

Justin choked as his air was cut off. The defiance was gone from his expression, leaving only the fear there.

"All right," he rasped. "I'll tell you what you want to know."

Ford released his hold. Justin coughed once, then put his hand to his throat.

"I took her to an old temple, out in the desert," Justin said slowly, as though the words were painful to him. He looked up at Ford tentatively. "I intended to leave her there until tonight. She wouldn't be hurt. I just meant to frighten her a little, to make her see that she can't just run off, she can't just leave me."

"Fool!" Ford hissed.

Justin nodded. "It was wrong. I know that now. I was a fool to think I could force her to love me." His expression grew sly. "I'll take you there. It's you she wants. The two of you should be together."

Ford felt a prickling at the back of his neck, a feeling he got when things felt wrong to him, not dangerous necessarily, just wrong. Justin's words seemed too repentant, his expression too cunning. Still, he realized he had very little choice but to go with Justin. He was sure his cousin knew where Amity was, sure there was no other way he might find her.

"Where is this temple?" Ford demanded.

"To the north, near Heliopolis. Not far from the ruins of the ancient palace."

Ford scowled. "I know of no temple anywhere near there," he said.

"It's there, I swear," Justin countered. "It's to the east, into the desert. I'll take you there."

307

Ford thought Justin sounded a bit too eager, but he realized he really had no choice in the matter. There might very well be a hundred temples in the area of which Justin spoke, places of which he had absolutely no knowledge. If there had been time, he could have found an expert, someone who could verify or disprove Justin's claim. But there was no time. He thought of Amity, left by herself, alone in the desert and terrified.

"Pray she isn't hurt, Cousin," he told Justin as he stood back and pulled him to his feet. "Because if she is, I swear to you, I'll see you pay in blood."

Chapter Seventeen

Amity woke with a start.

She was staring up at the ceiling of the cell, at smoothly planed timbers and unmarred white plaster. Her eye roved to the corner where the ceiling met the wall. Here the square stones were perfectly fitted, one to the next. For a moment her mind dwelled on the unlikely care that had been taken in the construction of her prison.

Slowly her memory returned. In her mind she relived the moment following her drink from the pitcher: the dizziness, the sight of the pitcher falling from her hands, the beautiful spray of its contents flying out and slowly drifting downward, and finally the sensation of falling toward the stone of the floor, watching it rise to her but never quite meeting it. It struck her as odd that the floor did not feel cold and hard beneath her.

It was several seconds before she realized she was lying on the small bed, not on the stone floor as she ought to have been. She had absolutely no idea how she had gotten there. She sat up slowly, putting her hand to her forehead as the movement made the dizziness return. Then she put her feet down to the floor. It was hard and very real beneath her feet. Her thoughts were still a bit muddled, but she told herself she could steady them by concentrating on the solidity of that stone.

She forced herself to concentrate, to look around her. It was only then that she realized she was dressed strangely. Her flowered dimity was gone, as were her stockings, petticoats, and the rest of her undergarments. She stared dully down at herself, taking in the filmy drape of pale-blue linen, the golden rings on her fingers and her ears, the surprising weight of the bracelets that circled her wrists and her arms.

She was immediately struck by a sense of familiarity with the strange clothing. It took her only an instant to realize she was dressed just as the girl who had been sacrificed the night before had been dressed. The thought was suddenly chilling. She was dressed for her own death.

She had not been alone in the temple after all. Someone had come into her prison while she'd slept, stripped her and dressed her this way in preparation for the offering. She felt her skin crawl as she thought of those strange hands touching her, lifting her to the bed and removing her clothing while she lay slack and unfeeling. She closed her eyes and could see strange eyes staring at her naked body.

She found herself filling with a sudden fury. Why, she thought, if they were going to do this thing to her, did they allow her to awaken? Why couldn't they at least have had the kindness to let her simply hold on to her dreams?

She pulled off the rings one by one and then the bracelets, flinging them as she removed them to the floor. They rattled against the stone with a sharp metallic sound as they landed. When she'd emptied her hands and her arms of all adornment, she reached to her neck and found it bare. Her hands began to shake. She thought of the girl who had gone so willingly to her death the night before, remembered the bare neck being offered up to the high priest's blade. Of course her neck would be left unadorned. It would not do to impede the priest's task.

There was a rattle at the door, the sound of the latch being drawn.

She looked up, wondering if she might run forward, if she could escape, as whoever it was out there was opening the door.

But when she got to her feet, she found herself dizzy and confused, her legs unable to bear her weight. She was unable to stand, let alone run. She sank back down and sat, staring blankly as two black-clad figures entered and the door was closed and once again secured behind them.

They were both elderly women, gray haired, amply girthed, and swathed in black. Both carried trays, one bearing food and a small flask and a cup, the other holding combs and brushes and a multitude of small, ornately decorated boxes. At first the women seemed surprised, perhaps that she was awake and not as they had left her. But they quickly smiled at her, and bowed their heads in a show of humility.

Amity felt the odd inclination to laugh at these unlikely apparitions. They seemed so much like walking heaps of cloth to her, short, rounded piles that had somehow grown heads. But her humor disappeared as she realized they were part of what was to happen to her. They were the ones who were making her ready for the sacrifice.

The one bearing the tray with the food stepped forward first.

"Into awes haga, ya sitt?"

Is there anything you would like, lady?

Her smile was pleasant, plumply grandmotherly as she held the tray forward to Amity, inviting her.

Amity shook her head. "No. Go away," she shouted, and made a pushing movement with her hand. It terrified her to think that these two pleasant-faced women were accomplices to murder. That knowledge made their appearance seem grotesque, and frightening.

The woman shrugged, obviously understanding the gesture if not the words. She bowed her head once more, and stepped back to place the tray on the table where the pitcher of drugged water had been. Amity watched her, suddenly wondering what had happened to the pitcher, wondering if she might not have the chance of escaping back to her dreams once more.

The second woman moved forward now, only rather than coming to Amity, she stared down at the rings and bracelets that lay scattered on the floor.

"Gawaher," she muttered crossly: the jewels.

Her heavily fleshed faced seemed to fold in upon itself as though it resented the necessity to frown. She bent down carefully, her body apparently uncertain that it could accomplish the feat. She began to gather up the golden rings and bracelets, scuttling clumsily across the floor as she reached for each piece and then placing it in the sack she made by gathering up the ends of her skirts. Her ill temper was short-lived, however, and when she'd finished, she was once again smiling.

Now the first woman was talking, her words indecipherable to Amity, but spoken softly, obviously meant to calm her fears. She lifted the flask from the tray she'd brought with her and poured some of the contents into the golden cup. Then she smiled at Amity, and once again approached her, this time holding out the cup in offering.

"No," Amity told her, shaking her head. *"La.* No. Leave me be."

The woman seemed surprised that she refused the drink. She smiled and nodded her head.

"Tayeb," she said. Good. She lifted the cup to her own lips and swallowed a sip, then smiled broadly, dem-

312

onstrating. *"Tayeb,"* she said again, *"kheteer tayeb."* Very good.

Amity let her eyes wander to the closed and locked door. There was no escape for her, that was certain. Perhaps it would be better to simply accept the drink, let whatever drug it contained do its work. There was no doubt in her mind but that the liquid was drugged. The woman seemed far too intent that she drink the contents of the cup for her to think anything else.

Her hand seemed to reach out and take the cup of its own accord. She brought it to her lips and tasted the liquid. It was thick and slightly sweet, but not unpleasant. The woman smiled at her and nodded encouragement, then put her hand to Amity's, helping her raise the cup once more and drain it.

It happened quickly, the feeling of euphoria swimming through her and making her feel as if she were floating. Her mind was unclouded, and her senses incredibly sharp. She marveled at how clear everything appeared to her — the rings the women were now pushing back onto her fingers, the gold sharply bright in the flickering torchlight. Even the folds of thick black fabric in which they were swathed seemed immensely rich with texture to her newly perceptive eyes.

She made no move to pull her hands away from them, letting them push the bracelets onto her arms, the rings to her fingers. She suddenly was past caring any more that she was being groomed for her death. She was floating, her body without substance or weight. She was, she realized, perfectly content. Nothing could harm her.

What knowledge these priests must possess, she thought idly, what a wealth of drugs they brewed: one that seemed like water and brought absolute peace and this sweet, thick brew that made her fears disappear made her feel as though she were immortal.

The women set industriously about their tasks. One

brushed and arranged Amity's hair, weaving golden threads strung with tiny gold beads into the braids she wove. The other painted Amity's cheeks with rouge and her eyes with kohl and gold-flecked blue paint from the small, ornate boxes she had brought on the second tray.

As they worked, Amity sat silent and thoughtful, considering the feel of the combs as they passed through her hair, the soft caress of the tiny brushes that touched her cheeks and eyelids to leave behind the colorful coating of the paints. Every hair, every pore of her skin, every cell of her body seemed awake to sensation. Everything—every touch of comb or bristle, every brush of the old women's hands against her skin—was a marvel to be considered and appreciated. Even as she wondered at this sudden wealth of feeling, she seemed to be floating above herself, looking down at herself and the old women, perceiving everything with such marvelous clarity, a depth of vision she had never known before. Everything was beautiful—the old women, the wrinkled folds of their dresses, the stone of the walls that surrounded her. She wondered why she had never seen these things before.

The feeling faded quickly, however, and Amity soon found herself falling, collapsing into herself. The loss was devastating, and she wanted to reach out and hold onto the vision and the sensations even as they seemed to be slipping away from her.

The old woman who had been braiding her hair apparently recognized the symptoms, for she put down the comb she was using, crossed the room, and refilled the cup. She returned to Amity, once again holding out the cup to her.

"*Akhtar?*" she asked. More?

And Amity reached out for it, eager to drink, unaware that her hands were shaking. Her only thought was to take the cup and drink, to swallow that sweet, thick liquid, to find once again the peaceful place that had slipped away from her.

The woman put the cup in her hands, and helped her bring it to her mouth so that her shaking hands did not let it spill.

Amity swallowed and closed her eyes, concentrating, waiting for the change to begin within her. She found her expectations met quickly. In only a few seconds she had returned to that lovely, peaceful place. She embraced it with joy.

The women finished their task and left her. Amity hardly noticed their departure. She was lost, wandering in a pleasant haze, her only disagreeable thought the fear that she might be forced to leave this lovely place.

The feeling had only just begun to ebb when two dark robed priests entered her cell. They moved directly to her, each putting a hand beneath her arm and lifting her. She absently considered their entrance an intrusion, and tried to shut them out of her thoughts. But when they began to guide her toward the door she found she had no will to defy them. She stumbled along quietly between them.

They brought her to the same room she had been in the night before, the one where Professor Sareef had removed his robes. He was there now, garbed once more in the gold robe and the headdress. When he turned to her, Amity realized the dark spots that decorated the front of the robe were splotches of blood. The thought swam around in her mind, and some part of her told her that she should be afraid, but she was not quite sure why.

Sareef turned to her, and she smiled at him. His long face seemed so fatherly to her at that moment, caring and benevolent. He moved forward to her, taking her arm and leading her to a chair.

"You have been well cared for, my lovely Amity?" he asked.

She nodded and stared into his eyes. They seemed so dark, so deep. There was peace in his eyes, she thought. She could fall into his eyes and float there forever.

He put his hand gently to her chin.

"You are beautiful, my dear," he told her. "The image of the goddess. A goddess yourself."

"A goddess?"

She was bewildered. Suddenly there were flashes of memory, images of the huge stone idol, the image of Bastet holding her cat, and then of Sareef, standing before the goddess, bringing the knife down and sending up splashes of blood. His eyes were no longer deep, no longer promised her peace. She was no longer floating, she realized, no longer was her body as thin and as light as air. She was glad she was sitting. She felt that she could not stand on her own, that her own weight was far too much for her to carry. She looked up at Sareef and was gripped with sudden fear. She pulled her head back, away from his hand.

He dropped his hand. He realized the effects of the drug were wearing off and knew she would soon become terrified and wild. He moved to a table in the center of the room, forcing his steps to be slow and calm, not wanting to frighten her. When he reached the table he lifted the small flask and gold cup that were set there, ready for this moment.

She was talking now, staring at him. He forced himself to concentrate on her words, to look up at her and appear attentive.

"You won't do that to me?" she begged him softly. "Not kill me, not rape me?"

He poured the liquid into the cup as he answered, aware she was watching, her eyes watching the liquid fall, then fastening anxiously to the cup.

"Rape?" He seemed genuinely shocked at the thought. "Oh no, my dear. The high priest makes an offering to the goddess. It is a holy act, an act of praise and sacrifice. Certainly not rape."

He moved forward, holding the cup out to her.

Amity watched him approach, and part of her wanted so much to believe, to take the cup from his hand and drink. She could not take her eyes from the cup, could not keep the thought of what it would bring to her from her mind. But another part of her cried out to her that it was all a lie, that she must not accept this, that she must fight it or she certainly would die. And the part of her that wanted to believe began to wonder. Where was she? What was happening to her? She was gripped with a biting fear.

Sareef took her hand gently in his and put the cup into it, wrapping her fingers around it and then smiling down at her.

"You have nothing to fear, my dear," he whispered. He pushed her hand gently upward, raising the cup. "Drink, Amity, and your fears will seem like folly."

His voice was almost hypnotic. Part of her felt as though she were one with the seductive call of it, anxious to open herself, to offer herself up to it. Surely there could be no evil behind so kindly and protective a call, surely that voice could never urge her to destruction.

Amity stared down at the liquid in the cup. A being inside her was crying out to her, urging her to do as he told her, to drink. Her body craved the contents of that cup, ached with the longing for it.

But still there was some part of her that fought, that refused to simply give up and accept her death. Her hands shook, and a few drops of the liquid splashed onto her fingers. *Pour it out, spill it onto the floor* a voice cried out at her in desperation.

Sareef pushed her hands upward, urging her.

"Drink, my dear" he whispered. "Drink and find paradise."

She raised the cup to her lips.

The sun was already beginning to lower itself in the sky. The oblique angle turned its light from a blazing sharpness to a warm, honeyed glow that transformed the desert sand into a wilderness of softly flowing gold.

Despite the beauty, the fading of the light seemed an ill omen to Ford. Each hour that passed seemed to be taking Amity farther and farther away from him. Since they had turned off the road between Cairo and Heliopolis, the feeling had been growing on him, filling him with an unpleasant sensation of impotent rage. He felt that if he did not find her soon, it would be too late.

He called out angrily to Justin.

"How much farther?"

Justin turned to him and offered him an absent, knowing smile.

"Not far," he replied, then turned away.

Ford felt the prickling sensation at the back of his neck, the same sensation he'd felt when Justin had offered to take him to the temple earlier that day. It was wrong, a voice within him was telling him firmly: Justin did not smile this way, with this absent sort of humor; and his manner was too distant, too evasive. Ford almost wished for his cousin's more usual open querulousness, however distasteful it might be. He was accustomed to outright antagonism from Justin, not this distantly sly malice. It put him off, made him feel uneasy.

He hadn't long to consider his mistrust of Justin,

318

however. Before he had decided what the uncomfortable feeling might mean, Justin raised his arm and pointed.

"There."

Ford stared into the long shadows cast by the sun setting to the west. The temple seemed to rise out of the sand, glowing like soft warm gold in the last of the daylight. It wasn't a large temple, but the face of it was perfectly proportioned, with four pillars supporting the portico, the granite gently smoothed, burnished by the desert sand and the passage of time.

He nodded to Justin, motioning him to speed his horse and then following, kicking his own mount to a trot. He did not know why, but he wanted to reach the place before the sun had set. Somehow the prospect of darkness seemed to bear with it the promise of disaster.

They reached the temple without incident, while there was still the glow of gold from the sun that had reached the rim of the horizon. Justin had been completely silent, and now continued to hold his own counsel as he dismounted. Ford followed suit, following him to the entrance of the temple.

Inside the stones were cool underfoot, and smooth with wear. Ford realized that he had not quite believed Justin until that moment, hadn't really believed there would be a temple in the desert. But here it was, undeniably real, a bare peristyle sided by a row of columns and a wide aisle on each side, and to the front a raised dais that supported an enormous carved idol, the figure that of an elaborately draped and jeweled woman holding a cat in her arms. Dozens of cats lazed about, napping in the patches of sunlight admitted by the open doorway.

Ford stared at the idol's face, suddenly struck with the similarity she bore to Amity.

Justin put his hand to Ford's arm.

"The goddess Bastet," he said lightly, and then started

319

forward, to one of the side aisles. "Follow me."

He led Ford forward, along the length of the aisle and to a set of stone steps leading downward. Again Ford felt the prickling feeling at the back of his neck. As he watched Justin light a torch he sniffed the air, wondering what the light scent it bore could be. Surely a deserted, ancient temple should smell of nothing more sinister than the dry desert sand, with perhaps an overtone of must. But there was something else there, something he could not place, incense perhaps. But why should there be the scent of incense in a long-deserted temple? And all those cats, he mused. Where did they come from and what did they eat?

Justin led the way down the flight of stone steps, and Ford followed. The temple lay still and quiet around him save for the occasional mewling of the cats, but he realized that it had seen human habitation recently, for the floors and walls were all clean, bearing no evidence of being home to the creatures that eventually found shelter in deserted places — no snakes, no rodents, no infestation of insects, merely an occasional beetle underfoot. And the cats. Once again his thoughts fastened on them. How could the cats survive so far from water, unattended in the desert?

As they neared the bottom of the stairs, Justin became suddenly loquacious.

"The ancient priests chose the site for their temple carefully," he told Ford. "It would have taken half a day to walk here from ancient Heliopolis, nearly two hours on horseback. Remote enough to ensure that only the truly devout would make the trip to observe the goddess's rites. And there is water here, a small spring, not large enough to support a real oasis, but apparently it yielded enough for the needs of the priests and their servants." He darted a look at Ford. "Can you imagine, building a temple around a spring? They had great imagination. And the spring, it has never gone dry, even to this day."

Ford nodded. He was well aware of other such springs in the desert, aware that the nomadic tribes depended upon them when they roamed. Often they were dry part of the year, and some were buried most of the time under the sand. It took a skilled scout to find them, one who knew the desert well.

"So that is how the cats live," he mused aloud. "Available water, and rodents and small animals that come for the water to feed upon.

Justin nodded. "This temple was dedicated to the goddess Bastet," he said. "These cats may very well be the ancestors of those tended by the ancient priests." His voice rose, as though he were in a hurry to get the words out, to keep Ford's attention. "She was the goddess of joy, and her worship is believed to have included ritual copulation in her honor." He turned to Ford, his smile knowingly sly. "Not an unpleasant sort of a religion, eh, Cousin?"

Ford felt nothing but distaste at the thought, even more at Justin's lecherous innuendo.

"You surprise me," he replied, his manner dry and distant. "I'd no idea you were so well versed in study of ancient Egyptology."

They had reached a narrow wooden door, and Justin was reaching out to it. Ford felt uneasy. This was too easy, he thought. And now he seemed to hear voices, a murmur of human voices.

Justin gave him no chance to listen. "This particular goddess, I must admit, appeals to me," he said, still eager to talk. Ford wondered if he was trying to cover the sound of those other voices with his own. "A goddess who encourages men to take their pleasure seems far more appealing than the desiccated god our own priests offer us, a god who condemns human passion as a sin."

Again he offered Ford the same sly smile. "But who knows? Perhaps it's simply our priests who find pleasure unacceptable, who wish to deny it to others because they have sworn to deny it to themselves. Perhaps even our own antiseptic paradise will allow us those things we have been denied here on earth."

"What makes you think either of us will ever be granted admission to paradise?" Ford demanded. "Personally, I find neither of us fitting candidates."

"True," Justin agreed with a loud laugh. "Such presumption is unbecoming in a gentleman."

He pushed the door open and then stood aside so that Ford could see into the room.

Amity looked up and saw Ford staring at her. She trembled. She had never thought to see him again, and yet he was there, in this horrible place, staring at her, moving into the room toward her. The cup fell from her trembling hands. She darted a look down at the spilled liquid, and realized she was glad she had not drunk it. She looked back up at Ford.

He seemed only to have eyes for her, only to see her. It was as though the others, Sareef and the two dark-clad priests, were not there.

"Amity?"

At first she did not understand his apparent confusion, the perplexed look he cast at her, but then she realized how strange she must appear to him, how odd the clothing she wore must seem. She pushed herself to her feet, wanting to go to him, to feel his arms close around her, to be assured that he would let no harm come to her.

And then she saw Justin moving up behind Ford, and the two dark-robed priests, all of them with their hands raised, ready to strike.

322

"Ford!"

Her warning cry came too late. Ford had not expected the assault and had barely turned when the first blows were struck. He was momentarily stunned by the attack. One of the priests used the instant to his advantage, bringing his hands down expertly to the back of Ford's neck. He fell to the floor, senseless.

"Ford!"

The two priests had withdrawn, but Justin seemed unsatisfied to have Ford finally at his mercy and leave him be. He lunged forward, pummeling Ford's face viciously.

"No!" Amity shrieked as she threw herself at Justin, striking him with her fists, trying to get him to stop.

For a moment there was chaos, and then Sareef's voice rang out.

"Stop!" he cried, his voice sharp with the sort of authority that demanded immediate compliance.

The sound of it seemed to galvanize Justin. He let his fists fall to his sides and he straightened up to stare down at Ford. A look of satisfaction spread over his face as he saw the bruises begin to color on Ford's face and the blood flow from his nose and lips. He looked up at Sareef for an instant, then turned back to Ford to deliver a coup de grace, kicking Ford's still body in the ribs.

Amity fell to her knees, putting her hand to Ford's bloodied cheek. Then she looked up at Justin.

"Bastard!" she shouted at him.

He ignored her. He moved to the far side of the room, to a shelf that held the high priest's vestments and paraphernalia. He grabbed up the scepter, pulling the blade from its ornate sheath as he returned to stand over Ford and Amity. There was no question but that he intended to use it to kill Ford.

Amity stared up at the blade, then threw herself across Ford's chest before it could fall.

But Justin's hand was stayed by Sareef's.

"This is the holy temple of the goddess," Sareef said sharply. His voice seemed to cut into Justin, to make him tremble. "There will be no murder in these precincts. I will not allow you to desecrate this holy place or the sacred blade."

Justin lowered his hand slowly, letting Sareef take the blade from him. He stared at the older man with a schoolboy's adoration that was tainted with shame.

"We can't let him live," he protested. "He'll bring the khedive's police down on us."

Sareef nodded slowly. "Yes, what must be done, will be done. But not here." His face grew calm again as he stared at Justin. "The sun has set," he said. "The ceremony must begin soon. You must hurry. You can take him into the desert and tend to him when it is done. But for now you have other duties."

Justin nodded and began to turn away as Sareef motioned to the two other priests to come forward and take Amity. They put their hands to her arms and held her despite her attempts to struggle, lifting her until she was standing facing Sareef.

She struggled against their hands, but fell silent as she saw Justin begin to remove his clothing. He turned and smiled at her.

"You did not know I was a priest, did you, Amity?" he asked her, his tone taunting. He was lifting a second golden robe, like the one Sareef wore, and pulling his arms through the sleeves. "Tonight I will be the one who makes the offering to Bastet," he told her. "Tonight you will finally be mine. Mine and the goddess's."

Sareef smiled at her.

"We have preliminary matters to which we must attend, my dear," he told her, smiling at her as he retrieved the fallen cup and refilled it. "This is a grave time, a time when rituals must not be ignored."

324

He moved forward to her and put the cup to her lips.

She jerked her head away. "Murderer," she cried. She looked up at Justin. "Monster," she spat at him.

Sareef put his hand to her chin and held her face firmly in his long-fingered grasp.

"Come, my beautiful Amity. I offer you paradise."

"Your paradise is hell," she retorted, then clamped her mouth shut as he pressed the cup to her lips.

He put his fingers against her jaw and pressed the bones sharply until she had no choice but part her lips. Then he poured the liquid from the cup to her mouth. She gagged and tried to spit it out, but realized she had swallowed some of it as the floating, uncaring feeling began to fill her and her body went slack.

She was going to die, a weak voice within her called out in warning. She would soon die and so would Ford. But the voice was quickly stilled. She could no longer bring herself to care.

Chapter Eighteen

The two dark-robed priests were faceless, character-less. They might have been statues themselves, or machines fashioned in the shape of men for all the emotion they showed as they stood at the far end of the dais and rigidly held Amity between them.

She realized her mind was wandering as she watched Justin make the first sacrifice. Somehow the sight of him carefully lowering the blade to the ram's neck was unable to rouse any feeling of fear within her, despite the nagging voice at the back of her mind that told her she would soon follow the ram, that her blood would be the next to flow.

She was still held too firmly in the drug's grasp for the fear of death to have any meaning for her.

But as the ram's corpse was lifted, she caught sight of its dull, glazed eyes. Somehow those eyes roused something in her, first pity as she realized the entity that had lived behind those now-unseeing orbs was fled, then anger as she thought of Ford, as she remembered being pushed past Ford's still body and out of the room toward the stairs.

She would soon be treated as the beast had been, a voice cried out to her in indignation. And when that act had been done, Ford would be killed as well, his body taken and left to be swallowed by the desert.

Once the ram's corpse had been removed from the altar Justin turned and motioned to the priests who stood at her side to bring Amity forward. His eyes, too, seemed glazed, almost as if he had been drugged by the sight of the blood, by the taste of it. She wanted to scream at him, to shout out a curse, anything but accept without a whimper what he intended to do with her and Ford. Despite her sudden spurt of determination, however, no sound came from her lips. Although at least a small part of her mind was waking and pulling itself from the drug's grasp, her body, it seemed, was still beyond her control.

She felt as though she were moving through a thick, clinging fog. The two priests who held her arms handled her with a distant expertise, their grasp sure and firm so that she appeared to walk as though she moved of her own volition. That small part of her that had managed to free itself from the drug was powerless to do more than force her to see the stains of fresh ram's blood on the stone altar, smell the blood on Justin's hands as he approached her and touched her cheeks and her forehead. The blood felt warm and sticky against her skin and the scent of it filled her nostrils, heavy and sweet. She felt as though she might gag.

A priest came forward holding the golden cup. He handed it to Justin who took it from him and then turned to offer it to Amity. As he did so, the two priests who held her arms released her. She stood a moment, swaying slightly, feeling as though she might fall. And then she stared down at the liquid in the cup.

It was no good, she decided, to try to tell herself she did not want the sweet liquid. Her stomach pulled itself into a tight ball with want for it; every cell of her body seemed at once to cry out to her to take it, to drink it.

She stared numbly into the cup, then reached out to

touch it. Here is peace, freedom from pain, her agonized body told her. Take it and drink. Drink and be finally at peace.

She looked up then and found Justin staring down at her with smug and expectant pleasure. He was, she realized, anxious, ready to take what he had obviously considered his right from the very first. The fact that she had denied it to him would justify, at least in his own mind, what he intended to do to her. This was his revenge.

Sareef might honestly believe what he had told her, that whatever horrors were committed in this place were simply religious acts of piety. She glanced quickly at him, standing mutely at the side of the dais. His eyes wore a glazed look, as emotionless and cold as the two priests who had held her. But Justin's expression was different. He would take pleasure in what he was about to do. He would prolong the act as much as he could and then he would feel pleasure when he took her life as well. To Justin, her end was an act of retribution, plain and simple.

His expression was enough to stir that part of her that refused to be meekly acquiescent. She could not let him do what he intended to do without at least fighting. She refused to give him the satisfaction of letting him believe she would enter willingly into an act that led to her own destruction.

It took all her will to force her hand to move, to lift the cup and fling the contents into Justin's face. But when it was done, she was glad, glad to see the amazed stare that swept over his face at her defiance, glad she had not gone to her death meekly and without protest.

There was a single, unified gasp from the priests and the worshippers. Apparently the act was unprecedented, an unheard-of sacrilege. She was glad of that, too, and hoped she had ruined their entertainment for them.

Once again her arms were grasped by the two dark-robed priests, and the cup torn from her hand. She was trembling, she realized, and without the strength to fight the steel hold of their grasp. But she had defied them, she told herself. If she was to die, at least she knew she had not accepted her fate with the same dull acceptance of the beast that had preceded her.

Justin moved close to her and took her face with his hand, his fingers biting into the skin of her cheeks.

"Fool," he hissed at her. "You only make it worse for yourself." He smiled then, as he realized that if she refused the drug, she would be completely aware of what was happening to her. "And all the more pleasurable for me."

She felt a wave of disgust as he spoke, and in its wake a sudden throb of strength inside her as though the resolve had thrown off the effects of the drug. She would fight him, she told herself. She would fight for every second of the life that remained to her.

"You want my compliance," she shot back at him. "Instead I give you my curse. As long as you live you will bear it. Damn you, Justin. Damn you for a rapist and a murderer. Damn you to hell."

She spat at him.

He froze for an instant, his face coloring with his anger. Then he wiped the spittle from his cheek with the back of his hand. Still bloody from the ram's sacrifice, his fingers left a trail of red on his cheek.

"Bring her to the altar," he ordered the two priests, his voice sharp with anger. "And hold her."

As they started to step forward, dragging her with them, Amity screamed.

Ford awakened in a sea of pain. His ribs ached sharply as he began to move, and he groaned as he forced himself to sit upright.

He realized there was the sound of chanting. The sound wasn't loud, but it was composed of many voices. Something was happening above him, in the temple proper. He knew instinctively that it involved Amity and that it boded ill.

The robing room was empty now, but he had no doubt that he had been left unguarded. He forced himself to stand, then rested for a moment, leaning against the wall as he mentally surveyed the damage done him. There was blood, clotted and hard, on his lips and chin, his jaw throbbed as did his left leg, and there was a sharply aching hurt in his torso, probably a cracked rib, he decided. Enough to slow him, but nothing remotely fatal.

At least not yet, he mused. He was sure that if he were to remain where he was, Justin would see that he would encounter ills of a seriously more permanent nature. He had to find Amity and get the two of them out of this place before it was too late.

The plain batten door was without a latch or any other device to make it secure. He did not remember seeing anything on the other side, either, when he had entered with Justin. That fact led him to believe that some sort of guard had been posted there to keep him from escape. He looked around the room, searching for something he might use as a weapon.

There wasn't much—a small table, the chair in which Amity had been seated when he'd entered the room, the shelves on which the high priest's vestments were stored. He lifted the table. It was compact and deceptively heavy—not exactly his weapon of choice, but better than nothing.

He went to the door and slowly pulled it open a crack. He had been right, he realized. One of the priests had been left there on watch. But this was obviously not a military man. He stood leaning against the far wall of the narrow corridor, and his attention seemed more acutely centered on the noises from the temple above than it was on his task. He obviously regretted the fact that he could not witness whatever it was that was happening.

Ford pulled the door open quickly and stormed out, the table held in both hands in front of him. His attack found the priest off guard, and he caught the man in the stomach with the hard edge of the table, knocking the wind out of him. It was a simple matter then, for Ford to place a well-aimed blow to his chin, then another to the back of his neck as he bent forward with the pain. The priest slumped to the floor.

Ford quickly stripped off the priest's robe and pulled it on over his own clothing as he started for the flight of stairs. The corridor was deserted and he moved unchallenged, save for an occasional questioning meow from one of the many roaming cats.

There was the sound of a scream, raw with terror, and he knew it could only be Amity. For a second the chanting stopped, the voices seeming to hesitate as one, and then it began once again. Ford raced up the stairs.

Once up them he found he had far underestimated the number of people who were assembled there. The temple was packed, body pressed close to body, all moving, swaying, intoning the endless chant as they stared at the dais. Ford turned and looked, too, and saw Amity being forced toward the great stone altar.

The robe seemed to make him invisible, for no one so much as glanced at his face. He was thankful for the lack of attention. He put his hand to shoulders and arms, pushing away bodies, forcing his way forward. There was blood on the altar. He had no illusions what Amity's fate would be once she was brought to it if he did not act quickly.

There was confusion among the other priests on the dais. Apparently Amity's cries and struggles were not the usual course of events. The disorder was decidedly to Ford's advantage, allowing him to move forward unnoticed. Once he reached the edge of the dais, however, he realized his apparent invulnerability would not extend so far as to allow him to pull Amity from the priests' grasp and race out of the temple with her. He would need to create some diversion if they were to stand any chance at all.

A quick glance at the statue of Bastet that dominated the front of the temple sent him racing forward, onto the dais. Ignored by the priests, he slipped to the rear, then edged his way along the wall until he was standing behind the huge carved stone.

He climbed the back of the statue, ignoring the hurt of his ribs, using his arms to pull himself upward in the narrow space between the stone of the wall and that of the carved goddess. When he had reached Bastet's shoulders, he eased himself so that his back was against the wall and his feet were pressed firmly to the goddess's shoulders.

He looked down to the altar, to where Amity was being forced to lie back on the bloody stone. There was a heat in the air, a heavy expectancy as the attention of every man in the temple was centered on what was about to happen. Far from disgusting those who watched, her struggles seemed only to excite them all the more. Ford decided it would be only fitting were he to disrupt their grisly convocation.

"Justin!"

Ford's shout echoed through the temple. The chanting ceased and a mass of faces, Justin's among them, turned to stare up at him.

He pushed. With all his might, his muscles straining, he pushed against the mass of the stone statue. For a moment it seemed as though it would not move, and then Bastet began to totter.

The movement was slight at first, but Ford encouraged it, pushing against Bastet's massive shoulders until she rocked insanely. Below there were screams as both priests and worshippers realized what was happening. Some began to run toward the door, anxious to be out of the way when the mass of stone fell. There were screams as people fell only to be trampled beneath the feet of others in their panic to be away.

The old priest, the one Ford had seen handing Amity the golden cup when he'd entered the robing room below, was running forward, staring up and crying out, ordering Ford to stop. He stood in front of the huge brazier, looking up at Ford, his voice ringing with outrage when he realized his orders were being ignored.

Ford didn't stop. He was clinging to Bastet's shoulders now, and pushing against the wall with his feet. The huge stone goddess listed, her movement seemingly hesitant, as though she knew she was about to be tumbled and was unwilling to relinquish her place. But Ford gave one final, muscle-wrenching shove and then, with a shudder, Bastet began to fall.

The hands that had held her fell away. Amity watched the priests turn to stare up at their goddess, to watch her sway with near human movement. And then they began to run.

Justin, though, seemed determined to finish what he had begun. He might be denied his pleasure, but he would not so easily give up his revenge. He held the knife above her. His eyes blazed as he stared down at her. He grasped the knife firmly with both hands and then he brought it down.

With an energy born of sheer panic, Amity rolled

333

away, sliding from the stone altar and falling to the floor.

She scrambled forward, along the length of the dais, knowing only that she had to get away from Justin's grasp. He lunged toward her, and she feinted, moving aside, keeping just inches beyond his reach. His lunge had unsettled his balance. He fell forward, to his knees. The blade fell from his hand and clattered on the stone of the floor.

Amity snatched up the knife, and held it in front of her, the blade facing Justin. He got to his feet slowly, not taking his eyes from her, his own glaring hate. She glared back at him, daring him to come closer and feel his own blade.

Around them there was chaos. People were fleeing, running toward the rear of the temple, trying madly to get away. Sareef alone among those in the temple seemed to think himself immune. He stood in front of the huge stone idol, crying out to Ford, warning him with the goddess's curse if he did not stop. And then there was a dully wrenching sound as Bastet was finally freed from the place where she had stood for centuries. The goddess began to topple.

Justin turned and looked up, and his eyes filled with sudden terror. And then he, too, ran, racing away from the falling mass of stone, rushing forward to the door.

Amity backed away, too. But she was afraid to follow Justin, afraid he might once again leap on her once they were away from the temple. And Ford. She could not leave without Ford. She ran to the side wall of the temple and pressed herself against the stone.

Ford rode on Bastet's shoulder as she fell, face forward, to the floor of the temple. There was a heaving shudder as stone met stone. Amity could feel the impact beneath her feet and in the stone wall behind her. Bastet's fall shook the very foundations of her temple.

And now all she could see was Ford, his body lying slumped and still on Bastet's back. She picked her way numbly among the burning bits of coal that had been scattered by the overturned brazier, her feet skirting the many small fires without her conscious thought. Her mind was fixed on Ford, and she stared at him searching for some movement, some sign of life.

She dropped the blade and scrambled up the side of the huge mound of the goddess's enormous torso, then across it, to reach him.

"Ford?"

She put her hand to his neck and felt the steady beat of his pulse. A wave of gratitude spread through her, and she offered up a wordless prayer of thanks. There was fresh blood on his forehead. She realized he must have hit his head against the stone when it fell. She was terrified that he would not open his eyes again.

"Ford, please wake up," she begged as she put her hand to his shoulder.

Now that she was beside him, she was becoming far more cognizant of the danger they still were in. The temple, although empty save for the two of them and the still bodies of those who had fallen in the melee, was nonetheless filled with noise. The impact of the statue's fall had sent a shock through the ancient structure, and it was adjusting to that shock slowly, tremulously. Stones were shifting in the walls and the floors, and cracks appeared, accompanied by loud, wrenching noises. When she looked up, Amity could see the pillars that supported the temple's roof were starting to shift as well.

"Ford, please, please answer me."

Her proddings had become more urgent now that she recognized what was happening around them. They had to get out of the temple, and quickly. There was no question in her mind that it was going to tumble, that

Bastet was bringing her temple down around her.

And then Ford's eyes opened.

He was staring up at the ceiling, and a puzzled, then pleased look spread over his bruised face. The effect was unsettling, to say the least.

"Damned if I didn't actually do it," he muttered with the sort of amazed intonation one might have expected from a schoolboy who had managed to fell the local bully despite all expectations to the contrary.

"Yes, you did it," she snapped in reply. "And what you did is going to get us killed if we don't get out of here." She pointed up, to the growing cracks in the ceiling and the slow movement of the capitals of the pillars. Her expression softened. "Can you walk?" she asked.

"It looks like I'll die trying if I can't," he replied grimly as he pushed himself up. He put his hand to his temple. "The ride was pleasant enough, but the landing was a bit rough," he said with a resolute grin.

She put her arm to his waist and, still dizzy, he made no move to push it away. Together they slid to the statue's side, and then down, to the floor.

"Wait," Amity told him.

She moved forward and knelt to retrieve the blade she had dropped there. The floor seemed to be shifting beneath her, but the shock that knowledge generated was nothing compared to what she felt as she saw the long arm extended from beneath Bastet's mass. The fingers of the hand were long and thin, and the arm wore a sleeve of golden fabric. A dark ooze of bright blood eked its way from beneath the goddess's body. Bastet had taken Sareef with her to her grave.

Amity screamed.

Ford put his hand to her shoulder. Still shuddering, she turned to stare up at him.

"We have to get out, Amity," he told her.

336

She nodded. The rumblings were growing louder, and she could see the scattering of coals from the brazier seem to move of their own volition, their bright bits of flames jumping first this way, then that as the floor shifted beneath them.

"Justin said this temple was built over a small spring," Ford told her. "The force of the statue's fall must have been great enough to shake the foundation. There's no telling what's happening beneath us."

She nodded and stood. He was not telling her anything she could not accept.

"Get the knife," he told her calmly.

She realized she had forgotten it in the surprise of finding Sareef's body and had started to stand without retrieving it. She knelt and quickly snatched it up, taking care not to look at Sareef's exposed arm. Then she stood and handed the knife to Ford. He put it into the pocket of the priest's robe he still wore. Then he put his arm once more around her shoulder.

"Some hero I am," he muttered. "I was supposed to rescue you."

He was leaning heavily against her, Amity realized, something he would never have allowed himself to do were it not necessary. She put her hand to his waist and prayed she was strong enough to get the two of them out of the temple before it became their grave as well as Sareef's.

"Good enough," she assured him. "Justin would have killed me if you hadn't sent his goddess to her doom before he had the chance."

"Let's just hope I haven't done the same for us," he replied.

They moved forward, and Amity could feel him hold himself firmly, not allowing himself to falter, to bring them down to the shifting surface of the floor. All around them the small fires burned, some of them reaching the trampled bodies and igniting their clothing, making gruesome human torches of the dead who had been left behind in the stampede to leave the temple. She would not let herself see those things, but kept her glance firmly on the door, wishing it closer even as it seemed to grow farther and farther away. Mostly it was the noise, though, that terrified her, the groaning, the shifting sounds, raw and brittle, as though the temple were tearing itself loose from the very core of the earth beneath it.

They were almost to the door when the first of the pillars, those closest to the front of temple where Bastet's great stone body lay, toppled. There was a huge roar as the stone fell, then a tremendous, thundering noise as the floor beneath them split and dropped inward.

Amity found herself lying on the floor. Beside her a huge slab of stone had suddenly given way. Ford was clinging to the side of it, his feet dangling downward into darkness.

She reached for him and screamed.

"Ford!"

"Get out," he shouted to her.

"No. Not without you."

She held tight to his wrists, refusing to let him allow himself to fall. He was struggling, trying to pull himself up and over the ledge of stone, groaning with the pain his injured ribs inflicted at the effort.

The noise was growing steadily until it seemed almost deafening. When she looked up, she could see the first pieces of the roof falling in at the far end of the temple, above the place where Bastet had stood. Closer to them, the pillars had begun groaning with the pressure of stones shifting above and below, as though they knew they could not long bear the pressure and remain standing.

"Please, Ford, try," she shouted. Her words were lost amidst the chaos of noise, but still she entreated him. "Try!"

And then he heaved himself, grunting in pain as he raised himself upward and forward. She grasped his arm and pulled with all her strength, helping him to push himself up and then roll onto the stone and away from the gaping hole in the earth that had threatened to swallow him. She scrambled to her feet and knelt to him, pulling him upward, somehow getting him to his knees and then to his feet.

They could not die now, she told herself. She would not let either of them die now.

Her arm around Ford, they stumbled forward. The open doorway beckoned with a dark emptiness, the blackness of a desert night. They fell forward to it, gasping with the effort, finally tumbling out into the darkness and onto the sand just as the last of the pillars toppled and the temple crumbled in upon itself behind them.

In her fall Bastet had turned her temple into her final monument, a monument of ruin.

Amity lay still in the sand, feeling her heart pounding in her chest. She could hear Ford's labored breath, could feel the warmth of his body lying in the sand beside her. For a moment she was not quite sure she could believe they both were still alive, that they had both escaped. The ruins of the temple lay just steps behind them, still angrily noisy as shifts below the ground continued to occur.

"I think we should move away," she suggested when she finally found the strength to speak.

She looked off into the darkness of the desert. There were noises, human noises, she realized. Bastet's priests and worshippers, those who had survived, were fleeing off into the night. Justin, Amity assumed, was among them. Still she felt wary, afraid they might come back, afraid they might decide to take some revenge for the wrong done to their goddess. Even though she was not at all sure that stumbling off into the desert at night would provide them much protection, she felt they ought to leave. She stared at Ford. He hardly seemed in any condition to put up much of a fight.

Ford grunted in pain as he pushed himself to his knees. "I think you're right," he agreed.

She held on to him, and the two of them staggered through the sand. When they'd gone a fair distance, Ford turned and looked at the shifting remains of the temple.

"This should be far enough," he said, and together they lowered themselves to the sand.

Amity stared at the pile of broken stone that had once been the temple. However horrible her experience there might have been, from the distance and in the mellowing glow of moonlight, the ruins seemed beautiful, romantic.

She moved closer to him.

"Cold?" he asked as he put his arm around her shoulder and pulled her nearer to him.

She was, she realized. The thin drape of the dress she wore offered little warmth against the desert night.

"A little."

"More than a little, I think," he said as he ran his hand over the bare skin of her arm.

He pulled off the dark priest's robe he still wore and then wrapped it around them both.

"Tomorrow we'll start off toward Heliopolis. It's a fair walk, but we ought to be able to make it by mid-day. With any luck, we should find some elderly duke on his wedding tour with his young bride roaming

340

through the ruins there and be able to convince them to give us a ride back to Cairo. If not, it'll be a long day tomorrow."

He stared at Amity, wondering if she could endure a forced march through the desert. She looked far too frail for such effort, especially dressed as she was. Still, she'd shown surprising strength back at the temple. There was, he decided, determination and unsuspected toughness hidden within that decidedly pleasant form.

He tore his eyes from her and looked around in the darkness. Although the night sky was deep and lustrous with a brilliant sweep of stars, the moon was bright enough to cast a silvery light on the landscape.

"It's a shame the mounts Justin and I left hobbled out here are gone. Probably stolen by one of the fine celebrants of that charming spectacle in there when he decided it was a propitious time to leave."

"What do you think will happen to them?" Amity asked him softly. "Justin and those others?"

He shrugged.

"Who knows? They'll probably disappear, just melt into the woodwork. The khedive won't bother too much with a crime that affects only the Copts. As long as the local civil power isn't disturbed, native Egyptians can kill each other in peace if they do it quietly. But Justin, he's a different matter. He's a dead man if he stays in Egypt. He's probably racing for Alexandria right now in hopes of finding some transport."

Ford pulled her still closer. He hoped he sounded reasonably confident, more confident than he felt. For he knew Justin wouldn't give up his life in Egypt, the life of a wealthy, landed man, without a fight. And the two of them, he and Amity, were Justin's enemies, the ones who could expose the atrocities he'd committed. One way or another, Justin would try to get to them if he thought he could do it safely.

341

One thing was certain in Ford's mind. If Justin thought a bit of killing could save his position for him, he was not above trying.

Chapter Nineteen

"Why would they do such a thing?" Amity asked. She waved her hands toward the place in the distance where the ruins of the temple lay, slowly working their way to silence and peace. She could not understand how any human being could do what she'd seen done there, how any man could do what Justin had intended to do to her. "Justin, I mean, and an educated man like Sareef?" she wondered aloud.

"Justin is a mystery to me," Ford admitted. "I'm only just starting to realize just how much of a mystery. Perhaps it was just the allure of doing something forbidden. I don't know. As for the others, who can say? Egypt has been conquered so many times through the ages, by the Greeks and the Romans and the Ottomans and God knows who else. Perhaps this was their way of clinging to their own past, reviving some small bit of their antiquity and making themselves a part of it. Perhaps it is just a way of affirming that they hold some small part of Egypt that cannot be conquered."

"But their rites involved murder!" she protested.

"Men have done worse in the name of religion, Amity," he replied calmly. "Were the Crusades anything but organized murder? Or the Inquisition? This was wrong. But it was certainly not the first time religion has been used to justify man's taste for violence. Nor do I think it will be the last."

She pressed herself close to him.

"In any case, I'm glad you decided to come after me," she whispered.

He turned and gazed down at her upturned face.

"In any case," he agreed, "so am I."

He put his hands to her cheeks and rubbed away the stains of blood and the bright rouge that had been applied to her cheeks.

"That's better," he whispered. "You know, you do look like an ancient goddess."

He kissed her. It was not a questioning kiss, nor a tentative one, but an affirmation, a man claiming what he had determined to be his. And Amity willing accepted it, parting her lips to the probe of his tongue, tasting his lips and his mouth while she felt her own passion growing inside her. She had felt so sure she would never see him again, that her life would end on the altar within Bastet's temple and she would die never knowing if he had ever really loved her. Now she had her answer. The power of it filled her, swept through her with a wave of deep, surging desire unlike anything she had ever dreamed could happen to her.

"Is that what you came out here to find, Ford?" she asked. "A goddess?"

"I came to find you, Amity," he told her. "To ask you if you could stand to live with an undistinguished British officer in a little house on the outskirts of Cairo with only one elderly servant and no cook at all."

She smiled. "No cook?" she asked, hoping she sounded properly shocked.

"None whatsoever." He went on, his tone implying that the interruption had not been required. "It would be a fairly boring life, with few of the diversions you're accustomed to . . ." He grinned then, slyly knowing. "Although I suppose a child or two might serve to oc-

344

cupy your time."

She stared up at him and her own expression grew prim.

"Am I to assume this is a proposal of marriage, Major Gardiner?" she asked.

His grin broadened. "You may so consider it if it pleases you to do so, Miss Ravenswood."

"Then you've reconsidered your position regarding those reasons why you could not marry?" she asked softly.

He shook his head and the grin disappeared.

"No, nothing's changed, Amity. I'm still a man without family or position, without honor as far as the rest of the world is concerned, not a heritage I willingly bequeath. But perhaps the world will see my son for his own worth, and not with the stain his father let fall to him. I only know that I can't live without you. I love you, Amity. And it's enough for me to know that you know me innocent, that you could possibly love me in return."

She put her arms to his shoulders. "I do, Ford," she whispered. "I do."

"Enough to learn how to cook?" he demanded.

She smiled. "Even as much as that," she agreed.

His arms were around her, holding her tight, so tight she felt as though she were melting into him, becoming part of him, and he smiled at her before he pressed his lips against hers, warm and hard. The dark robe felt back onto the sand, and he lowered her to it, his hands cradling her, holding her to him. The night no longer seemed cold to her, but heady and warm and sweetly moist, like the touch of his lips and his hands against her skin.

It seemed it couldn't come to either of them fast enough, and they pushed away each other's clothing, Amity wriggling out of the thin drape of her dress as

345

Ford pushed it down to let his lips find her breasts, she tearing at the buttons of his shirt until he finally shrugged it away.

The touch of his flesh beneath her hands was like poetry, pure and beautiful, something that filled her soul. He lowered himself, to kiss her breasts and her bare belly, and she pulled him to her, her fingers in his dark curls, accepting this knowing survey of her body as it filled her with liquid fire.

Finally he brought himself to the downy-soft forest between her legs, and this, too, he kissed, stroking her with his fingers and his tongue until she thought there was nothing left to her but the molten surgings of her own desire.

He left her then to pull at the remainder of his clothing, shedding it with indifference and then letting her reach out to him and pull him to her. He pressed himself into her, feeling her enclose him, surround him, an indescribable joining that completely filled his senses. There could be a lifetime of this, he realized, and never would the feeling of the wonder of it leave him. When he made love to her there was nothing else, nothing but this heady narcotic feeling that made everything else seem weak and insubstantial. With her in his arms he felt himself strong enough to hold the world in his hands and not feel the burden of it.

Amity reached up to him and pulled him to her, closer, wanting to feel herself part of him, and him part of her. They were meant for this, fated to be one together. There was no other explanation for the certainty she felt when she was with him. They could not have escaped each other had they chosen to do so.

But she had no desire to escape this particular fate, no desire to flee from the touch of his hands and his lips, to escape the heady, sweet press of him inside her. She wanted only to open her whole life to him just as

346

she had at that moment, open and vulnerable. There was no stronger way in which she could show him her trust.

She clung to his body, joining him, pressing her hips to his, feeling almost as though she were melting into him. She was made for this, she realized, made for her body to be one with his. The knowledge, like the liquid press inside her, was heady and sweet.

She welcomed the waves that rose within her, accepting them, and finally welcoming the shattering, tumbling release. She gazed up at the stars and felt as though she were part of them, glowing and brilliant, unique in her love for him.

He felt her trembling release and let himself join her, let the sweet hot flow explode from him. He gave himself up to it, to the wonder how each time seemed like the first with her, the passion unfathomable, the release an unknown sea of wonder. He could not understand how he had ever been such a fool as to think of letting her go.

He lowered himself to lie beside her in the sand, spent and content, staring up at the stars. He put his arm out and encircled her and pulled her close to him.

She lay quietly spent in his arms, then snuggled closer, pressing her head against his chest.

He winced.

She pulled back. "I'm sorry. Did I hurt you?"

"It's all right, Amity," he replied. "It seems I'm a bit sore just there." He motioned toward his side. "A cracked rib, I think. A gift from Justin."

"You should have told me."

He smiled at her. "I must admit that for a while there, I wasn't feeling any pain at all."

She smiled back, then leaned forward to him and kissed him.

"We have to get you to a doctor," she said, her ex-

347

pression filling with concern.

"A task that will have to wait for a bit, I'm afraid. Don't look so worried. It'll mend."

"It *is* over, isn't it, Ford?" she asked. "We'll get back to Cairo and be married and all this will be as if it never happened."

He put his hand to her breast, cupping it gently.

"I think there are a few facets I'm quite glad have happened," he told her.

She laughed.

"When we're married, will you take me out to the desert and make love to me?" she asked.

He raised his hand to push the hair away from her cheek.

"Wanton. Would you prefer that to a properly sanctified marriage bed?"

She nodded. "Decidedly." She sobered. "I don't ever want us to become like Charles and Beatrice," she said. "I never want to lose what I feel right now."

He shook his head. "No chance of that, my love," he assured her.

Then he put his hand to the back of her head and pulled her down to him once more. Unprepared, she fell against him, but he gave no sign that the impact caused him any hurt. He seemed, for a second time that night, incapable of feeling any pain.

It was just barely dawn when Amity woke. She found Ford lying beside her, his head propped up on an elbow, staring down at her. He had drawn the priest's robe over them, and beneath it their shared body heat was pleasant, warmly intimate.

She stared up at him, puzzled by the bemused expression in his blue eyes.

"Penny for your thoughts, Major Gardiner?"

He smiled. "Such formality from the lips of a naked lady, Amity."

She smiled smugly and ran her hands along his body.

"I think I've no need to pay for your thoughts this morning," he said. He caught her hand and it held it so that it rested between his legs. "And I must admit the possibilities are intriguing." He leaned forward to her and kissed her lightly on the lips, then reluctantly pulled her hand from him. "But the temple has completely buried the spring. We have a long walk with no food and no water. I think we'd better leave now, before the sun gets too high. We'll travel faster that way."

She nodded, and reluctantly pulled back the robe that had covered them.

"Look," she laughed and pointed to a tiny ball of black-and-white fur that lay curled up in the sand not far from her feet.

Ford snatched up the kitten and handed it to her. Surprisingly tame, it lifted trusting eyes to her and meowed.

"Probably crawled in with us to stay warm," Ford told her as she petted the kitten. "Can't really blame her. Most of her usual sleeping companions are doubtless buried under the rubble of the temple."

Amity stared at the kitten. Such a small creature, she thought, to be made a victim of wrongs it had had no part of making.

"Let's take her back with us," Amity suggested. "She'll die out here."

Ford nodded agreement. "As will we if we don't get started."

They dressed quickly and set off, walking to the west, keeping the rising sun behind them. Ford draped the dark robe over Amity's shoulders to keep her warm in the early-morning cool, and she found, much to her surprise, that the kitten seemed quite content to doze in the robe's pocket, with her head and front paws peeking out. Her tiny body was a soft small contrast to the contents of the other pocket, where Ford had put the high priest's knife Amity had taken from Justin the night before.

She found her hand dropping occasionally to feel the hard certainty of the blade. It was repellent to her, yet still she could not think to take it from the pocket and throw it away, into the sand. It was, she realized, a reminder that they were not yet safe, and that Justin might be out there somewhere in the desert, waiting for them.

Justin dropped to his knees beside the ancient well and scooped some water up to his lips. It was warm and brackish, but he was in no position to be excessively fastidious. His throat ached with thirst, and this water was the only that was available to him. He lowered his head to the water, wet it, then wiped away the drips that ran from his hair onto his neck before drinking again.

When he'd had his fill, he pushed himself back and stared at the stones of the ruined temple of Rah Harmachis. Two thousand years before this place had been the center of the great, flourishing city of Heliopolis. It was said that it was within the walls of this temple that the child Moses was educated in the ancient language by the priests. And now it was only ruin.

Like his life. Everything, it seemed, lay in ruins around him, or at least soon would. He had been initiated as a priest into a secret cult that made human sacrifices, and when that fact was made known to the authorities, he would face certain death at the end of a rope. The British and the khedive could not let such deviation pass unnoticed . . .

That was, if it were ever brought to their attention. He felt a fool now, that he had run in panic from the collapse of the temple. He had no way of knowing now if either Amity or Ford had escaped or had died in the destruction of the temple. One thing he did know: if either of them ever returned to Cairo, he was as good as a dead man.

He should have stayed, waited to see if they'd gotten away. But he'd been frightened, terrified as he watched the great stone statue of the goddess topple. And in his fear he'd run.

It was no good trying to go back and find them, either. There was too much desert for a man on foot to think of searching. If only he'd stayed and watched. Now he was vulnerable, his fate in Ford's hands. The knowledge made him sick with fury and shame that he'd ever let such a thing happen.

Of course, he told himself hopefully, they both might be dead. It was likely they had been killed in the temple. Or, barring that, they might be injured and wandering in the desert. That would lead to their demise as surely as if he'd plunged his knife into both of them there on the altar to Bastet. The desert took life willingly, indiscriminately. Perhaps they would die and be lost to the sand.

As pleasant as it was to contemplate the possibility, Justin realized he could not simply assume they were dead, return to Cairo and pretend nothing had happened. But he could wait here in Heliopolis for them. After all, without horses, Ford would definitely come here first just as he had, seeking water and hoping to find a ride back to the city. All he would need do was keep himself hidden for a day or so. If they hadn't come by then, he could assume they were dead. And if they did come, he could see they were hurried into the hereafter.

351

He put his hand to his boot and withdrew the knife he kept hidden there. Yes, he mused, it would be easy to see them off on their final voyage.

Justin leaned back against the stone and stared across at the ruins of the ancient city. The morning sunlight bathed them in a golden glow. Merely heaps of stone, yet they were strangely evocative of a cleaner, purer time. Even as they were, little better than rubble, they were strong if silent witnesses to man's folly. They were, he decided, quite beautiful in the warmth of the bright morning sunshine. He stretched his arms and yawned.

Perhaps, he mused, his future was not quite as dark as it had seemed only a few moments before. Perhaps the ruins of this ancient city waited silently to witness the resurrection of his own fate.

The sun was high and the air thick and shimmering with the heat when they finally saw the ruins of Heliopolis. Ford pointed.

"You see, Amity I told you it was just like a little stroll through the park."

She scowled. If the morning had seemed like a stroll through the park to him, it had been something else entirely to her. She was exhausted and parched. The robe that had seemed so pleasantly warm in the early morning chill and which Ford had insisted she continue to wear as protection against sunburn seemed to feel hotter and heavier with every step she took. She entirely doubted that she could have gone on much farther. Had Ford not kept his arm around her, supporting her, she doubted that she could have gone on at all.

She surveyed the landscape of the ruined city as they neared it. It was eerie, silent and still, a field of tumbled pillars and half-destroyed walls, much of it partially covered by a drifting curtain of pale sand.

"It has been my experience that a stroll through the park is not officially complete unless it is concluded with a proper tea," she said with a sigh. "I don't suppose that anything in the nature of a proper tea is in the offing, is it, Ford?"

"I'm afraid the best we're likely to find here is a drink of not entirely crystal-pure water."

"I'll take it," she returned immediately. The thought of water, any water, made her throat tighten in expectation.

"And once we're back in Cairo," he promised, "a wedding ceremony followed by all the champagne you can drink."

She looked up at him, and found he was staring down at her with eyes filled with a pleasantly anxious light.

"Followed by a honeymoon?" she asked.

"The best my meager resources can provide," he replied. "What would you like to see?"

She smiled. "The ceiling," she whispered, then laughed.

"Hussy."

But he smiled, not at all displeased with the prospect of showing it to her.

They began climbing a small mountain of toppled pillars and slabs of pale granite, approaching the ruins of the temple. Ford grew tense, staring sharply into the heaps of fallen stone. Amity could feel the change in him, the sudden awareness, the tensing of his muscles.

"What is it, Ford?"

"Just looking around, love," he replied. "If Justin had decided to look for us, this is where he'd be waiting. But I doubt he's here, so there's no need for you to be concerned." He tried to keep his tone light and unconcerned, tried not to let her see that he was not really all that sure that what he was telling her was

353

true. Then he smiled and turned back to her. "The place seems empty. Too empty. I was hoping for that elderly duke, limping his way though the stones, nursing his gout."

She ignored his attempt at humor.

"It really is over, isn't it, Ford?" she asked, her voice nearly a whisper, as though she were almost afraid to ask.

He put his hands to her shoulders. "For us, it is. When we get back to Cairo, I will give my report to General Stuart and let him decide what to do about Justin. But for us, it's over."

He leaned forward to her and kissed her gently on the lips.

"Now, this way, love, for that drink of water I promised you."

He put his arm around her waist and led her through the rocks to the old well.

Amity let the dark robe fall from her shoulders, then put the kitten down on the sand beside her so that she could offer her a drink from her hands. The animal looked at her uncertainly, and put her paw to the water, but made no attempt to even taste the water. Amity thought she seemed dizzy, almost too weak to drink. She stared up at Ford, uncertain as to what she should do.

Ford lifted the kitten and put her on a nearby rock, then brought several handsful of water to it, letting the liquid form a small pool in a recess of the stone. The kitten lapped up the water thankfully, and when it was gone, meowed for more.

Amity laughed and refilled the small recess. She felt ebullient, suddenly almost light-headed. Now that they had reached Heliopolis safely and she and Ford had satisfied their thirsts, it really seemed to her that they were, finally, safe. She shed her fear as a snake sheds an old skin, and let her spirits rise with the sheer joy of being alive.

"We ought to name her," she said, pointing to the kitten. "Have you any suggestions?"

"How about Bastet?" Ford proposed. Then his expression grew somber. "Or perhaps you would rather forget about the goddess?"

Amity shook her head. "No, it's no good pretending none of it happened. And Bastet is an excellent name for her. Goddess of joy. I think her finding us was a good omen. I think she'll bring us good luck."

"Then Bastet it is," Ford agreed.

Amity smiled up at him. "I'm desperately hungry," she asserted. "When do you think our elderly duke and his bride might arrive for their sightseeing expedition?" she asked. She narrowed her eyes and looked at him slyly. "You don't suppose he'll bring along a picnic hamper with him, do you?"

He laughed. "I doubt it. The expedition would call for a hearty lunch in his hotel beforehand to fortify him for the exertion."

Amity scowled. "Well, I hope he at least arrives soon."

Ford looked up at the position of the sun. "It's well past three, I should think. Just about time for the crowd from the Hotel Mena to be arriving after their lunch," he replied.

Amity groaned. "Please, no more mention of lunch," she begged.

Ford responded with a dutiful smile, but his thoughts were turning elsewhere. Once again he surveyed the heaps of rubble, realizing even as he did so that they were surrounded by far too many places for a man to hide for him to be comfortable. He walked a half dozen paces away from the well and considered the relatively vulnerable spot where Amity sat, surrounded by small mountains of fallen stone.

He realized he was getting that odd feeling at the back of his neck again, and decided this was not a good time to ignore it. He turned back to face her.

"Perhaps we should wait out by the road. If the duke's gout is bothering him, he might not bother to come this far."

Amity nodded, then lifted the kitten and stood. "We wouldn't want to miss him," she agreed.

As she began to move forward she saw movement from the corner of her eye. There was something or someone hiding in the rocks, she realized.

"Ford . . ." she began, but even as she uttered his name, she heard the sound, like a thick, dull thud, as a stone struck the back of his head. His body grew suddenly rigid, then he slumped forward and fell.

"Ford!"

Amity scrambled through the rocks to him, dropping down at his side. He was completely still and there was a thick gush of blood at the base of his skull. She could feel his pulse beating when she put her hand to his neck. He was hurt, but still alive.

She shuddered as her eyes strayed to the rock that lay beside Ford, stained with his blood. There was only one person who could have thrown it, she knew, and the fact that he was there, that he had hidden himself and waited in ambush for them, could only mean he intended to see them both dead.

"It seems we will have the opportunity to finish what we've begun after all, Amity."

The sound of Justin's voice sent a shiver of fear down her spine, even though she had expected to hear it from the instant Ford had fallen. She turned and slowly stood.

She found he was staring at her as though he could not be quite sure he could believe his eyes. His expression grew clouded and he seemed unable to see Ford, unable to see anything, in fact, but her.

"You were my goddess," he said softly as he approached her. He moved carefully through the heaps of jagged stone, descending from the rise of rubble in which he'd hidden himself and waited. "From the very first moment I saw you, you were my goddess. If only you had accepted what I had to offer, none of this would have been necessary."

His words meant nothing to her, nor did the lost expression in his eyes. She couldn't see herself as he did, clad in the thin drape of linen, her hair still arranged as the old women had placed it for her sacrifice, and holding the cat in her arms. She couldn't know that he looked at her and saw the idol of Bastet. All she knew was what she saw—the dull, unbalanced look in his eyes as he approached her and the flash of sunlight reflected from the knife he held in his hand.

Her eyes fixed on the blade. There was no question in her mind as to his intentions. Unless she could find some way to stop him, both she and Ford would be dead within the hour.

Bastet jumped down from her arms, and once again concerned herself with lapping up the remainder of the puddle of water with which Amity had provided her. Justin's eyes followed the cat for an instant, then returned to Amity. They seemed to clear.

"We have unfinished business, you and I," he hissed through tight lips.

Amity took a step backward. "You can still get away, Justin. You can go now, get to Alexandria, leave the country."

He grinned and shook his head. "Why should I do that, Amity?" he asked her. "It will be so much easier

357

to kill you and Ford."

At first she was struck by the calm, emotionless manner in which he spoke of murder. It chilled her far more than his anger might, or even the sort of malice she'd seen in him the night before in the temple. He was, she realized, beyond feeling anything, beyond caring. The thought chilled her.

Amity refused to accept the panic that threatened to overcome her. She told herself they had too much to lose now, she and Ford, to let this happen. She glanced quickly to the place where she'd let the dark robe fall. There was still a blade in its pocket, she reminded herself. If only she could get to it, she stood a chance.

"But there's no need for that," she told him, struggling to make herself sound as calm as he did, struggling to keep the rising panic within control. "We'd already decided that there is no need for us to tell anyone about you, about what happened," she said. She stepped slowly backward, away from him, closer to where the dark robe lay on the ground. "You have nothing to fear from us. All we want is to be left alone."

He stepped forward as she moved back, slowly, deliberately.

"You don't expect me to believe that, do you?" he asked. Then he grinned at her, his expression half foolish, half vengeful. "And even if I did, you don't think I'd actually let *him* have you, do you?" He nodded his head in the direction where Ford lay. "I wouldn't give you to any man, Amity. I'd first see you dead." The calm demeanor was suddenly gone. He could talk of her murder without emotion, it seemed, but not about losing her to Ford. "But Ford!" His voice rose hysterically. "Ford!" he screamed. And then he managed to get himself under control. He looked at her with derision. "You chose a fool over me," he told her. "A fool.

All these years, he's paid for a theft I committed." He laughed then with bitter satisfaction.

Amity shook her head. She knew what it was he referred to, but his words were as senseless to her as those he'd uttered previously. "But it was Kendrick who stole the necklace. He told us so before he died."

He shook his head. "My father was a fool, too. A weakling and a fool. The necklace, the rifles, all of it was my doing. I had only to lift my finger and my father did as he was told. All he cared about was his damned land. He made it so easy to control him." His voice fell. "But for you," he whispered.

Amity shook her head, bewildered by what he was saying. He stole the necklace and let Ford carry the blame all those years? And *he* was the one who controlled the arms sales to Ali Kalaf? It all seemed too fantastic. She realized, however, she had no time to unravel it all. He was moving closer to her. If she were to get the knife, she must do it now. There would be no other chance.

She retreated another step and realized she was standing beside the robe now, that the moment had come. She darted him one last glance before she fell to her knees and grasped it. He misunderstood the gesture, only saw her on her knees in front of him. He stood over her and smiled.

"You finally understand, don't you, Amity?" he asked, his voice calm once again. "There is no escape for you. You belong to me. Your life belongs to me. And I have promised it to the goddess."

She grasped the robe and looked up at him while her hands desperately felt the fabric, seeking the sacrificial blade.

"Your goddess is no more, Justin," she told him. "She fell and was buried in the ruins of her own temple."

He shook his head and his eyes grew once again withdrawn and distant.

"She lives," he told her, his tone certain, his conviction unshakable. "She lives in you. Don't you see? That is why you must die. A goddess lives only in paradise."

Until that moment she hadn't really accepted the possibility that he might be deranged. She had thought his only motive had been revenge, against her for refusing him, against Ford for whatever reasons he'd managed to find in the past. But now she realized that there was no logic left to him besides his own twisted reasoning. And she realized he fully intended to sacrifice her to the goddess he insisted she personified.

And then she felt the blade beneath the folds of the fabric of the robe. She grasped the hilt in her hand and slowly rose, obscuring the weapon in the folds of her dress.

"If I am truly your goddess, then you must honor me."

She wondered where she found the strength to speak as she did to him, forcefully, with unquestioning command. She found his eyes with hers and held them for a moment, surprised to see him suddenly deflate beneath her stare. She pointed to the knife in his hand.

"You do not threaten a deity."

For a moment he seemed cowed by her. His hand shook, and he let the knife fall to clatter against the uneven stones. Amity could not believe that he had given in so easily. She told herself she could manage him, that if she accepted the role of Bastet she could control him.

But she was wrong. His eyes narrowed and his expression grew sly. He stepped forward, closer to her.

"Of course, the rites must be observed," he hissed at her. "The priest must make his offering first."

He reached out his hands toward her.

She stepped back and pulled out the sacrificial knife.

"Take one more step, Justin, and I swear to you, I'll use this."

His eyes fell to the knife in her hand and he smiled.

"You even bring the holy blade," he whispered, as though this fact confirmed in his mind that what he was about to do was preordained.

He lunged toward her and Amity slashed wildly at him. The blade caught him on the side of his arm and there was a sudden spray of red. But she had no idea how to use a knife, and he was quick to grasp her wrist and hold it where the blade could do him no further damage. She struggled against him, but his hold was firm and unyielding.

He raised his slashed arm and licked at the flow of blood.

"The first blood is spilled," he intoned softly, his words echoing the chant he'd sung in the temple the night before as he'd watched her being forced to the stone altar. "The ram's blood flows. And now the sacrifice begins."

He wrenched the blade from her hand and pushed her backward, down onto the rocks.

Chapter Twenty

Amity fell to the stone, but she hardly felt the impact. Nor was she more than remotely aware of Justin's hand as it pushed her skirt up her thigh. Her eyes fixed on the knife in his hand and her mind on the murder he intended to commit with it.

She began to struggle wildly with him, her fingers reaching out for his eyes to scratch them, her legs kicking, her body twisting. But her efforts were useless. He seemed oblivious to her, intent upon the act he intended. When he felt the bite of her nails into the flesh of his cheek he simply raised himself from her and struck her once, very hard, in the abdomen. The blow knocked the breath from her. Stunned, she momentarily quieted.

But she screamed and thrashed wildly when she felt his hands move up her thighs. She would not allow him to do this, she told herself. She would not allow herself to be used by him.

And then there was movement by her head, a blur of black-and-white fur. She realized the kitten had jumped, landing on Justin's shoulder. Bastet yowled wildly and dug her sharp little claws into Justin's arm and back.

Bewildered and shaken by the attack, he rose up, backing away from Amity, trying to free himself from this unexpected enemy. While he struck out angrily at the kitten, Amity pulled herself back and away from

362

him. She started to run, scrambling up the rubble heap of the temple ruins.

And then Justin managed to brush the kitten from his shoulder. Bastet fell down to the stone and stared up at him with surprising malice in her tiny eyes. But when Justin made a threatening move toward her, she ran and quickly hid herself in a crack between the rocks. Dismissing her, Justin turned his attention back to Amity.

"You can't escape me," he cried out to her. "You cannot run away from your fate."

He raised the hand in which he held the knife and started after her.

Amity screamed.

"You there. Stop that! Leave that woman alone!"

The cry was gruff and loud. Amity hesitated for a moment and turned to see the outline of a round, lumbering form standing at the far side of the huge field of rubble.

"You won't get away with it, Justin," she cried. "You've been seen. There will be a witness to murder."

He glanced quickly around to where the ungainly shadow was slowly working its way through the rocks. Then he turned his eyes back to her.

"He won't get here soon enough to help you, Amity. Neither you nor Ford. If I leave two bodies here, or three, it's all the same to me."

Amity darted another glance back at the stranger. He was, she realized, just as Justin had said, too slow and too far away to help her. Whoever he was, he would not reach her in time to keep Justin from using the knife. And Justin, she now saw, was beyond being stopped by the thought that he might be forced to commit a third murder in order to protect himself.

She climbed. Scrambling with both hands and feet, scraping her fingers and knees against the rough stone, she fled Justin with every ounce of strength within her.

And he climbed after her, pulling himself up through the huge mound of the ruins of the ancient temple, determined not to let her escape him this last time.

She felt his hand against her ankle, grasping for her, trying to pull her down. She screamed again. She realized then that there was no hope she might outrun him.

She turned, and found him staring up at her, the same deranged look in his eyes as he had had when he first saw her standing with the cat in her arms. He reached up and clawed at her leg with his hand, single-minded, determined to catch hold of her and finish what he had begun.

Amity leaned back against the stone and kicked at the hand that reached out for her. Her foot struck his forearm, just above the wrist, and he pulled it back. He seemed stunned, more by the look of sheer hatred she leveled at him and her sudden ferocity than by the force of the blow.

He looked up at her, his expression calm now, almost beseeching.

"Don't you see?" he cried out to her. "I do this for you. I send you to paradise. Don't you see that I'm saving you from an ugly life, from ruining yourself with men like Ford who will only use you? Can't you understand that the goddess will keep you as you should be, ageless and pure?"

"No," she screamed in reply and kicked once more at the hand he raised to her.

"Stop! Stop that!"

This time the cry was closer, and Justin could not ignore it. The sound of it seemed to unsettle him. He raised the knife and lunged at Amity.

She pulled away, fleeing him once more, scuttling over a ridge of broken stones, slipping and nearly tumbling as the loose stone slid beneath her feet. Justin followed after her, leaning forward to her, lashing out with the knife.

And then his foot slid on the loose stone and he slipped and fell.

There was a sharp cry, then he raised his head and stared up at her. Amity turned to him, bewildered, wondering why he lay so still, why he simply stared that way at her. Then he reached up his hand for her. This time it was no longer holding the knife. This time it was empty save for the thick red ooze of his own blood.

Amity shuddered as she saw him try to lift himself, as she saw the knife protruding from his chest, and realized that he had fallen on it.

"Amity," he murmured, his voice bewildered, beseeching.

Then he fell forward and lay finally still.

She backed away from him, still shaking, still afraid that if she got too close to him he might suddenly rise up again, a phoenix intent upon dealing her death. But he lay completely still save for the slowly growing slick of blood that ran from his body onto the rock.

Amity ran then, down through the seemingly endless heap of rubble, returning to where Ford lay silent and unmoving beside the pool of water. She fell to her knees at his side and touched his face, then moved closer so that she could cradle his head in her lap.

"Ford," she whispered, knowing only that she had to tell him. "It's over, Ford. He can't hurt either of us anymore."

Suddenly there seemed to be noise and movement all around them.

"I saw it. I saw him try to kill her."

"Is this one dead, too?"

"I think there's something wrong with her. She doesn't seem to understand."

"My dear, are you hurt?"

Amity looked up. She felt strangely removed, dull, as though only some small part of her were actually there. Part of her brain took in the four of them, and recorded the details for her: the two old men, both better dressed for the Surrey countryside than for the Egyptian desert, one limping and using a cane, the one who seemed to be speaking to her. There was a woman, much younger than either of her companions, her expression one of absolute distaste at what she must perceive as the vulgarity of the scene. And finally their guide, dressed in a flowing white *aba* and striped *kaffiyeh,* the only one who dared approach close enough to her to touch her.

"Are you hurt, ya sitt?" he asked softly as he put his hand to her shoulder. "Will you let us help you?"

But Amity didn't hear his words. She was staring up at the elderly Englishman, the one with the cane. It was Ford's duke, complete with gout, she thought, come to give them a ride back to Cairo. She started to laugh, shaken with a sudden hysteria that changed without warning to tears for no reason she could understand.

And then the kitten appeared at her side, meowing softly, and rubbing herself against Amity's thigh. Such a strange little beast, Amity thought, and the realization came to her that it had been the kitten that had saved her life by leaping on Justin's shoulder. It had been Bastet's attack that had given her the chance to get away. She pondered that fact a moment, wondering why such a tame little animal would do what the kitten had done.

"It was the goddess," she told Ford as she stroked his cheek, speaking to him calmly, as if he could hear her words. "It was Bastet who saved us."

Then hands were lifting her, urging her aside as the guide reached down to Ford.

"You'll be fine once we get you to Cairo, my dear," the elderly man was saying to her as he and the young woman guided her toward the road. When she looked back to Ford, he patted her arm. "Don't worry. He'll be tended to as well. You'll both be fine."

She nodded, still too numb to speak.

Then she pulled away from him, ignoring the puzzled expression he leveled led at her as she pushed his hand aside. She ran back to retrieve the kitten, lifting her from where she stood, reproachfully meowing at being so completely forgotten, and settling her comfortably on her arm.

As she had suggested to Ford, the kitten had proved to be good luck to them. Or perhaps, she thought, it was the goddess, acting through her creature, finally determined that the killing should end. In any case, Amity had no intention of leaving Bastet behind.

Amity leaned over the rail of the balcony and looked out over the starlit expanse of deep blue water that lay spread out below her. The reflection of the moon sat like a fat, round water lily floating on the waves. It seemed almost too beautiful a view for her to think it actually real.

Such a calm night, she mused. How could she think of anything unpleasant on such a beautiful night as this?

"Amity?"

Ford came out onto the balcony and put a blanket around her, then stood close behind her.

"More dreams?" he asked her gently.

She nodded as she caught the edges of the blanket and pulled it around her. She'd been cold in the damp of the night air but hadn't wanted to return to the room for fear she might disturb him, might wake him and sob out the same words she'd told him a dozen times over in the preceding nights. She'd felt that if she talked about

367

the dreams they might seem less real, but that hadn't happened. And now that he was there beside her, now that he'd asked her about the dreams, her throat was suddenly too tight for her to speak. Instead, she leaned back into him and rested her head against his naked chest.

"It's all over," he whispered, his lips close against her ear. Then he put his hands to her shoulders and turned her so that she faced him. "Didn't I promise to love, honor, and protect you?" he asked her with a smile.

She found herself suddenly smiling back at him. He seemed so boyish to her, standing there naked, his tousled hair falling onto his brow, his blue eyes bright in the moonlight. And with the smile came the yearning to be close to him, to feel his arms around her.

"I am safe," she replied. "When I'm in your arms, I know I'm safe."

"And you'll never leave them," he replied. "That's what this means." He lifted her left hand, showed her the golden band he'd placed on the third finger only three days before.

He released her hand and pulled her close, putting his hand to the back of her head, letting his fingers drift through her hair as her cheek fell against his chest.

"Give yourself a little time, my love," he whispered. "As hard as it may be to believe right now, the memory will fade. And the nightmares will fade with it."

She nodded. "I know," she murmured. "But sometimes it seems so real, as though it were happening again. I close my eyes and I can see the temple, smell the incense, and he's there, leaning over me, holding the knife."

She didn't mention the terror that filled her when the dreams started, a terror that left her trembling and bewildered when she woke, a terror so real that she hated even the thought of sleep. There was no need. Each of he previous nights when the dreams had finally released her, he'd wake to find her lying beside him in the darkness, sobbing, the echo of silent screams that she could not voice filling her head. He'd held her in his arms until the fear ebbed, but still, even when he'd lie with his arms around her, she'd try to remain awake, fearing the return of the dream.

But this night the dream had not gone so far before she'd wakened. She'd not seen Justin holding the knife, not watched it begin to fall. This time there had been no silent screams, no waking with her body trembling. Instead, she'd forced herself from the dream before any of the real horror had begun, managing to wake herself before the real terror had begun. She'd risen, leaving him still asleep in their bed. Perhaps it really was beginning to fade, just as he said it would. Perhaps the next time there would be even less of the dream to torture her.

Only now, with his arms around her, she didn't want to think of the dream, nor of the real nightmare that had caused it. She raised her arms to his shoulders, not caring that the blanket he'd wrapped around her began to fall. She felt no cold with her flesh close to his. The contact set free a fire within her that could stave off a far greater cold than that of the balmy air that surrounded them.

"This is not a dream," he whispered as he let his hands move slowly against her skin. He felt the slope of her waist, the sweet swelling of her hips, warm and silken against his hands. Then he brought his lips to hers as the need for her began to build inside him.

Amity pressed her hips forward, encouraging him, eager to let him send away the last of the specters of her dreams with his passion. She parted her lips to his tongue, welcoming the sweet probe and the dizzying rush it provoked within her.

This, she told herself, only this was real. They had the

369

rest of their lives to explore this intoxicating realm into which he took her, and nothing could ever take that from her. Even the terror of all that had happened, even the horror of her dreams, all of it suddenly seemed to have meaning for her as it had brought them to each other.

And then he was lifting her in his arms, holding her close to him, smiling as he gazed into her eyes.

"I think it time you were abed, Mrs. Gardiner," he said as he turned and carried her back into their room.

She smiled, no longer thinking of the dreams that had haunted her in the bed to which he would take her, thinking instead only of the pleasure they had shared there. Then she laughed.

"I believe you had the same thought this afternoon about noon, Ford."

His eyes narrowed.

"And I would not be surprised if the same thought occurred to me again tomorrow morning, and perhaps at noon, and even again at teatime."

She threw her head back and laughed once more, only this time the sound of it was deeply throaty, more pleased than amused.

"Teatime!" she exclaimed with a not entirely successful attempt to sound shocked as he set her down on the already rumpled sheets. "I fear you will come to a bad end after all. How can an upstanding member of Her Majesty's armed services contemplate anything except tea at teatime? Doesn't that constitute subversion, the undermining of the empire, perhaps?"

He expression remained completely somber.

"I fear you have been grievously deceived, Amity," he told her. "Teatime was specifically devised so that an officer might retire with his wife and expend his very best effort toward providing the queen with an additional subject. It is a highly honored custom."

"No tea?" she asked.

He shook his head. "None whatsoever."

"Scones?" she persisted. "Little cakes? You're entirely sure?"

He nodded. "Absolutely positive. Those things you've mentioned are just diversionary tactics, let out to colonists and the like, to keep them from the truth. We can't be going around giving away state secrets, you know."

She grinned, but refused to give up. "Crumpets!" she exclaimed in triumph. "What about crumpets?"

He pushed her back against the pillows, then leaned forward to her and licked her breast thoughtfully.

"Well, perhaps a taste of crumpet," he agreed, and he set himself about the task of tasting, letting his tongue and lips tease her flesh until it grew taut with want.

Amity put her hands to the back of his head, letting her fingers riffle his dark curls. His touch sent off ripples inside her, eddying through her, a heated, expectant tide that began to fill her. She gave herself up to the flow, hungry for the feelings she knew he would awaken in her.

He raised himself to her once again, and he was smiling now.

"Do you understand?" he asked. "This is how it's done in the very best of families."

"Is it?" she asked, sure that the things she was feeling at that moment would be decidedly frowned upon in an entirely proper British household.

Then he was kissing her, and his hands were touching her, her breasts and her thighs and the soft mound of Venus, trailing through the small hillock of curls to find the moist warmth inside her.

She spread herself beneath him, hungry for him, eager for the sweet fire he ignited in her. And she softly moaned with pleasure as he slid into her, then pressed herself to him, locking him tight inside her in an embrace of welcome.

They made love slowly, with the more knowledgeable expertise the previous days had given them, touching each other, letting lips and tongue meet and part and taste. They had both found that the desire to bring the other pleasure had heightened their own, both discovered the secret language that only their bodies could speak, that could have meaning for the two of them alone.

And Amity clung to him, seeking the refuge he had promised her. She turned her back on the memories and the fear, denying them place within her, taking Ford inside herself instead and letting him fill her. He had been right, she told herself. The memories would fade, they would become unreal to her. Only this sweet, heady narcotic with which he filled her would remain.

The tides rose within her, higher and higher until they swept through her with such power she thought she might shatter from the force of them. She welcomed them, gave herself over to them and let them wash through her.

In their wake they left her clean and, for the first time in her life, completely free. She felt that part of her that had seemed incapable of releasing the past loosen its hold and then finally let go.

She let herself float on the ebbing flow, holding herself close to Ford, listening to the beat of his heart and the echoing beat of her own. She peered up at him and saw herself reflected in his eyes. Her image, she realized, looked happy, completely and unreservedly happy.

He put his hand to her chin.

"I love you," he whispered. "Have I told you how much I love you?"

She smiled. "Isn't that what we've just been doing?" she asked. "Telling each other how much we love one another?"

He nodded. "But I've just begun," he murmured as he lowered his face to hers and kissed her softly on the lips. "I've a great deal more still to say, and all of it means I love you."

She wrapped her arms around his neck and smiled up at him in contentment. "As have I," she said.

They made love again, both saying the words silently with their hands and their bodies as well as speaking them aloud, both aware that they would never tire of repeating or hearing them.

When he cradled her finally in his arms, she let the wave of exhaustion sweep over her. For the first time in days she realized she welcomed it, that there was no fear in her of sleep and the dreams that sleep might bring her. For the first time she slept peacefully, the memories that had haunted her at last impotent in the face of their love.

"I've been out here several times trying to find you, Major Gardiner."

The words "Lieutenant Colonel," not "Major" were on Amity's lips, but she bit them back. She realized that Ford was not yet quite easy with his promotion, that he felt it came to him swimming on a sea of blood.

"I regret the inconvenience you've been caused, Mr. Barrows. My wife and I have only just returned from a trip to Alexandria." Ford looked up to where Amity stood to the rear of his chair and offered her a smile. "It was a wedding trip."

A honeymoon, Amity thought, and yet something else. More a period of recuperation, of learning again to fall asleep, to walk in a street, to accept life without being afraid. Still, she would not have traded those days with him in that small hotel overlooking the Mediterranean. After everything that had happened to them, those healing days in Alexandria had brought them closer together than she had ever thought two people could be.

"Yes, yes," Barrows replied. "I was so informed by your commanding officer when it finally occurred to me to inquire." He pressed himself to offer Amity his best effort at a smile. "And my very best wishes to you both, of course."

He shifted uneasily in the room's single comfortable chair Ford had insisted he occupy and adjusted the spectacles that seemed determined to slip too far down his nose. Then he reached to the case he'd set on the floor near his feet. As he did, a small black-and-white kitten removed itself from the place where it had been hiding beneath the chair, stared at him with an oddly evaluating glance, then strode off, dismissing him as not worthy of her attentions. He saw both Ford and Amity smile at the creature as she stalked from the room and forced himself to hide the scowl that ached to be released. Not for the first time in his life he wondered how people could possibly be so tolerant of their pets. He certainly would never allow a smelly animal to share his home.

His hand found the leather case and he lifted it, then began hastily to unbuckle the straps.

"I wouldn't, of course, presume to bother you unless the matter were important."

"Certainly," Ford agreed.

He seemed a bit bored, but more than that, amused by the man's fussily uncomfortable manner. He reached up to take Amity's hand in his and held it.

"Are you sure I can't fix you some tea, Mr. Barrows?" she asked. "Or perhaps something stronger?"

Barrows shook his head. "Oh, no. Thank you, no. This business ought not to take but a few moments, and I won't think of having you put yourself out, Mrs.

374

Gardiner."

"It would be no bother," she prompted.

Again the not quite certain smile. *He probably thinks I couldn't manage to prepare decent tea,* Amity thought, then admitted to herself he was probably right. But that would change, she determined. She would be a perfect wife to Ford, or at least the best she could be.

"Thank you, no." The buckles finally unfastened, he reached into the leather case, withdrew a handful of papers, and considered them with an air of deep solemnity. "As I mentioned," he said after he'd rather noisily cleared his throat, "I was solicitor to both Mr. Kendrick Gardiner and Mr. Justin Gardiner. In that capacity, I've been entrusted with the final dispersal of both those gentlemen's estates." He looked up to Ford. "First, Mr. Kendrick Gardiner entrusted to me two letters to be delivered in the event of his death. The first, as per his instructions, I have forwarded to the firm of Soames and Harley, Fawkes Court, London . . ."

"But they were my father's solicitors," Ford interrupted.

"Quite," Barrows replied.

"I don't understand."

"Perhaps this will make matters clearer," Barrows suggested, and offered him an envelope. "The second letter was to be delivered to you."

Ford took it, then gave the solicitor a puzzled look. But Barrows settled back into his chair, for the first time starting to look comfortable now that he was in his own element. He was apparently prepared to wait for however long it took Ford to read this letter before he proceeded any further.

Ford shrugged, tore open the envelope and removed a single sheet of gray vellum covered with Kendrick's neat, even hand:

Ford,

As you are now reading this, I am dead. Letters of this sort, I believe, are rather old-fashioned. Still, I can find no better way to do this, and so I find myself asking you for the pardon I was too much a coward to ask of you while I yet lived. If I had been stronger, perhaps I would have found the strength to tell you that I was the cause of all you have suffered since that night when your grandmother's necklace disappeared. Perhaps I might even have taken on the blame that you should never have been forced to bear. As it is, I can only swear to you that you were the last person I ever wanted to see hurt, although I know that fact can hardly bring you any comfort considering all the harm that has been done you. I can only say what I have done, I have done for the sake of my son.

I can, however, make some effort at amends. Toward that end, I have instructed Barrows to forward a letter to your father's solicitors in London, explaining that you bear no guilt and hopefully clearing your name. Although it is too late to mend matters between you and your father or to return to you the estate that ought to have been yours, I can, at least, give you back the honor I stole from you.

I have thought a good deal about one last matter, and have come to the determination that despite his pretense, Justin's true love is his business. I have no doubt but that he will make his own success there. As I am sure he will have no need of the little I have managed to accumulate in my lifetime, I can leave to you the only object of value I own, Gardiner's Ghenena. I pray this will in some way compensate you for all I have unjustly taken.

I pray you will not remember me with too much
bitterness.

Kendrick.

"But that's wrong," Amity murmured. She'd been
reading, too, over Ford's shoulder, and had just come to
Kendrick's confession. "It was Justin. The necklace, Ali
Kalaf's rifles, it was all Justin's doing. He gloated about
it. I told you."

Ford looked up to her and nodded. "Kendrick tried to
protect him, I suppose. That was why he confessed to
me in the first place, or perhaps he simply felt guilty for
keeping silent about it all those years. For whatever reason, he decided to clear me and still protect Justin in
the only way he could, by taking on the blame himself."

Barrows maintained a air of distance while they
spoke, but when Ford fell silent, he once again cleared
his throat.

"I may now inform you that Mr. Gardiner has left to
you the tract of land known as Gardiner's Ghenena. As
the only liens against it are held by the estate of Mr.
Justin Gardiner, and as you are the closest surviving relative of that gentleman and thus his sole heir as well,
the estate is essentially free and clear—"

"Just a minute," Ford interrupted. "Do you mean to
tell me that Justin held title to the debt on his father's
land?"

Barrows nodded. "Precisely," he confirmed. "He purchased the outstanding loans several years ago."

"And Kendrick knew this?"

Barrows cleared his throat once more, this time with a
shade of embarrassment.

"It is my belief that he was never made aware of that
fact," he replied.

Amity turned to Ford. "Could he have actually done such a thing?" she asked. "Could he have been so much a monster as to force his own father to deal with Ali Kalaf by having him dunned for money on liens he himself held?"

Ford seemed as unable to believe it as was she. He leaned forward, to Barrows. "Did he?" he demanded. "Did Justin press his own father for payment of those debts?"

Barrows stirred uncomfortably. "I was, of course, not privy to either gentleman's private business. I can only tell you that on several occasions, payment was demanded against the outstanding debt."

"And you saw nothing wrong in acting as the middleman for these transactions?" Ford asked sharply.

"I am merely a solicitor, sir. Not a fiduciary adviser. I merely execute those instructions given me by my clients."

Despite the words, Barrows's pale cheeks colored noticeably. He had grown decidedly uneasy.

"Of course," Ford said, the words thick with sarcasm. "You were only doing your duty."

"Precisely," Barrows agreed, ignoring his tone. "Now, with regard to Gardiner's Ghenena, if you would care to review the transfer papers and sign them, I'll see to the details."

"Ford?"

He turned to Amity and saw her pained expression.

"After everything that happened there . . ." she began.

He nodded, understanding, and turned back to Barrows.

"My wife has resigned herself to the less than extravagant lifestyle of an army wife, Mr. Barrows," he said slowly. "I believe we would both rather see Gardiner's Ghenena divided and transferred to the *fellaheen* who have labored on it all these years."

378

Barrows seemed incapable of accepting the thought. "But the estate is worth quite a good deal of money, Major. If you choose not to hold it yourself, it could be sold for a handsome price, especially in view the fine crops that it has produced over the past few years."

Ford shook his head. "My wife and I both feel the land would fare better in the hands of those who have tended it over the years, sir." He looked back up to receive Amity's agreeing nod. "You will see to the disposal of the land as I have suggested to you."

Obviously not precisely pleased, but in no position to offer further argument, Barrows shrugged in resignation.

"As you wish, sir." He removed a pencil from the case, scrawled a note to himself in a small leather-bound book, then shuffled through the heap of his papers before he continued. "Now," he went on when he'd located what he had been looking for among the rest and removed it from the pile, "as to the matter of Mr. Justin Gardiner's accounts . . ."

Ford simply shrugged. "I don't suppose there's much there," he said.

After the way Justin had determined to try to save the shipment of rifles, Ford had come to assume its loss must have come close to ruining him.

Barrows looked up at him, his expression perplexed. "On the contrary," he said. "Mr. Gardiner left an estate in excess of one and a half million pounds."

Amity gasped.

"One and a half million? But that's impossible."

Amity heard Ford's words through a haze. She felt a bit weak. A million and a half pounds was an enormous fortune. She fell onto the arm of Ford's chair, suddenly not quite sure she had the steadiness required to stand.

Barrows shrugged. "I have the account books here, sir. I will leave them for your inspection. There will, of course, be the usual half-percent transfer charge, and my fees as well, but you should realize close to the figure I mentioned." He rose with the magisterial grace that the handling of true fortunes imparts and held out a sheet of paper to Ford. "If you will sign this authorization, I will be more than happy to tend to the details."

Ford took the sheet, scanned the half dozen lines written on it, then stood, crossed to his desk, and signed it. Barrows followed him and watched, apparently completely mesmerized by Ford's hand as it held the pen. Then he blotted the signature carefully, lifted the sheet and folded it, then placed it in his case.

"A great pleasure, Major Gardiner," he said as he began to refasten the buckles. That task completed, he held his hand out to Amity. "Again, my best wishes, madam. I hope you can excuse my barging in on you this way, unannounced."

"Not at all, Mr. Barrows," she murmured, incapable of saying more. She lifted her hand and let him take it. She still felt numb, still could not quite believe that Justin's death had brought them this unexpected wealth.

He shook her hand quickly and grinned at her, the expression making his round face appear owlish. Then he turned back to Ford.

"Major," he said, and once again offered his hand. "My heartiest congratulations on both your marriage and your good fortune."

Ford glanced at Amity's dazed expression then accepted Barrows's handshake.

"My marriage is my good fortune, Mr. Barrows," he said evenly. "What you have brought me is mere surfeit."

Barrows seemed as bewildered by this sentiment as by those that had preceded it, but he smiled, nodded pleasantly and bade them both farewell.

380

Chapter Twenty-one

They had walked the path from the house to the river in a companionable silence, and stood for a while staring at the Nile moving past them before Ford spoke.

"I've been examining Justin's accounts," he said.

Amity looked up at him, but said nothing. Instead, she waited for him to tell her what it was that was on his mind.

"There is one large entry, dating apparently from about the same the time Ali Kalaf's men began to appear armed with those first Meerschmidts, not much of a surprise, I suppose, after what you told me he said about Kendrick before he died. But most of his money came from the brokering of cotton. Apparently there has been a steadily rising demand for the best quality Egyptian cotton on the Continent over the past several years."

"There is nothing wrong with that," she said.

"No," he agreed. "But apparently the cotton he sold came mostly from Gardiner's Ghenena. To put it simply, he sold Kendrick's cotton for a fortune and returned to Kendrick only a small percentage of what he realized."

"You're saying he stole from his father?"

He nodded.

"But why? Presumably he would have eventually come into Kendrick's fortune."

"For the same reason he bought up the liens on Gardiner's Ghenena," Ford told her. "To keep Kendrick in debt to him. To be sure he could manipulate Kendrick when it suited him."

"As when he wanted to use Gardiner's Ghenena to illegally sell arms?"

Ford nodded.

Amity turned away to stare at the flow of water surging past them.

"The more we learn of him, the greater monster he seems," she said. She felt a wave of revulsion as she realized she had almost allowed herself to commit the folly of marrying him.

"I don't think there will be anymore," he said. "I think we can let him lie quiet now."

She turned back to look up into his eyes.

"And you, my love? Have you decided?" she asked.

The money and Kendrick's confession had set him free, and they had spoken of the possibility of his resigning his commission and returning to England. She had realized when he'd first broached the matter that he was of a mixed mind. She had taken great pains to tell him that she was perfectly happy, that whatever he chose, she would be content. And it was true, she had realized. She had never been happier in her life.

He took her hand and raised it to his lips.

"Are you unhappy with this life, Amity?" he asked her softly.

She shook her head. "No," she replied. "I even find I like cooking."

He smiled, but then grew serious.

"For the longest time I felt as though I was trapped here, with no other place to go. And now that I can leave, I find there's no place I want to go. The Army has been good to me." He put his hand to her cheek and smiled at her. "And so has Egypt."

"Then you've decided to stay on here, as we are?"

He pulled her close. "Not quite as we are," he replied. "I think we might find ourselves a larger house. And definitely hire a cook."

She permitted herself a small pout. "And I thought you liked my dinner," she objected.

"I did," he assured her. "But I think I can find a more worthwhile way for you to occupy your time."

"Really, sir?" she asked, and lifted her face for him to kiss her.

He obliged her with a lingering, heady kiss.

When he released her, she pulled slowly away. "I think I might like to stay here, in this house, for a while at least." She smiled smugly with the secret she was about to divulge. "It might seem a bit crowded in not too long a time," she said slowly, "but for the meantime . . ."

"Crowded?" he asked.

She nodded. "And perhaps even noisy," she said. "Babies are sometimes noisy, I believe."

Amity watched his eyes light and his lips turn up in a decidedly delighted smile.

Then he was pulling her back into his arms, enfolding her in them and holding her close. A wave of contentment stole over her, filling her, and she knew without question that he shared it with her.

His lips found hers and she accepted his kiss with delight, giving herself over entirely to the heady reaction she had to his touch.

When his lips left hers she once again pulled away from him.

"The grass here by the bank is quite soft, I believe," she whispered as she fell to her knees. She lifted her hand to his and tugged gently.

"As soft as the desert sand?" he asked as he joined her.

She laughed softly. "Why don't we see?"

She lay back and waited for him to follow.

He was, she found, more than willing to oblige.

383

Author's Note

The scene depicting worship of an ancient Egyptian goddess, the Lady Bastet, is purely imaginary.

Very little is actually known of ancient Egyptian religious practices. Because the priests and royalty perform the rites, keeping them secret from the populace, and because little written or pictorial evidence was left behind, even the vaguest conjecture regarding holy ritual is admittedly merely that, conjecture.

Animal sacrifice was certainly quite common in the ancient world, however, and it is not out of the question to assume that the priests of Bastet might actually have performed this act. Temple whores were common throughout the ancient Mediterranean, plying their trade not only for the comfortable living it provided them, but also as a holy rite. As Bastet was considered a goddess of joy, it is not unreasonable to assume sexual rites were part of her worship. There is, however, no evidence whatsoever that human sacrifice played any part in the goddess's worship.